THE THIRD DOOR

THE THIRD DOOR

by Jim Williams

atmosphere press

Copyright © 2019 by Jim Williams

Published by Atmosphere Press

Cover design by Nick Courtright
nickcourtright.com

No part of this book may be reproduced except in brief quotations and in reviews without permission from the publisher.

10 9 8 7 6 5 4 3 2 1

The Third Door
2019, Jim Williams

atmospherepress.com

To my teachers

BOOK 1, CHAPTER 1
November, 1992

An early autumn evening, not quite raining but a persistent mist saturating the air, everything damp and dark. The streetlights cast the boulevard in an orange hue, headlights glancing off the slick streets. A twelve-year-old boy in a gray hoodie navigated the sidewalk, keeping a wary eye out for cars darting out of shopping center exits. The boy's head was not hooded and the orange light accentuated his high, prominent forehead, and even in the half-light, the vulpine arrangement of his nose and mouth were plainly evident and made him seem shrewd beyond his years—still juvenile in stature, but in possession of a curiously adult air. He heard his name called from someone in a passing car, a girl's voice piercing the low-level rumble of city traffic; a single name—"Bobby." Bobby wondered if it was Layla, and he raised a hand and waved at the car in return, but he had resided in the neighborhood for less than two months and did not recognize the car in question.

Bobby had left the apartment in the first place because at about six o'clock he had checked the cupboard and the refrigerator—both of which were empty, which was hardly an unusual state of affairs—and except for a six-pack of

Miller High Life, he had not ingested any calories during the last twenty-four hours. He had staked out a mom-and-pop convenience store that had only one clerk and a minimal number of cameras, but the clerk picked up on Bobby's vibe as soon as he entered the shop and watched him warily, so Bobby left and continued up the boulevard. He passed a pharmacy but dismissed it out of hand—too many cameras, too many mirrors, probably full-time eyes on the aisles. Considering his options, he crossed a wet parking lot, his hands sunk deep into his hoodie, and concluded that the HEB, a large Texas chain grocery, was his best option. Bobby approached the store, making for a garbage dispensary just beside the entrance and grabbing a handful of discarded paper receipts as foot traffic milled around him. He leafed through a half dozen receipts until he found an itemized list that appealed to him: a 24-ounce Miller Lite, Twinkies, two packages of beef jerky. Bobby wadded up the receipt, put it in his pocket, and entered the store.

Grabbing an empty plastic grocery sack from an abandoned cart, he headed up an aisle toward a large bank of refrigerated shelves behind glass. An advertisement affixed to a glass door declared, in big blue bold letters, "Coldest Beer in Corpus Christi." He placed a 24-ounce can of Miller Lite in the sack, then tracked down Twinkies and the beef jerky. Bobby kept his head down, walking quickly, but without hurrying. As he approached the exit, he felt a momentary burning in his stomach, acutely aware of his surroundings. The doors opened and he was out into the night and he did not look behind him, keeping his gaze forward. He was already halfway across the parking lot before he heard a man's voice call out, "Hey, you! Youngster."

THE THIRD DOOR

Back at the automatic doors was a heavyset, middle-aged man in an HEB uniform. The man called out again. "Yes, you. Come back here."

Walking backwards away from the store, Bobby held up the receipt. "I've got a receipt for this."

"Just come on back here," said the man, waving. The man did not seem angry, merely resigned. "Receipt or no, you can't have the beer."

"My mom bought it," yelled Bobby, who turned back around, throwing the receipt on the ground. "I'm taking it to her."

He quickened his gait, not looking behind him, and arrived at the boulevard in seconds.

He hurried his way across, picking through the traffic, finding a side street and disappearing into the gloom. Taking the back streets, he listened for sirens but heard nothing. These streets were darker than the boulevard and he tried to blend in with the shadows, passing small, working-class residences—the houses modest with earthen driveways and small yards. He passed through an empty lot, jumping a chain-link fence and stepping through a small patch of wild grass, coming to his apartment from the rear of the building. Bobby trotted through a parking lot covered in gravel and grabbed the metal handrail of the stairs, taking the steps two at a time. When he reached the landing, he noted the tiny parking lot, the narrow stairwell. He took a deep breath, steeling himself, and entered the apartment.

The living room was dark, but amid the shadows Bobby could see well enough to switch on a lamp resting on an end table. In the next moment, a circular halo of light illuminated the brown carpet, a sofa, a TV on a plastic carton box, and the end table. The light was still low and murky, and in the gloom, its farthest walls not readily visible, the living room seemed larger than it really was. Bobby sat down on the sofa, popping open the beer and unsealing the beef jerky. He munched on the jerky while keeping his gaze fixed on the floor—at a light-blue blanket wrapped around a man who looked at least fifty. Bobby surmised the man was younger than that, but this only underscored his waste of an appearance—the stringy gray hair that receded in volume as it approached the top of his head, the thin ashen face, and thin white arms stretched out over the blanket. The man's eyes were open but empty; he stared at Bobby oddly, his expression remote.

Six and a half weeks ago, when Bobby and his mother moved into the apartment with Vyasa and Charlie, Bobby did not know how to judge Charlie, and this had made the man a bit of a mystery. Even in the beginning, Bobby did not fear Charlie. Charlie was too inward and emanated little presence, either physical or psychological; most days he remained immobile on the floor as he was now, like a sick prey animal, the blanket wrapped around him. Bobby wondered what was wrong with the man. Then, after less than a week in the apartment, Bobby came home one afternoon and found Charlie cross-legged in the living room with a needle stuck in the crook of his elbow, his sleeve rolled up and a thick band already removed from around the bicep. Bobby fled the apartment—at that point he had never seen anyone shoot up, and he felt so unsettled that it took him hours to come to terms with it. But he assimilated the experience quickly, and by the next day, he regarded Charlie as something between a benign ghost and a pile of refuse, a sometimes disquieting presence to be sure, but one that could be mostly ignored.

Bobby took a sip of beer and reflected on the

apartment's daily pattern. The adults were generally asleep well past noon—Vyasa and his mother in the bedroom, Charlie in the living room—but when they awoke, they recovered from the night before with beer and pot (they often let Bobby join in both) before Vyasa left the apartment to troll for more coke and heroin (these they did not share with Bobby). Judging by the man's vacant expression, Bobby guessed Charlie had done his evening fix while Bobby was out. This probably meant that Vyasa and his mother were off on a run as well and that he might not see his mother until morning, if even then. Bobby thought back to the store employee who called after him at the HEB and he felt a momentary anxiety—the man had gotten a good look at him and would remember him if Bobby returned. He brooded over this state of affairs before getting up and heading to the bedroom door, knocking.

He immediately heard a man's voice say, "Go the fuck away!"

Bobby stood immobile, but after an instant, he vigorously flipped off the door with both hands. He could think of any number of retorts but he knew they would not change anything. He called out. "Vyasa, we need to talk."

"No, we don't," the man said through the door.

"Something happened and I don't want it to fuck things up."

Seconds later, the bedroom door popped open and the man stepped out. (Seven weeks earlier, when mother and son still lived in their own place, his mother came home one afternoon with her new boyfriend and introduced her son to him, mentioning the boyfriend's name. Bobby asked about the unusual name, and Vyasa informed Bobby in no uncertain terms that his was a holy name in India. Bobby looked at the short, squat white man in front of him and thought to himself there was little about the boyfriend reminiscent of the India he had read about in a fourth grade social studies textbook.)

Confronted with Vyasa in the flesh once more, Bobby felt a small sinking in his stomach, whether due to fear or a concerted suppression of morbid laughter he could not tell. As always, Bobby first noticed the odd, disjointed haircut. Since Vyasa thought long hair would cause him to look like other dealers, he kept his hair short, but because he would not divert money from his habit, he cut his hair himself, oftentimes when he was high. As a consequence, Vyasa's hair resembled a patch of overgrown weeds attacked indiscriminately with industrial clippers, the hair receding and falling, ballooning up on one part, only to thin toward an almost negligible amount on another part of his head. There were also the muddled features and the sallow skin, both made indistinct by a high consumption of alcohol. And finally, the long pajama pants, apparently the only pair he owned, which he cinched at the waist with a string because he felt they looked "Eastern" that way.

Vyasa straightened himself, trying to be casually threatening. His accent was passably reminiscent of Southern California. "What the fuck is your deal, man?"

Bobby did not give an inch. "I nearly got pinched at the HEB."

Vyasa was not much taller than Bobby, but he was full through the chest and shoulders, his build like an upright brick. His face glimmered, a light sheen of sweat covering his cheeks. He was clearly disoriented but tried to conceal it. "What were you doing at the HEB?"

"Goddamn it, we've talked about this. There's never any fucking food here and you never give me any money. You do the math."

Even disoriented, Vyasa was sizing up Bobby's claim, trying to estimate what it might cost him. Vyasa went on the attack, seeking leverage. "I bet you snatched it like an amateur."

Bobby ignored the jab and parried, slapping his palm with the back of his hand. "I told you. Give me $75 every Monday and I'll make sure there's food in the house."

Vyasa laughed immediately. "Oh right, I'm going to give you $300 a month."

"Okay then, next time it won't be some fat manager who can't run me down; so they'll catch me and the cops send me somewhere for a while. Who will make the deliveries? You?"

Vyasa scratched the back of his head, following Bobby's train of thought and not liking where it was going. "You know I used to make all the deliveries."

"But now I do it, don't I? So that when the cops figure this little racket out, it won't be your dumb ass who gets caught with the drugs. Right? Just tell me I'm right."

Vyasa's agitation increased. He changed the subject. "How's Charlie?"

"I don't know. He never talks to me."

"It's all right. He's just old. Right, Charlie?" said Vyasa, calling out to the living room. Bobby heard a grunt, generally the fullest extent of Charlie's reply to a direct question. Vyasa appeared to consider the nuance in that grunt, but he soon seemed taken with a notion and inched closer to Bobby, proffering a slightly conspiratorial smile. "Hey," he whispered, still smiling. Bobby realized that Vyasa was attempting to charm him. "Did you try the pot?"

During the late morning and early afternoon, Bobby had smoked pot and drank beer for hours. "Yeah."

"Well, what'd you think?"

Bobby sized up Vyasa, taking a step back, trying to figure out the contours of Vyasa's approach. He lowered his voice. "It was good."

Vyasa leaned closer. "How good?"

"It was quality stuff," said Bobby.

"I've got more. I mean, I can get more."

Bobby thought there was a rote aspect to everything associated with Vyasa. There was the content of his speech, which centered on obtaining drugs or using drugs; his featureless gray T-shirts, some with holes in the armpits, some without; the cans of Miller High Life he consumed to come down from the extreme agitation of a crack cocaine high.

Vyasa continued his line of inquiry. "You got any friends who might like some pot like that?"

Bobby was catching on. "Yeah, sure."

Vyasa rubbed his glistening forehead. "Listen, you get some regular buyers, you know. A little revenue stream moving through here. You follow? I'll find you $300 every month. Everyone chips in, you see."

Bobby did not like it that Vyasa had regained the high ground. He thought quickly. "What if I can move a lot of it? So it's not a flat-fee arrangement. A percentage, maybe."

Vyasa's eyes went unfocused for a moment. He rubbed an unkempt set of whiskers on his chin, shook his head, and then appeared to catch his snap. "Goddamn, this kid." Vyasa put a hand on Bobby's shoulder and laughed, a short, little laugh. "Hey Charlie, guess what? The kid's negotiating with me. You hear that, Charlie? Twelve years old and he's negotiating." Bobby heard another grunt from the living room. "He's going to be an earner, Charlie."

"I've got people," said Charlie. "And I buy, too."

"Charlie, I know. I know, I know. Don't get upset. I'm

just saying. We got a prodigy in our midst."

Bobby still wondered at the bond that joined the two men. His theory was that Vyasa sheltered Charlie as a warning against a vision of himself in five years, a Dickensian ghost of Christmas future—Vyasa would become Charlie in five years. It remained to be seen if Charlie would last for another two years.

Vyasa turned his attention back to Bobby, putting a hand on Bobby's shoulder.

"Now look, don't get any big ideas. I'll do what I can for you. It all depends on how many people you can bring in." Bobby nodded and Vyasa lowered his voice. "I need you to make a delivery for me."

The deliveries were seldom difficult, and since Bobby no longer attended school, they gave him an excuse to leave the apartment. "No problem," said Bobby.

"You make this delivery and you can have all the beer and pot you want for a while."

"Can I have anything else?"

"Hey, listen to me. No hard stuff. You're too young and your mother wouldn't approve."

"How is my mother?"

Vyasa's concentration appeared to wane once more. "She's a beautiful person," he managed to say.

Bobby closed his eyes, frustrated with the repetitive drug-culture responses to ordinary questions. "No, how *is* she?" Bobby insisted.

"She's fine, she's fine."

"I'd like to see her."

"She's sleeping it off, okay? Let her sleep."

Bobby thought this was probably true, so he let it go. "So then, beer and pot later, right?"

"Sure. Now, listen. I'm going to give you something.

Just put it in your coat pocket. Don't open it, don't even handle it. Just go over to Rene's place and give it to Rene's mother. That's it."

"Not a problem," said Bobby.

"And don't give it to Rene, the little bastard."

"I won't."

"He might ask. Don't trust that little snake. Don't even let him know why you've come."

"He knows."

"He don't know. He don't know what you have."

"Do I collect?"

Vyasa laughed. "Hell, no."

"When can I collect?"

Vyasa laughed again. "What are you? A twelve-year-old gangster?"

"Maybe."

"Yeah, and maybe I'm going to kick your ass." Vyasa leaned into Bobby. "I collect. I always collect. You got it?"

"Yeah, yeah, I got it," said Bobby.

"So what are you doing?"

"Handing the package to Rene's mother."

"And to no one else, you got it?"

"Yeah, I got it."

"Okay."

**

Vyasa disappeared to his bedroom and did not return for almost half an hour. Bobby drank beer and watched TV, his eyes darting about the minimally furnished apartment. There was a thud on the other side of the bedroom door as someone ran into it, or tripped into it, then the rattling of the doorknob. At last, Vyasa managed to get the door open.

THE THIRD DOOR

Vyasa stood in the doorframe, swaying slightly. The hollow disconnect in his eyes suggested he was sniffing heroin in order to come down from a run on cocaine. Bobby eyed the man shrewdly as Vyasa crossed the living room to stand before him. "Okay," Vyasa said, concentrating so as not to slur his words. Vyasa handed Bobby an item the size of a man's fist, wrapped in a plastic sack. "Don't mess with this. Just walk it over. She's waiting."

Bobby felt a renewed sense of purpose after the immobility of the last half hour. After taking the package, he strode to the entry hall closet, put on a windbreaker and stuffed the package deep down into a pocket. He left the apartment quickly, closing and locking the door behind him.

He descended the stairs rapidly, grasping the cold metal railing the whole time, the stairs opening out to a small concrete walkway. No grass grew in the small islands surrounding the walkway; instead, these islands were filled with smooth glass chips. Bobby circled the perimeter of the building and arrived at a tiny grass lot enclosed by a plank-board fence. He cut through a gap in the fence and walked through another complex parking lot until he came out on a street. He was one block over from the thoroughfare; there were small apartment complexes and houses all around.

He passed a boardinghouse with a blue plastic kiddie pool in the front yard, filled with leaves and dirty water. From where he stood he could see several complexes and all of them had looped barbed wire strung over their fences, whether the fences were wood or chain-link. Bobby walked past a blue dumpster at the end of a driveway and took a path through a shallow ditch into a vacant lot, which merged into another residential street—that's when he saw up ahead, bathed in yellow light, the apartments that were his destination. He took another path, cut through an opening in a metal fence, and walked through the courtyard. Bobby climbed stairs that appeared brown in the dark and he knocked on a door.

An Hispanic boy, not much older than Bobby, answered. The boy had crooked teeth but grinned broadly, and they did a palm-to-palm shake. "Hey, man," said the boy. "It's good to see you."

"What's up, Rene."

Rene stood in the doorway and each boy sized up the other. Bobby saw that Rene sported new bright-red Air Jordans and Bobby felt a twinge of embarrassment as he looked down at his worn tennis shoes. This observation only reaffirmed what he had long suspected—Rene's mother was far better connected and higher up the food chain than Vyasa ever dreamt. Rene's grin turned smug, seeing that Bobby noticed the shoes, and Bobby heard condescension in Rene's tone. "I know where I can get you a pair cheap," he said.

"How much?"

"For you, I'd say fifty."

Bobby knew that Rene knew this was far beyond Bobby's price range. Bobby felt an intense rage but maintained a poker face. "Give me till next week," he said.

"Next week's good, even the week after. I like doing favors for a friend."

Bobby well knew that Rene never did anyone a favor. In fact, it was from Rene that Bobby learned that a favor was only the first step toward a future obligation. Rene stepped back into the apartment and ushered Bobby inside.

Bobby found himself in a warmly lit living room, one with the homey touches absent from Vyasa's apartment. A faint scent of jasmine permeated the room, with several scented candles encased in glass illuminating various depictions of the Madonna. As a room divider, small crystalline objects dangled from the ceiling on thin wires like fishing line. A comfortable sofa faced a TV, which was turned to an episode of *Roseanne*. "Where's your mom?" said Bobby.

"She's coming, all right?"

After a few seconds, Rene's mother appeared from behind a door at the back of the living room. She prowled across the room, her shapeless blue dress more like a nightgown than daywear, and she carried herself with a stern authority. Bobby had never seen Rene openly cross his mother or disobey a directive; if he did disobey, he did it with all stealth. "You got it?" she said to Bobby, not bothering with niceties.

"Yeah," said Bobby.

She eyed him. Bobby speculated she was searching for dissimulation, and if she found it, she would change strategy immediately. Bobby waited as she sized up the moment. All at once, she seemed satisfied. She stuck out a large, fleshy hand. "Well, give it to me."

Bobby reached into his coat pocket and passed her the sack. She snatched it from him. She held the sack in her palm, her hand bobbing up and down, seeming to weigh it. She nodded. "Good," she said. She looked at Bobby directly and nodded again, a veteran's affirmation. "You did good. Now look, I want you to stay here for a while. Hang out with Rene."

Bobby did not hesitate—he knew the code. A small reward was in order. "Can I have a beer?" he said.

The woman appeared perplexed, and then upset. But she nodded to Rene. "Get him a beer," she said.

"Can I have one?" said Rene.

"No!" she said, glaring at the boy. She slapped him lightly on the temple. "I should kick your ass for asking."

**

Rene and Bobby sat on the sofa, a window unit contending with the noise of the television. Neither boy tried to follow the sitcom and Bobby took slow, luxuriating sips on the can of beer. He could tell this upset Rene.

"Let me have some," said Rene.

Rene was about a year and a half older and bigger than Bobby, but his limbs were long and stringy, his shoulders close, supporting a thin neck. Bobby did not fear him. "Your mother said no. If she knew, she'd kick my ass."

Rene elbowed Bobby hard in the shoulder. Some of the beer spilled. "*I'm* going to kick your ass unless you give me some of that beer."

"Motherfucker," said Bobby, popping Rene on the side of the head with the back of his fist. They nearly came to blows, squaring off at each other. Bobby backed off, not seeing the point. "You can be a real prick."

Rene scrutinized Bobby with steady eyes, his mouth forming the slightest of smiles. Bobby knew he was searching for an advantage and was determined not to give it to him. Rene considered his options. "Okay, look. Just give me a pull on that beer and I'll cut you in on something much better later."

Despite better instincts, Bobby eyes went alight, and he lowered his voice. "Are you moving some?"

"Maybe. You'll thank me later."

"It better be good," said Bobby.

Rene could see he had the upper hand. "I don't think

you'll be disappointed."

Bobby instantly handed him the beer. "When can we go?"

"Not for a while," said Rene, taking the can and chugging. "She's cutting it right now. She's busy and won't come out for a while. But she wants me here when she's done."

Bobby asked the question slowly. "How much are you moving?"

"That's for me to know, fool," said Rene, his grin breaking more broadly than ever. This incarnation of Rene's grin possessed a certain gloating quality, one that Bobby had tried to replicate unsuccessfully in the past. "Just come with me later."

The boys heard a rumbling in the next room and Rene darted a glance at the door, popping a wintergreen Lifesaver in his mouth and passing the beer back to Bobby. Rene's mother stuck her head out. "Rene, I need some more plastic. The ones with the small black lids."

Rene got off the sofa, opened a drawer in the kitchen, and slunk to the bedroom, handing off some items Bobby could not see. As soon as she had them, Rene's mother disappeared into the bedroom again. In about ten minutes, she came back out.

"Okay," she said to Rene. "It's time."

"Bobby's coming with me."

Rene's mother regarded the boys dubiously. Finally she shook her head, her words carrying the weight of an edict. "He can go as far as the building. He can't see the apartment."

"Okay," said Rene.

"Under no conditions."

"I got it," said Rene.

"You got it, you got it," his mother said, mockingly. She handed Rene something Bobby could not see and Rene instantly put it in his pocket. "Don't trust anyone," she said. "Even this little white boy."

Rene nodded and smiled his arrogant smile. "Come on, Bobby. Maybe we can find you another beer."

"And don't you drink, Rene," his mother said as Rene opened the door and stepped out into the darkness.

Rene and Bobby took a path behind the apartment, in an area between a chain-link fence and one of the two buildings that comprised the complex. On the other side of the fence was the street. In this area, there were square brick houses with tar-and-gravel shingles, corrugated metal lean-tos over window units. Bobby heard chickens and saw a wooden hutch covered with wire. An empty shopping cart was pushed against a curb.

Rene took out a small plastic container. "Sammy always lets me keep one," said Rene.

"What is it?"

"'What is it?'" said Rene. "You moron, it's coke."

"I can't see."

"Seeing ain't nothing. Try some."

They found an air conditioner compressor behind a wooden fence. Rene poured a small amount on the flat metal surface and handed Bobby a dollar. Bobby took the dollar with a trace of reluctance—while he was now familiar with pot, he had never done cocaine and had seen with his own eyes what it was doing to Vyasa and his mother. But he rolled the bill up and took a hit.

"Hand it to me," said Rene indicating the bill and pouring some for himself. "So what do you think?" said Rene, rubbing his nose.

"Nice," said Bobby, who in fact felt very little.

"Give it a minute," said Rene. "I know this girl who does it with a needle, but she sometimes does too much and freaks out."

"With a needle?"

"Yeah, she shoots it up. Let's go."

They found an opening in the fence and came out on the street. After they had gone about half a block, Bobby felt a wired, jittery sensation coming on. He started jumping between steps, counting out three jumps to himself, then taking three steps.

"You fool," said Rene. "Quit bouncing."

"I think I feel it."

"You're such a dumbass."

They came to an intersection and Rene stopped. "I got to go this way. You can't come along with me now. People are watching."

"How much is one of those?" said Bobby, indicating the containers.

Rene smiled again, knowing all too well the dynamics of the street. Bobby would not find $50 for Air Jordans, but he would find the money for one of those containers. "For you, $30," said Rene.

"All right," said Bobby, nodding. He would make it a point to find out if Rene was giving him a fair deal or ripping him off. "I'll see you."

**

When Bobby returned to his apartment, he flopped on the sofa, a little wired but no worse for wear. He looked at Charlie, who was in his customary position on the floor, blanket wrapped around him. They did not exchange a word. Vyasa came out of the bedroom within thirty seconds after Bobby's arrival. Bobby could hear him fumbling around in the bedroom, the doorknob a puzzle whose solution briefly eluded him.

"Where've you been?" Vyasa said, stumbling out, too disoriented to be irritated.

Bobby remained on the sofa. "Rene's mother wanted me to wait," he said.

Vyasa cocked his head. He looked confused. "Why'd she want that?"

"I guess because if I left too quick it might attract attention."

"Oh," said Vyasa, his voice lacking true recognition. "Did it go okay?"

"It went fine," said Bobby.

Vyasa nodded. "All right," he said. "Someone might be coming over later."

"What about the pot?"

"The pot?" he said. "Oh yeah. Just give me a minute."

Vyasa disappeared back into the bedroom. Bobby knew there was no telling how long he would be, so he went back out to the living room and watched TV. After about twenty minutes, Bobby got up and rapped on the bedroom door twice, two short knocks. The door opened and his mother, Regina, stepped out, her balance unsteady, her dirty-blond hair damp with sweat. She caught herself on the doorknob before making two lunging steps toward the sink. She steadied herself again on the rim of the sink and hunched over, coughing.

Bobby watched her. Her cut-off jean shorts were worn and her black shirt, one of many concert shirts she had procured throughout the years, was turned inside out; Bobby could see the tag. The hollows of her cheeks were pronounced, her face narrow, her arms and legs thin. The youthful glow she could have summoned five years earlier had been displaced by haggard skin, with wear around her eyes. Bobby watched her as if he were at the zoo, quietly observing an animal in its habitat. Regina seemed entirely unaware that her son was there. She reached into a cabinet, pulled out a plastic cup, poured some water into it, and drank greedily. She coughed again, a hoarse, deep, hacking cough.

Bobby stared at her and then barged into the bedroom. There was nothing in the room besides a double bed with a nightstand, a desk along a wall. Vyasa was sprawled out on a gray sheet, which was coming off the mattress in one corner; Bobby could see the light-blue fabric of the mattress. Both a syringe and a straight were on a table next to the bed, along with a burnt spoon and some crack. Bobby stood at the foot of the bed. "What about my pot?" he said to Vyasa.

Vyasa nodded as if he'd heard, but then he just kept nodding.

"You said you were going to get me some pot," said Bobby, louder. Vyasa mumbled something, then turned on his side.

"Fuck," said Bobby, under his breath. He looked around the room and began to open up some drawers in the desk. He found a stash of pot, about an ounce. He took out several buds, setting them end to end so they formed a line. Once they formed the length and thickness of two fingers on a man's hand, he grabbed a baggie and wrapped them. "Vyasa, I'm taking this pot," he announced. Bobby closed the drawer and opened another. A two-gram packet of cocaine slid to the front. Bobby snatched it up and put it in his pocket. "Thanks, Vyasa. We're square."

When he left the bedroom, his mother was squatting on

the floor, her right hand reaching up into the sink, the hand dangling over the rim. Bobby took a step toward her but stopped. He stood there, frozen, considering the scene. He thought to himself, it was not always like this, not nearly this bad. But then again, he reminisced, it wasn't so great, either. When did he first realize it, the first clues that something was terribly wrong? He considered the question for the briefest of intervals, perhaps less than a second. His mind raced, but then, fixated on a memory of her as she was five years before—a thin face, dirty blonde hair and hollowed-out cheekbones that descended narrowly and abruptly down to the point of her chin; attractive, certainly, but with an overall appearance too complicated to be termed "pretty," often undercut by the frenzied enthusiasm in her smile when she was taken by a whim. Bobby came out of his reverie and exhaled, sick of fruitlessly lingering over his past, sick of Vyasa's apartment, sick of it all. "I'm going out," he said, more to the apartment in general than to Regina. "I won't be back until tomorrow."

**

He walked along the boulevard, cars rushing by. He passed a washateria, a nail salon, a car wash. He came to a weathered liquor store and walked in without hesitation. The floor consisted of dark tile and the walls were yellow with age, the overhead lights casting a grainy luminescence. The store was closing, and the clerk was preoccupied with a customer and did not notice that a preteen had made his way past the bourbons to the scotches.

Bobby stopped and looked around him. He knew little about hard alcohol, only stuff he had picked up listening to friends over the years. He knew that Everclear was very strong and was best mixed with punch. He had heard that Jack was good, but that brand was placed near the end of the aisle, in plain view of the clerk. He looked at the prices of the bottles near him and saw that The Glenlivet was the most expensive. He grabbed a bottle and walked out of the store. The clerk caught him leaving out of the corner of his eye and ran around the counter to the door, but Bobby had already disappeared into the night.

He walked about a half mile through a dimly lit neighborhood. Most of the houses were small, with dirt or gravel driveways, and many were spaced unevenly down the street. He heard a dog bark behind a chain-link fence. He approached Layla's house, which was shaped like a box. A cat crouched at the edge of an earthen driveway and scurried off into the dark. He stood at one end of the house, his hand small enough to fit between the black burglar bars, and he rapped on a window.

He heard a rumbling, and then a curtain parted. An angular face peered down at him from behind the window. "What the fuck?" said a girl.

"It's me, Bobby."

"Bobby?"

"Yeah."

"What do you want?"

He held up the bottle of whiskey. "Let's party," he said.

Layla met Bobby at the front door. She was older than Bobby by a year and a half, and she had dark hair and delicate features, a small nose and a Cupid's bow mouth. Her body was already developing into adult maturity. She stepped back into the tiny entry hall and let Bobby inside. "My dad's out, so we shouldn't have any problems here." She smiled knowingly at Bobby, who returned the smile.

The last time they'd hooked up, Layla's father was home, and so they had snuck out, found a vacant house, and whiled away the night in its garage. "He won't be back tonight, but my mom's here. She won't care if we go to my room."

Layla wore plain jeans and a light-blue T-shirt, her hips filling out the jeans. Bobby stared at her swaying pelvic carriage as she walked. She led Bobby through a dark living room stuffed with old furniture, then to the back of the house. At the end of a hallway they came to a bedroom in which a woman smoked a cigarette and watched TV. "Mom, this is Bobby," Layla said. "We're going to my room."

The woman turned her head slightly but made no other movements. She had gray hair and a pinched face, and Bobby saw the light of the TV in her eyes. He made no attempt to conceal the alcohol.

"What's wrong with her?" said Bobby as they went back down the hallway.

"Nothing," said Layla. She shrugged. "I don't know, probably nothing. She stays in her room mostly. Dad doesn't like to talk about it."

"Where is your dad?"

"With his girlfriend."

They went to Layla's bedroom. Layla kept the lights off and the only illumination in the room came from the pervasive yellow streetlights outside the window. Layla disappeared but soon returned with a couple of glasses containing ice. "Don't want to drink from the bottle," she said. "White trash free zone."

"You got any papers?" said Bobby.

"Papers?"

"I've got pot," said Bobby.

"I don't have any papers. My dad has a pipe."

"That'll work. We'll clean it when we're done."

"We don't have to clean it. My dad smokes more dope than the two of us combined."

They drank and smoked and talked as easily as old friends. The liquor burned Bobby's mouth and throat. Layla's dad's pipe was a marijuana pipe; Bobby had not expected that. He thought Layla came from a straight family—that she was kind of a black sheep. But when he considered it, it dawned on him that none of his current acquaintances were from straight families.

After a while, Bobby leaned over and kissed her. Layla kissed him back and rubbed him through his jeans; Bobby kissed her harder. He pulled away and Layla's eyes were distant. He undid the button on her jeans. She pushed them down, stood up, and stepped out of them. Bobby kissed her again, took off her shirt and panties, and made his way down her body, kissing her as he went. Layla grabbed the pipe and took a hit. "No, use your tongue," she said. "It's gentle. Like this." She pulled Bobby up to her face and put her tongue on his lips. "Like this," she said again.

"Okay," said Bobby.

"That's better," she said after a while, with the slightest of smiles. "You'll learn."

Bobby began to take off his jeans.

"You got a condom?" she said.

"No," said Bobby. He had already had sex on more than one occasion, but he had never used a condom.

"I won't do it without a condom."

"Okay," said Bobby. When he and Layla had made out in the abandoned garage, the garage was too cold and dirty for actual sex, and the condom issue hadn't come up. "I'll remember that. Fuck."

"Don't worry," she said. "I'll take care of you."

A while later, they were naked together, entangled on the carpeted floor. They were both relaxed, lying across each other. Bobby sat up on one elbow, rifling through his jeans. "Look what else I got," he said. He presented the packet of coke.

"Fuck yeah," said Layla, eyeing the packet. "One gram or two?"

"I'm not really sure."

"It looks like two. We should rock some of it out."

"Rock it out?" said Bobby. He knew what the term meant, but he felt a momentary chill.

"Yeah. You know, smoke it."

A scene ran through Bobby's mind, as if he were watching a sped-up film. He could see his mother stumbling through Vyasa's apartment, covered in sweat. "I don't know," he said.

"Oh, come on. It'll be fun."

"Do you know how to do it?"

"Yeah, a guy showed me one time."

Bobby hedged his bets. "Why don't we do a couple of lines? Then we'll see."

"All right," said Layla.

Bobby poured some of the coke on a dresser. He took out a dollar bill and divided up two lines. "Ladies first," he said, handing her the bill.

They both did a line and drank a shot of scotch. Bobby thought the scotch tasted especially good with the cocaine dripping down into his throat. "That's pretty good coke," said Layla.

"How much coke have you done?"

Layla considered Bobby's questions and shrugged. "A little. You know, my share."

Bobby nodded. "Yeah, I know."

They drank two more glasses of scotch and did a couple more lines apiece. Layla's expression became increasingly abstracted, and she looked at her hand, which seemed to open and close without her consent. Bobby could feel the effects of the alcohol and the coke counteracting each other, and he found it a highly agreeable sensation. He shook the packet and fought a craving to finish all the powder right there, but the impulse toward immoderation bothered him, and he scowled. He reached for the Glenlivet bottle and upended it, drinking straight from the spout. Layla looked at him.

"Easy," she said. "Go easy."

"I'm fine."

"I know you are," she said. "But still, go easy."

Bobby went silent, reflecting over her words. He stood up and looked out the window but soon turned back to Layla. He scowled. He almost whispered the words; they came out in a hiss. "So fucked up."

Layla's attention was diverted from her hand. "What is it?"

Bobby paused, seeming to ruminate. "My fucking mother," he said, at last. He nodded, his disjointed words mirroring the conflict in his mind. "I think it was the screaming match."

Layla was lost. "I don't understand what you're saying."

"When I first knew. Knew this was coming, something like this." He paused, again, his voice drained of feeling. "I was six. We had just moved to Corpus, my mother and me, moved in with a boyfriend. He was okay, the boyfriend, the first one. My aunt didn't know she was going to do it, the move. My grandfather neither. So she called back home to Cuero to tell them what she'd done and got in a screaming match with my grandfather. For the rest of the day, she drank, passed out that night. She looked deranged the whole time."

Layla placed a hand on his forearm, a compassionate gesture. "You want to talk about it?"

He pulled away from her touch, waving a hand, dismissive, seemingly angry with himself. "No, I don't want to talk about it. In fact, I shouldn't talk about it." He nodded, as if he had had a sudden epiphany. "I should never talk about it." Finally, he turned back to the window, his eyes inward. "Have you ever thought of getting out of here?"

"What do you mean?"

"Leaving. Leaving Corpus. Just getting away."

"Where to?"

"I hear Austin's cool, that it's a cool place."

"Don't be weird."

"I'm serious."

"Bobby. You're twelve."

"So? I know lots of people older than me who are less put together."

"How would you live?"

"I've met some people with friends. I'd have a place to crash for a while. All that would be left would be finding money for food."

Layla pondered the idea. She reached for the bottle, poured a glassful, and took a long swig. "You're insane. The police would pick you up."

"Fuck the police."

"No, really. You would stand out like a billboard. A billboard that says: 'Come arrest me.'"

"They wouldn't arrest me. They would just send me back." Layla laughed. Bobby leaned into her. He wanted to kiss her but he felt a powerful undercurrent from the drug, and he was determined not to allow the kiss to be a passageway to sensory overload. "I'm serious. Come with me. Even if it were just for a while. It would be fun."

"I can't."

"What's keeping you? What's here?" His voice rose slightly and he made full eye contact, emphasizing each word. "There's nothing here. This—this place—is all a great big nothing."

"I've got my family, Bobby."

Bobby turned to the wall. The light from the street illuminated the right side of his face. "I saw your mother tonight. You don't have a family, not a real family."

"My dad would find me. He would personally track my ass down."

Bobby went quiet. Layla could feel his silence radiate throughout the room, permeating every corner with a brooding, simmering energy. Of all of Bobby's characteristics, from the feral look of his face and the obscene way he held his mouth, like a young Mick Jagger, it was the power of his anger that attracted her most of all. She had to admit, he did not look twelve in any way except stature. He was, in fact, somewhat strange-looking—a miniature adult, fully formed. At one moment, vaguely ugly, too raw to be believed; the next, vital and wholly attractive. But still, she saw that he would be eaten up out there. It wouldn't be long; just a matter of weeks, or even days, and the streets would devour him. Devour him whole.

She touched his back. "I like you, Bobby," she said.

"I like you, too," said Bobby. He shook his head, his mood shifting from anger to regret and sadness. "Fuck."

"What?"

The effects of the coke had been subsumed as he considered his immediate fate. "This place. This fucking life."

"It won't be long," she said. "It won't be long and then you can leave."

"I'm not sure if I'll make it that long."

"You will. You have to."

Bobby nodded and turned to her. He was now exposed and vulnerable, even childlike. "My mother's boyfriend is a total prick."

"So's my dad's girlfriend," Layla said. "A pure cunt."

He took the measure of her statement. Then he nodded, as if he had finally come to a conclusion. "I want you to show me."

"Show you what?"

"How do you rock this shit out?"

BOOK 1, CHAPTER 2
March, 1993

    Bobby, wearing an orange jumpsuit, was led from a locked room with a one-way window, a small table, and two black chairs into a waiting area with a map of the city of Cuero on the wall. The uniformed officer who led him was young and deferred to a large, older man in brown slacks and a white button-down shirt. The older man paused momentarily, taking Bobby by the chin and gently repositioning the angle of his face, carefully scrutinizing the bruises around Bobby's eyes and the horizontal cut on his upper lip. The officer continued to inspect him, looking beyond the wounds in an attempt to assess the character of the person underneath. Despite being at the peak of adolescent awkwardness—Bobby's teeth were too large for his thin, vulpine face and his spindly arms and legs seemed gangly, at odds with his body—the boy nonetheless carried himself with a scarcely concealed, guileful self-awareness, a quality not lost on the officer. The man inspected the boy a moment longer, then unhanded him.
    "Follow me, son," said the man.
    They walked down a tiled hallway with yellow walls and harsh tubed lights, and Bobby cast vague glances at the

notices on the bulletin boards. The older man opened a door and indicated Bobby should enter. Inside the small, windowless space, his aunt, Tilda, and his grandfather, Elias, were seated at a conference table.

The officer gestured to Bobby to sit down and Bobby took a chair at the head of the conference table, the chair furthest from his relatives. For a moment, everyone eyed each other, and Tilda winced when she got a good look at Bobby. "Bobby?" she said, quietly. Bobby wondered if Tilda even recognized him; he had seen neither his aunt nor his grandfather since the move to Corpus Christi. "My god, Bobby, what happened?"

Bobby looked down at the table, remaining silent, not wanting to make eye contact. The officer waited to see if Bobby would say anything, and when Bobby didn't speak, the officer cleared his throat. "I'm Sergeant Pawalek," he said. He nodded at Tilda and Elias. "I'm glad you came quickly. We didn't want to keep him in a holding cell. We saw no reason to expose him in any way to the general population, but we couldn't hold him indefinitely without a formal charge. And we don't want to charge him."

"How did he end up here?" said Tilda. She was wide-eyed and seemed out of place. Bobby guessed that she had never been to a police station before. Although this was Bobby's first brush with the law, he had heard about the intake process a sufficient number of times from fellow street kids and knew the general protocols. For a thirteen-year-old, Bobby seemed remarkably at ease.

"We don't know a whole lot, either, quite frankly," said the sergeant. "We found him not far from here in the pouring rain about two hours ago, just a little after eight o'clock. We don't know what he was doing there. A trailer park wasn't too far away, and there were some houses scattered about. In any case, we expect he might have been holed up somewhere around there, but we don't know, because he won't tell us anything."

Elias, red-faced and fleshy, looked at Bobby with a severe expression. Bobby had only vague memories of his grandfather but remembered enough to know that Elias would hardly approve of a grandson in the hands of the police, regardless of the particulars. Bobby thought the sergeant and Elias looked somewhat alike, blunt features and big, bony hands—in Elias's case, the sort of hands that were roughened by decades of field work. Bobby could feel the energy Elias generated as if it were something palpable, the deep-seated conservatism of a rural Texan—not only a political conservatism, but one that went down to the very core of his being. Bobby guessed, correctly, that Elias had simple black-and-white notions of right and wrong and had little patience with shades of gray.

The sergeant continued. "The wounds you see on his face are recent, for the most part, probably sustained within the last several hours. We haven't done a comprehensive medical evaluation, but there are also bruises sustained to his person—his back, chest, the area of the torso in general. We would like to do a full medical to ascertain whether there's additional trauma, but he's not cooperating."

The sergeant went quiet and the word "cooperating" lingered in the room. All eyes turned to Bobby, who looked between Tilda and Elias. Tilda said, "Are you okay, Bobby? Are you in pain?"

To Bobby's surprise, despite the soundness of the beating he had taken only hours before, he was in some pain, but not a lot. As the seconds passed, Bobby realized the adults expected him to say something and he found himself thinking he was not a performing seal. He clenched his fists, fighting an urge to cry out or gesticulate. He searched for an appropriate response but his anger settled and deepened, and he lowered his head and folded in on himself, like a clam. "Fuck that," he heard himself say.

After a sufficient interval, the sergeant again cleared his throat. "Those are the first words I've heard from his lips," he said, "but they are consistent with his attitude." Elias glared at Bobby from across the table, offended by the use of bad language in front of an authority figure. The sergeant continued, direct and matter-of-fact. "We found paraphernalia on him, but no drugs."

"What did you find?" said Tilda.

"A crack pipe."

"Oh my god, Bobby," cried out Tilda. She asked the sergeant, "Is he high right now?"

The sergeant shook his head. "Crack cocaine produces an intense but short-lived high, lasting only minutes. We picked him up over an hour ago. He didn't seem particularly high then, and he certainly wouldn't be now."

"This is all so new to me," said Tilda. "What happens now?"

"We could hold him for the paraphernalia alone," the sergeant said, "but we don't think that's what he needs. We feel the support of family at a time like this is the single most important factor. The only thing he did tell us was to contact you and we took that as a good sign. Does he have any immediate family?"

"He has a mother," said Tilda. She struggled for words, but finally shook her head. "We haven't spoken in quite some time."

"Where is she?" said the sergeant.

"Corpus Christi," said Tilda. "I think."

The sergeant stared at Bobby closely. "You mean, you ran all the way from Corpus? Is that true, son?" Bobby's mouth transformed from petulance to a crooked smile and he seemed rather pleased with himself. Then the smile disappeared and he went still. The sergeant sniffed, neither laughing nor mocking. "In any event, we need to follow up with the mother. We looked for a missing person's report but we couldn't find one for this boy. Can either of you speak to the mother's state of mind, anything at all?"

"No," said Tilda.

"Okay," said the sergeant. "We put him in the jail garb because his clothes were soaked through and he was chilled to the bone. His clothes are almost dry and we would like to release him to you." Tilda and Elias looked between each other, for the first time confronting their own doubt and the large responsibility being dealt to them. "It's either that or he stays here until we find his mother."

Tilda paused, thinking. "We'll take him home," she said.

Tilda and Elias sat in the waiting area while Bobby changed clothes in a restroom. After he was dressed, the sergeant escorted all three of them out to the lobby, taking a last long look at Bobby as they passed through the sliding glass doors. The wind was still up from a recent rainstorm and Bobby saw gray, hurtling clouds against the absolute blackness of night. It was just before ten p.m.; Bobby realized the police station had few officers on duty and that it was surrounded by fields with high grass and a thicket of trees. For one wild instant, Bobby considered making a dash for the trees and the highway beyond. But as he considered this, he simultaneously realized he was extremely sore and tired, and as much as anything longed for a good night's sleep. His aunt opened the passenger door to the car and Bobby crawled into the backseat and almost immediately fell asleep.

He awoke when the dome light came on. The two adults got out but Bobby hesitated, trying to survey what he could from inside the car. In front of him, a silver yard light cast a sheen across the windshield, and it obscured whatever lay beyond. Behind him, he could see a black line of trees in the distance, and after that, nothing but night sky. He got out of the car slowly, keeping an eye on Elias, and he felt the cool wind billow against him. The night sounds of innumerable creatures formed an oddly reassuring melodic background.

He remembered little about the house, but when he saw it, it seemed immediately familiar: square with a low roof and a peak at the living room, white paint peeling on horizontal plank boards. Concrete steps led up to a wooden porch, and a workroom and a toolshed were separated from the main residence. The residence itself had rectangular windows illuminated from the inside by a yellow glow.

Bobby took in the scene a moment longer, scanning the live oaks and unmown grass out toward the toolshed, smelling the acrid, sweet odor of manure, unsure how to process the confluence of sensation amid memory. In one instant he felt an odd sense of renewal, and in the next he wanted to withdraw into himself entirely. His aunt stood only a few feet away and she watched him calmly, her expression open and rather curious. Bobby did not know how to interpret Tilda's quiet demeanor, and this unknown variable, along with his compromised autonomy, caused an unexpected rage to course through him. Then, to his intense embarrassment, his anger competed with an impulse to cry.

It was then that Elias stopped at the steps leading to the porch and pointed a bony index finger. "I want you to remember a couple of things, son," he declared. Bobby watched him, sizing him up. "You will have respect for the rules here. No cussing and sure as hell no drugs."

"Daddy," protested Tilda, "not now. He's been through a lot."

Bobby remained absolutely still, his face expressionless. He thought to himself that Elias was more than slightly stooped—bent at the chest was closer to the mark. Bobby remembered his grandfather as a large, sturdy man, but now his shoulders seemed squeezed together, and even in the relative darkness, Bobby could see exploded veins in his face. Bobby told himself that if it ever came to it, he could catch Elias unaware with the first move and likely take him.

"He needs to know the fundamentals," insisted Elias, staring malcontent at his grandson the whole time. In his gray windbreaker and black work boots, in the rigidity of his lips pressed together, he looked as though he might be the progeny of the pitchfork-bearing farmer in *American Gothic*. Once again, Elias raised a gnarled forefinger and pointed toward the emptiness of the countryside. "I'll kick him out so fast he won't know it."

Bobby's face betrayed no emotion, but he abruptly turned around and started walking the footpath toward the lane leading to the county road, the way they had just come from and, therefore, the way back out. Both adults watched him as a few steps quickly grew into fifty feet, then fifty yards. Tilda looked to her father for some manner of reconciliation and at least a muted plea for Bobby to return, but Elias simply shook his head. "Let him go," he called out, loud enough for Bobby to hear. "If he's going to be a horse's ass."

This seemed to embolden Bobby, who increased the tempo of his gait. Tilda watched her nephew recede from sight, quickly becoming a small gray figure against the enormity of night and threatening to vanish altogether. Tilda took a step forward, as if she were about to pursue him, but then she froze. "Bobby, stop," she cried out, a real alarm underscoring her words. "It's the middle of the night! There's nothing out there!"

In the distance, Bobby hesitated, stopping in his tracks. He tried to discern the distance to the line of trees, a place he figured he could hide until first light, but the darkness made mockery of any real estimate. He stood still, wavering. He took one more step toward the highway, but then reversed course and headed back toward the house, keeping his head down and avoiding eye contact as he headed up the long driveway to the threshold of the front door.

Once inside, he grappled with a series of competing impressions. It seemed to him he was in an alien environment, but one that was somehow very familiar. The house was from another time. The furniture was mostly wood and some of it was unvarnished. A sofa with a small tear in the light-blue fabric faced a TV, and an end table was covered with ceramic knickknacks, angels and overweight cherubs grinning in frozen contentment. "Be it ever so humble," read the inscription on one throw pillow; "There's no place like home," echoed another. A shelf next to a bookcase displayed a row of ornate Bavarian beer steins with pewter lids and thumb levers. But countering the anachronistic decor was a vent in the wall for central air and a circular shadow at the window indicating that the TV was hooked to a satellite.

Tilda, as silent as a ghost, moved up quietly beside Bobby, startling him. Tilda smiled wanly, seeming a little uncomfortable, and she made an odd hand gesture, one that seemed intended to convey hospitality. "I wish the circumstances were different," she said, a touch formally. "But, welcome. We're glad to have you here."

She led Bobby to a half-lit hallway, the walls bare. As they continued down the hall, the corridor darkened and the walls went from off-white to a dull gray. They came to a room and Tilda flipped a light switch.

"You'll stay here tonight." She appeared distracted, as if she were trying to recall a rote list of things to say to a guest. "You can have the run of the place, and get anything you like from the kitchen. The bathroom is further down the hall. If you need something, just ask me."

Bobby took in the room. The bed rested on an ancient rug, which covered a wooden floor littered here and there with dust bunnies. He saw an oak chest of drawers that supported a wooden bookshelf. There were no books. Instead, a collection of dusty porcelain dolls presided over the shelves, and their glassy eyes momentarily disconcerted Bobby. When he spoke, his voice was small. "Can I have a beer? I could really use one."

Tilda blinked. For a second, she seemed unsure of the correct response. Finally, she gathered the will to deliver the unfortunate news. "No, you can't," she said quietly. "Not here."

Bobby's face revealed nothing. For the first time, he took a long look at his aunt, trying to learn anything that might prove useful later. He could not ignore the obvious. A plain woman with a long, narrow face and mousy brown hair, approaching forty, still living under a parent's roof. Bobby assumed she still taught high school. Unlike her sister, Tilda's appearance was rather nondescript, but like her father, she could easily be the progeny of the farmers in *American Gothic*. Bobby's eyes were drawn to her hands; she wore no rings, and he pondered that telling detail. He then considered that she wore no bracelets, no necklace, no earrings—no jewelry of any kind. On top of that, Bobby tried to imagine what might lay behind her careful bearing and unchanging demeanor.

Tilda raised an involuntary hand to her mouth. "We need to call your mother," she said, rather urgently. "We have to tell her where you are."

Bobby furrowed his brow and lowered his gaze. Clearly Tilda believed that his mother must be worried. "She doesn't care," Bobby said, a resignation in his voice.

Tilda said nothing, and Bobby watched her face as she grappled with his statement. "Of course she does, Bobby," she said. "I can't believe that your mother doesn't care."

Her earnest naivety sent his emotions in several directions at once and he fought to contain them. More than anything else, he suddenly recognized an overriding need to protect his aunt. "No, she really doesn't."

"Bobby, I can't believe that."

He closed his eyes briefly, bracing himself for another moment of role reversal when he had to explain things to an adult in his life. "Okay, believe what you want," he said. "But it's too late now, anyway. They won't answer the phone."

"It's only ten thirty," protested Tilda.

"It's not that they're asleep," he said. "They're just not going to answer the phone."

"How can you know that?"

Bobby could no longer conceal his exasperation. "Call away, then," he said with a sweep of his hand. "You'll see.

And if they do happen to pick up, chances are you won't get many answers, believe me."

"How do you mean?"

Bobby considered telling her the plain truth, but he hedged at the last moment. "It's after six, it's night. They don't really . . . socialize after six."

"We have to try, Bobby."

"Well, call away, but I'm not going to talk to her," he said, a touch impatiently.

"What's the number, then?" said Tilda, Bobby's impatience momentarily rubbing off on her.

Bobby repeated the number twice. "I'm going to bed," he said.

"You sure you don't want to talk to her?"

"Why would I?"

He could sense Tilda observing him closely. "Well, okay then. Goodnight."

"'Night," said Bobby.

He wanted to say something else, not wanting Tilda to think he was irritated with her specifically, but she was already leaving the room. He could hear her footsteps as she traversed the hallway. Left alone in the room, with its dust, its homemade quilt, and the all-pervasive quiet, he felt unresolved. He suddenly wanted very much to hear what his aunt said to his mother, but he did not want to be in the same room as Elias. He took off his shoes, then stole down the hallway. He could hear the adults talking.

"Turn down the TV for a minute," said Tilda. "I'm going to call Regina."

"No telling what's up with that girl," said Elias. Bobby heard the rough texture that underlay his voice and thought he did not sound well. "I could have told her she'd raise her boy to be a runaway. Probably the best thing for him."

"Please be quiet, Daddy." Bobby heard Tilda key in the number, and Elias went quiet. "Hello," said Tilda. "Hello. I'm looking for Regina." She then repeated herself. "I said I'm looking for Regina." Bobby could feel Tilda's confounded patience—Vyasa had obviously picked up the phone high out of his mind. "I'm sorry, could you repeat that? Does Regina live there? I said, does Regina live there? Regina." Then Tilda hung up. "I wonder if that was the correct phone number," she said.

Bobby crept back down the hall, closing the door but not quite shutting it. He sat on the bed. In less than a minute, he heard a knock.

"Come in," said Bobby.

Tilda opened the door. "I just called your mother. A man answered and I couldn't understand a word he said. Does her boyfriend speak English?"

Bobby smirked, his face ultimately revealing a kind of disgust. "That was English you heard," he said. "Kind of."

"I don't understand."

Bobby waited, trying to find the right formulation. Finally, he shook his head, his voice raised slightly. "It was Mom's boyfriend. He's high right now."

"High?" Tilda was uncomfortable with the word. She looked at Bobby. "Are you sure that's it? He was incomprehensible."

"Well then, he's *really* high. Okay?" Tilda was momentarily immobilized. "He got so high once, I heard him howl into the phone."

"You mean, like a dog?"

Bobby nodded. He found it disagreeable to tell his aunt these things. "Yeah."

Tilda blinked. "Okay."

THE THIRD DOOR

**

Bobby awoke. It was still night and the bedroom was dark. In the murky light he saw one of the porcelain dolls, and it was then that he remembered his mother's doll collection and concluded that he must be in his mother's childhood bedroom. This kindled his anger, and he was about to sit up when a savage pain shot through his head. It felt like his skull was imploding. His mind instinctively sought escape from the pain and he felt a ghost rush as he imagined doing a hit. For a moment, he craved a real hit. His mind was beset by a chaotic assemblage of images, and almost instantly he connected that rush with lying in a strange bed in the dark fighting off disorientation and intense physical pain.

Hours later, bright sunlight showed through a pale-blue curtain, the rich light hurting Bobby's eyes. His head hurt worse than ever and he was unsure whether he could get out of bed. He tried to sit up but was almost overcome by dizziness. After a while, his head had cleared and he sat up fully and peered around him. Every object in the room stood out clean and sharp, and he wondered at the difference a few minutes could make.

He dressed and made his way out to the main living area. He could smell the toothsome odor of cooked sausage. He could not remember his last full meal, and his mouth watered involuntarily.

Elias sat at a dining table near the kitchen, eating a bowl of oatmeal, his face pink, his hair white. Elias wore gray work clothes and a pair of black work boots. Bobby slowed his gait as he approached his grandfather, but Elias pretended to ignore him, not quite able to put aside the notion of a young druggie grandson and the other dubious circumstances of their reunion.

Tilda's head popped in from around the kitchen doorframe. "Good morning," she said. Bobby thought she wanted to appear cheerful but was probably not. The reason she was not, Bobby realized, not without a bit of distaste, was him. "Are you hungry?"

"A little bit."

Bobby could see she was telling herself not to stare directly at the bruises on his face. "What would you like?"

"That sausage smells good."

"Anything else? Eggs? Toast?"

"Yeah, all that would be very nice."

"Daddy, make space for Bobby at the table."

Elias grumbled to himself and then sighed, getting up and moving some old radio equipment off the table. Bobby sat down and kept his eyes directed at the placemat in front of him; Elias stared at the newspaper. With his peripheral vision, Bobby saw Elias make a momentary chewing motion, as if he were swallowing something unpalatable.

Tilda appeared from around the corner with a skillet. "How are you feeling?" she said, maintaining an artificial lightness.

"Fine," said Bobby.

She smiled and nodded, but then paused. "You don't look fine."

Bobby was unused to being the subject of well-meaning adult scrutiny, and it embarrassed him. He gestured, frustrated and flippant. "It hurts a little, but I'll be all right."

"How about we go to the doctor later?" said Tilda. "Just a quick checkup."

"Really, there's no need. I'll be fine."

"Bobby, I've already called the doctor's office and

they're expecting us. We'll be back before lunch. It couldn't hurt things, right?"

Bobby found Tilda's logic irrefutable, and besides, he saw no way out. He had learned long ago that the first rule of the street is that nothing is free. Although he was positive his aunt had no ulterior motive, her unsolicited concern cut across years of conditioning and left him feeling trapped. He opened his mouth to speak and then closed it. "I can't pay you back," he suddenly exclaimed, a little loudly, surprising himself.

Tilda drew her head back, confused. Bobby felt excruciatingly embarrassed. He knew his aunt did not expect money in return. "I . . ." He sought the right words. "I'm sorry. I didn't mean that."

"It's all right," said Tilda. She, too, searched for an appropriate response. "You didn't say anything wrong."

Bobby nodded, mainly to himself. He knew this breach in etiquette was going to bother him for a while, but there was nothing left to do but accept the situation. He spoke slowly. "I could really use those eggs right now. If it's okay."

"Of course," said Tilda, smiling weakly. She deposited the eggs on his plate, and Bobby began to eat ravenously. The simple act of watching him tear into his food—the vulnerability of hunger, even in this street-tough boy—touched something inside of Tilda. "Of course, it's okay," she said, under her breath.

An hour later, Tilda drove over the gravel county road, a plume of dust following the car. Bobby's head rested against the window as he considered the green countryside going by, the image of the passing land stirring old memories, mind stuff he thought he had forgotten. He remembered this same rolling green countryside from long-ago trips into town with his aunt and his mother,

Tilda consoling Regina after a heated argument with their father or Regina prattling on about a new boyfriend.

"I am interested, you know," said Tilda, breaking the silence. Bobby, interrupted from the midst of his reverie, looked at her. Tilda wore tan khakis and an unadorned white top, her shoes not quite tennis shoes but clearly meant to be sensible. "I'm interested in whatever you want to tell me. Like, what you were doing in Cuero. How you got hurt. And especially, I'd like to know about your mother. How's she doing."

"I don't want to talk about my mother," said Bobby.

Tilda thought about that for a moment. "We used to get along, Bobby, your mother and I," she said. "We weren't terribly close, I think because we're not much alike, but I could see the good in her, which pains me right now because I have to ask this." Tilda shifted in the driver's seat, by all appearances steeling herself for the worst. "Did she do this to you?" Tilda nodded at the bruises on Bobby's face. "Or her boyfriend? Did she hurt you, Bobby?"

Bobby considered evading the question, but finally he shook his head. "No, my mother has never touched me. She's never let anyone hit me. I can say that much for her."

Tilda digested that bit of information. When she spoke again, she sounded confused.

"So, why did you leave home?"

Bobby seemed to search his feelings but then his eyes went hollow and he once again put the side of his head against the passenger window. His vacant stare reminded Tilda of a documentary she had once seen about survivors in Hiroshima. This sudden withdrawal from the moment troubled her; she had seen it in abused or neglected students. She weighed the benefits of trying to draw him out, but the fixed nature of his absent eyes persuaded her to leave him alone.

At the doctor's office, Tilda sat on a wooden bench in the tiled waiting area. She had brought along a briefcase of student papers, along with a copy of *The Scarlet Letter,* and she jotted down notes into a spiral notebook. The doctor appeared from a hallway and they went to an empty examination room. Out an unfrosted window, Tilda could see a field, bright spring sunlight on green grass and live oaks with twisted branches. She had known the doctor for over a decade, one of only a handful of general practitioners in the area. The doctor was tall and slender, his face and hands tanned in contrast to the white medical coat he wore, a professional competence present even in his movements, in his hand gestures and the tilt of his head.

"There doesn't appear to be any serious damage," said the doctor. "The wounds on his face are ugly, but superficial. He's young, he's resilient. At the same time, make no mistake—he's been through a lot."

"Nothing permanent, though," said Tilda.

"Physically, no, nothing permanent."

Tilda hesitated. "Was your examination comprehensive?"

"It was a thorough examination."

"And you didn't find other evidence . . ." She found the formulation she was seeking. "Of trauma?"

"There's no evidence of further assault, if that's what you're asking."

"Are you sure about that?"

"I'm sure there's no evidence of it." The doctor eyed Tilda intently. He was an anomaly for the area, an Atticus Finch type, somehow not quite part of the community, but still deeply committed to it. "But if you're asking what I think you're asking, some details might be impossible to find without the full cooperation of the patient. And he's not really cooperating."

Tilda looked pained but she nodded. "Thank you, doctor."

**

Tilda placed mustard and mayonnaise on the dining table, along with cold cuts, bread, and sliced cheese. It was just before noon and Elias was out in the fields. Tilda watched Bobby as he ate one sandwich, then two, then drained half a glass of milk. Bobby was entirely preoccupied with his food. Tilda ate part of a sandwich, scrutinizing her nephew carefully, his ragged jeans and long, lank air, his negligible arms and thin torso.

"The doctor says you're fine," said Tilda.

Bobby chewed the remnants of his second sandwich. "Good to know," he said, entirely uninterested.

"Do you feel okay?"

"Sure."

"Do you want to talk about how you feel?"

Bobby swallowed and looked at her, his face betraying no particular emotion. "Not especially."

Tilda set aside her plate. "You see, Bobby, what I want to know as much as anything else is this—even if the doctor says you're fine, are you?"

Bobby understood the implications of the question and remained nonreactive. He drained the last of his milk in a few swallows and rubbed a hand across his mouth. "I suppose you could say I'm about as good as can be expected," he said.

"Well, to tell the truth, Bobby, I'd like to talk about all this a little bit more. About all the things we haven't talked about yet. We could start at any number of places, but I would like to start with the obvious. I'd like to know who hurt you."

Bobby could summon animal-like stillness at will. He eyed his aunt slowly, only his eyes moving. "I think I feel tired," he said finally, coming up with the one avoidance mechanism that his aunt could not refute. "If you don't mind, I'd like to go back to bed."

"You don't want to talk?"

"I really think I need a nap."

Tilda clasped the back of her neck with her right hand. "We'll need to talk about these things at some point, Bobby."

"I appreciate all this," said Bobby. "All you've done for me. I do. But it's been a long day already, and I'd like to sleep for a while."

"Of course, Bobby." Tilda clearly wanted to say more but reverted to the fundamentals of decorum. "Remember, you're a guest here."

Bobby did not enjoy frustrating his aunt. He stood up from the table, turned into the bedroom and laid down, pulling the sheets and quilt over him. For several minutes, he rested on his back and stared at the ceiling. When he had said he wanted a nap, he thought it merely a convenient means of avoiding a question he didn't want to answer, but he suddenly felt a real need for sleep. He fought the effects of oncoming drowsiness as long as he could, but in a short time he was sound asleep.

When he woke up, the light in the room was much dimmer, and he could tell by the sun's reflection off the window that it was late afternoon. His head hurt badly, so much so that it affected his vision. At the periphery of his sight, the world blurred, and the unfamiliarity of the experience frustrated him. He wandered out to the living room, where his aunt was reading on the sofa.

"Do you have an aspirin?" he said.

Tilda seemed surprised by the sound of his voice. "Yes, of course," she said, putting down the book and getting up. "What's wrong?"

"I have a headache," he said.

Tilda went into a bathroom and returned with a bottle of pills. "What does it feel like?"

"Like I've had the shit beaten out of me," said Bobby, without sarcasm or any attempt at drama. Tilda simply nodded.

"Take these," said Tilda, who gave him two aspirin.

"Are you sure I can't have a beer to wash these down?" said Bobby. "My mother lets me drink beer."

"Your mother's not here right now," said Tilda. "And this is my house."

For reasons he could not divine, Bobby felt the need to justify himself. "I was just asking," he said.

"Well, that's the second time you've asked. And you know the answer now."

Tilda was not short nor was she impatient, yet Bobby felt something he had not experienced before. Over the past several months, beer had become a daily fixture in his life, and he had routinely managed to get hold of whiskey as well. But here and now, his need for alcohol, for the first time ever, went beyond mere craving. From the most fundamental depths of his being, he needed a drink. Tilda stood before him, her expression sincere and eternally constant, but Bobby had no words to articulate what he felt, so he withdrew into himself. For what seemed an eternity he fought a riot of impulses, but over it all he heard himself exclaim that it was only one fucking beer. At last, when he could wrest control of his anger, he saw Tilda's face. She did not appear upset with him, merely concerned.

He said nothing to his aunt. His sense of confinement magnified dramatically, and he headed for the front door without a word of explanation. Tilda called after him but he ignored her and continued on outside, assaulted by springtime scents and the thin blue sky high above. He looked back once toward the house; his aunt watched him from the doorway. Before he knew it, he had reached the end of the lane, and the gravel county road unfolded before him, hugging the contours of the green, rolling land. He walked for about a quarter mile and then stopped. He calculated that it was at least a few miles to the highway, and he told himself that with a little bit of luck he could hitchhike his way to Austin by midnight.

He held on to that idea a moment longer, but then felt confused. Sitting down in the grass beside the road, he grabbed a stick and began prodding the ground. He guessed that his aunt had let him leave because she assumed this was merely a high-temper fit, and that once it had run its course, he would come back. If he didn't come back, he strongly suspected, his aunt would call the police, and out on the open road, he would be a sitting duck. He prodded the ground some more, his anger dissipating, his craving for alcohol subsiding. He told himself that his aunt had been straight with him so far, that she seemed to have his best interests at heart, even though he recognized that the need for both alcohol and autonomy would return. He looked up the road and saw his aunt bending a curve. She halted in her tracks momentarily when she saw him, but then continued on toward him. Even if he desperately wanted to get to Austin, he reminded himself—standing up and walking back toward the house—in all likelihood it would not be tonight.

By the time dinner was served, Bobby had restored emotional equilibrium. All three ate in relative silence, and each consumed his or her entire portion of chopped steak, mashed potatoes, and mustard greens. As dinner wound down, Elias and Bobby shifted in their chairs, away from each other. After several rounds of this, Elias appeared frustrated.

"I'm going out to the toolshed," he announced, rising. "Son, you help your aunt clean up the table."

"Why aren't you helping?" said Bobby.

Elias acted as if he did not hear this and walked out the front door into the evening air. Bobby was again alone with Tilda.

"I'll clean this up in a minute," said Tilda. "I'd like to talk to you."

"Okay," said Bobby. He'd known this was coming, but after his outburst in the late afternoon, he was far more amenable to Tilda's questions.

"Let me say, first of all, it hasn't escaped my attention that you haven't asked us anything about returning home," said Tilda.

"Why would I?" said Bobby, simply.

"Because most twelve-year-old boys—"

"I'm thirteen," said Bobby. "I turned thirteen in February."

"Thirteen-year-old boys," said Tilda, not skipping a beat. "Most of them like to be home, with their families."

"I'm beginning to think you're not listening to me."

"I am listening, Bobby," she said. "But you're not telling me very much."

"What do you want to know?"

"Who hurt you?"

"That's my business. It's only between me and the guy who did it."

"Okay then, how did you get here? Did you hitchhike?"

"Sort of. I got a ride with a friend of a friend."

"Did you know the person driving?"

"No."

"Isn't that dangerous, considering your age?"

"I'm still in one piece," said Bobby.

Tilda did not speak but sat squarely in her chair, facing her nephew earnestly. Finally, she nodded. "So, why did you leave home?"

Bobby tilted his head and rubbed his chin as if he were thinking, clearly not relishing this moment. He considered saying something evasive but at last he shrugged. "I couldn't stand it."

"Why not?"

"It was a freak show."

"How do you mean?"

Bobby didn't find the question unfair, but it was unclear to him how he might adequately describe the situation to his aunt. "They were all lost," he said, slowly. He shrugged again. "To a person, completely lost."

"Including your mother?"

"Especially my mother," he said. Tilda swallowed, as if Bobby's answers caused her physical pain. Bobby could tell he would need to redirect his aunt, and when he spoke again, he sounded resigned and a little tired. "Where do you want me to begin?"

"How's Regina?"

"Not very good."

"No?"

"No."

"What do you mean? Does she have a job?"

"After we first settled in Corpus, she did. Several. She was a waitress."

"But she doesn't have one now."

"She quit over six months ago."

"And she has a boyfriend?"

"Yes," said Bobby. "Vyasa."

"Come again?"

"Vyasa. She's living with a guy named Vyasa."

"What kind of name is that?"

"Hindu, I think," said Bobby. "I don't really know. His real name's Larry. But he calls himself Vyasa."

"Why does he call himself that?"

"It's supposed to be a holy name. He says he talks to God."

Tilda's eyes grew wide. She looked baffled. "Is he a minister of some kind?"

Bobby laughed. "You mean church?"

"Well, I guess."

"No."

"What does he do, then?"

"He thinks he's a shaman."

"A shaman," she repeated.

"A healer."

Frustration crept into Tilda's voice. "I know what a shaman is." She paused. "Does he have a job?"

"He deals." Tilda appeared baffled. "He sells drugs."

Tilda's lips stretched over her teeth and lost some of their color. At last, she said, "How is my sister doing?"

It hurt Bobby to look at Tilda's face. He almost said the first thing that came to mind, which would've been glib and somewhat nasty. But he thought about it, thought it through, and then said, slowly, "She's crossed over."

"I don't understand."

"It's something one of my friends says. It's polite." He hesitated, but then the words were out before he realized it. "It means she's bitched."

Tilda swallowed again and went quiet. She nodded, indicating that Bobby should continue.

Bobby clenched his jaw. He thought to himself that even from a hundred miles away his mother made his life a hell. Right then he saw himself, his entire life, the utter meaninglessness that shadowed him. He felt the street rise in him, and then the words were out of his mouth before he could filter them. "It means," said Bobby, "that she's a fucking addict. A crack-smoking, junk-shooting addict. And I lived in this goddamned apartment with her, her goddamned junkie-dealer boyfriend, and his bitched-out junkie best friend, Charlie, for over five months, and watched her go from crazy, alcoholic, occasional user who couldn't keep a boyfriend or a job for a month to plain old junkie bitch."

Tilda's eyes were riveted to Bobby's face. Bobby suddenly found himself without his feelings, without any feelings, looking into the gentle face of his aunt. For the second time in a span of hours, so many dynamics were occurring that even Bobby, hardened and attuned to observing nuance in a twitch of a mouth or a blink of an eye, could not keep up with them. "I'm sorry," he said, and he felt a wave of revulsion.

"My god," said Tilda. "Was this all in Corpus Christi?"

"Yes," said Bobby.

"Can you take us to where she lives?"

"I know the neighborhood. If I was in the neighborhood, I could find the apartment. But she sold our car a long time ago and I didn't get around town very much. I probably would have a hard time finding it from here."

"Do you remember an address?"

"Yeah."

"I've got to talk to her."

"I don't want to talk to her."

"She's your mother."

"Not really. Not anymore."

"I can't believe this," said Tilda, mostly to herself. "I can't believe it."

"I don't know if you should see her," said Bobby. He put together the next sentence carefully, then spoke it without affect. "It's like a nightmare."

Tilda was firm. "I've got to see her," she said.

"I'm not sure if she'll see you."

Tilda went into the kitchen and returned with two glasses of iced tea. Bobby looked at his glass with disinterest as Tilda sat back down. "You're not exaggerating all this, are you." It was more a statement than a question. Then Tilda tried a new line of inquiry. "Where did you go to school?"

"I didn't. I haven't been in school since last May, long before we moved in with Vyasa."

"Didn't someone—the school—try to find you?"

"Not especially," said Bobby, simply.

"What have you been doing with your time?"

"I watch a lot of TV."

"Do you want to go to school?"

"Not really. I don't see the point."

"You know that I'm a teacher."

"Yes."

"Would you try it out? Give it some time?"

"I don't know," said Bobby. He paused. "You're going to send me back, aren't you? To Corpus."

"I haven't really thought that far ahead, Bobby."

"I would leave again. As soon as I could."

"Bobby, we could try to make it different for you. If what you say is true, we could try to help your mother. People do change. And she is your mother."

"You haven't heard me."

"Bobby, I would not send you into a situation where you're going to be hurt. But whatever I might do for you, please remember one thing—I'm not your mother."

Although Tilda did not intend to be hurtful, Bobby flinched ever so slightly, the reminder of his harsh reality like a boxer's jab to the gut. He reminded Tilda of the country dogs that prowled the edge of their property, dogs that had long ago learned the patience and guile necessary to survive. A wave of dejection seemed to reanimate him and recast his face with a haunted, regretful aspect. Tilda imagined he was weighing his options, and that once again he couldn't find a single winning card in the deck. At last, Bobby sat up straight in his chair, and the aspect of regret disappeared. "One thing," he said to Tilda, his voice clear, "I do have a question."

Tilda waited for the question, but Bobby paused. "Yes?" said Tilda.

The paused continued, but at last, Bobby looked at his aunt directly. "Did she ever talk to you about my father?"

Tilda was surprised. She felt as though this was the first time he had engaged her, and his chief concern was not his mother but his father. "No, she didn't."

The questions arrived in rapid succession, a persistence to the asking. "Did she mention a name? Where he lives? What he does? Anything?"

Tilda hesitated. She could tell this was important to him, but she could do nothing but confer bad news. "No, Bobby, she kept the issue dark. If I were guessing, I don't think she wanted our father to know."

Bobby's expression soured. At last, he nodded. "Figures."

**

When they were done talking, Bobby went to the living room and watched a basketball game on TV. Tilda remained seated at the dining room table, drinking her tea. Elias came back inside and Tilda called to him. Bobby could hear faint voices in the adjoining room but he made no attempt to listen to what they said. After a time, Bobby heard Elias raise his voice.

"What?" Elias said, and then Bobby heard a crash.

"Daddy," said Tilda. "Daddy, sit down."

"Where is he?" bellowed Elias. "I want to talk to him."

Bobby felt galvanized and sprang up, bounding to the wide doorframe of the dining room. He grinned involuntarily, savoring the prospect of a real confrontation with his grandfather, reminding himself that getting in the first blow might prove critical. If they came to blows, he was ready to hit the road and hitch his way to Austin.

"What's happened to Regina?" Elias demanded. "What's happened to my daughter?"

"I told her," exclaimed Bobby, indicating Tilda. "Ask her."

"I'm asking you," said Elias.

"She's doing great," said Bobby, acidly. "She's doing just swell."

"Daddy, sit down and lower your voice," said Tilda.

Elias was so full of rage that he tottered. "I'm talking to him. I'm talking to my grandson."

"You're not talking to anybody," said Tilda. "Now calm

down."

Elias's fury reached such an emotional pitch that he seemed immobilized. He put his hand to his eyes and bent over. He shook his head, and then he seemed to shrink, in a moment going from an enraged giant to a spent old man. Bobby's posture relaxed, and he began to pity the sight before him. "I'm sorry," said Elias, blinking back tears. "I'm sorry."

And with that, Elias fled from the room.

**

Bobby started and woke up fully. It was pitch-dark in the bedroom, save for the residual light from the yard lamps outside. Bobby decided he was no longer tired and sat up, checking the clock next to the bed. One fourteen. He remained sitting up, his eyes adjusting to the dark, when he heard a sound from elsewhere in the house. He got up and dressed, already tired of the shirt he was now putting on for the third straight day. From the hallway, he could see the living room bathed in blue light and he stopped at the threshold and peered around the corner. Elias sat at one end of the living room sofa, a half-empty liter of whiskey beside him on a table and a small glass in his hand.

Elias spotted Bobby. "Hey, son," he said, a resonant brightness in his voice. "Come on in," he urged, welcoming Bobby with a wave of his hand. "Come on in. I won't bite."

Elias wore baggy shorts and an old T-shirt that looked gray in the blue light. In the bloodless pallor of the TV, his legs appeared thin and white. Bobby considered going back to his room, but something held him there. He couldn't quite bring himself to enter the room but he couldn't retreat either.

"You think I'm a real bastard, don't you," said Elias. "Come on, let me make it up to you. How about a drink? You want a drink?"

Bobby's thoughts turned back to the late afternoon, when his craving for a drink proved almost more than he could bear. He wondered if his yearning for autonomy conflicted with the nearly overriding need for alcohol. Alcoholism was a form of slavery exactly like that to which his mother had submitted and he considered that he might be better off refraining from a drink. In the next instant, he dismissed this mode of reasoning, quickly discovering his voice. "You sharing with me?"

"Sure, why not? Why the hell not? What's a drink or two between a couple of guys?"

Bobby sped to the kitchen. "I'm getting a glass."

"Yeah, yeah," said Elias. "Even I don't drink straight from the bottle." Bobby retrieved a glass and handed it to Elias. "You probably want a little bit of ice and water there, son."

"I like it better straight."

"You've had it straight?"

Bobby checked out the bottle. "Evan Williams? No, I've never tried Evan Williams."

"No, I meant whiskey. You know a bit about whiskey?"

"I've had whiskey," said Bobby, simply.

"I see," said Elias. There was a slur to his words. "My grandson is twelve and knows about whiskey." Without further ceremony, Elias poured Bobby a drink.

Bobby sat at one end of the sofa, Elias at the other. Elias was watching a black-and-white John Wayne Western that Bobby had never seen. Bobby drank his glass quickly and passed it to Elias, who poured Bobby another. "Don't drink too fast," said Elias.

"I'm not drinking fast," said Bobby.

"That's what a lot of guys say. And then it hits them." Bobby nodded, shrugging. "You're kind of a tough kid, aren't you?" Elias said.

"I don't really like to fight."

"You're still kind of tough," said Elias, who watched his grandson from the corner of his eye. "Guys who fight, they ain't necessarily tough."

"Yeah, I guess."

"I was a lot like you once. More than you know."

"Yeah?" said Bobby.

"Yeah," said Elias. He nodded, looking doubtful in spite of his affirmation. "Believe it or not."

They drank in silence. Bobby began to enjoy the movie. From time to time, Elias would take a deep breath, exhale loudly, and look around him. He rubbed his eyes and said something to himself, so softly that Bobby did not understand. After that, Elias got up and went to the kitchen, then returned with more ice. "You're a good kid," he said, sitting down. "I can tell. You're basically a good kid, just full of hell. I understand. I understand that."

More silence ensued. Elias's drinking sped up. Bobby noticed that he was now drinking whole glasses in a swallow. "My wife left me, you know. A long time ago. It was my burden that drove her away. Tilda was just a girl, Regina was a baby, and she just left. Left me with two daughters, alone. I don't even know exactly where she went. But it was my fault. All along it was me. My burden. She couldn't take it. All the yelling. I'd lose it over nothing. Like today. I don't even know what happens. Sometimes I don't even remember. Everything just goes black and I might as well be an animal, a snarling dog or something." Elias looked at Bobby, his expression so unguarded that

Bobby looked away. "You don't even hear me, do you?"

"I'm listening," said Bobby.

Elias nodded, but soon his eyes receded. "Regina has it too, you know. The burden. The anger. You know what I'm talking about, don't you, son?"

Bobby did, in fact, know what his grandfather meant. "Yeah, I know," he said, a bit reluctantly.

"I could never talk to Regina. Never. Tilda's nice as pie, level-headed. And Regina, always one goddamned stupid notion or another. She came home one day when she was seventeen with green hair. Said she was a punk. I said, 'Yeah, you look like a punk.' She said it meant something, something in England. Hell, I still have no idea what she was talking about. I bet there was nobody within a hundred miles of here who knew what she was talking about. I told her to fix her hair, make it go back. She just started screaming at me, and I went black, and the next thing I knew, I hit her. I hit her with my fist. Green hair or not. Green hair or not."

Bobby imagined a younger version of his grandfather, the big hands and the broad shoulders, the force that must have propelled such a blow. "Where did you hit her?"

"What?" said Elias.

"I said, where did you hit her?"

"Here," said Elias. "Here in the living room."

"No, where on her? Her face, her gut?"

Elias raised his chin, seeming to ponder Bobby's question at length, his shoulders tightening. "I don't remember."

"She's never hit me, you know." Bobby's voice was a clear sound in the quiet.

Bobby looked at Elias, who looked as though he might be pondering a question of high philosophical import. "I just wanted you to know that."

Elias nodded robotically, obstinately silent. He poured another glassful, which finished the bottle, so he got up, went to the kitchen, and returned with a full bottle. He sat down again. "I always keep one in reserve. You want another drink, son? You look like you could use another drink."

"Sure," said Bobby.

"You're a good kid, like I said. You probably been raised wrong. That's all. Just don't take drugs."

"Why not?" Bobby said. "Why not take drugs?"

"They're bad for you."

"So's whiskey."

"Hard to argue with that," said Elias, and he paused. "What are they like?"

"What?"

Elias tried to conceal his curiosity, but failed. "Well, drugs."

"Which drugs?"

"I don't know. I've never done them."

"Well, they're different."

"Yeah?"

"Yeah," Bobby reaffirmed, sounding as though they were discussing the virtues of a brand of motor oil. "I think you'd probably like pot."

"Marijuana?"

"Yeah." Bobby looked at his grandfather, whose face had become purple and bloated due to the alcohol. "You probably shouldn't do coke," said Bobby. "Never."

After a few minutes, Elias tried to take another sip from his glass but instead spilled half his drink on himself. He didn't seem to notice.

"You okay?" said Bobby.

"I tried. I did try." He took another enormous sip, finishing half the glass in a swallow, spilling more in the process. He stood up shakily. "I did everything I know." He gestured with his free hand. "Now look at this. You're a runaway. She's on drugs. My daughter's on drugs." He paused, unsteady on his feet. "I mean, I tried. I raised them churchgoing, made sure they were at school on time every day. I didn't drink in front of them, didn't have women in the house. They were always fed, always had clothes on their backs. I did everything I could. I tried." He sat down, placing the cold glass to his forehead. "I tried. I did try. I did try."

Elias muttered something unintelligible, but soon thereafter, his head sank backwards into the cushions and his eyes closed. Bobby stood and took the glass from Elias's hand, then observed his grandfather. He tried to dispassionately evaluate the situation, but to his surprise he found that he did not have it in him to calculate an advantage. Instead, he reached forward to shake the old man, to rouse him and get him to his room; but at the last moment, Bobby pulled back and sat back down. Even if Elias was no longer an adversary, Bobby still couldn't quite forgive his conduct during the past twenty-eight hours. Bobby finished his drink and poured another, watching the movie as Elias snored loudly beside him. Bobby thought to himself that the whiskey bottle was still half full and the John Wayne movie still had a ways to go before the end.

**

Tilda put her hand on Bobby's shoulder and shook him gently. "It's after nine. You need to get up," she said. "I'll make breakfast. We're going to see your mother."

"I don't want to go," said Bobby.

"You have to go, Bobby. Only you know where she lives."

Bobby ate in silence. Tilda read the newspaper but appeared jumpy and impatient.

"Where's . . ." Bobby was at a loss for words. What should he call Elias? Granpa? Elias? Him? "Where's Gramps?" he said at last, and after saying it, he liked it.

Tilda looked up from the newspaper, surprised by Bobby's term of endearment. "He went to town. He won't be coming with us."

"Why not?"

"It's probably for the best, don't you think?"

Bobby thought that Tilda did not seem like herself at all, and she ate only half of her English muffin. She seemed to be reading the newspaper as a means of distraction, but she flitted from one page to another, her attention never settling on any one article. "We don't have to do this," said Bobby. "Have you called?"

"Yes," said Tilda. "I talked to her right before I woke you up."

"I'm surprised someone answered."

"I think I woke her up."

"Did she answer, or a man?"

"A man answered but passed her the phone."

"What did she say?"

"She knows I found you, she knows we're coming."

"We really don't have to do this. At least, not today."

"Yes we do, Bobby," said Tilda. "We have to do this."

They drove in silence. The land flattened as they approached the coast, the Gulf plain scrub hurtling past their windows. For as far as Bobby could see, they were the only car on the highway. After a while, Tilda turned toward

Bobby, keeping an eye on the road. "What does she look like?"

"Mom?"

"Yes."

Bobby thought about it. "I'm not sure what you're asking."

"Does she look like herself?"

"Yes and no. She hasn't turned into a monster, if that's what you're asking. But she's probably different from what you remember."

Tilda leaned toward the steering wheel, her shoulders hunched as her neck craned forward. It seemed to Bobby as if she were preparing herself for the worst, like a boxer absorbing the blows of a sparring partner. "What's the apartment like?"

"Well, it's just an apartment."

"How many bedrooms?"

"One."

She nodded ever so slightly, as if she were confirming an anticipated answer. "Where'd you sleep?"

"On the sofa."

"In the living room?"

"Yes."

She nodded, again. "Is the apartment a mess?"

"There's not enough stuff in it for it to be a mess."

Tilda hesitated. It seemed to Bobby she was leading up to a final set of questions. "Did you ever see your mother take drugs?"

"No, not exactly. I saw a lot of cocaine and heroin and I saw her high lots of times."

"Where did she go to do all that?"

"Her bedroom. That's where they keep the drugs. Under lock and key."

Tilda nodded. She appeared momentarily satisfied. "Okay, I think that's enough."

As they neared Corpus Christi, Bobby became aware of an increasingly uncomfortable feeling. It was not exactly fear, but a generally gray feeling, like a pall across a blue sky—a feeling as if he were attending a funeral, although he had never been to a funeral. He noticed that his fingers drummed against his leg, and this same leg shook very lightly. By turns he was aware that he was angry, then morose, then there was nothing, just a blankness in the hollow of his chest. As they drove, downtown Corpus Christi arose from the plain, and simply the sight of the town caused his feelings to range across a wide gamut.

"It's not much farther," he said, as much to himself as to his aunt.

Bobby was surprised to see that Tilda was perhaps equally affected. She nodded, but her mind was clearly elsewhere.

Bobby found himself in his neighborhood. They passed a fried chicken joint, a drugstore with a local gang's tag on the side of a dumpster in the concrete parking lot. A line of low-flung strip malls sped by the passenger window. He began directing Tilda to the apartment building, and within minutes they were parked outside of it. It was a clear day, bright, and a spring scent filled the air.

"Which apartment is it?" said Tilda. Bobby told her the number and directed her. Tilda got out of the car but Bobby did not. "Aren't you coming?" said Tilda.

Bobby looked at the little collection of buildings, at the tiny stairwells and gravel stairsteps, the gray walkways, the native grass. The parking lot itself could accommodate only a few dozen cars, and Bobby wondered how such a small place could loom so large in his imagination. "No, I'd like to stay here," he said, finally.

Tilda appeared disappointed. "Bobby, I think your mother would really want to see you."

"No, I think it has more to do with you. That you really want me to be there when you see her."

"Let's not argue, Bobby."

"I'm not arguing."

Tilda grappled with Bobby's stubborn refusal but relented. "Okay. Keep the doors locked, then, and don't be surprised when I bring her down here to you."

Tilda turned up the walkway and began climbing the stairs to the second-floor landing. Bobby watched her, feeling detached, as if he were watching a scene in a movie. As Tilda climbed the stairs, the wind blew her hair and the spring sunlight reflected off her white shirt. She seemed small and forlorn, like a mouse about to swim a body of water. The feeling of detachment passed and all at once he felt a tremendous empathy with his aunt as she turned a corner on the landing and disappeared from view. Bobby got out of the car and trotted across the parking lot and headed up the stairs. He caught up with Tilda just before she knocked on the apartment door. Tilda nodded, almost as if she were saying *We're both in this together now*. Tilda rapped twice on the door. Bobby brushed past her and rapped several times, hard.

"They may not hear it," he said to Tilda, a little sheepishly.

Bobby feared she might lose the power of speech. Bobby heard the rattling of locks, and then the door opened. Regina stood at the threshold in her newest pair of jeans and a long-sleeved T-shirt, blinking in the noon daylight. She was not obviously high, but her eyes were puffy and red. Bobby assumed she probably had smoked a little pot to calm herself, and he wondered if Tilda would notice such a thing. In the light of day, Bobby thought his mother looked older than she should, the wear of several years fully taking hold, her dirty blonde hair almost brown and the skin around her eyes thin and wrinkled.

Tilda took a breath and smiled self-consciously. "Hi, little sister," she said.

"Hi," said Regina, keeping a poker face, backing up and refusing to make eye contact with Bobby. "This isn't the Taj Mahal, but come in."

Tilda went first, and Bobby followed her into the living room. Although it had been only three days since he left home, Bobby felt as though he were seeing the room for the first time—the TV on the plastic carton box, the musty sofa and brown carpet, the dust floating in the air and the consequential silence interrupted by the thin, tinny babble from the TV. Bobby thought the interior had the elusive, unmistakable feel of a drug house. Once again, he wondered if Tilda could read this. To top it off, Charlie was on the floor, wrapped in his ragged baby-blue blanket.

"You have a guest," said Tilda. Both women seemed on their best behavior. "I hope we're not intruding."

"That ain't no guest," said Bobby. "That's Charlie."

"He's a friend of my boyfriend," said Regina to Tilda, hurriedly.

"Where is your boyfriend?"

"Larry's out doing a job."

"Too bad. I wanted to meet him."

Bobby could see that his mother wore the long-sleeved shirt to cover the bruises on her left arm, and that she was doing everything she could to minimize her lurching, chaotic manner.

Tilda walked over to Charlie and extended her hand;

Charlie stared up blankly. "I'm Tilda," she said, keeping her hand extended.

Charlie did not take her hand. "Charlie," he managed. He turned back to the TV.

Tilda rejoined her sister. "Does he stay here?"

"He's a good friend," said Regina, avoiding the question.

"He's there all the time," said Bobby. "Just like you see him now."

"Is that the sofa you slept on, Bobby?"

"Yes."

"Did this man sleep next to you at night?"

Regina's mouth parted, aghast. "I don't think I got any coffee," she said in a clear effort to change the subject.

"I don't need any coffee," said Tilda.

"Well, good, because I don't think I got any."

At last Tilda said, "How are you, Regina?"

"I'm fine."

"Really?" said Tilda.

"Well, yes," said Regina. She seemed to think about it. "I'm not gonna lie. I'm not gonna say there haven't been rough patches lately. But I'm fine. I'm getting better."

Tilda smiled weakly. "We're concerned about you. All of us are."

"Well, I'm working things out, you know. But I'm good. I'm good."

Tilda found a delicate voice. "Bobby says differently."

Regina frowned and several opposing emotions seemed to cross her face. But at last, she said, "I can't control that boy any more than I can control the weather."

"He's your son."

"He's hell on wheels."

"You haven't seen him in days, he's beat up, and you

don't seem particularly concerned about him."

This stunned Regina, as if someone had struck her in the face, but she recovered, gesturing elaborately. "Believe me when I say it, sister, it's not the first time he's stayed away, and it's not the first time I've seen him roughed up. When he turned up missing after a couple of days, me and Larry found out from a friend that he told a neighborhood girl that he's trying to get to Austin. I mean, what are you supposed to do with that? He's wild. Just wild."

"Did you call the police?"

Regina again looked aghast, but seemed to realize how this might appear and covered it up quickly. "Well, of course I was worried. How could a mother not be? But you should try living with this boy. He's an endless source of torment."

"He seems agreeable enough to me," said Tilda.

"You don't know the half of it, sister."

"Does that mean you didn't call the police?" persisted Tilda.

Regina stammered and a wild light filled her eyes as an instant stretched into seconds and she struggled to find the right answer amid the many conflicting ones that were not quite appropriate. Finally she said, "Larry's had some run-ins with the cops before. He's still bitter about it."

"I see," said Tilda, who took a cleansing breath. "Little sister, I love you."

Regina seemed unsure of the best way to respond. "I love you, too."

"What would you say if I asked you to come back home right now? We could fix you up a room, and you could stay there for as long as you liked. I bet we could even refit the work room, and you could have a place to stay, away from the house, away from Daddy."

Regina smiled as if she had just heard a particularly funny joke. "You're talking crazy, sister."

"I'm being dead serious."

"I can't go back, Tilda. With all we've been through with Daddy, you know that. You should know that in your heart."

"You can't stay here, either," said Tilda, avoiding taking the bait with the reference to her absent father. Tilda did not want the conversation to become about Elias. "I wasn't sure what to expect driving here. Bobby told me some things, and in my head, it was all just imagination. Now that I see it, it's real to me."

"What are you saying?"

"I don't know exactly what you're doing here, but I understand this place now. I was going to ask you a bunch of questions, but that's not necessary. All I know is one thing—you shouldn't be here."

"This is my life," said Regina. "My life is here."

"This life has nothing in store but a bad end." Tilda seemed to reflect on that statement. "Are you sure you won't come home?"

"I can't."

"Okay." Tilda hesitated but then plowed on. "Would you tell me where you keep Bobby's clothes?"

"What?"

"Where do you keep his clothes? I'll go get them."

"Why do you want his clothes?" said Regina.

"Because he can't stay here."

Regina was stunned. "You want to keep him? He ain't no pet."

Tilda repeated. "He can't stay here. Not like this. He can't live like this."

"Well, Christ, Tilda."

"You can get him whenever you want. When you're ready. He'll be right there."

"I don't believe this."

"Just show me where his clothes are."

Regina looked at Bobby. "Did you know about this?"

Bobby looked from his aunt to his mother. "No."

"Are you going to say anything?"

"I don't think so," said Bobby.

"Just tell me where his clothes are," insisted Tilda.

"Sister—"

"Do you really want him?" said Tilda, with a sudden fierceness that caught everyone by surprise, including Tilda herself. "It's a question. Do you want him? If you do, straighten yourself out. Otherwise, he's coming with me."

Minutes later, Bobby and Tilda scrambled into the car, Bobby's clothes forming a small pile in the backseat. Bobby looked to the window of his mother's apartment and imagined he could see the shadow of a person behind the blind. Bobby could not tell if it was a trick of light, and when he looked again, the shadow was gone.

"Do you know what you're doing?" Bobby said.

"I can't leave you here, Bobby."

"I don't even know what to call you."

"Aunt Tilda. Call me Aunt Tilda."

Despite the domestic turmoil that he was fleeing from in the first place, Bobby felt a wave of anxiety and wondered if he could adjust to the sort of life Tilda would expect him to lead. Along with that thought, he wondered if he might prove to be a millstone around his aunt's neck, a constant source of trouble. "Do you know what you're doing, Aunt Tilda?"

"No." The keys rattled in her hands as she put them in the ignition and started the car, clearly grappling with the new life situation she had just accepted. "What's past is past," she said, slowly. "What you've done up to now, you had to do, and I understand that. But you see, I don't want you to turn out like that. You're safe now. You're safe."

Tilda pulled to the edge of the parking lot and waited for an opening in the traffic, preoccupied by the road in front of her. That was when she heard the sniffling noises. She looked to Bobby, and despite the irrefutable scene before her, she could scarcely believe it. Bobby wept openly, rows of tears on his cheeks, his mouth contorted and red. "Aunt Tilda," he said, the sound of his voice distorted to the point that it resembled that of a crying child. "I don't want you to get the wrong idea. I am grateful for this. I am. But the thing you should know is, I don't feel safe. I don't know if I'll feel safe for a very long time."

BOOK 2, CHAPTER 3
September, 2003

Bobby awoke suddenly, opening his eyes and propping himself up on one elbow. A keen sense of panic ran through him until, by degrees, he realized he was in his own bed. He sat up, resting the pillow behind him on the wall. He reached for a cigarette on the nightstand and lit it, taking long, deliberate drags. He coughed, quietly at first, but the expulsions grew longer, until he was hacking from an area deep in his lungs. The coughing stopped and he took a full breath.

Based on the angle of the sunlight on the Manila blinds, Bobby guessed it was close to noon. He noted the bedroom, with its constant color motif of gray and off-white. He ashed his cigarette in a ceramic cereal bowl, putting his fingers to the bridge of his nose, and considered the night before. Splinters of memories formed reluctantly against the haze in his mind. Dinner at the Jackalope, a cheeseburger; a walk amidst the congested foot traffic of Sixth Street; a brief stop in the head shop to chat with a clerk; turning on his phone about five o'clock; a quick couple of bourbons before going out. Sales were strong, so strong that he quit about midnight. He then sat on the outdoor roof deck at Monks, drinking purposefully and watching the stars wheel through the night.

He got out of bed. The floor was covered by a thin carpet of nondescript color. Sometimes he thought the carpet beige, other times light brown. Today it looked pale gray. As he made his way to the hallway bathroom, the floorboards creaked beneath him. He peed, ashing his cigarette in the toilet and contemplating the resulting dark film on the water. On the way out of the bathroom, he stopped briefly at the mirror and gazed at his triangular face. He had retained his high forehead, coupled with his mother's pointed chin and sandy-colored hair. He had relinquished long ago the easygoing features of youth; there was a worn quality to his countenance, like a domestic animal left too long in the wild. But his eyes were patient and unassuming—they were eyes that waited for others to make the first move.

In the empty hallway, he listened to the ambient noises of the two-story house, classic rock music played on a radio at low volume, the subtle frequency of a woman's voice, her words indistinct but her tone suggestive of flirtation. The playful feminine murmuring came from the room of one of Bobby's three housemates, Steve. Bobby walked the length of the hallway to the stairwell, and his eyes became internal and remote when the murmuring was superseded by soft laughter. He descended the stairs, taking out another cigarette and lighting it with his first. The kitchen was standard Sun Belt fare, tiled floors and particleboard cabinets, and the grainy late-summer sunlight washed out the color in the room. He opened a cabinet, removed a three-quarters-full liter bottle of Evan Williams, and poured himself a drink. The metal legs of a chair screeched over the tile as Bobby sat down at the kitchen table. He listened again for the woman but heard nothing. He drank slowly, letting the alcohol flow through him, settling the irritation that had taken control of his mood.

Rick wandered into the kitchen wearing a black Led Zeppelin T-shirt. Bobby's housemates were in a rock band together. Unlike his other two bandmates, Rick had a college degree, but lacked confidence due to a minor weight problem, his belly slightly protruding. Rick wore black-rimmed glasses and tan shorts. The two men nodded, so familiar with each other that perfunctory greetings were unnecessary.

"Breakfast of champions," said Rick, indicating the bottle.

"That's what I hear," said Bobby.

"You mind if I have a snort?"

"When have you ever been denied? I'm not greedy."

Rick collected a highball glass. "I'll pay you back."

"I'm more concerned that you guys make rent."

"We always make rent."

"Well, you do," said Bobby. "Eventually."

Rick poured a drink and both men lapsed into silence, sipping their whiskeys thoughtfully. "How was last night?" said Rick.

"Fine, I guess," said Bobby. "That is, the usual, more or less. Jason's being a dick. And you?"

"Same. It was a good show," said Rick. "The usual."

Bobby quickly grew dissatisfied with the silence. "Who's the girl up there with Steve?"

Rick's eyes rested on Bobby for the briefest interval. "Someone he met at a show."

"Last night?"

Rick shrugged. "No, about a month ago."

"Is it serious?"

"Steve? Serious? Is that a joke?"

"You know I can't keep up with you musician types."

"Well, there was a time when we couldn't keep up with you."

Bobby looked away from his housemate, concealing his displeasure with that observation. "Lately I can't seem to find a girl who's halfway normal."

"Normal? When has normal been important to you?"

Bobby considered the question and did not have a ready answer.

Rick formed a bemused grin. "Besides, when it comes to a woman, what is normal anyway?"

Bobby's eyes went opaque. Although he realized he had already said too much, he nodded and breathed out, indicating a kind of primal agreement. "Fuck if I know."

**

Bobby returned to the second story where he showered and shaved, putting on well-worn black jeans and a pale-blue button-down shirt and looking about his room. To his thinking, the room wasn't very much. The bed was unmade, a wad of gray sheets and a balled-up, dark comforter. There was a composite wood desk, a chair with a tear in the black vinyl seat, a nightstand with a drawer that had bottomed out and would not open. Bobby ceased his pessimistic observations and turned on his phone. It went off within two minutes, and Bobby answered immediately. "Damn, Claire, is that you again, girl?" Bobby listened. "Okay, okay, keep your shirt on. I'll be there in a minute."

He hung up and looked at the phone, dissatisfaction evident in the twist of his mouth. He tossed the phone on his bed and went to his closet, pulling down a steel, fireproof combination box he kept concealed under a white blanket on the top shelf. He opened the box. Several neat rows of one-gram packets of cocaine were carefully arranged on black felt. He took twenty-five grams and placed it in his pockets, setting aside one final gram and pouring the contents on his desk, arranging four lines. He took a plastic tube from his nightstand, and in several deft passes, he hit the lines. He stood and rubbed his nose, his mood appearing to veer between satisfaction and its opposite. Finally, he shrugged, as if to say, *Whatever*. He grabbed his keys and headed out to his car.

He motored toward downtown, getting stopped at a light at MLK and the I-35 feeder, the enormous granite dome of the Capitol partially obscured by university buildings. The lunch rush traffic wheeled around him hectically, cars darting about the crowded streets. He took I-35 south and exited at Oltorf, bearing east, and he turned down a street ringed with apartment complexes and condos. Claire's complex had no gate. Bobby drove the length of the parking lot down a small hill and turned into a space. He performed his usual ritual before a sale, slowly observing his surroundings, seeing nothing out of the ordinary. The complex itself was not well maintained, accentuated by a small laundry room with peeling paint and exposed boards. Bobby trotted up some stairs and knocked on Claire's door. A large brown stain formed a straight line from the doorknob to the ground.

The door opened. Claire was small and blond. At one point she had been a student, but had flunked out, and if she had a job, Bobby did not know it. Bobby could never decide if she was a good person gone bad or if she simply enjoyed being bad in the first place. "Come in," she said, eyeing him intently.

Jessie, Claire's closest friend, smoked on the sofa. "Hey, Bobby," she said. "You never call me."

Jessie was thin, her face gaunt in a manner suggestive of heroin chic. She was a little younger than Claire and emanated an overindulged, suburban quality. Bobby wondered if her parents had the first clue they were financing their daughter's substantial habit. "You're busy, usually," he said.

"I'd make time for a drink with you," she said.

Jessie's pallor was pale due to a long run on the coke, but despite this, she was attractive in the perilous manner of youth flirting with self-annihilation. Bobby peered at her, considering the short- and long-term ramifications of making a play. "I'm available now," he said, his voice low.

Jessie was the first to look away. "Well, not *now*," she said.

Bobby quickly dismissed his exasperation. At last he smiled at her, underscoring the irony. He had made his point. "Well, another time, then. Let's see what we can work out." He paused. "What do y'all want?"

"Eight ball," said Claire.

Bobby nodded. Claire wore a loose T-shirt and Bobby noticed that the bones around her shoulders were starting to protrude. "Didn't we just do this last night?"

"Are you counseling us?" said Claire.

"Not really." He fished around in his pocket and placed the packets of coke on the pass-through to the kitchen. Claire handed him the cash. "Have either of you seen Tamara lately?"

"Yeah," said Jessie, her eyes never straying from the drugs. "The other night."

"I haven't heard from her."

"She's been locked up."

"No shit," said Bobby.

"Yeah," said Jessie. "She passed out in her car at a convenience store. The cashier thought she was dead. The cops found paraphernalia."

"I thought she was a little more together than that," said Bobby.

"You've obviously not gotten high with her," said Jessie. She shifted gears, her question marked by a measure of persistence. "You want to ask her out?" Bobby closed his eyes, ignoring the question, weary of Jessie's game. "Well, you can, because they released her."

Claire stood before the pass-through holding a spoon darkened on the bottom, mixing the coke with baking soda and applying heat with a lighter. "It would be easier if you guys just snorted this shit," said Bobby.

"It would be easier," said Claire, intent on her work, "if you just sold us crack."

"I don't do that. You know that."

"Standards," said Jessie. She seemed aware that Bobby had stopped listening to her, and she was beginning to sound shrill. "Boundaries."

"No," said Bobby, more to the room in general than to Jessie. "I just don't want to deal with crackheads."

"You deal with us," said Claire, letting the mixture cool.

"You guys are different. We have history."

"That's sweet of you, Bobby," said Jessie.

Bobby continued to ignore her, speaking only with Claire. "I don't see why you don't find a crack dealer," said Bobby.

"They're unreliable and tend not to make house calls," said Claire. She produced a glass tube stuffed with burnt Chore Boy. "You want to join us?"

Bobby peered at the cooling precipitate, his eyes vague and regretful. "I used to do a lot of that shit."

"It might be fun," said Jessie.

Bobby sounded tired. "I don't remember much fun about it."

"Stay anyway," said Claire. Her approach was direct and matter-of-fact, lacking Jessie's obviousness. "Just hang with us."

Bobby eyed Claire evenly, taking in the solidity of her compact frame, the easy sense of cool she could produce at any given moment. He was fully aware that in the past this situation would have led to him hitting a couple of lines while the women smoked, with Bobby hoping they would not get too high to double-team him. "That's very nice of both of you," he said. He looked at Claire again, wondering for a split second if she was girlfriend material, in the next instant reminding himself that those who smoked crack were a different breed. Although he told himself he was making the right call, he felt a twinge of regret. "Y'all take care now."

**

He sat on a stool in an Irish pub, eating a bowl of potato soup and nursing a whiskey. The lunchtime business had receded considerably and the bartender talked on a cell phone. The place was old, with concrete floors and high ceilings and the humid odor of years of spilled drinks. The bartender's voice reverberated in the emptiness and Bobby gazed at an old advertisement on the wall, a cartoon ostrich eyeing a pint of dark beer—"My Goodness, My Guinness."

His phone rang. "Hey, Cal," he said. "Yeah, I'm downtown right now. Give me fifteen minutes." He hung up, polished off his whiskey, and handed the bartender a ten. The bartender gave him change but Bobby immediately dumped it in the tip jar. He got up and cast a furtive glance around the establishment. Once he was satisfied that the place was reasonably empty, he shuffled to the bathroom and locked the door behind him, cleaning off a section of the bathroom counter. He deposited half a gram on the porcelain, made two lines, and hit them one after the other.

Waiting at a light in the downtown traffic off of Guadalupe, Bobby sank down in his seat to take two large swigs from a bottle of Evan Williams. The light turned green and he tapped the accelerator, sunlight reflecting off a glass skyscraper and refracting in his eyes. He called Cal. "Meet me on the street in about two minutes. No, I don't want to go inside."

He pulled up into a restaurant mini-lot, where a middle-aged man in a gray suit stood waiting. Cal could not be more obvious. Still, Bobby unlocked the passenger door, operating under the premise that Cal's general air of cluelessness protected them both.

"Hey, Evan," said Cal, taking the seat. Bobby used an alias with customers who only knew him peripherally. Cal was slightly overweight, agreeable, and quiet—a mid-management type, recently divorced. Bobby had never seen him without a coat and tie. Cal knew he was not cool and didn't try to be, a quality Bobby appreciated.

Bobby reached into his front pocket. "Work treating you okay?"

"They haven't fired me yet," said Cal.

They made the exchange. "You be careful now," said Bobby.

"I always am."

Bobby smiled slightly to himself, rolling down the passenger-side window as he turned around. "Call me if you need anything," he said. Cal nodded.

Before Bobby could exit the lot, his phone went off again. "Kelly, where are you?"

He drove under the freeway and headed due east on Seventh Street before turning right, then right again, heading west on East Sixth. The skyscrapers disappeared as he passed under the freeway, the buildings becoming older and smaller, highlighted by a distinctive Mexican influence which was underscored by three reputable mom-and-pop Mexican restaurants on three consecutive blocks. Kelly waited outside a one-story brick bar. She wore a sleeveless T-shirt and cutoff jeans so short they revealed her front pockets. Bobby pulled to the curb and Kelly trotted to the driver-side window.

"What are you up to?" said Bobby.

Kelly was thin and had the distracted air of someone who lived primarily in her own mind. She had once told Bobby in passing that she was getting an advanced degree in mathematics. "Differential equations."

Bobby passed her the packets. "Can you do math on this shit?"

Kelly pocketed the packets, seeming resigned but at peace with her habit. She shrugged, mainly to herself. "Probably better than when I'm sober."

**

Bobby turned off his phone when he entered Samson's. Samson's had originally fashioned itself as an upscale watering hole, but those days were long gone. The hardwood floors were scuffed and badly finished, and one could not escape the unpleasant impression that the interior was covered with a film. A haze of smoke floated in the low light, smoke which was supposed to be forbidden by city ordinance. Bobby's eyes slowly adjusted to the dim.

He found Ellen with a whiskey neat and a lit cigarette at a hardwood table in the very back. She was staring at the gray windows in the front, tendrils of smoke curling around her. She seemed entirely unaware of Bobby as he sat down.

"Here, again?" he said.

With deliberation, Ellen snuffed out her cigarette and lit a fresh one. She continued to stare at a point out in space. "I don't care what anyone says, I like this place," she said. A trace of sandpaper underpinned her voice. She paused, seeming to search for just the exact turn of phrase. "It has character."

"A bar's bar," said Bobby, helpfully.

Ellen wore a dark business suit with a precisely tailored skirt, but Bobby concluded she had already left work for the day. He tried to control where his eyes rested but was unable to ignore her ample figure, subtly emphasized by her clothing. Ellen had once told Bobby that she sizably increased her sales simply by adjusting her neckline. She finished her drink. "At least it's not some fucking self-congratulatory idiot joint for the young and the beautiful."

"It's certainly not that," said Bobby. "How many is that for you?"

"I'm older than you," said Ellen. She moved her blond hair away from her face. "I get to ask those questions."

Bobby lit a cigarette. "So, what's up?"

"I'm waiting."

"For what?"

"For you, among other things."

Bobby reached into his pocket. With callous indifference to their public setting, they made the exchange. "I'll be back," said Ellen. After a couple of minutes, she returned. Her only indication of use was the gentle tapping of her long, polished fingernails on the hardwood table. She followed Bobby's eyes to her fingers and the tapping stopped the next moment. "It's over between me and Javier."

"I see that."

"Do you?"

"Well, not until you said so. But now it all falls into place."

She tilted her head, her demeanor turning peevish. "So, I'm transparent."

"Don't take it personally."

Ellen wavered. She seemed disgusted with herself. "I won't." A cocktail waitress appeared from behind the bar and they both ordered whiskey. The waitress nodded, then disappeared into the gloom. "I'm living at a Residence Inn off of Ben White. I couldn't stand being in my own place."

"Alone?"

"Yes, alone. What do you think? Jesus, Bobby, don't rub it in."

"I'm not rubbing it in." He looked at Ellen steadily, at the fullness of her curves. "There's an extra room at my house. You wouldn't have to be alone."

"Bobby, don't."

"It's a no-strings proposition," he heard himself say, even though he knew it was a lie. "We're both way beyond that."

"An extra room?" said Ellen, her head tilted down as if she were looking at him over her glasses. "In the house with the band?"

"Yeah."

"Oh my god, Bobby."

"It's a sincere offer. Take it or don't."

"Fuck, where's that whiskey?" said Ellen, under her breath. Her hands shook as she lit another cigarette. The cocktail waitress appeared with their drinks.

Before the waitress could even depart, Ellen tapped her glass on the table and swallowed her drink whole. "Another," she said.

Bobby eyed Ellen as the waitress walked away. "Let me take you home," he said.

"Jesus, Bobby, I'm just a little upset." She looked away from him, ashing her cigarette into an empty whiskey glass. "I can find my way home without you."

"I don't doubt that."

"I'm not a child. I'm not a goddamned child," she said, a little too loudly. Bobby clammed up, hoping that some silence would diffuse her. At last, Ellen stood up. "I'll be back." She went to the bathroom. Within a minute she returned and resumed smoking her cigarette, rocking slightly in her chair. "I don't know, Bobby."

Bobby was beginning to worry she would overdo it with the whiskey and coke in meteoric fashion. She had once called him for an eight ball and he found her passed out on a barstool on Sixth Street, the police having already arrived. Bobby managed to talk them out of a public intoxication arrest, concocting a lie about a recently deceased parent. "What don't you know?" he replied.

"Sometimes I feel like I live in an empty universe."

"You need to get some sleep."

Ellen refused to make eye contact. "You don't know what I need."

"A good, hot meal. And sleep."

The waitress returned with Ellen's drink. Ellen swallowed a little bit of it, tentatively. She rested her forehead in her hand but her head collapsed down on her upper arm. "You'd think I'd learn. After all this time. There must be something wrong with me."

Bobby stood up. "Come on," he said firmly. He took Ellen by the upper arm. "Come on, get up."

"A learning deficiency," said Ellen, rising halfway. Her knees buckled slightly.

"I'm driving," said Bobby.

"Obviously," said Ellen, more than a bit unsteady. "Obviously. Just like me."

**

Bobby maneuvered through the afternoon traffic while Ellen sank down in her seat, taking one-hitters off of a key. Her skirt had bunched itself high on her legs and Bobby cast a discreet glance at her full thighs. After one such furtive peek, Ellen noticed her exposed legs, shrugged, then resumed her focus on the cocaine.

"You want any?" she said.

"No, thanks."

"Come on, don't be boring. I hate it when you're boring."

"I've been called a lot of things," said Bobby, "but seldom boring."

The hotel was only a quarter of a mile from the freeway and Bobby could feel the energy of the rushing cars. He pulled in front of the entrance and waited for Ellen to get out.

Ellen turned to him. "You're not coming in?"

"I'm meeting someone."

Ellen looked him over. "Why don't you come in?" They exchanged a glance. "Just for a minute."

Even though they had never really dated, there had been a months-long period when they had weekly sex. That was a couple of years ago. It had been a few months since they had last hooked up, though Ellen bought coke from him at least twice a month. Bobby considered her breakup and her constant need for attention from men, but then he simply nodded and parked the car. Ellen's high heels clattered on the tiled lobby floor. They passed a bank of elevators; a strong scent of disinfectants filled the air and the patterned carpet was neat and newly vacuumed. Bobby saw in it the vision of a manager who loved checklists. They walked down a first-floor hallway together, until Ellen stopped and looked at a door.

"This is the wrong hall," she said.

"Jesus, Ellen."

"Don't worry. We're close."

They found Ellen's room, and after several attempts, she unlocked the door with her card key. She had left the TV on. Bobby turned on a light. The room had two double beds, a dresser, a small desk in the corner, and a mid-sized kitchen with a refrigerator. A bottle of scotch rested on the desk.

"I've got some whiskey," said Ellen. "Do you want a drink?"

"I'm worried that we might overdo it."

Ellen realized she was the "we" in question. "Bobby, it's been one hell of a week but I'm fine right now. Really."

Once again, Bobby considered the offer, but only for a moment. "Do you have ice?"

"I put the ice bucket in the freezer." Ellen's voice lowered in timbre; Bobby heard it distinctly: "Will have one. Just one." She had turned her head, her face in profile, her expression neutral.

"Okay," said Bobby, his voice becoming small.

Ellen took off her shoes and Bobby noticed that her feet were tanned and her toenails painted light blue. He stared at her legs as she prepared a couple of lines.

"You want a hit?" she said.

"Sure," he said.

Bobby hit a line while Ellen poured the drinks, then she took her turn. They both sat down on the bed, drinks in hand. Neither one of them spoke. After a moment, Ellen stood up, taking off her top. She lowered her breasts to Bobby's face and took off her bra.

"I'm a bad girl," she said.

Bobby took in Ellen topless. As welcome as the sight was, he realized that the events of the next several minutes would have no bearing on their relationship once he left the room. He could not tell if this disappointed him, or only encouraged the fetishist within him. "Yes, you are a bad girl," he said.

"No, Bobby, do you hear me? I'm a bad little girl."

He noted that she often returned to this game but didn't know its significance. "A little girl?"

"Yes," she said. "A little, little girl."

**

Bobby drove through streets lined with residences until he came to a newly paved road through an open field. After passing old houses and a collection of double-wides, he saw an old house, surrounded by several trucks, alone on an embankment. Bobby imagined that at one time it was the only residence in the vicinity. The place was a mess. There was no lawn, just a dirt yard and some scraggly native plants, with a big black pickup parked in the dirt just outside the front door. Bobby parked behind the pickup and got out.

The front door was cracked and Bobby heard pulsing rock music. Hearing no answer to his knocking, he pushed the door open and called out, "Jason, it's me."

A couple of ragged couches and a dented table with several chairs were arranged haphazardly about the living room. A man in a T-shirt, jeans, and boots slept on a couch near the door. Another man sat at a table, wearing a black button-down shirt and a bolo tie, smoking a joint and drinking a Miller Lite.

"I'm looking for Jason," said Bobby.

The man nodded. "I know you."

"Yeah, we've met. Bobby."

"You here for a pick-up?"

"No," said Bobby. "Not today."

The man puffed on his joint. "It don't matter. He's in the back."

Bobby walked down a hallway that smelled of stale beer, a huge Stevie Ray Vaughan poster dominating one wall. Bobby passed empty rooms with more sofas and an occasional bare mattress before he came to the final bedroom, the door parted slightly, emitting a narrow band of light. Bobby knocked.

"Who the fuck is it?" said a voice within.

"Me."

"Bobby?"

"Yeah." Bobby pushed open the door.

"Hey, motherfucker." Jason, in washed-out jeans and a black button-down shirt, sat at a table and looked quizzically at Bobby. The two men eyed each other, trying to get a read on the other. As the staring contest continued beyond a beat or two, Jason grinned crookedly. The table was empty save for a bag of cocaine and some cut lines. A square bottle of Jack was on the floor at Jason's feet.

"The security here is first rate," said Bobby, sitting down.

In keeping with the other denizens of the house, Jason, too, wore boots. His face glistened slightly from the coke. His hair was dark and combed back and he wore a gold necklace. "They know you," he said.

"I don't know them. At least some of them. It's a new crowd every week."

"Not you, though," said Jason. Like Bobby's, there was a worn quality to Jason's eyes, young but not youthful. "You're a mainstay. You want any?"

"I just had some."

"Probably time for more, then."

Bobby waved off the invite. "Later," he said.

"Your loss," said Jason, hitting a line. Whenever Jason grinned, Bobby thought he appeared quite pleased with himself, a characteristic that Bobby hated. Jason picked up the whiskey bottle and cradled it in his lap. "I'm having a little party later. Hang around. It'll be fun."

"Any girls?"

"Fuck, yeah."

"I'll see what I can do."

"You'll see what you can do?"

"Yeah."

"What does that mean?" Bobby stared straight into Jason's eyes. Jason did not look away. "Is there something you want to tell me?"

"Yeah," Bobby said. "You're being a prick."

"Am I?" said Jason. Bobby stared resolutely into Jason's

eyes. "First of all, stop it with these little pussy games."

"I'm not doing anything."

"Okay. What's this about?"

"You lied."

"That's a strong word, Bobby."

"You quoted me a price, and then when I'm about to come over to claim the goods, I get this call from one of your boys who quotes me a different price. A higher price."

"I don't think that exactly qualifies as a lie."

"Are we arguing about word usage?"

"Don't be an asshole."

"I'm not the one who reneged on a deal."

"Okay," said Jason, sitting up. "Let's cut through the bullshit. The price went up because of factors beyond my control. You know me. You think I enjoy that kind of thing?"

"I think maybe you found yourself a little short. So you turned to your friends."

"Come on, man," said Jason. He actually appeared hurt. "Something's happening in Mexico. I don't know what exactly. Ray told me a couple of stories and people are starting to die. It drives the price up."

"Ray? Why would our boss tell you anything about what's going on down in Mexico?"

"Did you just hear what I said? Dudes are getting shot."

"All right," said Bobby, reframing the conversation. "Put aside that people getting shot is nothing new to this business. There's the principle of the matter. You welched on a deal. You changed the price after an agreement was made. I mean, what's going on here? We're not slinging shit down on Rundberg."

"Bobby, I had to do it. I can't afford to break even. Come on, it's business. It happens."

Bobby relaxed a bit, turning thoughtful. "This has nothing to do with high-stakes poker? Maybe some bad luck in Vegas?"

"How long have we known each other? When has personal bullshit ever interfered with business?"

"You can be a cocky bastard, man," said Bobby.

"And you can be a moody fucker, you know."

Bobby grasped the point of his chin with his thumb and index finger, seeming to think. "All right," he said, "I've had my say. We split the difference on this next buy, and we go with the new price from here on out. I can live with that."

Jason considered the proposal. "You're always driving a deal, Bobby."

"No, I'm not."

"All right, you're on. Of course, you're on." Jason extended his hand, and Bobby shook it. "Now, look. There's going to be a party. Seriously. Stick around. Let's have a good time and forget about this shit."

"I'm going to grab something to eat," said Bobby. "I'll be back later."

**

Bobby found a place on the East Side not far from Jason's that served whiskey and flank steak. He sat at a booth by himself, eating slowly and relishing his drink. For reasons he could not determine, his waitress was angry and argued constantly in the back with the manager, essentially leaving Bobby alone, which was fine by him. The sun was setting in various shades of orange and indigo, and Bobby watched football under the pink light of a beer gewgaw. When the waitress finally returned to check on him, Bobby smiled, but the smile was not returned. She walked off with his empty plate, still in a snit. Bobby left her a fifty percent tip.

When he returned to Jason's, it was dark and the party was getting underway. A line of cars had already formed on both sides of the street and the front door was open. Bobby, equipped with a liter bottle of Evan Williams, spotted Jason in the living room and they shook hands, Jason engulfing Bobby's in a two-fisted shake.

"I'm glad you came back," said Jason. "Let's get fucked up."

In the kitchen Bobby made a drink and sat down with a cigarette, ashing into an empty plastic cup. There were now well over a dozen people in the living room—all of them young, with a preponderance of men over women. Bobby kept to himself, drinking and smoking. When he got up to get ice and returned, an attractive woman had taken his seat.

Bobby retrieved a lawn chair from the backyard and set it up next to the woman. He introduced himself. She was college-aged, lithe, with a deep tan—a young woman who appeared as if she had never wanted for anything in her entire life. She was hardly his type, but then again, he reminded himself, sitting alone in a crowd of people was hardly preferable.

By this point, the stereo was blasting at full volume. "Bobby Kaufmann," he repeated, shouting over the noise. "I'm a friend of Jason's."

"I'm Deena," said the woman. "I've heard Jason's parties are great."

Bobby surveyed the room and concluded it was not much of a scene. There was a keg on the concrete floor, surrounded by a bunch of guys who were beginning to carry on much too loudly. The women had formed into a discrete clique. "Well," said Bobby, "I'm sure if you stick around long enough, something interesting will happen."

Deena nodded and smiled, a mischievous glint to her eye he could not interpret. She brought her mouth closer to Bobby's ear. "I hear Jason's shit is great."

Bobby now knew the interpretation. He laughed. "No doubt you heard it from him."

Deena smiled brightly, revealing a mouthful of straight white teeth. Bobby guessed that she came from a prosperous family and was a student at the university. "Everyone says so," she said.

As with most women roughly his own age, Deena struck Bobby as young, and it was unclear to him whether this might be a deal-breaker. Still, his uncoupled status weighed on him and he decided to press his advantage. "Is that why you're here?"

Deena looked away, shrugging coyly. "I came with a friend."

"You didn't answer the question."

"I don't have to," she said.

Bobby could not quite dismiss her immaturity, but neither could he ignore her uncomplicated good looks. "Come on," he said. "Follow me."

"Where are we going?"

"Just down the hall. We don't want everyone looking over our shoulder."

The room he took her to was empty, except for the lone sofa along one of the walls and a card table in front of it. "Jason's not that much into decor," said Bobby. He fished out a packet of coke and formed a couple of lines. "God bless," said Bobby, handing Deena a $5 bill.

Deena took a line and Bobby followed. She rubbed her nose, looking at Bobby and then looking away. She seemed suddenly smaller, as if she were retreating internally. She breathed out.

"Another?" said Bobby.

"Sure," she said, her voice high, oddly childlike.

Deena went first again, and Bobby could see her posture stiffen as the drug took effect. He looked into her eyes. Her lips curled slightly, and Bobby leaned in and kissed her. She kissed softly, tentatively. When he pulled away, she appeared confused.

"You want more?" he said.

Deena's eyes searched the empty room. She placed one foot on top of another, crossed her legs, then resumed a normal stance. Finally, she said, "Where are you from?"

Bobby shrugged. "Nowhere special."

"Dallas? Houston?"

"No, nothing like that."

"Are you from Texas?"

Bobby could tell she was not going to leave this alone. "Yeah, a place a couple hours south of here. Near Cuero."

"Where's Cuero?"

"It's not important."

Deena smiled, slightly. "Do you go to school?"

"No."

"What do you do?"

Bobby was unable to conceal his frustration. "Look, I'm just a guy. That's all."

"Do you work with Jason?"

"We're friends. We've known each other a long time."

"I see." Bobby felt as though he could read her thoughts—it was one thing to score some drugs from one of Jason's crowd, but quite another to sleep with one of them. Certainly his pitch, to be successful, would have to include a decadent sleigh ride, but Bobby could not muster the enthusiasm to sell her on it. After a moment or two, she became smaller, oddly passive, looking down at the floor. "Let's go back to the party."

"You sure you don't want more?"

"Maybe later."

"Well, just hit me up, then."

"Yeah" she said. "Let's get back."

"I'm not stopping you," said Bobby.

"Yeah," she said. "We'll talk later."

They went back out to the living room, Deena leading the way. More people had arrived and the room felt crowded. Bobby went to fill his glass, and by the time he returned, Deena had joined up with a group of girls that were conspicuously off by themselves. Bobby found a place along the wall and leaned against it. Although he had hardly actively pursued her, Deena's ready dismissal of him suddenly pained him and he asked himself: was the easy access to coke the only reason he was interesting to women? The question had never bothered him before but now it did. He drank his whiskey in a couple of swallows, returned to the kitchen, refilled his glass, and drank that where he stood. Then he drank two more.

When he rejoined the main party in the living room, he stood at the periphery of a group of guys. Bands dominated the conversation, until the subject veered to the women at the party. Bobby listened with feigned uninterest.

"What about her?" said one of the guys about Deena. "She looks likely."

Another stifled a smirk. "She can be an animal, but it's a one-off. If you run into her again, she'll pretend she doesn't know you, unless she's jonesing. If she is, you'll get lucky again, but really, as far as I can tell, she wants to date a guy in the law school."

This bit of intelligence further stoked Bobby's agitation and he stalked out to the backyard, lit a cigarette, and watched the stars. When he went back inside he made his way to the back of the house and knocked on a bedroom door. Nobody answered. When he opened the door, a nude couple rested on a mattress, the woman straddling the man. Bobby found another bedroom. He went inside and sat down, smoking. He cut himself a couple of lines and then finished his drink.

The living room had become cacophonous. Several dozen people crowded the space and the stereo was louder than ever. He found a chair and sat in it. Deena was talking to Jason, smiling and laughing, and Bobby drank, watching them. Deena laughed again, her expression a mixture of grinning deviousness and abject intoxication, and obviously Jason had sold her—they disappeared together to the back of the house. Bobby retrieved the bottle of Evan Williams and returned to the chair. He sat there, his mind blank, and he drank. The music and the clamor crowded his thoughts and he focused on an empty wall.

The room became very still and dissolved into the immaterial. The fluorescent lights of Jason's kitchen gave way to natural sunlight. Bobby awoke on a cot in a room bathed in early-morning light. The apartment was quiet. He sat up, a radiating feeling in his chest, and he clenched and unclenched his fingers.

He got out of the cot, opened the bedroom door and peered into the living room. Beer cans and whiskey bottles covered the table in front of the sofa. At the foot of the sofa, Regina was prone on the floor. She had no blanket or pillow and had apparently slept where she had fallen down. Her eyes were closed. Bobby stood in front of her, unsure what to do. He said, quietly, as if not to wake her, "Mommy."

Regina did not even flinch, her face wine-colored and bloated. It occurred to Bobby that she might be dead. The radiating feeling in his chest heightened and he felt his own heartbeat. He reached out to touch her but then retracted his hand. Finally, he got down on his belly, his head turned to face hers. She stank of alcohol. He said again, more loudly this time, "Mommy." Regina did not move.

Bobby was wrenched out of his reverie. A drunk young man was howling in the face of a friend and their laughter ate into Bobby. Pearl Jam's "I'm Still Alive" poured out of a nearby speaker.

With no further provocation, Bobby threw his glass to the concrete floor, smashing it. The room suddenly went dead still, the only sound the blaring stereo. All eyes turned to Bobby, who was keenly aware of the change in the room. Finally, he barked, "Fuck." He paused. "Motherfucker," he barked again. He looked at one of the young men. "I hate Pearl Jam. I hate motherfucking Pearl Jam."

The partygoers looked around at each other. Then one of the men started laughing, then another and another. Soon laughter had engulfed the room. One of the young men cleared a space and threw his glass to the floor. "I hate Pearl Jam, too," he shouted. "I hate motherfucking Pearl Jam."

The party quickly moved on. A couple of guys slapped Bobby on the back. Bobby remained seated, staring straight ahead.

**

The lights of the city rolled by on the drive home. Bobby kept to the back streets, driving much too quickly, his tires squealing when he braked in front of his house.

THE THIRD DOOR

It was just a little after two o'clock and the band was gone, still out at a gig. Bobby climbed the stairs to his room and got undressed. In spite of the varying degrees of invitation from Jessie, Claire, and Ellen, not to mention Deena, he realized he was going to crawl into bed alone. He opened the blinds and looked out the window. The lights of Austin blinked and glowed, filling him with reproach. They suggested a tranquility and harmony at which he could only guess.

BOOK 2, CHAPTER 4
September, 2003

Bobby awoke the next day with a sharp pain shooting through his skull, his room pale grey with late-morning light. For the most part, the house was quiet. He sat up and lit a cigarette, trying to work through the murky residue in his mind, feeling a sharp jab of shame as clearly and as physically as if he had been poked with a bony index finger. He got up and trudged to the bathroom. The door was closed, so he knocked.

"Occupied," a woman's voice called out.

Bobby stood still momentarily, wondering if this was Steve's girlfriend or someone new altogether, whether coupled with Steve or with Rick. Contemplating the various permutations served only to accentuate the pain in his head and he sighed, making his way down the stairs and trying the bathroom under the stairwell. This, too, was occupied by a woman, so Bobby relieved himself next to a live oak tree in the backyard.

He sat alone in the living room in shorts and a T-shirt and nursed a whiskey as the house came to life. Bobby watched a woman descend the stairs wearing nothing more than a long T-shirt. She took little note of him, and

Bobby eyed her warily. She was blond and cute, and he guessed this was Steve's girl of the moment, knowing Steve's predilection for attractive, innocent types. Steve himself followed the woman a moment later wearing wire-rimmed glasses, his face lean and suntanned, his hair full and sandy—he was effortlessly good-looking, with the amiable, capricious manner of a musician. He nodded at Bobby and disappeared into the kitchen.

Less than two minutes later, Rick rumbled down the stairwell, followed by a shorthaired brunette more than passably attractive. It was not lost on Bobby that even Rick, with his mid-sized belly and perpetual shyness, was in the game. Rick noticed Bobby off by himself and asked him if he wanted to go out to breakfast with the group. Bobby declined. The proximity of the women had Bobby brooding about what kept him from making a harder push for Deena the night before.

Minutes later, the two new couples left together, and Bobby leaned forward on the sofa, rubbing his knees. He was sure that neither of the women were his type, yet he was also equally sure he was jealous of the idea of them, thinking also that his musical roommates seemed to treat women as a kind of unlimited currency, easily obtained and easily discarded.

The stillness and quiet of the house was palpable. Bobby grabbed his bottle of Evan Williams and retreated to the musty sanctuary of his room, sitting on the bed and staring at the drywall. At last, he was struck by a notion and stood up, pouring a drink without ice and getting out a black notebook and pen he kept in a desk drawer. Flipping through the pages, he noted that he had made ten entries in the past three months. He found an empty page, its blank whiteness almost ominous. He nearly closed the notebook but stopped himself. Finally, he wrote:

I feel.

The pen stopped. It moved aimlessly above the page and refused to make contact. Then Bobby continued.

I feel like this shit will never end.

He paused again but then urged himself to press on.

Five years. Five fucking years I've been in this town. How will next year be different? Probably the only change will be that I'm living with another band. Some new customers, who I don't know. New clubs. But otherwise, it will be the same. No real girlfriend. Nothing but a series of alcohol and coke-fueled freak shows, adding up to nothing.

Bobby read over the text and finished his drink in one swallow. He poured another, his face impassive, as blank as the notebook's empty pages. He looked around his room with disgust, put the notebook away, flopped on the bed and uncapped the bottle. He drank slowly, thoughtfully. After making his way through a good portion of the liter, he stood up abruptly and grabbed his phone, scrolling down the call list until he arrived at the name and number he sought—Kayla, usually his girl of last resort.

The call went to voicemail. "Kayla, it's me, Bobby. I know it's early and you're probably at class but I just wanted to say hello. Give me a call back later. I'd love to see you."

For a moment he was pleased with himself, sitting on the bed and wearing a half-smile. But the smile faded quickly, his eyes clouded over, and he raised the bottle and took a long pull, then followed that with another one, then another and another. He removed the mouth of the bottle from his lips with a pop, his eyes considerably dulled. He took another drink and then set the bottle on the floor. From a desk drawer he removed a plastic bottle of Xanax and swallowed two of the pills. He waited, his eyes empty. At last, a sense of conscious recognition reanimated his features. He put the tips of his fingers to the bridge of his nose and rubbed his eyes with his thumb and index finger. He took out a black address book from the top desk drawer and unfolded the pages, his eyes following his index finger down the page as he scanned the names. He picked up his phone.

A woman answered and Bobby gave her just enough time to say hello. "Christi, it's me."

The woman paused a beat, her tone suspicious. "*Me who?*"

"Bobby."

"Bobby?" She paused again. Her tone changed, revealing a sort of stunned surprise, but not pleasant surprise. "You mean Bobby Kaufmann?"

"Yeah, Bobby."

"You've got to be kidding me, Bobby. What the hell do you want?"

He could picture her, sullen, her hand on her hip, never shy about confrontation. He opened his mouth, almost stammering, then pressed on. "I'm just curious. What went wrong between us?"

A silence ensued, and with each passing moment the chill it induced turned colder. "Jesus fuck," she said, and the line went dead.

He sought in motion what he could not find in stillness. He trudged out to the car, putting the whiskey bottle on the floorboard and the Xanax on the passenger seat, tooling south on I-35 across town and exiting at William Cannon. He drove hesitantly, sure of his destination but not his purpose. He followed a car through an automatic gate into a generic Sun Belt apartment complex and pulled into a space. He scanned the parking lot for a light-brown Honda Civic and found it. Bumper stickers of every ilk covered the back of the car, commenting on a range of topics from veganism to witches to local bands. Watching a particular second-floor balcony, he chased a Xanax with whiskey and made a call.

Kendra's voice was soft and husky, far too mellow to be suspicious. "I don't know a Bobby," she said. Then a note of recognition. "You mean, *Bobby*?"

"Yeah, Bobby."

Kendra's question moved at the same cadence as Christi's, but without the unpleasant edge. "What the hell do you want?"

"I'm downstairs. I'd like to see you."

"You're downstairs?" she said. She peeked through her window blinds; through the shadows, Bobby could barely see her face. Her voice displayed curiosity, with only a hint of trespass. "Why do you want to see me?"

He strained harder to get a glimpse of her. For a moment, he was at a loss. "I think I just want to understand."

"Understand what?"

"Look, you can see me. I'm right here. I'll be in and out so fast you won't know it. Then I won't come back." He waited. "Come on, at least give me that."

"Is that a promise?"

"Yes."

She spoke slowly, as if thinking about the placement of each word. "All right. I will say this, you never broke a promise."

He shuffled up the concrete steps, his footfalls plodding and unsteady. As he climbed, he grasped the rail for support. After knocking, he swayed slightly as he waited.

THE THIRD DOOR

The door opened. Kendra regarded him frankly, her expression equal parts doubt and empathy. Her face was square and strong, more arresting than attractive. It had been a year since he had seen her and she had put on some weight, but had the same haircut, short in the back and not quite touching her shoulders. Although she was heavier, he found her to be curvy in all the right places. He raised a hand and waved by lowering his fingers one after another, starting with his pinky. It was their customary greeting and she smiled slightly, backing out of the doorframe and allowing him inside.

The interior of the apartment was as he remembered, stuffed with old furniture to the point of clutter, with a color tendency toward brown and black. Knickknacks of all variety were crammed onto shelves—in one glance, he spotted a ceramic unicorn and a skull—and he remembered her predilection for things "pagan." An entire bookshelf was filled to the brim with vinyl record albums, and as always, music was playing, a band he didn't know with an '80s New Wave sound. He sat down in an empty chair upholstered in black leather. She wore gray shorts and an aqua-blue T-shirt depicting a cartoon Speed Racer.

"You're drunk," she said. He internalized her observation but was fully aware of the sweet herbal scent in the air. He felt no need to counter that her eyes were puffy and bloodshot, and he could see that she recognized this. Finally, she exhaled. "At least I'm not showing up at your doorstep, Bobby."

Bobby smiled slightly, content to let the matter pass. "Who are you dating now?"

"A guy who plays a little guitar. You?"

"Bupkis."

Her mouth remained nonreactive and she didn't smile,

but Bobby saw a wryness in her eyes. "Have you come to ask me for my hand?"

It began to come back to him, why they had dated in the first place. Even though they fought often, they generally understood each other. "Nah, sweetheart. I'm just having a time of it today." He paused. "You want a Xanax? For your trouble?"

She looked at him, her expression canny and forthright, evaluating the contours of the offer and the ramifications if she accepted. "Okay, fair deal." He shook out three pills from the bottle and handed them to her. She swallowed one and deposited the other two on the table. "So, what's this about?"

"I don't know," he said. He reflected for a moment, then made a dismissive gesture.

"Things aren't adding up lately. If they ever did."

She squinted. "And?"

"And nothing. I just wanted to ask you what you remember."

"What I remember?" she said, emphasizing the I.

He wondered if she meant to be ironic, and he hoped the tenor of the encounter would not deteriorate. "Yeah." He waited, allowing time for the air to clear. "Look, I don't want to rehash the obvious," he said. "I know I drank too much, didn't communicate enough, didn't have a regular-type job." He despised the confessional aspect of his own voice, but continued. "But you know, you were hardly perfect either. And about me dealing, you had plenty of friends who dealt for a little side cash, so I thought it was all cool." He reflected a moment longer. "The thing is—I really liked you, you know."

After the last remark, she seemed momentarily pained, and he could see she was processing a lot. At the very least, he told himself, she took him seriously enough to go through a certain amount of uncomfortable effort, and for that he was grateful. She seemed to arrive at a conclusion and smiled briefly. "Didn't communicate enough. Is that how you'd put it?"

He paused. "Well, I guess. I mean, that's just how it came out."

"Didn't communicate enough," she said softly, mulling over the phrase. She tilted her head, looking at him. "So, those three things—you think that was all that was wrong?"

If he were truthful, he would have said yes, that was overwhelmingly the main part of all that was wrong, but he knew her to be too feminine and non-linear to accept an absolute. "Well, no, not the sum total," he managed.

She waited, giving him time to say more. When he didn't, she smiled again. "So then, according to your silence, those were the problems."

He loathed the moments when she started in on the inductive reasoning. He was frustrated, felt backed into a corner. "Well, Kendra, I'm not saying it's everything. As in *everything*."

"But wait," she said, "I just want to be clear. You're saying you think it's the main part?" She counted off on her fingers. "You drank too much, weren't communicative enough, and dealt to make a living?"

"Well, I'm sure I could say it another way, too."

She raised a hand to cut him off. "Give me a minute. You drove across town to hear me out, so hear me out." With each passing moment, her presence seemed to grow, becoming increasingly enthusiastic about the situation in which she unexpectedly found herself. She went silent, her face intimating that she was considering a number of things to say and straining to select just one. Finally she spoke, and was clearly proud of what came out. "Why?"

Bobby wondered if this was a trick question. "Why?"

"Yes, why?"

"Why what?" he said.

She couldn't conceal her disappointment. "Why to any of it. All of it." Bobby just stared. "Let's take it from the beginning. Your first observation. You drank. Why?"

He thought for a moment. "Because it's fucked up."

She nodded, content with his reply. "Because it's fucked up."

"Well, yeah."

"But why, Bobby?"

"I don't know where you're going with all this, Kendra."

"Okay, let me reframe the question. Let's take me. I'm twenty-six years old, underemployed, sitting in my squalid little apartment stoned on a Saturday afternoon. Why?"

"Same answer. Because it's fucked up."

"Because it's fucked up. Yes, I agree. But why?"

Bobby thought for a moment, tilting his head as he looked at her. "Shit, Kendra, because your dad's an asshole who ran out on you. Your mom's fucking crazy. And let's not even get started about your sister waiting tables at a titty bar doing fuck knows what else to keep her meth habit going—"

Kendra raised a hand again. "Okay, okay. That's it. You got it. But here's my question: why do you drink?" Bobby suddenly saw what she was driving at and he remained quiet. When Kendra spoke again, her words carried the power of pure declaration. "You never told me once about your family, other than a tiny bit about your aunt. Besides a nasty quip or two in front of friends, I never heard shit. Nothing. Not about your father. Whether you have brothers and sisters. Least of all about your mother, who you mentioned once or twice high out of your mind, then when I asked again, you covered it up like a nuclear secret." Kendra took a deep breath through her nose and looked at him directly. "I always liked you, too, Bobby. But if you want a place to start, you might want to start there."

**

Back at home later that night, the blue light of the television turned his skin a silvery gray. He watched a football game but did not follow it, and at his feet an empty liter bottle sat next to a half-full one. He was damp with sweat and his face was swollen. At first he thought about Kendra, but as each minute passed, he felt more comfortable contemplating Jason and Deena. His thoughts swirled around, going forward then stopping, never quite forming a conclusion. He found himself clinging to a simple assertion—Deena's a bitch and Jason's an asshole. He did not think it a particularly fair or impartial assessment, but he could not seem to let go of it. In fact, the longer it whirled around in his brain, the more gratifying the thought became.

In his besotted state, he mustered up his full concentration to consider the matter, and he wondered if severing ties with Jason would be a welcome change. He asked himself if he could see a downside to such a move, but the question never went forward, and his head began to nod. He passed out before ten o'clock, sprawled out on the worn sofa, snoring loudly.

**

Two days later Bobby turned west on Rundberg from

the I-35 feeder road. He wondered what the average person thought of this place as he made his way from under the freeway out onto the two-lane thoroughfare. True, it displayed the normal trappings of a city, the usual leavings of an urban landscape—gas stations, hotels, pawnshops. Except along this particular road, the hotel had been boarded up for several months and the pawnshop was protected by razor wire. A motley congregation of street regulars had set up an open-air crack market outside a gas station, and Bobby wondered: Do ordinary people see the homeless, and if so, do they realize that though they may be without permanent shelter they are not necessarily without a trade? Do they think that only young black men travel by bus? That might be the conclusion one would draw, since the bus stops seem to be the exclusive domain of these young men. Bobby turned right on North Creek Drive and left Rundberg behind.

Brownie Lane was lined by square, four-resident apartments that seemed to have sprung up from the ground like mushrooms. One could see them, one after another, as they continued north like a derelict collection of dilapidated boards. It was hot outside, the violent blue sky remote. There were men in ragged t-shirts and grey trousers in groups of two and three, women putting laundry out on lines with clothespins, children kicking a tattered soccer ball. A boy about thirteen, wearing a wife-beater, practiced dance steps in the gravel.

"Is this Red's place?" Bobby asked. The boy stopped moving his feet. He looked at Bobby, his face inscrutable. Bobby waited for an answer but then understood that none was forthcoming. He moved to the front door, the boy watching him the whole way.

His knock was answered by a man about Bobby's age

with light black skin, wearing a hoodie and long red shorts down to his knees, chewing on a toothpick. The man observed Bobby was on time down to the minute and he stepped back and gestured. It was dark in the living room, somewhat cave-like. A lamp tossed a yellow patch of light against a wall, illuminating a section of ceiling. The room was crowded with old furniture, and a woman of about forty reclined on a faded green sofa and carefully observed Bobby as he entered. On either side of her were a gray-haired man, about sixty, and a woman of similar age whose black skin seemed overlaid with a hue of yellow, her hands shaking uncontrollably. Bobby wondered if the shaking was the result of a terrible disease or of drug overuse. The young man indicated an empty chair and they both sat down.

Each man eyed the other and neither spoke. Finally, Bobby sat up straight. "Ray once told me that Carter runs this part of town. So when I called Ray to get permission to talk to someone besides my usual supply, he gave me Carter's number. Then when I called Carter, he gave me your number. Everything I've ever heard about Carter is that he runs a square shop. Not running a bunch of nickel-baggers looking to rip off their customers by dealing two rocks for $50, instead of three. Cheap shit like that. Anyway, here's my pitch—I buy powder in bulk and the offer will be fair, it will be regular, and I've never fucked over anyone in my life. So that's why I'm here."

"I know all that," said the young man, and he said nothing else.

Although the man was resolutely silent, Bobby detected no rudeness. "I'm Bobby. Glad to meet you."

"Red."

"I'm looking for a new supplier, Red," said Bobby.

"That's it."

There was a short knock at the door and Red showed a momentary exasperation. He gestured at the woman on the sofa, and she got up and let in a small white woman.

"I need to re-up," she said to Red, weakly. She could tell she was interrupting. "A hundred."

His expression never changed, and while neutral, was impossible for Bobby to read. Red reached into his pocket and opened his palm, counting out the white rocks. The woman took them, smiled at Bobby a bit flirtatiously, and left. Red turned back to Bobby, patiently. "Quantity?" he said.

"Like I said, enough so you won't feel like it's a waste of your time."

"What's wrong with your current supply?"

"A personal thing."

"Which is?"

"I think he's a dick."

A faint smile raced across Red's lips and vanished just as quickly. "Carter says you're okay and that's enough for me. When?"

"Whenever. Now, if you like."

"Tomorrow," said Red.

"You're on," said Bobby. "If this works out, there'll be more." Bobby paused. "But there's just one thing, Red. I was told Carter is tight with Ray. My loyalty is to Ray."

Red repositioned the toothpick. "Nobody fucks with Ray."

"Well, that's what Carter said. If I find out different, I've got to move on."

**

Bobby made sales the rest of the afternoon, basking in a certain satisfaction in light of his new arrangement. At a little before five, he turned off his phone and pulled into the parking lot of a weathered Asian restaurant with algae on its cement foundation and stains on its exterior walls. Bobby considered the inexpensive sushi entirely adequate and the staff knew him, calling him Evan. As he waited for the miso soup to cool, he considered calling Jason and telling him that he and he and his shitty supply could fuck off. His satisfaction deepened as he rejected the idea, thinking it too easy—Jason would find out soon enough. It was at this precise moment that his phone went off. He looked at the number, picked up, and began walking out of the restaurant.

"Ellen," he said into the phone. "How are you, girl?"

Ellen's laughter mingled with that of another woman. "Bobby," said Ellen, much too loudly.

He stood in the parking lot as cars passed on the street. "You having fun?" he said.

"Bobby," Ellen repeated.

"I'm here," said Bobby.

"Meet us at Hannah's place," said Ellen, insistently.

Bobby was at a loss. "I don't know who Hannah is, darling," he said. "I don't know where she lives."

"She lives south," said Ellen.

"Where south?"

"Not too far from downtown."

"I need an address, girl."

"Okay, okay," said Ellen. "What the fuck's your address?" Bobby heard more laughter, and then he heard Ellen squeal. "Goddamn it, watch the road!" Finally, Ellen said, "She lives on Frederick Lane."

"Where's that?"

"It's off Lamar."

"Well, Lamar's an awful long goddamned road," said Bobby.

"No, not Lamar," said Ellen. Bobby heard the other woman's voice in the background. "It's off Congress. Near Woodward. It's a dead-end street heading west right off St. Ed's campus. I'll text you the address."

"Okay, look," said Bobby, "I'm eating but I'll be done soon. You get to Hannah's in one piece and I'll meet you."

Within thirty minutes, Bobby pulled up to a one-story house with a stone exterior on a residential street, a cul-de-sac that ended after a few hundred yards. Bobby guessed that the house was built sometime in the sixties and that, at that time, it was near the edge of town. But no longer—Congress teemed with traffic and the tumult of a busy city filled the air. A giant live oak dominated the front yard, and the grass was yellow in patches and dried out. Bobby thought he knew most of Ellen's friends, but he had never heard her mention a Hannah. He rechecked the address as he crossed the lawn and knocked on the door. Through frosted-glass panes, he could see a figure run to the door, which opened after a flurry of turning locks.

"You must be Bobby," said a raven-haired woman breathlessly, her cheeks flushed. She seemed a little drunk but extended a cordial hand. "I'm Hannah."

Hannah appeared to be in her early thirties. She wore black pants, a crimson top, and a multicolored decorative scarf, a formal attire distinctly at odds with the jeans-and-golf-shirt tendency of the city. Bobby assumed that when she wasn't drunk, she was composed and serious. "Ellen's told me all about you," said Hannah, all ebullience. Bobby wondered what that meant as she backed away from the door, and presented the interior with a sweep of her hand.

"She says you're a good man to know in a pinch, so come in, come in."

Hannah's offhand remark led Bobby to conclude that he had been called in on a professional basis. He stepped into a living room with an overhead light fixture, brown carpet, a dark leather couch, and an old easy chair. Bobby thought the room under-decorated, and in Austin terms, this most likely meant that Hannah was a student or a musician. The most vivid color in the room came from a hand-painted portrait of Willie Nelson on a far wall. The living room was adjacent to a generic Sun Belt kitchen with Formica counters and a tiled floor.

"You live here?" he said.

"I do," said Hannah. "But my lease is ending."

Ellen appeared, wearing a royal-blue top and black jeans that contrasted dramatically with her fair skin and blond hair. She smiled at Bobby and glided to where Hannah stood, kissing her on the neck and then the lips. It was a long kiss with darting tongues, and as it progressed, Bobby veered between voyeurism and impatience. At last they parted, but Ellen could not resist running her fingers through Hannah's dark hair.

"Isn't she hot?" said Ellen. "She's just so fucking hot."

Hannah smiled, embarrassed. Ellen leaned into Hannah again and the corners of Bobby's lips curled downward. "Okay, okay, break it up," he said to Ellen. "You've got company here."

"You're just jealous," said Ellen, who was now standing behind Hannah with her arms draped around her neck.

Bobby had heard Ellen talk about women before, but this was the first time he had encountered a girlfriend in the flesh. It occurred to him that she had rebounded from Javier in just a matter of days, and this left him with a curiously hollow feeling, an emptiness that took him by surprise. He sat with that feeling, then buried it. "What can I do for you, Ellen?" he said.

"Well, you can be happy for me."

"I am. What else?"

Ellen seemed put out. "You could show some fucking curiosity."

Bobby eyes flicked about the room, rather blankly. "Like what?"

"Like when did we meet? Where did we meet? And just who is this ravishing girl, Ellen?"

"No disrespect here. I thought that would come in time."

"In time," said Ellen, with a snort. Ellen tended toward a giddy exuberance when she was happy and alcohol only heightened the tendency. "Well, here's one for you, Bobby. Did you know Hannah's brilliant?"

"Stop it," said Hannah. "You're being annoying."

"She's getting her Ph.D. Double emphasis in English and women's studies."

"That's interesting," said Bobby. "We should have coffee sometime. But why did you call me?"

"Well, shit, Bobby," said Ellen. "You're the coke dealer. Break out the eight ball."

Bobby winced. "Fuck, Ellen," he said. "That was rude."

"God made me this way, Bobby. You of all people should know." Bobby shook off the indiscretion and placed the drug packets on the Formica counter. Ellen handed him a wad of cash, then began pouring some of the coke onto the countertop. "Have some with us, Bobby."

"Yes, please, Bobby," said Hannah. "Let us make it up to you. After all this." She conspicuously tilted her head at Ellen, who laughed again. "We're just a little happy, and drunk."

Bobby discovered that he was more curious than annoyed. "You got any whiskey here?"

**

An easy social dynamic developed. Hannah and Ellen sat on the leather sofa, Bobby in the easy chair. He felt the undulating energy of the coke. Ellen sat practically in Hannah's lap, one leg draped over Hannah's thigh. The two women laughed constantly.

"Where are you from, Bobby?" said Hannah.

"Near Cuero," said Bobby. "A place near Cuero."

"You've never told me that," said Ellen.

"Well, you've never asked."

Ellen put her hand to the side of her mouth, concealing it from Bobby and speaking in a stage whisper. "He must really like you, Hannah," she said, smirking. "He doesn't really like to talk about himself."

Bobby was instantly reminded of Kendra. "Well, Christ, Ellen. You're not exactly one to talk about yourself either."

Ellen spoke as if she were fifteen and talking down to a little brother. "Don't be a drama queen."

"I'm not from Texas," said Hannah, seeking a neutral topic. "Where's Cuero?"

Despite his irritation with Ellen, Bobby moved on. "Don't feel bad," he said. "Most Texans don't know where Cuero is, either. I guess you could say it's near Victoria."

"Where's that?" said Hannah.

Bobby waved a hand. "It doesn't matter." Then he added quickly, "Down by the coast."

"I see," said Hannah. "Near the ocean."

"Yes," said Bobby. "Not too far from the ocean."

"Are you in school?" said Hannah.

Bobby smiled. "No."

"How did you meet Ellen?" Ellen laughed, rolling her eyes, and in spite of himself, Bobby laughed, too. "Okay," said Hannah, who was starting to laugh herself. "Now I really want to know."

"He hit on me," said Ellen. "Came on like a horny teenager. At a club."

"No, wait," insisted Bobby. "Tell it right."

"Yeah," said Hannah. "Tell it right."

"It was on Sixth Street," said Bobby. "At this rave club called, of all the fucking silly names, Pandora's Box. I thought it sounded like some underground sex club. In any case, Ellen was there, dancing. I mean, dancing like she was X-ed out of her mind."

"I was a little drunk," said Ellen.

"A little," snorted Bobby. "You're lucky security didn't have a SWAT team over or something. Anyway, about half the club's watching her. I was, too. But after a while, I felt like I was starting to get what she was doing out there, that all these freaky contortions were starting to make sense. At that moment, I was thinking I must be as crazy as she is. But I was concerned. Did she come alone? If so, who's going to take her home?"

"Oh, oh, so you were like some saint that night," protested Ellen.

"I'm telling it like I remember."

"And you didn't come at me with every trick in the book?"

"Okay, I'll admit it. I thought you were cute."

"Thank you."

"What happened?" said Hannah.

Ellen laughed again. "Well, he had some coke on him.

When does he not?"

"I took her aside, got her sobered up just a bit," said Bobby. "I drove her home and she seemed like an interesting person."

"You slept with him?" said Hannah, mildly outraged. "You didn't even know him."

"We talked before we did anything," said Bobby, as if it explained everything.

Ellen looked Hannah in the eye. "I didn't know you either, sweetheart, before we did it." Hannah looked at Bobby, her face grave. Then both women stared into each other's eyes, until little by little, they were both laughing so hard they were practically crying. Their faces reddened and Bobby was galvanized by a sudden expression of tenderness on Ellen's part, a side of her she had never shone to him. The women drew back from each other with serious, questioning glances, and Bobby struggled with several competing emotions, foremost being anger.

"All right, enough," said Bobby, raising a hand with a sudden jerk. Both women started and Bobby realized he had raised his voice. He felt intensely embarrassed, and tried to cover it up. "What about you, Hannah?" he said quickly. "Where are you from?"

Hannah eyed him quietly, a patience to her eyes that reminded him of his Aunt Tilda. "I'm from the Midwest," she said. "St. Louis."

"Isn't that great, Bobby?" said Ellen, a little too persistently. Bobby sensed that Ellen realized it had been unfair to put him in this situation, but she continued on, keeping an eye on him. "A Missouri girl. What could be more all-American?"

"I've never been up that way," he said. He tried to communicate with his eyes that he was not upset or jealous, at least not of Hannah.

"It's nice," said Hannah, watching the both of them. "A nice town. I miss it sometimes."

"Well, this is great," Bobby said, after a long silence. "Just great. I'm happy for both of you."

"It's about time, right?" said Ellen. "What with the shit I've put up with."

"Yes," said Bobby, concealing his doubt about the viability of the relationship, especially at such an early juncture. "You've been through a lot." He tried to smile back sweetly but he could not quite pull it off. He sought normalcy by checking his phone. "I gotta go."

"Go?" said Ellen. She seemed disappointed but relieved. "We're just getting started."

"I gotta make a living, Ellen."

Hannah looked between them. Finally, she stood. "It's nice to meet you," she said, crossing the room and giving Bobby a gentle hug. Bobby felt oddly moved. "I'd like to catch up one night. You know, hear some life stories, stuff like that."

"That'll be the day," said Ellen, good-naturedly.

"You're on," said Bobby, still locked in embrace with Hannah. He pulled back and nodded at her, his expression soft and familiar. Then he headed for the door, unable to look directly at Ellen but hitting one more line along the way. Ellen followed him out to the front steps and shut the door behind her. Before she could say anything, Bobby spoke. "Don't think twice about it, okay? It's not what you think. I'm very happy for you."

"I can be a real bitch sometimes, Bobby."

"No," he said, and he leaned over and kissed her on the cheek. "I mean, you can be a bitch, but a very sweet one."

She pulled back from him, her head down, contrite.

"Christ, Bobby, you should be angry. I know you care."

He contemplated her statement, not without a hint of sadness. "I know you care, too, but we both know this would never work." He indicated the house with a nod. "Now get back in there with your girlfriend. I like this one, so don't fuck it up."

Ellen swallowed, watching him as he crossed the lawn. She called out to him as she opened the front door and stepped back inside. Bobby waved back, then got in his car and sat still. The final remnants of daylight formed a baby-blue hue in the Western night sky, and Bobby pondered the last vestige of sunset. He put the tips of his fingers to his forehead, his head bent, then he checked his messages. Three clients had called since he entered the house and he methodically listened to each voicemail. The undercurrent of desperation in their voices, no matter how carefully concealed, sounded pathetic to him. He closed his phone in disgust and then reopened it, looking at the readout and trying to decide his next move. Finally, he selected the number he wanted and called.

"Kayla," he said. "How about I come over?"

"Bobby, it's a school night," Kayla replied. "I've got a midterm paper I need to work on."

"Oh, come on now, you can't tell me you can't do that tomorrow. I'm not taking no for an answer. Not tonight. Come on, it'll be fun. I promise."

**

Kayla lived in a garage apartment in a residential neighborhood just north of Forty-Fifth on a quiet Hyde Park street. The neighborhood was in a state of transition; modest, decades-old houses squatted next to enormous new McMansions that filled almost every inch of their lots. Bobby parked in front of one such residence. Kayla's place was a converted space on the second floor, and he climbed the wooden staircase to the landing and knocked. It didn't take long for the door to open.

Kayla looked Bobby over, smiling slyly. "Well, come in," she said. "Come in if you're going to."

With Kayla, Bobby dismissed his predilection for older women, and it was easy to see why—she was extremely attractive, fresh-faced but not immature. She was of medium build, with small hands and an angular face with large, expressive eyes. She wore shorts and a T-shirt with no bra and Bobby wasted no time, telegraphing his approach. He kissed her, tilting her head back slightly, and she kissed him back.

When she broke away from him she said, "You've been drinking, you bad boy."

"When am I not drinking?"

"Touché." She kissed him again, then led him inside. The apartment consisted of a small living area with a partially demarcated bedroom. The pine bookshelf was stuffed with books about marketing, advertising and business law, as well as paperbacks displaying Kayla's Anglophilic indulgences, which included Agatha Christie, P. D. James, and Ruth Rendell. Kayla always had the apartment brightly lit, which Bobby thought reflected her infectious energy as much as anything else.

"It's good to see you, girl," said Bobby with a bit of detachment, not wanting to seem overly happy to be there. He passed his eyes over her. "You're looking healthy."

Kayla laughed. She opened a cabinet and brought out a bottle of Jack Daniels. "You want a drink?"

"What do you think?" said Bobby.

"Ask a stupid question . . ." She peered at him over her shoulder, bringing out two glasses and pouring the drinks. She placed a handful of long, slender ice cubes in each glass and marched over to Bobby, offering up the drink with a large, mischievous grin. They both sat down and Bobby took a long swallow.

"What's been going on with you?" he said.

"Well, you know, school. And school. And school. After I'm done with my bachelor's, I want that MBA. But then, there's all that crap I don't care about. Whoever told me that anthropology with Dr. Schwartz would be a fun elective is an idiot. What about you?"

Bobby had been in town long enough to be familiar with academic-speak. Still, he laughed, a short little self-conscious laugh. "This and that," he said. He sat up slightly. "I'm cultivating a new business associate."

"Yeah?" said Kayla, who knew nothing of the specifics of Bobby's life. At one point, Bobby told her he was a salesman, which entirely satisfied her. "Are you still thinking about opening that bar?"

"Yeah," said Bobby. "That's still in development, I guess you'd say. But when the time's right, who knows?"

"Sure," said Kayla, who shrugged and sipped her drink. She blinked and smiled. "So, why the sudden need to see me?"

"I don't see you enough," said Bobby.

"Well, I guess," she said, her tone coquettish. "You can be so impulsive." She smiled again and ran her finger over Bobby's shoulder. "You got any of that white powder?"

Bobby smiled back at her, but not fully. "Probably."

"Well, what's holding us back?"

They did several lines off a dining table, then shed their clothes and retreated to Kayla's bed. In twenty minutes they were done. Bobby retrieved the bottle of Jack and sat it on the floor next to the bed. Kayla lay across the bed lengthwise and Bobby lay on his back, staring at the ceiling. They were both still damp with sweat and Bobby asked the question impulsively, without premeditation, "You wouldn't want to go out sometime, would you?"

Kayla poured a small bump on the back of her hand and hit it. "What do you call this?"

"I'd call this staying in."

"I thought guys preferred staying in."

"Well, I'm not saying I dislike this," said Bobby. "Obviously."

"Obviously," said Kayla, and she kissed him. She rested her head in her hand, stretched out over the bed. "Wait? Am I hearing this correctly? Are you saying you want to date?"

"That's an awfully loaded word," he said. "I mean, *dating*."

"Yeah," said Kayla. "Dating. It kind of sucks."

"Hard to argue with that."

"Only women pursing their MRS degrees want that." Kayla leaned over and spoke softly into Bobby's ear. "What does a typical sorority girl say in the throes of orgasm?"

"I don't know."

"Mauve. The curtains should be mauve." Bobby forced a chuckle. "It's funnier at a party," she said.

"Yeah," said Bobby. "How about this? Let's not use the word 'date.' Let's just call it being friends. There are all sorts of ways of being friends."

"Yeah? What does that mean?"

"It just means we've never been friends on a Saturday night."

"Bobby," said Kayla, and she sat up, laughing with her

hand over her mouth. "I never thought I'd hear this from you."

"Hear what?"

"I always thought you were in this for a hard, head-clearing fuck."

"Well," said Bobby, backtracking. "Look at us. I am."

"That's a relief."

"Is it?"

"Well, yeah," said Kayla. "What has this always been? You call. Generally out of the blue. We drink. Do a little powder." Bobby nodded, his expression blank. "I mean, it's nice. It's really nice. I like you. I think you're an interesting guy."

"Oh, come on, Kayla," said Bobby, not sharply but briskly. "You're reading too much into this."

"Okay," said Kayla. "Good. I want to keep on with this."

"Because of the powder?"

Each held their gaze steady. Finally, Kayla broke into a half-smile. "Noooo."

Bobby smiled. The tension was broken. "Are you sure?"

"Yessss."

"Well, all right then," he said. "You should call me sometime. When you're in the mood. Either for powder or for me."

"Bobby," said Kayla, laughing. Bobby noted that the cocaine didn't dim the brilliance of her complexion. "I don't know anyone like you."

**

It was a weeknight but not yet eleven o'clock. Bobby drove toward downtown, answering calls, telling each client they would have to meet him on Sixth Street. He set up shop at a small blues club, a place where he was familiar with the bartender. He spaced out five clients, meeting them at five-minute intervals. After the fifth client purchased an eight ball, Bobby turned off his phone and moved into the shadows at the back of the club.

He drank and did hits in the bathroom and listened to the music, brooding over Ellen's apology and Kayla's frankness, realizing that neither woman would see him so readily if not for the easy access to coke. He did so many hits, in fact, that he began to hear a rushing noise, like the sound of falling water. He sought out the bartender and traded two grams of coke for a bottle of Jack. The bartender unlocked the storeroom and Bobby sat on a crate under an exposed light bulb and took huge swigs of whiskey and breathed. The sound in his ears began to dissipate, and before one-thirty, he was out the door and into the night.

He drove west on Eighth Street, buildings going by in a velvety blur. He continued on, turning south and then heading west on Sixth Street, through the intersection at Lamar and finally coming to the underpass at Mopac. He drove along Lake Austin Boulevard for a quarter mile, before turning left and descending down toward the bridge over the Colorado River. He parked under the bridge and got out with the bottle of whiskey in hand, crossing a dirt embankment, descending all the time, finally arriving at the shore of the great black river. The ground there was damp and mud clung to his shoes. He found a large stone and sat on it, cradling the Jack and continuing to drink, watching the river flow and letting the alcohol relieve an unpleasant awareness that he was once again alone. He took another huge swig, negating any conscious thought.

BOOK 2, CHAPTER 5
September, 2003

The next day, Bobby sat at the breakfast table in the kitchen, staring down at a half-empty glass of bourbon on the rocks. It was early afternoon but he had just awoken, the pain in his head almost beyond endurance. The sky had clouded and he saw through the window only a watery gray light. He tried to piece together the previous night. Everything was clear until he'd arrived at the blues club, at which point things became progressively fragmented. Then there were bits of sensory information, something about mud and a river and the feel of a stone, but after that he remembered nothing, a void of consequence in which he knew he participated but operated out of a perfect id, as if he were a marionette guided by an unknown hand.

He closed his eyes, the alcohol making inroads toward settling a persistent nausea. A fleeting image of Kayla from the night before troubled him like a bothersome insect, and he muttered something inaudible. After a time, the image of Kayla faded, but he found himself thinking that today was yet another day he was going to waste, another loss in the zero-sum game of life, and he raised his glass again, seeking whatever comfort he could find there.

By late afternoon he had collected himself and showered and dressed, ready for an evening of sales. He drove deliberately. Even though overcast, the outdoor light hurt his eyes and a thin fog in his head lingered. From time to time, he found himself gently shaking his head, as if that would dissipate the fog. When his head refused to clear, he gripped the steering wheel tighter, his lips forming a solid line of irritation. When he arrived at the condominiums, his anger had escalated to a point where it roiled through him, flowing as if it were a physical liquid affected by inertia and gravity. He turned into the driveway and passed a line of expensive cars and a couple of boats covered with tarps in special places to park them. He maneuvered his car into a visitor's space after a lawnman cleared it of leaves with an electric blower.

A grinning young man in plaid shorts and a polo shirt opened the door and beamed at Bobby. "It's my *dawg*," the young man exclaimed, overemphasizing the last word.

Bobby nearly turned and walked away but restrained himself. "Quiet down, Joel," he commanded, with no special emphasis. He waited half a beat. "You going to let me in?"

"Yeah, yeah, sure," said Joel, his voice much reduced.

The entrance hall was tiled and a small, tasteful light fixture dangled from the ceiling. The living room boasted a high ceiling and custom bookshelves built into the walls. The bookshelves were empty. A loveseat, a sofa, and a couple of chairs with roses printed on the cushions surrounded a large coffee table.

Bobby surveyed the room. "Who decorated?" he said. "Your mother?"

"Yeah," said Joel, missing the insult. "I mean, in a sense. This is my parents' old living room set. They're letting me have it until I'm done with school."

"Set?" said Bobby, trying out the word.

"Yeah."

Bobby turned around once, as if he were there to suggest improvements for the interior. "Where you from again?" he said.

"Houston."

"Where in Houston?"

"Bellaire."

"Bellaire?"

"You know it?"

"No," said Bobby. He turned once again. "Your parents must do okay."

"They do all right. We're not rich or anything but they're both lawyers."

Bobby stood still, overlooking for the moment that he was there to make a sale. He stared at the lonely bookshelves, then detected the odor of shoes and dirty clothes—the humid, testosterone-laden smell of young man. On the coffee table, a pizza carcass decayed inside its box and a porn mag poked out from under the sofa, its cover showing a woman's soft-focused face with her mouth liquid and open. Joel himself seemed to be the predictable outcome of this environment—an adult boy who would be lost if forced outside of his upper-middle-class milieu.

Bobby took it all in, letting the particulars wash over and through him. He had almost forgotten why he had come in the first place when he saw Joel eyeing him expectantly, as impatient as a toy dog waiting for his afternoon treat.

"Okay, what do you want?" Bobby said, the question emerging tiredly.

"Three hundred."

"Three hundred? You doing it alone?"

"Well, yeah."

Bobby grimaced. "Okay," he said. He began counting out the packets. "Where's the fucking money?"

"On the table."

"Bring it to me."

He had counted out six packets when a light wave of dizziness settled over him. He put his fingers to the bridge of his nose, listening to the muted roar of leaf blowers outside. He turned to Joel. "How much again?"

"Three hundred."

"Oh yeah."

"Hard night?" said Joel, with the proper meekness.

Bobby considered not answering. After a beat, he shrugged. "In a manner of speaking." The question came out like an accusation. "You have a girlfriend?"

Joel eyed Bobby closely, with curiosity. "Well, yeah. Don't you?"

Bobby nodded, but he couldn't deny the apparent truth—this moron had managed to find a girlfriend, while he had not. He suppressed a violent rage. "I'll let myself out," he said, unable to look at Joel. "If it's all the same to you.

**

He was out the door and advancing up the walkway next to the brick exterior when he stopped. Bobby formed a fist and looked at it, then unclenched it, but the next thing he knew he was stumbling backwards and nearly falling. He stood still, fighting off a hazy darkness. His eyes lost focus, but he took a deliberate step forward and clarity returned suddenly, all objects standing out with a sharpness that was startling. Then came an immense pain, which seemed to be everywhere but most specifically in his head. Without considering this further, he continued to his car. A lawnman saw him and did a double take, then stared at him with a fixity that Bobby found unsettling. "Que pasa, amigo?" the man cried out. Then, in English. "You okay?"

Bobby climbed into his car, blood dripping into his eyes. He took a couple of heavy breaths, seeking an internal steadiness. Instead of a tenuous equilibrium, the sense of rage heightened, and he pounded on the steering wheel repeatedly. He looked around. If anyone had been within twenty feet of his car, Bobby might have ended up in a fight. His breath continued at an uneven tempo, heavy and ragged. He dabbed his forehead with a shirttail and then looked at it, the fabric saturated with blood. He ripped the shirt at the collar and pulled it apart, rolling it into a ball and placing it to his head with his left hand.

**

"Jesus, man," Steve said as Bobby strode through the living room, genuine alarm underscoring his words. "What the hell happened?" Bobby pulled the shirt away and a swollen knot, the skin around it torn, stood out on his forehead like the half-shell of a large nut. Steve took a closer look and grimaced, his usual unflappable cool subsumed by the gruesome sight. "Bobby, what the fuck?"

"I need some ice," Bobby replied.

"No shit," said Steve, continuing to appraise the wound. "I'll go get some. Sit down."

"I don't need to sit."

"Don't argue with me, Bobby."

Bobby circled a chair once before he eased into it,

reluctant and weary. His anger had settled, replaced by self-disgust. Steve reappeared with a dishtowel wrapped around a bunch of ice cubes, as concerned and earnest as a Boy Scout, a side of him Bobby rarely saw.

"No whiskey?" said Bobby with irritation.

"I'm not your goddamned servant," Steve said.

"I'll get it, then," said Bobby, beginning to stand.

Steve shook his head, gesturing. "No, sit down, goddamn you," he said. "I'll get it."

"Just bring the bottle."

Bobby held the glass of ice with his left hand, the whiskey with his right. Both men were seated and a kind of normalcy slowly asserted itself. Steve had reoriented himself, his effortless sense of cool slowly returning. He looked at Bobby quizzically. Bobby met his gaze for a long moment but then looked away. Finally, Steve sighed and glanced at the ceiling, as if imploring the heavens. "Well?" he said.

"I hit my head."

"That's a revelation. On what?"

"A wall. A brick wall."

Steve waited. Bobby took a swig and looked down at the floor. He could sense Steve's growing impatience. "Should I even ask?" Steve said.

"I sort of did it."

"Sort of?"

"All right, I did it. I did it. A head butt." Steve opened his mouth but no words came out. "Look, Steve, it seemed like a good idea at the time." He held out the bottle. "You want any of this?"

Steve feigned a moment of mild displeasure. "Only you, Kaufmann." He shook his head. "Yeah, I need a drink."

After twenty minutes they had reached an unforced

mutual silence, both men drinking slowly and steadily. The wind whistled through the cracks in the house, and Bobby reclined on the sofa, his drink placed on his thigh.

"How's it feel?" said Steve.

"Better," said Bobby. "As well as can be expected."

"You should get it checked out."

"All right," said Bobby. "I will. Where's Rick?"

"Out. Business. Girlfriend."

Bobby grimaced, the reference to a girlfriend causing a wave of gray feelings to wash over him, a momentary sinking in his stomach. He remained like that, his gaze far away, the silence mounting in intensity. "You like how it's turned out?" he said at last, his voice small.

"What do you mean?"

"Your life," said Bobby. "You know, everything. Is this what you thought it'd be?"

"Well," said Steve. "Some parts of it. There's always room for improvement, I guess."

"Yeah," said Bobby. "Improvement." He went quiet again, slumped in his chair and his shoulders rounded, looking like a man who had been given bad news and was coming to terms with it. "Sometimes it's a crock of shit, right?"

"Well, sometimes."

"Day after day sometimes. It just keeps coming. The next thing you know, you've head-butted a wall."

"You sure you're okay?" said Steve.

When Bobby spoke again, he sounded as if he were talking from the depths of a hypnotic state. He breathed out, the words acquiring the texture of a pronouncement. "I'll tell you what," he said. "I can't keep doing this."

The statement lingered in the air. "Yeah?" said Steve.

"Yeah. This is no kind of life. No kind at all."

Steve observed him, unsure whether to nod in affirmation.

"Things have to change," continued Bobby. He leveled his gaze at Steve, both surprised and mesmerized by this series of statements. "If they don't? I don't know what. It's ugly."

Steve waited for more, but none came. "Well, that's a big goal," he said. "Where will you start?"

A moment passed before both men realized the galvanic nature of Steve's question. Steve appeared embarrassed at asking such a bald question. "I appreciate this," Bobby said, suddenly casual. "Your candor."

"No problem."

The introspection dissipated. It was as if Bobby had already forgotten the conversation. "I've got shit I need to think about." He touched his head. "You think a couple of Band-Aids will be enough for now?"

"No," said Steve. "You need to get that looked at."

Bobby waved a dismissive hand. "It'll keep until tomorrow."

**

He did not leave the house again that day. He retreated to his room and ferreted out a pint he kept stashed in his closet. He sat on his bed as the sun set, as the sky changed to hues of orange and red, and he sniffed coke through a straw, all the time looking out over the roofs of the houses on his street. He heard boys playing somewhere nearby, the underlying joy in their laughter, and he slumped ever so slightly. A little ice remained in his glass, which he placed on his forehead, the pain of the injury considerably lessened.

He climbed out of bed and went to his desk and opened the drawer containing the black folder. He thumbed through the pages, his thin handwriting passing before him, a parade of blunted introspection. He arrived at the first blank page and squared himself, and after several seconds, he picked up a pen.

Change one thing.

He looked at the entry. It filled him with a dissatisfaction he found hard to explain.

Change several things.

The pen circled above the remaining section of blank page. He fought an urge to break the pen in half. After a moment he relaxed, and at last began to write:

But which things do I change? Dating? (Bars or the regular scene? But's what's regular?)

He looked at the words and experienced a mild disgust.

Profession?

The starkness of the word held him in thrall. Once again, he placed pen to paper.

Sobriety?

This word held his attention the longest, but it was not immediately clear what he thought about it. At last, he stood up and stretched, as if he had just completed a long day's work. He found a packet and spread out a couple of lines and closed the notebook so he would not read the word "sobriety" as he hit them.

**

The following night, just after ten o'clock. He had decked himself out in a newly pressed, long-sleeved blue shirt and black jeans, the head wound stitched at a local clinic and professionally bandaged. (He laughed off the incident to the nurse who attended him, claiming his cat got under his feet and he tripped into a wall.) Parked near the Warehouse District, he sat in the darkened car, peering across a park to the vivid bright lights of the bars, clubs, and restaurants, watching the perpetual ebb and flow of human activity. Then he read the entry he had made earlier that night in his pocket-sized spiral notebook.

Observe quietly. Make an easy approach. No pressure. You're just glad to be there.

He looked over the words and considered them reasonable enough. Before he realized it, he had removed a packet of cocaine from his pocket. He simply held the coke, turning it over in his hand, studying it. Then he put it back in his pocket, and in the shadows of the car, he wrote.

Do not lead with the coke. Under any circumstances. Don't even let on that you have it.

The joint was a fusion bar/coffee shop, pretentious but inviting, sporting new wooden floors and black metal light fixtures and glass bins with baked goods. This was the first time Bobby had ever been inside. It was almost a point of pride with him that he did not frequent any place that mingled premium coffees with alcohol. Still, whenever he was near this place he inevitably saw women of all varieties inside. He sat at a small, round table with high wooden chairs near the middle of the main room. It was still early enough that the customers, most of them sitting in front of laptops, sipped coffee rather than beer or whiskey. Bobby had opened his little spiral notebook and, eyeing a man through a window outside on the deck, he wrote:

Black shirt and dark jeans, wearing sunglasses with orange rims, even though it's night. Douchebag? Or is this what the ladies go for?

He continued to take in the man's appearance, making

note of the hint of facial hair, the full tousled aspect of his haircut. Bobby couldn't tell if this man was alone or waiting for someone. He then turned his attention elsewhere, a new subject catching his eye.

She had short blond hair parted on the side and small, round black-rimmed spectacles. She peered earnestly at her computer. A bookish sort with a checkered, long-sleeved shirt and a black skirt, from the university perhaps, or maybe a fully functioning professional. Based on superficialities—the checkered shirt seemed collegiate and preppy, and the fact that she was the sort to frequent an upscale coffee shop to work in the first place—Bobby gathered they were light years apart. Still, he thought she conveyed an introvert's openness and freethinking bent. He began an involuntary sort of daydreaming. She would overlook their differences, just as he would. He thought she might be a fun date. They could catch a good movie at the Drafthouse perhaps, maybe coffee and conversation afterwards. This little fantasy floated through his mind like a Taster's Choice commercial and then dissipated like smoke. He felt the momentary adrenaline rush, the small, lonely pit in his stomach, before the approach. He stood up and drifted to her table.

"Hey," he said, in a small, familiar voice, somewhere above a whisper. "I was wondering what you're reading."

The two women adjacent to her looked at him immediately, their expressions unreadable. As approaches go, he wished this one were funnier and a bit more edgy, but he made allowances due to his limited information base. When the woman looked up, he made sure to maintain an easy eye contact and a smile. Bemused, she took a moment to process the situation, and seemed to repress a small smile. He saw calm, abiding eyes, the stillness and patience of a mature intellect. A graduate student, perhaps, finishing out her coursework. True, Bobby liked mature women, but most of those were offbeat in one way or another, and Bobby guessed this woman had moved beyond her angst. It set him on his heels.

She leaned forward, a little conspiratorial. "I'm with my friends right now," she said, sweetly and not unkindly.

"Well, okay then," said Bobby.

"Best of luck," she said.

"Of course," said Bobby. "Nice to meet you."

"Nice to meet you."

She maintained polite eye contact a moment longer, but Bobby saw little interest, and she immediately returned to her computer screen. Bobby forced himself to turn away before it got awkward. He found a different table, one from which he wouldn't inadvertently make eye contact with her. He opened his notebook and wrote:

Rome wasn't built in a day.

The rebuff had left him unsettled, so he ordered a whiskey. As he sipped it, a blond with a bright-yellow knit cap stood up from the bar and walked out. He managed only a fleeting glance at her face; he couldn't identify any characteristics other than the hair and the cap, but still, acting on impulse, he stood and followed her out. The sidewalk teemed with pedestrian traffic and Bobby maintained a proper distance, but as he moved along the sidewalk, he felt a growing sense of doubt, questioning the social dynamics underpinning the situation. He thought to himself morosely that stalking was seldom the best basis for establishing a new relationship, and when the woman turned down the steps leading to the Cedar Street stage, Bobby let her go and continued down the sidewalk.

He soon entered the heart of the Warehouse District

and its dizzying array of humanity—male patrons of gay bars, some with black leather vests or other such attire, mingled easily with professionally dressed, middle-aged couples out for an expensive meal, and noisy, jeans-clad undergraduates beginning to get their drink on. Bobby began to experience a deep sense of isolation which crowds only tended to exacerbate but fought this feeling and reminded himself that he should have very limited expectations for the evening, that this is the way it was. As groups of women of all ages passed, he kept his head down and soldiered on, as if fighting his way through high winds. He decided that a familiar venue might help soothe his alienation. He paid the cover at Monks, got himself a drink, and moved out onto the upper deck, letting the music wash over him. A sense of place, of normalcy, reasserted itself.

After his second drink he began the business of scanning the clientele. She sat a table across the deck, sporting a simple gray hoodie, her brown hair pulled back into a short ponytail. An athletic type, with tanned skin and a lean face, naturally attractive without the artifice of elaborate hair and makeup. Her glass was nearly empty and she was alone. Bobby trained his eye on her and she noticed. He raised his glass and smiled, and after a moment she smiled back. Bobby walked over to her.

"You're running low," he said.

"Observant," she said, eyeing him casually, demonstrating neither anxiety nor the burden of expectation.

"It's a sad state of affairs," said Bobby.

"Are you trying to buy me a drink?"

"If you like."

"Well, I won't turn down a drink."

Bobby raised a hand, getting the attention of a waitress,

who arrived in short order.

"We need to re-up. Bourbon on ice here."

"A mojito."

Bobby sat down. "A sweet drink."

She shrugged. "I think they're good."

"Well, they are good." Bobby liked the ease of their repartee. "Bobby."

"Joanne."

"Hi, Joanne. Mind if I stay for a minute?"

"Suit yourself." She smiled. "Bobby."

They talked across the table as casually as old acquaintances. Bobby reminded himself that he'd had only four drinks all evening, hardly an amount that would have even a minimal effect on him. This comforted him, instilling a quiet measure of confidence.

"Well, I suppose this is where I ask what you do," said Bobby.

"I think you're right. I think that is the next question."

"Well, what do you do?"

"Data," she said.

"Data?"

"Yes," she said. "Lots of it. In fact, taken in certain very small bits, the amount is so large that there's no number for it. Just a math equation."

"And what do you do with this data?"

"This and that. I analyze it."

"Like a shrink?"

She laughed. "That's good. That's very good. In fact, sometimes that's what it feels like. Like I have this really complex, really neurotic patient who needs constant attention."

"I see," said Bobby. "Did you go to school for this?"

"Yes," she said. "Cal Tech. You heard of it?"

Bobby nodded. "I've heard of it. I mean, this is a college town."

She pointed at the bandage on Bobby's forehead, which was mostly covered by his hair. "That looks painful."

"An accident. My cat tripped me."

"I hate when they get underfoot."

"Me, too."

For a split second it seemed the conversational thread might end, but Joanne picked it up immediately. "So then, where did you go to school?"

"Oh," he said. Several possible replies occurred to him—that he had gone to technical school, that he went straight into business out of high school—but he decided that the lack of a college degree would hardly impress a graduate of Cal Tech, and in fact would probably be a deal-breaker. "I'm boring. I went here."

"No shame in that," she said.

"I suppose not."

"What did you study?"

"Business."

"Just business?"

"I'm a simple man," said Bobby. The back of his neck began to tingle and he realized that he might blush at any moment but he wrested hold of this feeling and buried it. "I think you have to be direct about life," he said.

When their drinks arrived, Bobby, forgetting himself, sucked down half of his bourbon in one gulp. But Joanne, her focus turned inward, as if evaluating his words, hadn't noticed. "That's a good attitude," she said, eyeing him with a flicker of interest. "You know, that's a good philosophy to get behind. So what do you do?"

Bobby realized she believed him entirely. "Well, I suppose it follows. The basics. I'm in sales."

"That does follow. What product?"

Her questions were changing, becoming rapid, more specific. She was clearly taking him seriously. "Pharmaceuticals."

She looked at him with heightened interest. "I hear there's good scratch in that," she said.

"I make ends meet."

"I have a friend who has a friend in that. He just built a house in Rob Roy."

"Well, I'm not quite there yet."

She grinned at him with a certain slyness. "Is that where you're headed?"

Bobby fought to mask a feeling of disgust—whether at himself for misleading her or at her for being taken in, he could not tell. "Well, I don't dislike money."

"Neither do I," she said. "In fact, I'm bucking for team leader. There's this one MIT dickhead in my way. I think he may leave. If I make that, I think I'm moving."

"Where?"

She smiled, seeming both mock embarrassed and rather pleased with herself. "Maybe one of those new, way overpriced condos on Fifth Street, maybe a small place near the lake. I don't know. Where do you live?"

Bobby once again buried an oncoming impulse to blush. "Basic again. I'm an East Side guy."

"Delwood area?"

Bobby thought it revealing that she cherry-picked the neighborhood directly across the freeway from the university, an eclectic blend of students, commercial artists, and university personnel. Bobby lived nowhere near Delwood. "Yeah, Delwood," he said, less enthusiastic than ever for the web of lies he was weaving. "How'd you ever guess?"

"If I lived on the East Side, that's where I would live." She paused. "Listen, I'm supposed to be meeting someone here and I think technically I'm not supposed to be talking to you."

"Technically?"

"Well, you know, *technically*. Look, he's not my boyfriend or anything, and I don't want you to get the wrong idea. I don't play around. You got your phone?"

"I don't," said Bobby, who did, in fact, have it in his front pocket.

"Well, low-tech is still good." She took out a pen and scribbled on a napkin. "Here's my number. Call me. I'd love to have dinner or something. You know, good food. We can talk about business models."

"Sure, business models."

She looked at him again, the slyness returning. "Nice meeting you, Bobby. Call me."

**

He stayed on the deck, plowing through a bourbon, and then another, peering at Joanne discreetly. Halfway through Bobby's second drink, a man in a black leather jacket and jeans sat down at her table, and Bobby watched the couple from the corner of his eye, employing all of his skills to remain unassuming and unseen. The man looked about thirty and had the easy bearing of a successful young professional. Bobby felt a sudden pain from the head wound, a persistent throbbing. He stood abruptly, and without a backwards glance, he left Monks.

It was well past eleven and Sixth Street was more crowded than ever, lots of pedestrians, a riot of traffic noise. He ducked into a bar and crumpled up the napkin with Joanne's number and deposited it in a garbage can, relieved to be rid of the offending item. He absent-mindedly fingered the drug packets in his front pocket, then removed his hand and placed it on the table where he could keep an eye on it. His drink arrived. The bar was crowded, a football game showing on multiple televisions. He tried to immerse himself in the game but his mind returned to the open-air deck at Monks and involuntarily replayed parts of the conversation with Joanne, how any one of the lies he told buried his chances.

He decided a long walk was in order. He crossed Congress and passed the Driskill Hotel and the street pulsed like a thing alive. It was after midnight and most everyone was drunk. He was borne along the street as if immersed in a powerful current, the persistent noise causing a throbbing in his frontal lobe. He looked at those who passed—a woman in a shoulder-less red dress, an old man with a silver-handled black cane. He ducked into a head shop and studied the various glass bongs on the shelves behind the clerk. He noticed a rack of T-shirts, one of which read "On earth as it is in Austin." He left the head shop and moved up the street, reaching into his pocket and pulling out a packet, keeping it clutched in his hand. He was just about to pass a club when, at the last moment, he ducked inside. It was dark inside and full of the younger set, just kids really, and although he was their age, that was how he thought of them.

He climbed a set of stairs that opened out into a room with multicolored lights and a persistent strobe, the music mechanical and metal-driven. The dance floor was full and he pressed against a wall, avoiding the hyperactive bodies. He looked around furtively, then opened the packet, turned to the wall, and sniffed through a straw. The coke reframed his thoughts and all he saw was a hellish chaos of bodies, smiles without joy, inebriation without epiphany. A high-pitched metal refrain advanced over the bedlam and the sound reached the uttermost depths of his ears and the repeating *waaa waaa* signature left him faintly nauseated. The pain in his head had evolved beyond a dull throbbing quality into something different—a stabbing sort of pain, as if a small creature had been released inside his skull and was trying to exit by creating a new orifice.

The cool air of outdoors. A kind of equilibrium returned as he walked north on Neches and left Sixth Street behind. As he walked, his head cleared. He passed a bank of tattoo parlors, then two homeless men who were headed in the opposite direction, jabbering nonsensically. He stood under a sign—AROUND THE CLOCK BAIL BONDS. A car roared out of an intersection and the driver leaned on the horn, a pealing wail emptying out over the street. He saw street graffiti displayed on a wall, a scene with elongated one-eyed stick people, bat-like with their tongues out, Boschian, naked souls seeking a scarcely sought solace. He set his purpose on a bar up Red River and made his way there.

The floors were concrete and the beer selection vast. An Irish venue, or at least an attempt at it, whether the proprietors possessed Hibernian blood or not. He sat on a stool and cast his eyes about, his lips forming a pursed, thin line, his signature expression indicating conflict or irritation. He pulled out his notebook and scribbled a simple entry: *Fuck it*. He looked around for any reason to stay out among the denizens of the early hours and found one in short order. She was large-boned with high cheekbones, bleached-blond hair with pink-and-green highlights. Not unattractive, but somehow overused, a woman who carried her failures palpably, someone accustomed to drink and late nights, loneliness and rejection. He smiled slightly at her, and so steady was his gaze that she did not look away, and finally was coaxed into smiling back. He got up and went to her table, the smile still present on his lips.

"It's been one hell of a night," he said, not even inquiring whether she wanted the pleasure of his company.

"Yeah?" she said.

"Yeah," he reaffirmed, as if they were resuming a conversation from earlier that evening. "For better or worse." He extended his hand. "Bobby."

"Teresa."

"Hi, Teresa," he purred, his aspect vampirish. "What brings you out at one o'clock?"

Their eyes met and locked. So singular was Bobby's focus that it seemed she gave way in front of it. She hesitated, unsure which social convention to follow.

"Well, I don't know how to say it." She seemed to regain her footing and regarded him with a scrap of doubt. "Men are shit, you know."

"They sure are," he said.

She didn't smile. "You're a man."

"Well, forget that for a moment." He sized her up one last time and then pressed ahead. "I make no judgments here. You seem like a person who would refuse a bunch of bullshit, and I'm fresh out of bullshit tonight." He lowered his voice to just above a whisper. "Besides, I have some goodies."

**

The motel was just off I-35, south of Oltorf, cheap and run-down, the carpet thin and worn, with fake wooden furniture and a bedspread stiff and abrasive. The bed was wrecked, but that portion of the evening was over and their attentions had turned elsewhere. In the bathroom they did lines off the washbasin, the lights fluorescent and harsh. They powered through an eight ball in an hour and started on another. She was the type who talked when she got high and she regaled him with her life story and then started on her most recent breakup. Bobby only half-listened, and he rubbed his nose and did more coke, the light hurting his eyes but he did not care, and what she said sounded garbled and nonsensical and then he simply refused to listen at all and would simply nod from time to time, saying sure, sure.

When he awoke, he couldn't remember where he was and he panicked and threw off the covers, until he saw Teresa next to him and the night came flooding back. The red numbers of the clock radio read seven twenty-one. He got out of bed slowly, trying not to wake Teresa. He stepped into his jeans, dropped a twenty on the table, and wrote "cab fare" on the notepad. He looked at Teresa for a long moment and then added another twenty.

When he got in his car, he pondered the parking lot, which was sprinkled with cars but devoid of people. He put his hands on the steering wheel as if seeking ballast and stayed like that, almost preternaturally still, staring straight ahead. He could not escape the conclusion that the previous night was simply one more in a long string of failures and he punched the horn, the single sharp blast seeming to soothe something deep inside him.

He took the freeway heading north, and within minutes was confronted by a wall of traffic. Up ahead he could see the lights of a police car. The traffic crept forward incrementally and Bobby's mind swirled, thoughts battering the inside of his skull—thoughts about the elusive girlfriend and how his way of life frustrated the singular endeavor of finding one. He put his fingers to his temples and lowered his head, glancing at the road periodically but his attention focused almost entirely inward. He was lost in a reverie when he suddenly came out of it.

In an instant, he saw flares and a cop directing traffic into the two most leftward lanes. On the right shoulder, there was a series of three cars, each more damaged than the last. The first car's front was caved in and the second car had been smashed in the back. But it was the last car that seized Bobby's attention. There was no ambulance, but he could not imagine anyone surviving such a wreck. The twisted metal seemed to heave like an ocean in distress and Bobby could not take his eyes from the carnage when he realized that the car had been split in half. He braked to look at the scene, as if it were an exhibit in a museum with an aesthetic purpose, then he continued down the freeway.

BOOK 2, CHAPTER 6
September, 2003

When he arrived home, the sun had crept over the horizon and a soft light overlaid the sky. He sat in his car and looked up the gray street. It was a Sunday morning and the street was empty, utterly bereft of pedestrians or vehicles. He struggled to collect himself and he suddenly felt confined by the seatbelt and he got out of the car in a hurry. As he walked to the house, the sense of confinement persisted and he came to understand its origin—the circumstances of his life had forced him into a niche, a corner. He also understood he could remain where he was indefinitely but his options for moving "forward" (he balked at the word) were limited.

He opened the door and stood in the tiny entry hall, peering into the living room, its furniture placed without care for the arrangement. There was a T-shirt dangling from an armrest, a pair of old tennis shoes turned on their sides in front of the sofa, a couple of greasy white sacks from a local burger joint on the coffee table. He remarked to himself that the misbegotten presence of all things male revealed itself before one could take two steps beyond the front door and his displeasure in this observation was plainly evident. He crossed the room hurriedly and almost lunged for the stairs, racing for the sanctuary of his bedroom. The sense of confinement would not abate and he undressed and clambered into bed, grabbing a pack of cigarettes from the nightstand and smoking as the minutes passed slowly.

His thoughts turned to the night before. His encounter with Joanne played like a film loop in his skull, but he discovered that a night's passing had allowed him some distance. He played the conversation again, but this time he slowed it to see if he could extract a lesson from it. A question formed and his lips moved slowly as the thought translated into words. He said out loud to the empty room, "What if I had told the truth?"

That simple question spurred an awareness of the minimal nature of his surroundings—the negligible furnishings of his room, clothes piled indiscriminately into a laundry basket in the corner, the blanket on his bed a cheap gray one bought at a discount store. These were the material contents of his life. He imagined Joanne, with her upwardly mobile air of congratulatory self-satisfaction, confronting this room for the first time. What he knew implicitly found formulation in his mind—any relationship with her would involve a shell game. How long could he keep her from this room? How long before she would want to meet his friends, work colleagues, family?

He had no acceptable answers to those questions and his sense of confinement began to magnify and the room appeared to shrink until he felt as though he could reach out and touch the far walls, the feeling of claustrophobia intensifying until the room seemed to stretch and elongate. His vision was distorted and he breathed as if he had the dry heaves, his heart racing. He gathered himself and flopped down to the floor. He went for a bottom desk drawer and a whole liter of Evan Williams slid to the front, and he sat with his back against a wall and drank in huge gulps. At one point, he noted that he had downed a pint in less than a couple of minutes but he continued drinking, and then without entirely realizing it, darkness descended.

He was unaware, until something shifted in his mind, something inchoate and unreal. He was in a room, not his own. It was daytime, and he faced a bank of windows overlooking some rooftops. He was aware of himself in that room; he could see himself. Although he had no memory of the place, the spectral version of himself seemed to be familiar with it. There was a rudimentary bed, and clothes littered the hardwood floor, a woman's clothes. He became distinctly aware that he was not alone, and he turned his head toward a woman's voice. She had dark hair and a round face, smooth limbs, not long but well-proportioned, and she and Bobby faced each other, neither avoiding the other's eyes. He didn't recognize her. The room began to fade and the image went dark.

**

He came to in the early afternoon, a ferocious pain in his head. Slowly he realized that he was downstairs on the sofa. He hung his head to lessen the pain, and on the floor he spotted a largely empty liter bottle that had been turned on its side, only a couple of swigs remaining. He could not recall drinking so much so fast. His eyes passed over his person and he saw he was naked.

At first he simply sat up, resting his head in his hands, grateful to find relative quiet in his mind. The band was out of town, and as a consequence, nobody would have stumbled over the offense of him unclothed in the most public part of the house. This thought contented him, until he began to feel self-conscious and he stood, launching the whiskey bottle across the floor with a single kick, sending it clanging against the sliding glass door. He gazed at the bottle, his expression petulant, and then he shuffled to the stairs and began to climb.

Back in his room, he put on shorts and a T-shirt and sat at his desk. He placed his elbows on the desktop and once again rested his head in his hands, and he sat like that for several minutes, his mind barely stirring, the blankness creating neither reassurance nor conflict. The put-upon feeling persisted, then subsided, and the undeniable facts of his life intruded into his reverie, facts the formed a rudimentary list. It was early Sunday afternoon. He was in his room in a house he rented with a local band, and a motley collection of eclectic folk served as his friends and enablers. He had a car, a nest egg he never touched, a steel box full of cocaine. Meager as these were, these were the items in the plus column of the list. He reminded himself what he did not have—no close friends nor true gainful employment, not to speak of something so grand-sounding as a career. And of course, no significant other.

Although his circumstances were no different than they'd been three days earlier, everything seemed subtly changed. He had bounced from day to day for so long that he had forgotten the meaning of planning. When he opened his black notebook and glanced at the entries, he wasn't surprised that he stopped at one of the first he encountered, an entry from two days before. He looked carefully at the single scrawled word and his mouth formed the syllables carefully—*Profession?* He scratched through the word and then sat for several moments.

THE THIRD DOOR

He picked up his phone and before he could change his mind he sent the text: *Tim, does the offer still stand?*

**

He got out of his car on East Sixth and gave the low-flung, brick bar a once-over. Tim had originally painted the building a soft lime green, but the sunburnt color had faded and only the slightest tinge of green remained. According to rumor, Tim had bought the place with an uncut quantity of speed that helped pay off the former owner's gambling debt. Bobby and Tim were still close then, but Bobby had never asked whether the story were true, mostly because he knew he wouldn't get a straight answer anyway. *El Dorado*, the sign read, *cocktails, beer, wine, coffee*. Bobby crossed the street and entered the building through a metal door which squeaked when opened.

The interior consisted of a concrete floor and a wooden bar, Formica tables, and chairs with rubber cushions that could have once been used in the library of a public school. Antique sofas lined a far wall, which was painted a bright yellow, and the opposite wall was aqua blue. Bobby stood in the center of the room. Several daytime patrons—including a knitting group for recovering addicts, who drank coffee, and a man painting with watercolors—sat at the bar or at the tables, which also looked standard government-issue. The elegance of the old sofas juxtaposed against the utilitarian design of the chairs and tables was a blatant nod to hipster aesthetic—if a place aspired to be chic, it belonged on the other end of Sixth Street.

Bobby ordered a drink and grabbed a booth in the corner. He was several minutes early, as planned. No sooner had he settled in than a small, wiry man with a thick, dark beard and sunglasses entered the bar and, upon spotting Bobby, revealed the barest of possible smiles. Tim tilted his head, and Bobby followed him to the back of the establishment, past a small lounge area, until they came to a little office in the back. Tim gestured at an empty chair in front of a desk and Bobby took it. The desk was littered with all manner of paper.

"Is that Evan?" said Tim, indicating Bobby's glass.

"Awww, honey," said Bobby, "you remember what I drink."

Tim ignored Bobby's tomfoolery. Whether this represented a heightened level of maturity on Tim's part, Bobby couldn't tell. "You want something better?" said Tim. "Maker's, Crown?"

"Evan's fine."

"Let me get a bottle."

"Tim, it's just me. You don't need to get a bottle."

Tim peered at Bobby. "You still drink, right?" Bobby made a face, no words necessary to underscore the ridiculous nature of the question. "Then let me get a bottle."

Tim came back with a liter of Evan Williams and sat down in his black boss's chair. Bobby was struck by Tim's unclouded complexion—either Tim's drug use was greatly diminished or he had stopped altogether—and Bobby could tell that Tim was sizing him up as well. He pointed at the bandage on Bobby's head. "You must have caused her offense," he said, the glint in his eye revealing that he hadn't changed completely.

"What can I say?" said Bobby. "She likes it rough."

"You must be back with Stephanie, then."

"Fuck you."

Tim laughed. He eyed Bobby for a moment, the playful

smile still evident, but then it faded, replaced by an all-too-adult confrontation of the moment. "So," he said, folding his hands on the desk, "what's the news, Bobby?"

Bobby suddenly understood why Tim had grown the beard. It filled out his face considerably and made him appear more adult, more credible. Bobby reached over and swung the door closed. For a long moment, he mock assessed his fingernails. "You know why I'm here, right?"

"I have some idea," said Tim. "Probably something about a fifty-fifty stake, maybe?"

"Maybe. We can talk."

Tim assessed Bobby carefully, taking in the nuances of body language, tone of voice. "I'm actually surprised it took you this long."

Bobby remained still, only his eyes moving. "Well, business has been good," he countered.

"Yeah, but you know and I know it's a shit business."

Bobby remarked to himself the poker game was on. "How long have you been open, Tim?"

Tim smiled slightly, clearly pleased that the first negotiating question was a neutral one.

"Two years."

Bobby nodded. He knew that already. "Two years?"

"Well, two years, four months, and . . ." Tim checked a calendar. "Twenty-seven days."

"You look like you're doing okay."

"It's different," said Tim, "I'll say that."

Bobby waited a beat, indicating that this question was intended to be textured. "Different than what?"

Tim smiled slightly and appeared to think hard. "Well, I sleep nights now."

"Yeah?"

"Like a log, my friend." Tim smiled, a wry smile,

revealing that he had no intention of allowing Bobby the upper hand. "I think you know what I mean."

"You know I know, Tim. You know I know." Bobby paused, attempting to determine Tim's thought process. The beard hid his mouth so completely it made him considerably harder to read. "Can you still afford the ladies? A bit of time in Vegas?"

Tim seemed to realize that the questions had multiple levels. If anything, he further relaxed—Bobby was nobody's fool. "I could, but I don't really have the inclination any longer." He held up his left hand, revealing a gold band.

"You got lassoed."

"All too true."

"How'd you meet her?"

Tim laughed. "How do people meet now?"

"I don't know," said Bobby, smiling tersely. He was truly curious what Tim would say. "How do people meet?"

"Online. I met her online."

"Really." Bobby nodded and looked away but then resumed eye contact. "Children?"

"We're expecting."

"Well, congratulations are in order," said Bobby, and he raised his glass. "Salud."

Tim followed suit. "Salud."

"I must say, I wouldn't have called this five years ago."

Tim's mouth formed a bemused line but he didn't exactly smile. "You know, I would wager a month's earnings that the line on me had it I'd be dead by now."

Tim's observation struck a nerve in Bobby, not least because it was entirely accurate. Finally, Bobby shrugged. "People, huh?"

"Yeah, people."

Both men went quiet, lost in their respective thoughts.

Bobby saw there was nowhere to go but forward, and he shifted in his chair. "Well, Tim, you once said I could hit you up if this got off the ground. At the time, it didn't sound like bullshit. Was it?"

Tim saw no advantage to gamesmanship. He cleared his throat. "Let's go out back. And don't say anything about buying in around the bartenders. I don't want them spooked."

**

They stood on a smallish cement slab that served as a parking lot. It was behind the bar and could hold about a dozen cars and was adjoined by an alley that acted as a delivery artery for two restaurants and a handful of small retail businesses. A garage was next to the bar, and its dirt lot held a number of cars in various states of repair and disrepair. It was a typical urban milieu, no different than a thousand other street corners, but Bobby understood that every business has a backside, and it was as fundamental to the business as its entrance. Observing the bar's underbelly summoned an uneasy question—he knew plenty about drinking in bars but what did he know about running one?

Tim pointed at a dirt rectangle between his place and the garage. "You see, there's space here. I couldn't buy it all two years ago; I couldn't afford it. But you see, if I did buy it, I could set up an adjoining room, another lounge. I'd have access to this area in the back, and that means another bar out here, music at night. That's three times the capacity I have right now. I suppose there's no guarantee that added capacity means more customers, but on the weekends the line's out the door and people go somewhere else. In any event, three times the capacity means there's the possibility for three times more revenue, and even divided up, that's fifty percent more for me."

Bobby considered Tim's analysis. "A line out the door? Sounds like the joint's hopping. Why don't you just do it on your own?"

Tim's posture eased, his body language turning thoughtful. "I do all right, Bobby. The place does okay. If I weren't married, it might be different, but I am. I've gone in full hilt. A mortgage. A kid on the way. I do all right but not that good."

"No temptation to do something on the side?"

Tim didn't seem angry, but Bobby heard an unmistakable dissatisfaction in his voice. "Is that a joke?"

Bobby held up a hand, indicating the question was not intended to incite. "It's never occurred to you?"

"I don't want my child to see me for the first time behind Plexiglas. I hope that's not what you're here to propose." Tim was quiet for a long moment. Bobby recognized further physical evidence that Tim had changed; his torso was bereft of the baby fat of constant drink. "Ray didn't put you up to this, did he?"

"Tim . . ."

"I'm not trying to be a dick, Bobby. But I know Ray. He might need another place to run . . . money through."

Bobby scuffed at the cement with his shoe. Finally, he looked up. "Let's get this nice and clear right now. Ray doesn't know I'm here. I don't want him to know. Not yet. That's as clear as I can make it."

It was Tim's turn. He looked up the alley, then once again at the back of the bar. "No, I think it could be clearer."

Bobby raised his chin, his single nod almost imperceptible. "What's on your mind, Tim?"

"I think you know."

Bobby's gaze remained level. "I would never do anything to hurt you, Tim."

"Does that pass for an assurance?" Tim waited for an answer but one did not readily follow. "I run a square joint, Bobby, everything nice and above board."

"What is it you want to hear? Do you want me to promise not to sell to the customers?"

"Don't get hot, Bobby."

Bobby looked down and kicked at some gravel, clearly impatient. "Come on, what are we really talking about? Not in the abstract but in the concrete?"

Tim spat, then looked at Bobby directly. "You mean, the actual?" Bobby nodded. "If I had $100K, it could be sweet."

Bobby felt a measure of satisfaction that a proposal was now on the table. "Is that a firm amount?"

"It's a preferable amount, but I'll listen to anything."

Bobby considered lowballing but then thought better of it. "I've got eighty, Tim. That's what I got. I could have it to you tomorrow."

"Just like that?"

"Like that."

"Cash?"

"What else would it be?" Bobby kicked at the gravel again. "You're thinking Ray would have to launder it?"

Tim considered the question. "No, I don't think so. Not for that amount." Tim looked west down the alley and Bobby followed his gaze. "So, fifty-fifty, right?"

"I don't think it could work any other way."

Tim pursed his lips, thinking. "Why do you want to do this?"

Bobby could think of a dozen answers, but at last, once

again kicked at the cement. "I want to sleep nights, too."

Tim nodded and his posture sank ever so slightly. "I've always worked alone, Bobby. More or less."

"So have I."

"You'd have to be here. You can't just drop off the money and not be here. You have to help run it."

"If I need to start as a bartender, I will. I'll learn the business. You've seen me."

"I wouldn't be talking to you, Bobby, if that weren't true." Tim shook his head. "I'm still not sure I get it. Why me? Why now?"

"Why not now?" Tim was clearly not satisfied with that answer. Bobby reconsidered. He grinned slightly, shaking his head, trying but failing to hide his embarrassment. "Would you believe me if I said I was looking for a girl?"

"Bobby, don't shit me."

"No," said Bobby. "Actually . . ." He paused again. "Actually, that's not bullshit."

"Bobby, I've known you to have any number of girls."

"Maybe this time I'm looking for a regular girl."

"A normal girl? You?"

"Crazy, huh?" Bobby felt a momentary misgiving that he needed to explain himself like this. "And maybe I don't want to lie to this normal girl."

"I didn't think lying bothered a guy like you."

"Truth is, I might be changing, Tim."

"Does a guy like you ever really want a normal life?"

"You seem to be living proof."

"It was hard, Bobby, I gotta say. It was hard in the beginning."

"I'll take my chances, Tim."

"This is my business, you see. It's serious, Bobby. It's blood."

"I know that, Tim. You know I know that."

"Yeah," Tim said. "I know you do." He faced Bobby. Whether any one thing convinced him that Bobby was playing it straight, Tim kept it to himself. "I've got to talk this over with my wife."

"Yeah," Bobby said. "I would expect nothing else." He cast about in his mind. "I need a few things, too. I have to look at your books."

"Absolutely," said Tim. "You considering other deals?"

"I'll consider anything. But you're the first person I've asked."

"I appreciate that, Bobby. I appreciate the consideration."

"I appreciate this, too, Tim." Bobby looked again at the brick building. At that moment, he felt some relief that a deal was yet to be forged. "When are you getting back to me?"

"Tomorrow probably. The end of the week at the latest." Tim looked at Bobby. "What is it? You got this look."

"It's nothing," said Bobby. He glanced at the bar again. "It's nothing, really." Bobby extended his hand, which Tim looked at briefly, then shook. "You let me know what you think. I'll be waiting."

"Now don't you get cold feet on me," said Tim.

"Who said anything about cold feet?"

"Nobody, but I know what this is like. When I began all this, I had my doubts." Tim reflected, then nodded. "Another round?"

"I'm good, Tim. I'm good." Bobby scanned the bar. He couldn't help but wonder if such a small place could serve as a source of livelihood for two men. On the edge of his peripheral vision, Bobby was very much aware that Tim watched him the whole time.

Bobby hadn't even driven to the end of the block before his phone went off. He looked at the number and picked up.

"You going somewhere important?" Tim said.

"Not especially."

"Can I have a minute more of your time?"

Bobby circled the block and parked in the same space he just occupied. Tim stood on the sidewalk, waiting for him, and opened the passenger door and climbed inside. "I've known you too long, Bobby. I could see it a minute ago, I can see it now. You get quiet, removed, when you feel uncertain."

Bobby turned his head, his eyes forward. He thought about mounting a lame protest but he knew Tim would see through it.

"I know how hard this step is," Tim said. "I called you because I don't want you to talk yourself out of it. And let me just say, I'm not being generous here. I'm being selfish. In this case, I'm damn selfish."

"What are you saying, Tim?"

"I'm ready to shake on it. In principle. Eighty thousand, fifty-fifty."

"What about your wife?"

"She'll understand."

"You sure?"

"She'll understand that if I'm going to open a second place, I need this. This is too good a hand, Bobby."

Bobby looked at Tim. "It's not unreasonable to take a night and think on it."

"You see, Bobby, I figure that what it all comes down to

is this. Back in the day, you never did anything other than exactly the way you said you'd do it. Every time. There were no fuckups, no fucking around, no stories, no bullshit."

"I haven't even seen your books, Tim."

"I'll get you those. Just one concession. I can't begin paying out until the expansion's done. That's the one thing I'll ask."

Bobby carefully evaluated what he saw when he looked at Tim. He could see little vestige of the twenty-three-year-old punk coke dealer who routinely tried to start fistfights with cops stopping him for minor traffic violations. "You're driving a deal here, Tim."

"I know a good thing when I see it."

"Get me the books. I'll need to see Ray before I agree to anything final. And I want it written down in black and white. All legal."

"That's understood. But just one thing. I'll only ask it once, but it's important. In fact, it's a deal-breaker. I need you to answer yes or no. You're getting out, right? That's what this is about. You're getting out?"

Bobby's eyes shifted. He saw Tim evaluating every nuance, utilizing his full concentration. Bobby used all his powers of dissimulation to hide his secret doubt. "Yeah, that's right. I want out."

"I'm not trying to be a prick here, Bobby, but you didn't quite answer the question. Now look, I'm not your social worker. I don't care how much you drink, what you put up your nose on your own time. But this won't work if you're still with Ray. That simple. Cut and dried."

The moment had arrived, and for the first time, Bobby had to fully confront whether all this was real, whether he could even do it. He struggled briefly, but quickly he arrived at an elegant formulation—his present life led nowhere and this was the way out. Still, Bobby was surprised to find that four little words could feel so heavy. "Tim, I'm getting out." The two men locked eyes. "I'm getting out, and that's the god's truth."

"Okay. Your word's good enough." Tim waited a moment, then he extended his hand. "You have a partner now."

Bobby looked at the extended hand. For an instant, he thought about qualifying the deal, underscoring its still tentative nature. But at last they shook, each man smiling. Bobby was surprised at how good it felt. "Hey, partner."

"Partner," said Tim, trying out the word and laughing. They shook for several seconds, and then at last they let each other go. "What are you going to do the rest of the day?"

"I'll call Ray," said Bobby. "Don't say anything to anyone."

"Who would I tell?"

Bobby smirked. "Nobody. But you know Ray. He probably already knows." Bobby faced forward again. "So, you met your wife online?"

"Yeah."

"How'd that work out for you?"

**

Bobby was well clear of the city when he turned down a road that veered east from 183, a road covering ground in the midst of rolling flatland, with tall yellow grass and few trees. He passed a Church of Christ and a lonely machine shop, but the only other buildings in view were houses built decades earlier, houses that seemed to be decaying back into the ground, and even these were few and far between. He arrived at another road without a street sign and turned south. For a long stretch there was no sign of human habitation apart from a barbed-wire fence and the road itself. Reaching a metal gate, Bobby got out and opened it. A gravel track with a grass furrow in the middle advanced through the rolling landscape, and Bobby followed it.

He motored on, noting absently the undulating land, barren and starkly beautiful in its vastness. After a quarter mile he rounded a turn and saw a brick ranch house nestled in a grove of live oaks. He parked next to a wooden windmill that had rotted long ago. His footfalls crunched on the gravel and the heat emanated from the ground, as hot as air from a convection oven. The pervasive dusty smell of dried-out grass filled his nostrils. A stone path led to a front door, which was covered with a metal plate. The house had few windows but these, too, were protected by metal bars. Bobby found no doorbell and rapped on the exterior, the metal absorbing the impact with a dull thud.

After a few seconds came the sound of metal screeching over metal, followed by a hollow boom. The door opened. A woman in a black satin robe that ended well short of her knees blinked against the light. Her legs were tanned and shapely, her bust full, but her face was lined and looked as though it sagged down into her neck. A platinum shock of brittle hair barely moved as the breeze passed through it. She regarded Bobby with a hint of disdain, her eyes moving with a casual disregard over his person. Bobby followed her into the dim of the living room. She dipped a finger into a line of cocaine on a mirror and rubbed it into her gums.

"He put this out for you," she said. "Of course, you're welcome to as much as you like."

"That's very cordial," said Bobby.

"He's still getting ready."

"Yeah, of course."

"He said to make you a drink. You do want a drink?"

"You got bourbon?"

"He has everything."

"Evan, then," said Bobby. "On ice."

"Evan Williams?" she said, the disdain lingering. "Can't you do better than that?"

Bobby's sense of effrontery was aroused but he did not care to argue the details. "All right then, a Maker's. On ice."

He passed his eyes over his surroundings, noting briefly a fabric recliner, his gaze continuing through the room until he arrived at a hall. In surprise, he almost exclaimed out loud. A painfully thin young woman wearing only panties stood in the hall and peered at Bobby. Bobby had never seen her before but recognized immediately that she was hooked by the coke—her sallow, clouded skin and her confused look of obsequiousness told him everything he needed to know. She regarded him, then called out down the hall. "I think it's him."

"Well, okay," a man called back. "He won't bite."

The woman's statement carried with it an element of pained surprise, as if she were coming to terms with the veracity of her statement. "I'm not wearing anything, Ray."

"I know that," the man called out, his accent deeply Texan. "I promise, he doesn't mind."

The young woman gave Bobby a sidelong glance, as if further examination of him warranted ever more suspicion. Bobby thought her youthful to the point of indecency—she could have easily passed for the older woman's teenage daughter. She continued to observe Bobby oddly, then shuffled forward and did three lines in succession off the mirror. She threw a backward glance at

Bobby and disappeared back down the hall. Bobby was left momentarily alone. *Never a dull moment with Ray,* he thought. His attention was reabsorbed by the everyday and mundane, by the living room furniture—the recliner, a plasticine sofa, a couple of folding chairs around a gaming table, stereo equipment, and an enormous TV. The TV was a large screen that projected, eighties fashionable but an odd sort of time portal, an anachronism of another era. He heard the tinkling of ice cubes, and then the older woman returned with his drink.

"Thanks," he said. "I'm Bobby, by the way."

The woman, moving immediately back to the drugs, couldn't have cared less.

Bobby was more than a little pissed at the snub. "You have a name?"

"I do, I certainly do," she said, her attention on the mirror. In five deft movements she did five lines, and followed them with a shot of colorless alcohol. As she stood, she seemed to cross an internal boundary she should not have, and with each passing moment she appeared more disoriented. She reached inside her robe to rub her chest and the robe came open and she seemed entirely unaware of this. Her fake breasts protruded oddly, each at variance with each.

"Amelia, fly right," Ray said, not unkindly, standing at the mouth of the hallway. His jowly face reminded Bobby of a heavier, coke-using Winston Churchill. The woman stumbled forward and kissed Ray, a hint of tongue darting out. Ray took her by the shoulders to straighten her and she took an awkward step back. "That's enough for the time being. You go keep Janice company."

Amelia lurched forward, not unlike the younger woman who had preceded her, and disappeared down the hall. It was Ray's turn at the mirror. He cut some lines with a credit card, keeping his back to Bobby. "You want any?" he said.

"I'm good, Ray."

"Don't be bashful on account of me. Did Amelia fuck up your drink?"

Bobby took a sip. It tasted like bourbon. "She got it right, Ray."

"Well, she can still do that, at least," said Ray. He made two quick inhalations, then disappeared into the kitchen and returned with a sweating glass of brown alcohol. His jeans were pressed and he wore a black button-down dress shirt, with only white socks on his feet. One of the shirt buttons was out of alignment and the garment was thrown slightly askew. He looked very much like a man who had dressed reluctantly. Ray was large but carried his excess weight with a thoughtful integrity. He sniffed, his right hand shaking almost indiscernibly. At last, he eased into the recliner and Bobby followed suit on the plasticine sofa. Ray's eyes rested on Bobby, who had never learned to feel entirely comfortable under that gaze.

"Long time since I've seen you in the flesh, young man," said Ray.

Bobby thought about it. "I think the last time we hung out was the Vegas celebration three years ago, right?"

"Sounds right." Ray gestured at Bobby with his glass, an affirmative gesture.

"You, Jason, and the boys were selling the hell out of the town that summer."

Bobby didn't like the reference to Jason but he assumed a humble demeanor. "Good product that year. The shit sold itself."

"Any problems getting here?"

"I remembered the way."

"Good." Ray tapped his fingers on the armrest. "You hear from anybody?"

"Well, I've pretty much stopped seeing any of the boys."

"I don't think Jason's pissed off any longer."

"That's a relief."

"Smart mouth," said Ray, with no special emphasis or inflection. Ray tilted his head, as if trying to change his perspective. The words were so quiet Bobby could barely discern them over the faint whispering of the wind outside. "You called me."

Now that the moment had come, Bobby felt an intense, though not unexpected, uneasiness. He coughed, trying to clear his throat. "Do you remember when you first sat me down?"

Bobby thought a reference to their long history was an appropriate gambit but it struck him suddenly as transparent and rather lame. "You might need to remind me," said Ray. Something in Ray's tone suggested to Bobby that Ray thought the same thing.

Bobby coughed again, feeling rather foolish. He pressed on. "Well, there I was, five years ago. Eighteen years old and Jason never shut up about you. He went on and on, said you owned half of Sixth Street and that you ran this town, at least the parts not run by our Mexican cousins. And there's me straight from Cuero, everything so small. You took me aside and said you wanted to talk to me about exposure. That was the word you used. *Exposure*."

Bobby tried to gauge the effect of his words. He heard the girls talking quietly in the back. The sound of the wind. Ray's eyes draped lightly over him. At first glance, Ray could have been anybody—an insurance salesman, a car dealer, a country lawyer, any professionally oriented rural

Texan. But when he was still, the insidious thread of the menace he posed somehow came to the fore. It was so subtle, one hardly noticed. Bobby thought it a matter of juxtaposition—the glad-handing country veneer gave way to a man whose judgments were impossible to read, and before one realized, a lethal stillness, a caginess, quietly insinuated itself. The knot in Bobby's throat seemed to expand, increasing his discomfort. He coughed again.

"It was the way you said it, Ray," he said, thinking his voice sounded tinny and thin. "Exposure. As fundamental as gravity. Fly low. Know the people you know. And five years later, I'm still here."

Ray waited for Bobby to continue. The seconds stretched on. Bobby swallowed twice but could not manage to form words.

"Yeah, you're still here," said Ray.

"Yeah, here I am," he sputtered. Emotion welled inside him, a deep pool, alternating nerves with an inexplicable sadness. "I don't . . ." His voice cracked. "I don't want to be exposed any longer, Ray. I'm going to get out."

A light gust of wind blew against the side of the house and whistled quietly in the door. "Give me your glass," said Ray, and he stood up. "What are you drinking?"

"Maker's. But I think I'd prefer Evan."

Ray took Bobby's glass and shuffled to the kitchen. He returned with a fresh drink. "Something happen? Something I haven't heard about?"

"No, Ray, nothing like that."

"I won't turn my back on you."

"I just want out, Ray. It's time."

"A regular life? Is that you?"

"We'll find out."

"What are you going to do?"

"I'm buying in at Tim's place." Bobby's discomfort was fully evident. "I wanted to tell you face-to-face."

"It's a free country, Bobby."

Bobby nodded, remaining quiet until he made a choking sound, concealing a sob. He was astounded by his own reaction. "I didn't want you to hear it on the street."

"That's good of you, Bobby. Really, it is." Ray waited a moment. "What if we sweetened the deal a little? Took some new boys from Jason's crew? You could show them around, take a piece of what they make. Show them everything. The cutting, the scales, finding clients, all of it. Make it grow, take it somewhere. Expertise is a valuable commodity, Bobby."

"You mean, a mini-crew?"

"Call it whatever."

Bobby folded his hands, considering Ray's offer. He told himself that Ray was playing him like the pro he knew Ray to be, appealing to Bobby's vanity, to his sibling rivalry with Jason. A month earlier, Bobby would have jumped at the chance and not looked back. He considered the offer, but then imagined dissembling to a woman like Joanne. "My mind's made up, Ray."

"In that case, you'll meet with one of Jason's crew. At some place public. I know some bars in South Austin that are suitable."

Bobby saw he no longer needed to continue with any remarks. He was confronted with the shame-inducing reality that whatever words he prepared—not to mention his emotional outburst—were inconsequential. He felt momentarily lost. "What for, Ray?"

Bobby noted that Ray's Texas accent lessened slightly when he transacted business.

"Just be ready to give an accounting of your clients, at

least your best ones," Ray said. "Before the meeting, call up at least a couple dozen, tell them the truth, that you're getting out but you know a friend who can help them. There will be a phone number they can call. If they spook, reassure them, even promise to meet them. If a meeting is involved, I'll pay for your time, a fair wage, believe me. This is all I ask, Bobby. For five years, I expect it's not a problem."

Bobby nodded. "It's not a problem, Ray."

"If you want to sell me back, I'll give you a good price."

"I'm keeping what I got. For my own use."

"Well, you know where to get more. Friend prices. You hear that? Friends." Ray sat back in the recliner.

Bobby could not hide his sense of uncertainty. "Yeah, Ray, sure. Friends. Always."

Ray stood up with his right hand extended. Bobby shook it, his hand swallowed up in Ray's large, fleshy grip. "You take care now, son."

"You too, Ray."

It was over so quickly, Bobby didn't have time to regain his bearings. He stepped out into the daylight, throwing one last backwards glance at the living room. Ray was watching, but his eyes were blank. It reminded Bobby for the hundredth time that he had no clue who Ray really was.

He blinked, the sudden transition to outdoors and late-summer heat causing minor disorientation. He looked around at the scrub and long yellow grass, feeling the steady persistence of the sun, thinking to himself he liked the heat. He stood still, unsure how he felt and what to do next. Then he felt a sudden lightness, an increase of energy and a keen uplift in mood. He pumped a fist in the air, like a boxer's jab.

He got in his car and turned the ignition, the roaring of

the engine heightening his sense of well-being. When Ray's house was no longer in view, he turned on the radio and searched for a station. Normally he hated the radio, but now he felt grateful for it, as if he were being reintroduced to a long-forgotten friend. He stopped at an Iggy Pop song and sang along, full-throated and loud. The road was straight and deserted. Bobby tipped the accelerator hard, and the speedometer shot past 120 and into the area where speed was no longer measured. Bobby screamed at the road, no words forming, both hands on the wheel.

**

Some three hours later, he came to a sudden halt in front of his house and got out of the car with a large brown sack sporting the logo of a local liquor store. He navigated the walkway, laughing, his balance uneven. He dropped his keys, then picked them up in a single fluid motion. He stumbled inside, the interior of the house cool and dark. He grabbed some ice and a glass from the kitchen and lumbered to his room with his two new bottles of Evan Williams.

The sun had just set, a fast dissipating glow on the horizon. He took a few swigs while his laptop booted up, then navigated to a popular dating site. "Lonely tonight?" the banner read. "Meet the one who's right tomorrow." His expression darkened as he pondered the image of a generically attractive blond in the arms of an equally generic, tall-dark-and-handsome type. The obviousness of the advertising bothered him. From a menu he chose "Man Seeks Woman," then made selections indicating that he was looking for someone aged twenty-two to thirty living within twenty miles of Austin. Headshots began to fill the screen. Bobby looked at them one by one and felt the stirring of apprehension. He had ceased being a cocaine dealer for little more than a few hours and he asked himself, was he ready for all this?

Bobby filled in every field of his profile except for a screen name. The site had provided an example: *Mr. FlirtALot.* Bobby raised the bottle to his lips, took a swig, then hovered his hands over the keyboard. *Mr. GoFuckYourself,* he wrote, then deleted it before entering it. He didn't know if Rick and Steve were home, but he called out down the hallway. "Y'all back? Any of you motherfuckers?"

A head poked out of a room. It was Rick.

"You got time to provide some moral support? I got booze."

Rick sat on Bobby's bed, cradling the freshly opened bottle in his lap. The only light in the room came from the screen. "Apparently I need a dating site to meet somebody."

Rick wore another of his many Led Zeppelin concert T-shirts. *World Tour '71* this one read, the black shirt depicting a shrouded figure holding a lantern on top of an outcropping of rock. "Christ, Bobby," said Rick. "I never thought I'd live to see this."

"They want me to do a screen name," Bobby said. "Some cutesy fucking screen name."

Rick gazed steadily at the monitor. "How about *TrueGangster*?" he said.

"No," said Bobby. "Nothing like that. I'm trying to play it straight, Rick. Straight."

"Why?"

Bobby raised his hands, as exasperated as he was drunk. "Because all that shit. That punk-ass shit. I want it behind me. It's not me anymore."

"It's not?"

Bobby heard the inflection in the question. It cut into him. He looked down at the floor. "I'm starting a new chapter," he said.

"Of what?"

"Of me."

Rick looked imploringly at Bobby. "You mean, I can't buy from you anymore?"

Bobby shut his eyes and provided the faintest of nods. "That's right."

"Fuck."

"We'll all get used to it."

Rick couldn't conceal his disappointment. "Do you know how convenient it is to have your housemate double as your dealer?"

**

They had returned to the task at hand. "Do some variation of your name," Rick said. "*BobbyK*. And then follow it with the month and day of your birthday. That way, you're not really being cutesy. You got a digital picture of yourself?"

"My camera's old-school."

"Don't worry," said Rick. "I've got a camera."

As they continued making the profile, Bobby felt an ever-deepening sense of regret. "Drink is one of the descriptors," said Bobby, his mouth grim. "There's no category for pathological alcoholic."

"Sure there is," Rick said. "*Routinely*. Besides, who ever called you a pathological alcoholic?"

"My state-appointed therapist."

"He sounds like a winner. When was this?"

Bobby ignored the question. "God. *Body type?*" he said. "This is so fucking weak."

**

Bobby stood before a blank white wall in the hallway. Rick glanced at the readout, then lowered the camera again. "Come on, man," said Rick. "You look like you smell a fart."

Bobby looked down at the floor, like a condemned man about to receive his sentence. "The last indignity," he said.

"That's no fucking attitude. Now smile." Bobby showed his teeth. "For Christ's sake, you look like you're going to eat the camera."

"Maybe this is a bad idea."

"You got this far. Besides, could it really be worse than dating Stephanie?"

At the reference to the long-departed Stephanie, Bobby smiled—a genuine smile, if not a little rueful. "You're the second guy to mention Stephanie lately."

"Well," said Rick, "she was memorable." The flash went off and Bobby blinked. Rick looked again at the readout. "Got it," he crowed.

Bobby peered at the image. He was bright against a dark background, his high forehead almost pure white under the light of the flash. He didn't appear cheerful exactly, but the usual downward gravity of his demeanor was obscured by the smile. For a fleeting moment, he saw in himself an ordinary, if not even attractive, young man.

**

"It's official," said Rick as he made Bobby's profile

public. "You're off to the races."

Bobby took the neck of the whiskey bottle and lowered it so Rick could take it, which he did in short order. "You keep it. Services rendered."

"Hey, you want to go out?" said Rick. "I'll buy the first round."

"I need a minute," said Bobby, shaking his head. "Come find me in half an hour?"

"Yeah, sure, Bobby," Rick said, concealing his disappointment. "Of course."

**

When Rick returned to Bobby's room, Bobby was sprawled out on the bed, snoring loudly. The computer was on and it hummed contentedly, its screen light muted. Rick considered waking Bobby but finally decided against it. He thought back over the evening, at the improbability that Bobby Kaufmann would resort to a dating site to find a woman, and a small smile graced his lips. He lingered at the threshold of the bedroom and finally shook his head ever so slightly, the small smile turning sad, then disappearing. Rick returned to his room but grabbed his keys and headed out of the house.

As he lay there, Bobby turned a couple of times and muttered something unintelligible. He became aware of a darkness, and then realized that he rested on a mattress, his head turned to the left, his cheek flush against the fabric. He tried to rise, but his chest felt stiff. He wanted to cough but found he couldn't. Then he heard her. She had dark hair and wore shorts and a T-shirt but no shoes. She looked at him and spoke, but he couldn't understand what she said. He told her he wanted to leave. She said that he was close but not quite ready. He asked her why and she only shook her head. Then he felt a flash of real terror. Waking up startled, he found himself in his own room, his own bed, the computer humming quietly. He rubbed his face, trying to shake the dream off of him.

He got out of bed and sat down at the desk. He touched the mouse and the computer screen lit up. Under "Hair Color," he navigated to brunette. A couple dozen headshots came up and he went through them carefully.

He clicked on one attractive woman to open her profile. She was a college graduate, never married, no children, and she was twenty-six. Her screen name was not entirely to Bobby's liking—*Lookingfortruelove11*—but Bobby had yet to see a screen name that he did like. He hit the reply button and a small email box came up. He placed the cursor in the field, but it simply blinked at him. He read through her profile some more but discovered little in it that provided the key to the magical first sentence he sought. He found himself imagining meeting *Lookingfortruelove11* in person. He smiled slightly and nodded at the emptiness before him. He said out loud, "Bobby Kaufmann, wonderful to meet you. I'm the owner of the El Dorado."

He stopped. The sound of his voice crawled to a halt in the oppressiveness of his room. He cleared his throat, waiting a short interval then trying again, trying to strike a new chord with his voice. "Bobby Kaufmann, lovely meeting you. I just bought into the El Dorado on East Sixth."

Again, silence covered his words as soon as they were spoken. He cleared his throat, this time with an exaggerated emphasis. He did this twice, shifting in his chair and extending his hand, smiling. "Bobby Kaufmann, owner of the El Dorado." He waited. "Yes, I'm Bobby

Kaufmann. I'm from Cuero by way of Corpus. I own the El Dorado." Again. "Bobby, Bobby Kaufmann. I like . . ." He paused. "I like sports, music, going out. By the way, I'm a business owner. I own the El Dorado." He clenched his hands into fists. "Bobby, Bobby Kaufmann. Robert Fitzgerald Kaufmann. Yes, I know. RFK. My grandfather was a Republican and my mother wanted to needle him a little. Named me RFK. She got the middle name wrong. My mother was like that, you see. She was . . . She was . . ."

The room went as quiet as a tomb. Bobby put his elbows on his desk, his head sunk in his hands. He looked up again. "Bobby, Bobby Kaufmann. I'm Bobby fucking Kaufmann. I stopped being a drug dealer today. Instead, I've hooked up with my old friend Tim in an unlikely venture but I'll probably be back dealing within the year. I'm an alcoholic with a drug problem, you see, but you don't need to know that just yet. You'll find out soon enough."

BOOK 3, CHAPTER 7
October, 2003

A square dining hall, with two walls painted a dull purple and a third a muted red. The fourth had a large opening which led to the kitchen, and a gleaming tile of black, purple, and gold surrounded a pass-through area and glimmered faintly as late-afternoon sunlight reflected off car windshields just beyond the glass entryway. A curious light fixture jutted from a metal base above each of the black booths, a curved horn transparent on the ends. Bobby sat under one of these light fixtures, a discordant figure amid the finery, and he leafed through a three-by-five spiral notebook, preparing to meet a woman who was a complete stranger.

In three weeks online he had met a handful of women, but only one conversation had led to a date. The downtown restaurant was her suggestion. Bobby took in the details—a metal screen partially hid a corridor leading to the kitchen; the waitstaff was decked out in black, their dark shoes squeaking on the polished floor. Bobby wondered if her choice was indicative of an urbane sensibility or if she were simply selecting a place that was both central and tasteful. After considering that question, his mouth drooped at the corners as he thought to himself that he hated the senseless speculation before a first meeting.

He considered the likely progression of events: the hurried greeting, the initial assessments, the stop-and-start conversation interspersed with attempts at cleverness, all directed toward moments of buoyancy but rarely succeeding. He sought for something concrete to occupy his mind, so he flipped through the notebook and rechecked the basic information he had copied from her profile. Her name was Lara. He gathered that she was a college graduate and had lived in town most of her life, but her profile showed few specifics. A black-box profile, he had come to think of them. He had printed a picture of her and taped it to the last page of the notebook. She wore little to no makeup and faced the camera full on with only the barest of smiles, her dark hair parted in the middle. She was hardly a knockout, but Bobby found he paused whenever he considered her picture. He checked his watch. Seeing that she was running a little behind and this was still happy hour, he ordered a margarita.

She walked in wearing faded jeans, sandals, and a pale blue shirt, the shirt fabric resembling denim. It struck him as an informal, Southern sense of fashion. Bobby found her even more attractive in person—an angular face that curved to a strong chin, eyes that seemed open to the unfamiliar. He raised a hand and got her attention, aware of an acidic burning in his stomach. For a brief moment she regarded him, then she strode over to the booth. Bobby thought he saw a faint smile form, but if so, it disappeared instantly. He stood up, ready to shake her hand, but she merely sat down, depositing a black backpack in the seat next to her. Bobby sat down as well and the next moment they were introducing themselves.

"Bobby," he said. "Bobby Kaufmann."

"Lara Jennings," she said quickly, as if she wanted to dispense with the nervous formality of meeting. Her backpack, Bobby noticed, was well-used and full, and as in her picture, she wore little to no makeup. After some uncertain body language, she squared herself in the booth, taking in the situation fully. "You emphasize the *mann* portion of your name," she said. "Like a German."

Her accent was nondescript, flat but carrying a slight lilt, a brogue typical of Austin. Bobby liked the specificity of her observation. "It was the way I was taught."

"Are you from Texas?"

"I am."

"So, you're from Fredericksburg or Weimar. Some place like that."

"Some place like that," said Bobby. The more he looked at her, the more he realized she had the stamp of Austin all over her. He saw it specifically in the wryness at the edge of her smile, suggestive of someone eclectic, outside the ordinary range of Middle America. "You want a margarita?" he said. "I'll buy."

"Alcohol?" she said, sitting back in her seat. "Plus an offer to buy?"

"Only a friendly drink." He pointed at the sweating glass on the black tabletop in front of him. "As you can see, I'm not holding back."

She smirked. "Some women consider alcohol a no-no."

Bobby felt a burning in his stomach and wondered if she objected to drinking. "Why's that?" he said. "Do they have something against margaritas?"

"Well, no," she said, her voice low. "No, not usually. But some women think alcohol sends the wrong message. Like maybe you're here to party. And accepting an offer to buy is like taking a small bribe, or dating as if it's 1961."

The burning in his stomach instantly minimized—she was simply articulating a dating norm. "Well, personally," he said, "I think that's the silliest fool thing I've ever heard."

She didn't quite laugh, but she signaled a waiter, looking at Bobby as she ordered. "I'll have a margarita, too. Frozen with salt." She smirked at Bobby again. "But I'm buying for myself."

He held up both hands, palms out. "I won't interfere," he said. "I promise."

A silence ensued, both of them unsure which direction to go. Lara's expression changed, and she leaned forward earnestly, suddenly insistent and business-like. "Will you humor me?"

Bobby regarded her coolly, noting the active way she leaned toward him. "Well, sure, of course. If I can."

"Do you sketch?"

"I can't say I do."

"Well, I hope this isn't too soon, but I hate beating around the bush and doing a lot of role-playing. I'd like to get your opinion."

Bobby leaned forward too, intrigued. "I'll help any way I can."

She was already rifling through her backpack, and as her drink arrived she was pulling out a hardbound black sketchbook. She took a rapid sip of the margarita, flipped through several blank pages of rich Manila paper, and placed the sketchbook flat on the tabletop. A single page drawn in pencil depicted a man's face, wide with high cheekbones and thick dark hair. "What do you see?"

Bobby looked at the precise, intricate pencil strokes, then at her; he could tell this was important to her. He looked at the sketch again and went for a minimalist statement, not wanting to say anything wrong. "A man."

He instantly regretted the observation, thinking it far too obvious, but she didn't seem frustrated in the least. She asked the next question slowly, as if she were thinking through the implications. "Anything distinctive about him?"

Bobby tilted his head. "He looks Indian."

"You mean Native American."

He winced. He could not decide if he was embarrassed by the slip in etiquette, or miffed that she corrected him. "Yeah, sure. Native American." He adjusted the page, tilting his head again. He pursed his lips, concentrating. "He looks angry."

Lara blinked, her eyes widening. She placed her fingers on the sketchbook, turning it to face her, scrutinizing the page. "You think so?"

He was firm, decisive. "Yeah, I do."

She gently bit her lower lip, then released it. She didn't sound convinced but seemed open to the possibility. "What makes you say that?"

Bobby shook his head. "I don't know," he said. "Just look at him."

"Do you think it's overt?"

"What do you mean?"

"Well, I guess what I mean is, does it seem as if I intended to make him look angry?" She waited, looking carefully at the sketch. "Or does it seem like a kind of subtext, something not overt but between the lines? Maybe even something I didn't intend?"

Bobby thought about it, taking in her capacity for absorption. He shook his head. "Christ, Lara, I don't know."

She merely nodded. "Well, he's not supposed to be

angry, although he certainly was frequently enough."

"So you know him."

"An ex. Of sorts." She appeared to experience a moment of self-disgust but it quickly evaporated. Her next statement seemed almost rehearsed. "He's going to be a character in my graphic novel. I'm part of this group; I just joined." Her eyes soured. "This jerk in the group thought the drawing was disrespectful."

"Why? Because he's Native American and he's angry?"

"No-oo," she said, turning the negation into a two-syllable word. She squared her shoulders and waved a dismissive hand over the drawing. "This fucker's not that observant. He thought I exaggerated the features, which, if you knew the guy in the sketch, you would know I did not. But anyway, this guy had some fucking quip like, *Where's the headdress*? I mean, talk about disrespectful. Asshole." She paused. "Do you really think he looks angry?"

"Maybe I'm seeing him through my own lens."

She considered his remark, then reached into her backpack again and pulled out a snapshot, placing it next to the drawing. Bobby saw the same man in jeans and tennis shoes, the picture rich in sunlight. Behind the man, a purple mountain loomed.

"What do you think?" said Lara.

Lara's self-evaluation regarding the accuracy of the sketch was dead on—the face depicted was eerily similar to the picture. "I think you're good at sketching. Where was this photo taken?"

"New Mexico. Taos. Ever been there?"

"No."

"I went there to draw. Learn more about oil painting."

"You just picked up and left?"

"My grandmother died earlier this year." Lara sat back

in her seat, grabbing her drink and taking a long, fluid sip of her margarita. Bobby watched her, gauging fluency with alcohol the same way other people might weigh personality. "Anyway, Grandma left me something, so money wasn't a big issue and I just went. You know, to get away, get away for a while." She shook her head, again intimating a certain level of self-disgust. "And now I'm at a crossroads, as they say."

Bobby let the words sink in. "Well," he said, "we have something in common, then."

"What's that?"

"I guess I'm at a crossroads, too." She nodded, as if to say *proceed*, but he tried to downplay the announcement. "I'm buying into a business. A bar. With an old friend."

She took a moment to reflect on that. "A business owner. And you're all of twenty-five."

"Twenty-three."

"A younger man, no less." She took another long sip. "Where's the bar?"

"East of here."

"Downtown?"

"No, east of downtown."

"On Sixth?"

"Well, East Sixth."

"Don't undersell it," she said. "The whole city's moving that way."

"I hope so. We'll see, I suppose."

She looked at him closely, as if preparing to examine him through an eyepiece, and the words followed evenly, a steady progression of thought. "It must be expensive, buying a place like that."

She didn't seem like the type who was interested in money but it seemed to him she was seeking to know if he was. "Not that expensive."

"It is if you're twenty-three," she said.

"I've been working since I was eighteen."

"No school?"

"No school."

She looked pained again. "I nearly dropped out of college twice and now I wish I had."

"What's your degree in?"

"Job-seeking futility," she said, the set of her mouth indicating the possibility for ever-widening, self-effacing remarks. "Double major, art and English, euphemisms for job-seeking futility."

She was a distinct type, Bobby thought—the caustic graphic novelist. "What do you want to do with that?"

"Something different, not nine-to-five. I'd suffocate." She seemed to ponder her immediate future. "You see, all I want now is to finish my novel and let the chips fall where they may." She sat back in the booth. "And you, new bar owner. What do you intend to do with your business?"

"Get it off the ground."

She put her elbows on the tabletop and cupped her chin in her hands. "That sounds humble."

"More like realistic."

"So, a realist's perspective?"

Bobby thought about it. "I wouldn't necessarily characterize it that way."

"How would you characterize it, then?"

"Let's just say my perspective is complicated."

"Complicated?" she repeated.

He instantly regretted the word. "Well, yeah."

"I don't know if complicated is a useful word or an overused word."

Bobby leaned forward again, as if he were about to

intimate something confidential. "In my experience, it's a word that's overused but misapplied."

She laughed. "'Overused but misapplied.' I like that one." Lara finished her drink. Bobby had already finished his. "Well, what have we learned?"

Bobby thought about it. "That you're Austin to the core."

Her expression froze momentarily, followed by a small, wan smile. "Am I?"

He counted with his fingers. "You're an artist, a writer, and you see your career in doubt. Sounds Austin to me. And what about me? What have you learned?"

"That you know the true meaning of complicated."

"Is that all?"

"Well, that's a lot."

"You think so?"

"It is," she said. They looked at each other—a short interval that stretched a second too long. Bobby cleared his throat but she beat him to the punch. "You're finished with your drink and I'm finished with mine. Short but sweet. Is it time?"

"It might be."

She scooped up her sketchbook and placed it in her backpack. Bobby wanted to say more but couldn't think of anything. He dropped $5 on the table and she followed suit. They walked out together, stopping on the sidewalk as downtown foot traffic hurried past.

"It's been nice to meet you," he said. "I mean that."

"Yeah, same here," she said, and she raised her phone. "Don't smile," she said, and snapped a photo.

He thought she might explain herself but she was preoccupied with the readout. "That was a first," he said.

She gave the briefest of smiles. After a moment, she

seemed satisfied with the photo and put the phone away. "Will you pick up if I call?" she asked.

The question did not sound flirtatious, merely curious. "We'll have to see," said Bobby. "When you call, that is."

She knit her brow, appearing to concentrate. "Well, okay then."

Bobby watched her walk away, remained where he was, and tried to unravel his thoughts. Even half a block away, her light-blue shirt twinkled in and out of view among the moving pedestrians.

**

Lara did not immediately get in Bobby's head. In fact, the next night he went on a date with someone named Taylor. Their night followed a usual course—dinner and a blues concert downtown, the venue bathed in orange light. It was a warm October night, and Taylor, dressed in a secondhand skirt and a gray shirt, drank Miller Lite and Bobby drank whiskey as flying insects buzzed around the stage lights.

Taylor told him that she lived on the East Side in a small house with three other women. She was "half-employed," as she put it, and was thinking about returning to school, but didn't say for what purpose. Bobby let it slip that he had ownership stake in a bar, and Taylor half-smiled. She was pretty in that off-center way akin to so many East Side women, but conversation never got off the ground and Bobby drove her home largely in silence. They both smiled weakly as she got out of the car—Bobby unable to determine if her hipster aesthetic was put off by the conventionality of business ownership.

For the rest of the evening, Bobby remembered the

encounter with Lara fondly but she continued to recede in his consciousness. In fact, he had half-forgotten the meeting when he ran by the El Dorado and checked out the progress, conferring with Tim in his office over a newly minted blue print. After a half hour of shop talk, Bobby and Tim chatted amiably, laughing over a couple of glasses of Jack. Afterwards Bobby visited a bar on South Congress and watched a football game. He made it a point to count his drinks and stopped at five. Hardly alcohol cessation, but Bobby thought it represented a kind of progress.

The next day, he awoke late, made a little breakfast, and had a single glass of bourbon, which he was determined would last him until the evening. He spent a couple of hours on the dating site, taking time to craft each email message. After lunch at his favorite taqueria, he spent the afternoon in front of the television. After a while he craved a drink, but told himself that he could wait. By five he was freshly showered and out the door. As he made his way downtown, he felt a lightness in his mood. For the first time in a long time, he thought his life was moving in a positive direction and it shored up his confidence. He reviewed a mental list: he had left the cocaine at home; the bar was proceeding, a bit slowly but nicely; and he was going to find himself a girl, maybe not tonight, but soon.

In the midst of these reflections, Lara called.

When Bobby looked at the readout and saw it was her, he considered not answering, almost as a point of pride. This was only the day following their first meeting. But he reconsidered, reminding himself that he hated little games. "This is unexpected," he said.

Her voice sounded thin, partially drowned out by background noise. "Is it?" she said.

"I didn't think I'd hear from you so soon."

"Yeah, I considered that, the whole you-should-wait-three-days-before-phoning thing. But the fact of the matter is, I hate being conventional. What are you doing?"

"I was going to hear some music tonight. What are you doing?"

"I'm at Zilker Park. You have time? I'd like to get your opinion again."

Bobby decided this surprise was not unpleasant. "Are you nearer the springs or the river?"

He arrived in less than thirty minutes, parking in front of a children's playground which was ringed by a slatted metal fence, kids maneuvering on climbing equipment and zipping down a yellow slide. It was still before six, with plenty of daylight left. The playground was next to Barton Springs, and Bobby detected a wet, mildewed scent in the air. Lara was seated at a wooden picnic table and Bobby waved. She waved back, and Bobby felt oddly gratified by it.

She wore gray shorts, a light-green T-shirt, and a royal-blue bandana in her dark hair. A closed sketchbook rested on the table and Bobby pointed at it. "Does that thing go with you everywhere?"

"Just about."

"What are you drawing today?"

"I'll show you in a minute." She flipped to a page, which opened to the same man she had showed Bobby the first time they met. "I took this home and couldn't stop looking at it. I opened a bottle of wine, had a glass or two, possibly three."

Bobby smirked. "Possibly three?"

"I don't know. Four maybe. I just kept thinking about what you said. Then I saw it, too." She waved a hand over the drawing. "The eyes are focused, like they're boring into you. He could be a bit intense, you see, and I thought that was what I was drawing. But then I saw the mouth, the lips pressed together, which was how he looked when he painted. *Then* I saw the rigidity to the lips, which wasn't customary for him. He is angry, if you look at it the right way. And I had no idea. I drew it, but I was blind to it."

Bobby pulled out a pack of cigarettes and shook out two. "You want one?"

"Sure."

Bobby cupped his hand over the flame, lighting her cigarette, then his own. He looked closely at the sketch. "Well, damn, girl. What do you think he's angry about?"

She concentrated on the sketch, adjusting her bandana and running a hand through her hair. "Well, that's the thing. He's not angry. He can't be—he didn't draw it. I drew it."

Bobby looked at her closely. "What does that mean?"

"That it's not about him."

"So," said Bobby, blowing out a plume of smoke, "you're concluding that you're angry."

When she concentrated, her voice slowed. "I must be."

"At what?"

"At him, I think."

"Did he do anything to you?"

Lara gazed at Bobby matter-of-factly. "Does he have to do something for me to be angry?"

"No, I guess not."

"I mean . . ." She made a small gesture with her hand, then the words began marching out, each one slightly more forceful than the one that preceded it. "A lot can happen in six weeks; you can really get to know somebody. I mean, he was entirely self-involved, the worst sort of neurotic, and he cared more for his art than for me." Bobby made a keep-it-down gesture. "Sorry," she said.

He sat back. "No problem." They simply eyed each other, preoccupied with their cigarettes and their own thoughts. "So, what do you make of all this?"

"I think it means you're a good observer."

He began slowly. "Well, it stands to reason." He paused, fighting an instinct to say as little as possible. "I suppose you could say I've been watching people my whole life."

"Yeah?" she said, her eyes far off.

Bobby nodded, the affirmation simple and unforced. He wondered why he felt the need to tell her something true about himself. "Yeah."

"That sounds like life-story material to me," she said.

"Too soon?"

"I didn't say that."

"I mean, it is our second date," said Bobby.

"Are we calling this a date?"

Bobby couldn't tell if she meant to be playful or not. "If you like."

"Well," she said, "I'm all ears."

He chose his words carefully. "I suppose it all goes back to just trying to survive."

"Survive?" The inflection in her voice suggested doubt about the word.

Bobby stood firm. "Well, maybe that's a bit much, but then, maybe it's not. There were times in the past when in order to eat I had to look people in the eye, know what they were thinking."

"What did you say you did before now?" she asked. "For a living?"

Bobby had rehearsed answering that particular question. "I didn't say. I was a salesman."

"What did you sell?"

He wondered if he spoke too quickly, like a man in a hurry to move on. "Lots of things, actually, before I settled on a single product line." He reflected on his answer, content with the outcome. He hadn't lied. She was about to pursue more answers, but he made a crisp, decisive gesture. "The point is not what I sold, but how I related to people, how I read them. People give themselves up in a hundred ways. You just have to read it right."

Her eyes never left his face. "Is that so?"

"Well, yeah." She appraised him closely, a gleam in her eye. He changed the subject. "You said you had something to show me."

"Yeah," she said. She laughed to herself, an unguarded laugh. She then flipped to a page of her sketchbook. Bobby sat back, unsettled, and gazed at a drawing of himself in pencil. She had drawn a neutral line to his mouth and his eyes stared straight ahead. "Tell me," she said, "since you were so insightful last time. What do you see?"

Bobby considered whether it was strange that she barely knew him but had already sketched him. He looked at her and decided that he could sense nothing amiss, that she was an artist and perhaps a bit eccentric, but not in a way that was off-putting. He studied the drawing and tried to break it down into parts. The features were right—the high forehead, the sharp chin, the ambiguity in his eyes. He wondered at the neutral mouth, whether she was trying to make him look serious or if that was something he was reading into the sketch. He tried to imagine what she had been thinking as she'd worked through the drawing, yet he could see nothing that suggested she thought less of him. But after a moment, he shook his head.

Lara frowned. "Well, don't fucking sit there and shake your head and not say anything."

"Sorry," he said. "I feel like you've drawn a race car driver."

"What?"

"Yeah, something like that. Like I should be wearing goggles." He looked at her. "Or a scarf."

She scrutinized the page, her mouth annoyed, her expression opaque. She began nodding. "I did it from memory."

"You did?"

"Yeah, this one. I tore up the first one I did. It was from the picture I took."

"But we just met." Bobby paused. "That's sort of incredible."

"I had already sketched you once."

"But the details. The details are right."

"But not the overall effect . . ."

"Well, you asked me what I thought. So I told you."

She nodded thoughtfully. "No, you're right. Honesty is good. Honesty is always good." She went quiet, then said, "A race car driver? You might have something."

"I don't follow."

"We've already established that it's not you I'm drawing. I'm drawing a memory of you." She thought about it and Bobby waited. "My memory."

She laughed, and it was Bobby's turn to be nonplussed. "What's so goddamned funny?"

"I'm sorry." She raised a conciliatory palm. "My first impression, seeing you sitting there. If I didn't know better, I would have thought you owned the restaurant. That was my first thought. That this guy is the swinging dick type. I almost laughed out loud."

"So that's what the smile was about."

"Did I smile?"

"Briefly."

"Shame on me. But you see, that's how all this works. Because I looked again, and it got complicated."

"That word again. How?"

"I thought your profile said you were twenty-five but you didn't look twenty-five to me. In fact, if you had asked me to guess your age, I would have said . . ." She raised a hand, turning it up and down, one way and then another. "Twenty-nine."

"Twenty-nine?"

"Well, I guess I'm being nice, because I thought you looked older than that even. It even occurred to me to wonder if I was being scammed." She stopped to see if Bobby was hurt. He only stared back at her, his expression even. She continued. "But then I looked again, and then I didn't know what I thought, except that you had a complicated face. Not a bad face, just complicated."

"Well, go on. You can't leave it like that."

"Then you tell me you're twenty-three and you're going to open a place on East Sixth, and apparently your daddy's not rich, because you've been working since you were eighteen. And maybe that's what you see here, because only a swinging dick type can pull that off." At last, she shrugged. "But then, you're not the swinging dick type, I can tell, and I probably wouldn't like you if you were."

Bobby let it all settle, then lit another cigarette. "So, you're saying you like me?" He watched her closely but she didn't react. "You don't have to say anything."

"Well, good, because that question is a bit premature, no matter what the answer is."

Bobby nodded. "Okay, how about this question? Would you want to do something Friday night?"

She cupped her chin in one hand. "Yeah, sure."

"Okay," said Bobby. "Good."

Bobby was about to break the silence when Lara held up a hand. "Will you hold still for a second?" She began scrutinizing his face.

"What are you doing?"

"I'm trying to get the overall effect right."

She stared straight ahead, her eyes steady. At first, he thought that being stared at might be annoying but he found her capacity for absorption interesting. "What do you see?"

"I can't tell. There are so many moving parts."

"Yeah?"

"It's like. . . I don't know. Like you might be more than one person."

Bobby smirked. "Maybe it's just because I'm a little nuts."

"Well, I don't doubt that," she said. "But in my experience, crazy people can be monotonously one-dimensional."

**

Friday arrived quickly. All day Bobby reminded himself that it was only a date, and he was determined not to put his eggs in one basket, not to get carried away. He had been working the dating site as if he had never met Lara, going so far as to set up another first meeting early Saturday evening. He talked briefly with Lara Friday afternoon, and they agreed to skip dinner altogether and meet at Anthony's for the nine o'clock show. Bobby understood that by meeting at the club, he wouldn't find out where she lived, not that he was upset by that gambit in the least. In fact, he thought it a shrewd move on her part.

He went out for an early meal at six and was back home by seven fifteen to get ready. He took time to select his wardrobe—black slacks newly pressed at the cleaners, a dark-blue shirt, and black dress shoes. He examined himself in the mirror and felt reasonably satisfied. Just before he left, he took three grams of coke out of the steel combination box in his closet. He strode down the hallway but stopped at the crest of the stairs. Even spaced out over the course of an evening, she was bound to notice if he inhaled three grams, and who knows where that might lead. He went back to the closet and put all three packets back inside the box, but before he locked it, he pulled out one packet and returned it to his pocket.

The club was a venue big enough for two bars, with a large open area in front of the stage designed to accommodate hundreds of people. A single wall displayed dozens of brightly lit beer gewgaws and, even between acts, the lights were kept low. Although it was early, the place was at least half-full, and Bobby could not immediately spot Lara in the crowd. He grabbed a stool in the back and texted his location. Within twenty seconds, she emerged from the press of bodies. She wore faded jeans and a light-green button-down shirt, sporting a black leather wristband, and Bobby thought she looked as though she were dressed for an afternoon graduate seminar. He hopped off the stool and bellied up to the bar.

"What are you drinking?" he said.

"What are you having?"

"House bourbon on the rocks."

"Bourbon and ginger ale, then," she said.

"I'm getting the first round." When their drinks were served, he turned around and faced the stage. "The club's going to be packed tonight."

She scanned the crowd, displaying no signs of early date jitters. "Are the bands good?" she asked.

"The headliner's good. I've heard them before."

No sooner had he spoken than he heard his name being called.

"Bobby Kaufmann," a man exclaimed, easily audible over the low-level din. From behind the bar, a man in his thirties advanced toward the couple, his hair short and immaculately groomed and his hand extended. "No, excuse me," the man said, "Bobby *fucking* Kaufmann." He wore a houndstooth coat, a suit shirt and slacks, and polished black shoes with a gold buckle. Although he was shorter than Bobby, he engulfed Bobby's hand in his own and pumped twice.

"Douglas," cried out Bobby, visibly happy to see the man. "I didn't know you worked here." Douglas let go of Bobby's hand and he turned to Lara and lowered his head, suggestive of a minimal bow. "Douglas, this is Lara," said Bobby.

"A pleasure," said Douglas, taking her hand.

"Weren't you working at the Velvet Turtle?" said Bobby.

Douglas released Lara's hand and his courtly manner vanished momentarily, his eyes dismissive. "Fuck that place," he said. "Fucking owner." His dissatisfaction passed like a small rain shower and he stood up straight, chest forward with a wide smile. "What are you having?" he said, his best manners returning. "Evan?"

Bobby turned to Lara. "This man never forgets what anyone drinks."

"It's my job, Bobby," said Douglas, who got the attention of the bartender. "Next time they order, it's on the house." Douglas locked eyes with Bobby. Bobby recognized the look immediately but casually refused to acknowledge the cue. A silence formed and it didn't take Lara long to pick up on it. Finally, Douglas made a rumbling sound deep in his throat. "You got a moment, Bobby? Alone?"

Bobby looked a bit sheepish. "I need to talk to him for a second," he said to Lara. "I won't be long." If Lara read anything into it, she didn't give it away.

Bobby followed Douglas behind the bar, down a short hallway, and into an office. Douglas shut the door. "I don't mean to be rude, take you from your date," he said. "But this town's dried up. I can't find anyone holding."

Bobby raised his chin slightly. "This is new, so word's not reached you."

"What?"

"I'm out."

Douglas clearly did not want to believe what he had just heard. "You're out? As in completely?"

Bobby raised his hand as if he were revealing that he held nothing in them. "I'm altogether out. I don't sell anymore."

Douglas made no attempt to hide his disappointment. "Well, Jesus, Bobby." He waited a beat. "That's great, I'm proud of you. What are you doing?"

"I bought into the El Dorado."

"The El Dorado?"

"Yeah, on East Sixth."

Douglas concentrated. "Oh yeah, that place." He continued, but hesitantly. "It's a nice place but a bit small."

"I checked it out. I checked its books. Besides, we're expanding."

"Expanding? Terrific, terrific." Douglas stood there, no longer upright, his shoulders sagging a bit. The ensuing silence spoke volumes. Douglas hurried in, seeming to fear the silence. "Well, I'm happy for you, man," Douglas said, his defeated tone at odds with his words.

Bobby stared at Douglas, then reached into his pocket. "Okay, here's the thing. I don't want any money. Besides, I shouldn't have brought any in the first place." Bobby unpocketed the sole gram he carried. "This is all I got. This is for friendship. You got it? For old times."

Douglas resembled a thirsty man given reprieve with a drink. "Sure, Bobby. Thanks." Bobby turned to leave the room. "Hold on. Take this." Douglas signed three cards. "It's some passes. It's the least I can do."

**

As soon as she saw Bobby, Lara formed a bemused smile. "What was that about?"

Bobby was glad to see she wasn't put out. "He's an old friend."

"Who is he?"

"He's the manager. He used to manage the Velvet Turtle."

Lara appeared amused. "You make it a point to know club managers?"

"It'll get you a free round of drinks."

"Yeah, I guess," she said. The expression of amusement persisted. "Any more surprises tonight?"

"Well, maybe. Telling you would defeat the purpose of a surprise."

The show started in a matter of minutes. They settled at a table toward the back of the club. Bobby's encounter with Douglas had turned his mood—although he had already told his best clients that he was leaving the business, he hadn't spoken with peripheral clients like Douglas, and he realized that the same scene would replay itself any number of times. He ordered a second drink. Lara was occupied by the act and rocked gently in her seat, occasionally mouthing the lyrics. Bobby was struck by the frank innocence of the moment—he was out on a date with a young woman and she was enjoying the music. Impulsively he reached out and gently clasped her hand, then let go just as quickly. Lara smiled but it faded as Bobby felt a hand on his shoulder. Douglas leaned toward Bobby's ear. "I just need another moment of your time."

Douglas already seemed partially impaired, and coming back a second time, especially when Bobby was on a date, seemed to Bobby a real breach of etiquette. Despite his fondness for the man, his anger ignited instantly. "Are you kidding?"

"I swear, it'll just take a second."

Bobby stood. He looked both ways as if checking for traffic, and then he raised himself to full height, glowering at the older man. "I don't believe this shit." Douglas took a step back. "What part did you not understand?" Douglas opened his mouth to say something but Bobby cut him off, pointing an index finger at Douglas's chest, then making a slashing gesture with the flat of his hand. "What part of 'I'm out' did you not understand?"

Bobby's peripheral vision was suddenly at maximum effect. The bartender saw that a customer had berated the manager and froze in mid-pour. A bouncer watched the drama unfold and was left momentarily stunned. Douglas simply walked away as if he'd had no part in the encounter. Bobby spun around to Lara, wondering if their date had just ended. But Lara was riveted, her mouth revealing a pleased disbelief.

"Come on," Bobby said. "We need to leave."

She nodded, standing up, and Bobby took her hand. As they neared the exit, the bouncers stepped aside and cleared a path to the door. On the street, traffic whizzing by, Bobby strode purposefully toward the car, his rage not yet subsided.

"Hey, wait," cried Lara, pulling out of his grip. "Wait."

Bobby breathed out and leaned against a concrete wall. "What?" he said.

"What happened?"

"You were there," he said. "Nothing happened."

"What was that about?"

Her question clearly came from curiosity, not outrage. Like air from a burst balloon, his rage disappeared. He passed a hand over his face. "The nerve of that asshole. I'm on a fucking date."

Her appearance of pleasant disbelief had disappeared and now she simply seemed concerned for Bobby. "What did he want?"

Bobby searched for the right formulation, taking care not to lie. "I used to work for this guy. We—me and that manager—both know him. Basically, the manager wanted me to get something from the guy."

"What?"

"Nothing important." He finally allowed his eyes to meet hers. "This goes back a long ways. Can I just leave it at that? That it has nothing to do with me anymore."

"You're telling me to mind my own business."

"I don't mean that exactly."

"It's okay, if you are." Her voice changed, the amusement returning. "You stopped the whole club."

"Well, not really. A couple of employees maybe." Her eyes suggested a suppressed glimmer of intrigue. "What's that look for?"

"Nothing," she said. "Really, nothing. It's still early. Are we off to anywhere else?"

Bobby considered some options, happy that the date had not ended. "Do you like a little adventure?"

"I kinda feel like I'm on one."

"Well, we could head east," he said. "I know a place."

"What kind of place?"

"The kind where you might have some beer thrown on you. But it's all part of the fun."

Lara, who had taken a cab downtown, agreed to go to the club in Bobby's car. Bobby wondered if this represented newly earned trust. They took Seventh Street out from downtown and the crowds quickly thinned once they crossed under I-35. The darkened streets of East Austin unfolded methodically, past the near-east bars and small retail shops, the scattered pedestrian traffic on the walkways. Quiet pervaded the car, but it was an unforced quiet. Bobby glanced at his date from the corner of his eye and realized she was looking directly at him. They briefly made eye contact before Bobby turned his attention back to the road.

"You're not callow, are you?" she said.

"I don't know how to respond to that."

"That manager. He treated you with deference."

"I blew my stack."

"No, before that, too. He respects you. Most college-aged types, they can't pull that off."

"Most college kids have never had to scratch to survive."

"You see, that's what I'm talking about. College kids don't know that." She seemed to reflect over her statement. "I think I'm done with boys."

THE THIRD DOOR

They were amidst the remote neighborhoods of the far East Side when Bobby turned down a side street and passed an old, wooden warehouse, its white paint peeling. A large dirt yard served as its parking lot, and it was almost full, numerous motorcycles and a scattering of bicycles near the entrance. The building seemed to pulse as if it contained enormous machines.

Lara looked for a sign indicating the name of the club but couldn't find one. "What's this place called?" she said.

"The Dead Rabbit."

"That's an awful name."

"Perhaps," said Bobby. "But it's fitting."

"What kind of music?"

"I don't know what they call it. Neo-punk was the last I heard. Let's just say it's loud."

The doorman, who was at least fifty, wore black leather pants, a white-T-shirt, and a black leather vest. He cried out happily when he saw Bobby, doing a palm-to-palm shake and slapping him on the back. Bobby presented his date and they were allowed to pass without paying the cover. As soon as the door opened, a sonic wall of noise rolled over them.

They eased their way into the club. The bar area was bathed in yellow light, the stage in red, but the rest of the building was dark, the floor packed toward the stage. The band members were little more than post-pubescent boys, but they thrashed on their instruments skillfully, hopping around in ragged jeans without shirts, pale and sweating. At the lip of the stage, the crowd moved as if it were a single organ and held out their hands in a supplicant's entreaty, as if starved, if not for food, at least fulfillment. At the bar Bobby got two shots of tequila and handed one to Lara. "Up and in," he shouted, barely audible over the noise. "One motion."

"What is it?"

"Patron."

Bobby did his shot in a single motion. It took Lara two passes. Bobby smiled. "Another?"

Lara smiled back. "Yeah," she said. She seemed to loosen, arching her back and stretching as if she were warming up for an athletic event. "Fuck yeah."

This time she downed the shot in a single gulp. He took her by the hand and they waded through the crowd, inching step-by-step to the stage. They finally arrived at the stage's rim; they could have reached out and touched the lead guitarist. The lead singer pranced forward and backward, bleating into the microphone like a manic goat. They stayed at the front for two songs, but then Bobby grabbed her hand, and they picked their way across the floor to a stairwell. Another bouncer guarded the stairs, but Bobby whispered in his ear and slipped him a twenty. The bouncer signaled a cocktail waitress, and she followed Bobby and Lara up the stairs.

The stairwell opened onto a landing resembling a small lounge. A ragged sofa with some of the stuffing coming out of the armrests was against a wall, along with a table ringed by several wooden chairs. Bobby and Lara sat down at the table.

"Thanks for coming up, darling," Bobby said to the waitress. "We had to get away from the crowds." He gestured at Lara. "What would you like?"

"Vodka and Sprite."

"A bourbon," said Bobby. "On the rocks. And two tequila shots, house tequila. Thanks so much."

The waitress withdrew. "What is this place?" said Lara, indicating the room.

"It's for the musicians. Mainly for the musicians. I used to come here a lot and the owner's a friend."

"Do you have friends at every bar?"

"Well, a few." Bobby appeared at ease and completely within his element. Lara looked at him, thoughtfully. When the waitress brought their drinks, Bobby slipped her a twenty. He handed Lara her shot. "One more, okay?"

"Sure," she said, taking the glass. "Of course."

"What should we drink to?"

Lara answered immediately. "To being different."

Bobby considered her answer. "I can drink to that."

They touched glasses and downed the alcohol. Bobby was running his hand over his mouth to dispel the acrid taste of the tequila when he saw Lara out of the corner of his eye. He turned to her, her eyes steady, fully concentrated on him.

"Come here," she said, her voice low, her smile enigmatic.

"I am here," said Bobby.

"No, here," she said, but her head did not move. "Closer."

Bobby leaned forward, his face only inches from hers. He felt a thrilling tendril of satisfaction. This was a girl who seemed to like him for who he was, not what he could get. "Is this close enough?" he said.

She smiled again. "Closer," she said. "Just a little bit."

He could detect the cloyingly sweet smell of tequila on her breath. They kissed gently, but it lingered. Bobby looked at her intently. "Are you okay?" he asked. "Is this okay?"

This time she leaned into him and placed her fingertips to her mouth, her eyes remote. She began nodding, as if she had asked herself an internal question and had discovered the answer. "Yeah, it's fine, just fine." She stood up. "Well, come on," she said. "Come on."

"Where are we going?"

"Somewhere quiet. I'm tired of the noise."

"Anywhere specific?"

"How about my place?"

Bobby felt a momentary uncertainty about whether this was a good idea so soon, but as he thought about it, he realized there was something to the two of them—they could relate on several different levels. He realized there was no way he would turn her down. "Are you sure about this?" he said.

She never broke eye contact. "I've already said it. I'm not conventional and I don't believe in drawing these things out. When it's right, it's right."

**

Foregoing a seatbelt, she nestled in the crook of Bobby's arm. Although he'd had several drinks, he drove with assurance. Lara spoke only to give directions. They crossed over Lamar on Fifteenth Street and Bobby turned left not long thereafter. There was a side street with a number of complexes and Bobby drove up a short hill into a parking lot, which was filled with yellow light.

Lara cast an elongated shadow as they crossed the lot. The complex was older than the norm and had been built before Sun Belt amenities became a staple of most apartment buildings. They stepped down a mildewed walkway and Lara opened the door.

Lara turned on a lamp, but the interior remained half-dark and shadows congregated on walls and flitted across the ceiling. Bobby saw a living room tiled with brown, fifties-era flooring, unpacked boxes stacked along a wall, a white sofa, a nice TV. The unpacked boxes made it seem as if the apartment were in a state of transition, as if she hadn't quite moved in and was still seeking some grounding. To the left was a small nook next to a kitchen in which she had positioned a small breakfast table, various pencil sketches covering its surface.

She stood close to him. "I've got some whiskey," she said.

"What kind?" he replied.

"Canadian whiskey and vodka."

"Where?"

She pointed to a cabinet, which Bobby opened, pulling out a bottle of brown alcohol by its neck. "Don't you want some ice or water or something?" she asked.

"That's not necessary." He leaned over and kissed her again, whispering in her ear. "You good? Is this okay?"

"Yeah," she said. "I trust you."

He considered her words. "You lead the way, then," he said.

They kissed in the gray darkness of her room, a streetlight through the curtain casting light shadows and pools of blackness. He liked the way she smelled, a subdued dusty scent, like dried flowers. Everything felt soft—her mouth, her hands, the small of her back. She whispered to him, saying, "Slowly, slowly." They removed articles of clothing steadily, a little at a time, and Bobby watched her, making sure she was comfortable. There was a lot of kissing, a lot of hesitant exploration with their mouths, but hardly any foreplay, and a half hour later it was over. She kissed him a final time, grasping his hand and draping his arm over her. He settled into the bed, turned on his back and looked at the ceiling, where there was a rectangle of light, small shadows crawling through it. She fell asleep quickly, and he could hear her rhythmic breathing. His mind moved slowly, and he was largely bereft of thought. After a while, he, too, was asleep.

BOOK 3, CHAPTER 8
October, 2003

Bobby sat on the sofa in Lara's living room wearing only his underwear, smoking, contemplating the early morning and listening to the sound of birds. Lara had yet to wake. A certain agitation manifested itself in the light shaking of his right leg, and his mind turned evenly but relentlessly. He told himself he should be at peace, that he had come so far in just a matter of weeks, and that he had finally found an interesting woman who liked him for his merits. But that quickly led to a disquieting reminder—that Lara was the first woman in recent memory he had slept with without using cocaine as at least an indirect lure. He held that observation and then attempted to discard it, but the thought refused to abate. All at once he was seized by a feeling he could scarcely categorize, not panic exactly, but fright, and he fought off an impulse to get dressed and head for the door.

He grew irritated, remonstrating himself that he did not want to ruin it all due to early-relationship jitters. He peeked into the bedroom at Lara, her hair dark in contrast to the white pillow, a length of lightly freckled arm draped over the sheets. More questions troubled him. When she woke up, what would they talk about? In the cold light of morning, would she feel the same about him? The questions left him stewing in his own unease, until he saw an out, grabbing hold of an idea that things were better when in motion. As silent as a cat, he grabbed his clothes off the bedroom floor, dressed in the living room, and jotted a quick note that he adhered to her bedroom light switch. When he left the apartment, he locked the door behind him.

At a grocery store, a gust of air conditioning hit him when the sliding glass doors parted, and he strode out on the newly waxed floor, canned string music issuing from the speakers overhead. He stepped up a wide aisle devoted to salty snacks, finding some corn chips and a salsa he liked. A bank of refrigerated shelves behind glass revealed a vast beer selection, and he debated his options before choosing a six-pack of Shiner. He figured nobody from Texas would dispute a cold Shiner. He found a styrofoam cooler, and at the register he bought a bag of ice, placing it still packaged inside the cooler.

He drove back to her place and rapped on her apartment door gently, and after a moment, it opened. Through the doorway they peered at each other, and Lara leaned forward toward him as if somewhat suspicious.

"I was about to be pissed," she said. "I thought you'd left me here alone."

"I didn't want to wake you, so I left a note. Didn't you get it?"

"Well, yes, but not until I cursed your name up and down."

He detected no regret about the night before and his fears were temporarily assuaged. "Well, all I did was go to the store."

She continued to eye him dubiously. "Why'd you do that?"

"Have you ever watched the sun rise over the lake?"

During the drive, she kept the passenger window parted, cool air rushing into the car. The horizon was gray, the sky a mosaic of thick clouds burnished yellow by the approaching day. It was a cool morning. Lara took Bobby's right hand and held it in her lap, creating a wordless intimacy. He wore his clothes from the night before and she wore a windbreaker, shorts, and a simple pale-blue T-shirt. He handed her a beer from the cooler, which she nursed as they drove out on 71 and approached the lake from the west. They paid the park fee and drove until they found a quiet cove, the cedar and mesquite trees growing reluctantly from the limestone. A panorama of gray cliffsides jutted from the water, and they strode toward the rim of the cliff at the end of the cove. They sat at the edge, well over thirty feet above the lake's surface. The full extent of morning had yet to take hold and a slight chill lingered in the air. Bobby looked down at the water lapping up against the cliffside and pondered the depths directly beneath him.

She once again took hold of his hand and took in the view. "I don't get out here enough," she said.

Bobby clasped a beer in his other hand. The sky and water fused together and the vista was vast, the water running in both directions to the edge of sight. "Neither do I."

They sat there, silent in the midst of aesthetic reflection. A handful of boats churned a path on the surface way out in the middle of the lake and these boats seemed small, like toys.

"I always wanted one of those," said Bobby.

Lara turned her head, the breeze blowing her hair into her face. "You don't seem like the type," she said.

"Do you have to be a type to want a boat?"

"Well, no, not exactly. I guess." She squeezed his hand and laughed. "But you wouldn't look like you. Think about it. A hat, sunglasses. T-shirt and tanning lotion."

His lips curled reluctantly, perhaps recognizing she was right. "It would still be fun."

"I didn't mean anything by it."

"I know," he said. The reluctant smile persisted. He leaned over and kissed her, briefly and gently, then finished his beer. "It's just that my mother and I used to go downtown when I was young and I'd see the boats out on the bay, and I always thought they were really hot shit."

He realized that he'd alluded to his mother, and he tensed up, wondering if he had let this detail slip on purpose and whether Lara would see the difference, if she could feel his shoulders tighten. His mind raced through the times he'd stonewalled Kendra and all the other women in his life, and he told himself he shouldn't repeat the same mistakes again and again. But in an instant, he searched himself and discovered that on this particular morning he had no interest in talking about either Corpus Christi or his mother. To his disappointment, it seemed that Lara could read between the lines, enticed by his throwaway observation. "The bay? Where was this?"

Bobby felt conflicting emotions, conflicting impulses. He looked her in the eye, then he looked away. "Corpus."

"Corpus Christi?"

"Yeah."

She pursued the matter. "Is that where you were born?"

"No," he said simply. He cleared his throat as if he were

going to say more but then he went quiet. He reached into the cooler. "You want another?" he asked.

"No, I'm good." She watched him twist off the cap and take a long sip. "Where were you born, then?"

He continued avoiding eye contact. "Victoria."

"Texas?"

"It's the only Victoria around I know of."

"I don't know. People are from all kinds of places."

"Well, I'm not. I'm from here and this is where I'm staying."

"What were your parents like?"

He realized that his stubborn refusals to elaborate only drew her out further. He told himself to be forthcoming but cherry-picked his answer, thinking that an allusion to his father was the most emotionally neutral response he could find. "I didn't know my father," he said, a little too quickly.

"At all?"

He usually thought that he was long done with the issue of his absent father, but in moments like these, with his stomach churning, he knew the matter was far from resolved. "Not at all," he managed, clearing his throat. "Never met him, don't even know his name."

"How'd that happen?"

"Probably he couldn't stand my mother."

"Your mother? What's her name?"

He struggled for composure. "Regina." He paused a beat. "What's your mother's name?"

She ignored his diversionary tactics. She seemed almost amused by his discomfort, as if she thought he were an ordinary withholding male and just needed to be drawn out a little bit. "Regina. What is she like?"

"You're full of questions," he said, not meaning to raise his voice.

She didn't seem put out, only further intrigued. She leaned into him, a little playfully. "I seem to recall we slept together last night," she said.

His mood further soured. "And?"

She flinched slightly, her playful curiosity transforming in an instant into irritation. "And I'm interested in the man I'm sleeping with."

Bobby was angry, both at himself and her. "Interested?"

The words bounded from her lips. "I'd like to know a few things about you, goddamn it."

Bobby squared his shoulders and set his mouth in opposition to her. "Well, I was born in Victoria, lived in a place near Cuero until I was six. After Cuero, I spent a lot of time in Corpus. With my mother. And that's where my mother drove next to the bay and that's where I saw the boats, where this whole thing started." He turned back to the water and did everything he could not to make eye contact. He was dexterous in the face of anger, plenty quick on his feet.

"These are pretty basic questions," she said.

"Basic," he said, with no particular inflection, shaking his head. His anger mingled with disappointment and he wondered if this was a scene that was going to repeat itself his whole life.

Her anger didn't escalate. Instead it diffused quickly. In its sudden absence, she seemed adrift. "Well, yeah. Basic," she muttered.

"Christ, Lara, how long have we known each other? Since Monday?"

When she spoke again, he could hear that she was hurt. "That was unkind."

He stopped scanning the lake and looked at her, his

eyes lingering over her. He turned back to the water and took another long sip of beer. He shook his head again, his voice becoming conciliatory, and his discomfort gave way somewhat as he sought out the proper tone. "I'm sorry. My mother and I didn't get along," he said. "I am sorry. I shouldn't take it out on you."

He watched her internalize the apology; the genuineness of it seemed to diminish her sense of being offended. She cocked her head, seeming to break down his remarks. "Didn't get along? As in past tense? Does that mean she's dead?"

She waited for an answer, only to find his eyes fixed again on the water. He didn't focus on anything, deeply involved in something interior, and she let the questions go. She put her head on his shoulder, and not long after, he encircled her with his right arm and they remained that way for a long while.

**

They got back to her apartment just before noon. The sun had burned off the early-morning clouds and it shone high and bright in the remote, brittle blue sky. Bobby pulled into a space but left the engine running, thinking to himself that so much had changed since the night before.

"This has been great," he said.

"Yeah," said Lara. "It has."

"Sorry about that shit with my mother earlier." He tried to say more but his voice trailed away and his words were inaudible. "Anyway, sorry," he managed.

"No, I'm sorry." She smiled, rather sadly. "I get carried away and maybe start to pry a little bit. Sometimes us girls can be like that."

"Well, I'll call later."

"Would you want to come inside? Have another beer? Maybe a little whiskey?"

Bobby thought about it. She already knew so much about him. "I don't want to intrude."

"Goddamn it, Bobby, you aren't . . ." She formed the word as if there were marbles in her mouth. "Intruding."

"I didn't mean it like that."

She seemed disappointed in herself. "Yeah, I know."

"Anyway, I really should go." He indicated his clothes. "I've been in this shit for two days now and soon I won't be able to stand being near me. I'll call. Promise." She leaned over and kissed him, then pulled away. They looked at each other. "That was nice," he said.

If it was meant to be a form of consolation, it seemed to work.

**

He did not drive recklessly but he sped the entire way home, weaving in and out between cars on I-35. He remonstrated himself for his behavior at the lake, telling himself he had pulled a dick move with a nice girl who just wanted to get to know him. Once the thought took hold, he could not seem to expel it, and he fumed as he braked in front of his house, his tires screeching. He tried to collect himself, then opened the front door and peered inside. Steve and Rick were sprawled out on the sofa, wearing baggy shorts and T-shirts, the floor littered with beer cans. Bobby detected the cloying scent of pot and a glass bong of bright blue rested on the coffee table in front of them.

They grunted as he sped past but he found the scene sophomoric and wanted no part in it, not wanting so much as to glance at them. He took the stairs two at a time, shutting the door to his room and whipping off his shirt and shoes. In his stocking feet, he paused, only to discover that he was breathing deeply. Evenly, but deeply.

For a long while, he rocked gently on the bed. At last, he took his pillow and sat back against the wall and remained like that, the minutes passing. His eyes receded and his thoughts turned inward and he found himself in bed with Lara, her bed, and it was night. The light from the bathroom was on and it spread an arc across the room. He was on top of her, naked from the waist up, and she kissed him slowly and softly. Then she turned him over and in a single motion she unbuttoned his pants, smiling slightly, a vague residue of control and triumph in her expression. She held him with her eyes like a cat staring down a bird, the small smile persisting.

He snapped out of his reverie at the moment of orgasm, his pants and underwear lowered midway down his thighs. A thin sound issued from his mouth as his back arched and he tensed one final time, then went limp and lay there a short while, finally kicking off all his clothes. He closed his eyes and opened them after what he thought was only a couple of minutes. As he sat up, he could tell by the sun that it was mid-afternoon; he had been asleep for at least two hours. His mouth was dry and a sticky unpleasant film caused the tip of his tongue to adhere to the back of his teeth. He mustered the effort to get up, pulling on his jeans and trudging to the bathroom.

He drank greedily at the faucet, then splashed water on his cheeks and the back of his neck, remarking to himself that the vulpine shape of his face was more pronounced than he cared to admit. He was standing like that, appraising his reflection, when he raised his right hand to his mouth. He placed the tips of his fingers to his lips and he froze, as if his body were recovering a memory physically. The ghost of her lips moved across his and he remained still, using every fiber of his being to remember what was not there. After he could no longer sustain her incorporeal presence, he breathed out once.

He stalked back to his room and sat on the bed, confused, looking down at the floor. The questions started again: Had he blown it at the lake? Would she see through him to his life of meager equanimity? Before realizing he was doing it, he took the combination box from the closet and opened it.

After he had joined the dating site, he asked himself more than once whether he should rid himself of his stash, whether it would ultimately prove to be a wedge in any relationship, but he could not quite dispose of it. The packets of coke numbered in the dozens. He took one out and shook it, but the cocaine inside didn't stir. In the next instant, he put away the packet and returned the combination box to the closet. He snatched up his phone and stared at her number, then held the phone to his ear and counted the rings. After the fourth, he began to feel doubt. Then she answered.

"Bobby?"

He merely stood there, pausing a beat. "Hey," he said at last. "I know it's only been a few hours, but I'm just calling."

For a moment she didn't say anything. "What are you doing?"

"I took a nap," he said.

"I did too," she said. "I think I needed one."

"Did I wake you?"

"No," she said. "No, not at all."

"The truth is," he said, "the truth is I'm thinking of you." Silence. To Bobby it felt like a chasm opening up. "Lara?"

"I'm here," she interjected. "I'm here." Another pause. Finally, the statement came out deliberately. "The thing is, I've been thinking of you, too."

He waited, seeking to moderate a momentary elation. "You're not angry?"

"What for?"

"I lost my cool at the lake."

"Didn't you apologize for that?"

"Yeah, but—"

She cut him off. "Are you angry with me? For prying like a schoolgirl?"

"You didn't," said Bobby. "You weren't prying; those were just questions." He waited. "You see, Lara, I want to see you."

"Yeah," she said, her voice rising a half octave, then lowering. "I want to see you, too."

It wasn't a sexual advance, but still he felt a sudden stab of physical longing. "How about now?"

"Yeah, now," she said. "I think now is good."

**

The walkway leading to her door, with its dampness and the odd smells of jasmine and curry, already felt entirely familiar. He passed an apartment with the door cracked, Asian flute music emanating from within. She answered his knock within seconds. She stepped backward, an unspoken invitation, and shut the door behind him. They stood face-to-face, inches from each other, and Bobby put the back of his right hand against her right cheek. She rested her cheek there for several seconds, then reached up and interlaced her fingers with his. He leaned forward and felt her breath on his face, reaching around to the small of her back and pulling her close. They kissed. She took hold of his hand and led him back to her room, sliding into bed and eyeing him closely. They kissed again, and he took the hem of her shirt and pulled it off of her.

"Are you good?" he said. "Is this all right?"

"Shhhhhh." She shook her head, putting a finger to his lips. "Don't say anything. Not now, not a goddamn word."

**

They were flat on their backs, still breathing heavily, drenched in sweat. "You're staying, right?" she said, her eyes on the ceiling.

He swallowed. "Of course I'm staying."

Lara exhaled, wiping her brow. "Maybe we can order in for dinner."

A while later, they clambered out of bed but were soon entangled on the sofa, Lara in panties and a T-shirt, Bobby only in jeans. They remained immobile and silent for several minutes, staring out into nothing. Bobby eyed the half-empty bookshelves and a stack of unopened cardboard boxes. He hadn't asked her yet how long she had lived in the apartment, but he imagined it was only a matter of a few weeks.

"I was born here, you know," she said. "Here in town. One way or another, Austin will always be my home."

Bobby remarked to himself at the coincidence of thought, wondering if they had a special connection. "Yeah?"

"Born at St. David's," she said. "My father worked for

the state; he was an engineer. My mother stayed at home and took up sculpture. I graduated from McCallum."

"Sounds very Austin," said Bobby. "Very middle class."

His inflection on the term "middle class" seemed to give her pause. "We were comfortable," she said. "But we didn't really have a lot."

He wondered if he had intended to be classist, but then disregarded the thought. "You stayed in town for college," he said.

"Yes, I did. My father got sick and he couldn't work, at least not full time. There was less money. I lived at home. I didn't inherit my father's gift for numbers. Besides, math and science, they always bored me, bored me silly. I took up photography when I was fourteen, hung out with the kids in art class. We were all misfits. I got it in my head I wanted to be a commercial artist—you know, book cover designs, maybe work at an ad agency, that kind of thing. For a life like that, college seemed beside the point. I wanted to apply to RISD, Parsons, but there was no way we could afford it, and I didn't want all that debt hanging over me for the next twenty years. So I bit the bullet, took fine arts classes at the university but lived at home, and made the best go of it here in town. The professors were encouraging. Some of the students, you could tell that their teachers were being patronizing, but I began to hear a consistent message, that I could really draw, that I could make a go of it in this racket one way or another."

She stopped. Bobby realized she was waiting for him to say something, to trade a story. Bobby felt his abdomen tighten but cleared his throat, summoning his will and beginning slowly, starting at a place he knew would interest her. "My mother wanted to be a writer."

Lara pulled back, looking at him. "No shit? That's a bit

of a coincidence."

"Yeah, no shit. And maybe it's not a coincidence."

"What did she want to write?"

"Novels, I guess. I guess that was the idea."

"What kind of novels?"

"It was never really clear."

"Did she ever publish anything?"

"No." Bobby paused. "No, not even close, just all these spiral notebooks that she scribbled in. I never read any of it, couldn't even fake an interest." His voice lowered and he could feel the tension in his torso. "To this day I don't know what she thought she was doing." He could feel his face redden, and he tensed once again, but closed his eyes and breathed. He spoke again, almost apologetically. "I had some counseling when I was young, and as one shrink put it, the whole mother thing is all sort of unresolved for me. I think that was the word he used. *Unresolved.*"

Lara made easy eye contact and her lips parted, but then she closed her mouth and shook her head as if ejecting an impolitic thought. She put her head back on his chest. "My grandmother died in the spring," she said. "Talk about unresolved. When my dad got sick, she came and lived with us, like a third parent, a really cool and sweet one. I'm still sort of fucked up about losing her. Anyway, she left me a bit of money—I don't have to work, at least not anytime too soon. I wasn't doing much of anything, interning at an ad agency here in town, writing copy and helping the designers when there was a crunch. Just one notch above gofer work most days. So anyway, I took the money and headed for Taos. A former professor was friends with an artist who ran a studio, and this professor said I could learn a lot from the guy, the only price being I would have to produce cheap New Mexico tourist art. Crap, really. Mesas and mountains and Native American motifs, but the professor said it would be good discipline, working to meet deadlines and learning something of the commercial art business.

"So, anyway, I get there and there are artists everywhere. If you threw a rock, you'd hit one. And all these little boutiques. I got ahold of my contact, and he was a very cool guy; he set me up in a tiny apartment not far from downtown. I got work, and they sat me in a back room with three other artists and we were supposed to paint for a few hours a day in exchange for studio time, along with a commission if we sold a painting. I gotta say, when I sold my first piece, which I thought I hated, I made sure to take a picture of it so I wouldn't forget it."

"No shit? You got that picture?"

"I do."

"Well, goddamn, girl, let's see it."

Lara scrolled through her phone, her smile almost childlike in its transparent pride. She held up the phone so Bobby could see—it was a painting depicting dusty flatland desert, with a black seam running through it.

"Near Taos," said Lara, running her index finger down the seam. "There is this chasm formed by the Rio Grande coming down out of Colorado, and the chasm is close to a thousand feet deep. I was terrified of it, really. So I had to paint it, you see."

Bobby assessed the picture. The black seam was jagged, like a medical textbook depiction of an operation scar. "I like it," he said at last. "I really do."

"Yeah, there were some things about Taos that were good. It was also there that I met Michael, the Native American guy in my sketchbook. Maybe that's not so good. To his credit, he was different. He got into RISD, had this laid-back air, the internalized demeanor of a real artist. But he was lazy and he loved pot and thought about his work only when it suited him. But he could paint. God, he could paint, and he was fast.

"So, a thing started up. Michael seemed genuinely cool—mellow, and nothing got him down in particular. He was from Santa Fe, which is a lot like Austin, and I think it was this as much as anything that gave us a common vocabulary. In the final analysis, though, he was spoiled—his mother, I think, dotes on him—and I had no interest in being a caretaker. I got tired of running interference whenever he didn't show up to work at the studio. And when he did decide to grace us with his presence, he was condescending. I think he thought it beneath him to have a job. And to top it off, he was always a little lit up, whether it was pot or booze. After about six weeks of his shit, I took my stuff one morning and piled it in my car and started driving. I barely told Michael anything, I didn't really say a proper goodbye. Not really.

"I headed west, not having any idea where I was going. I found this deserted highway that led north into Utah, and I just followed it. The landscape was tremendous, desolate and huge, and I ended up in a motel in Moab, sort of like the end of the earth, and there was a national park close by, so tourists came and went. That was how I met Steve and Janice. They were bikers, they were a bit older, and we'd go out in the desert at night and light a fire and smoke pot and drink and talk. It went on for about ten days, and it was the most fun I've had, maybe ever. They were the greatest. But one day they left, they never stayed anywhere too long. And I saw this as my sign. It was over. The adventure was over. I drove back, took my stuff out of storage. Three months out west. I arrived back here in September. The summer was passing, so I decided to stay, start over here at home."

Bobby was quiet while she spoke, but her anecdotes left him with a handful of lingering questions. "You like adventures, don't you?" he said.

She sat up, placing her hands in her lap, the tenor of his question not lost on her. "Well, yeah. Don't you?"

"Is that what I am to you? An adventure?"

"Well, I will say . . ." She bit her lip. "I will say, you aren't a lot like most other guys I know."

"What does that mean?"

"Well, some of my girlfriends, they want their boyfriends to be college types, lawyers or bankers, that kind of thing. The money thing, a nice house in Westlake thing."

"Sounds god-awful to me."

"Well, I don't disagree. I mean, look at us. A sensible husband—and I mean that in the Jane Austen sense of the word—would be maddening to me."

"So a business owner is not sensible?"

"Well, they can be, but one look at you . . ." Her voice trailed away. "I think some girls might be a little afraid of you, Bobby."

He thought about this. "Really? I've been as gentle as a kitten."

"Well, I'm not sure that club manager would see it that way." They stared at each other. Bobby was about to reply when she cut him off. "The thing is, Bobby, I'm already quite fond of you, and truth be told, I'm not sure yet how I feel about that. But if you're asking whether I'm casual about all this, I'm not."

He nodded, taking it all in, and then with a flick of his eyes he put it away. He straightened in his seat and turned his full attention toward her. "Listen, I want you to hear it from me, okay? Right here, right now. I'm not casual, either. I've had a lifetime of being casual, of being less than casual, and now I want something different."

Her eyes stilled, and she looked down at her folded hands. "Well, that's the other part about you, the part other women maybe wouldn't get. You see, most of the time I don't have to wade through three feet of bullshit trying to figure you out. It's just that . . ."

"What?" said Bobby. "It's just what?"

"I think I gave it away. I said 'most of the time,' didn't I?"

He nodded.

"It's the other times. The times when I look at you and I have no clue what you're thinking, who you are, where you've been. Especially that last part. And wherever you've been, sometimes it feels a little dangerous."

They sat in a palpable silence, but then Bobby leaned into her gently and took hold of her hand, his voice cutting the fabric of the quiet. "Come on, let's have fun tonight."

Lara put her hand to her forehead, instantly seeming upset with herself. "Jesus, Bobby, what I said sounded terrible."

"No it didn't."

"You and dangerous in the same sentence? God, yes. Yes, it did."

"Forget it, forget all about it." He softly pinched the cleft of her chin and kissed her. She looked doubtful, but a second kiss seemed to placate her. "Now let's just stay inside, get some Thai delivered, watch a movie. Let's break out some whiskey and have a good time."

"Okay," she said. "But I think we're low on whiskey, though."

"Not a problem," said Bobby. "I've got some in my car."

"In your car?"

He headed for the door, all smiles. "You don't think I plan for contingencies, girl?"

She grinned back at him and he was out the door, striding briskly up the walkway. He turned a corner, moving down a short corridor, when his gait slowed. In the parking lot, he detected the faintly sulfuric odor of asphalt blacktop. He opened the driver's side door of his car and his mind replayed the scene he had just exited, lingering over her characterization of where he had been, and by extension, who he really was. He replayed the way she said that one particular word, *dangerous*, and he parsed the inflection in her voice. After a moment of this, he reached under the front seat and pulled out a fifth of Evan Williams by its neck. He looked at the whiskey and smelled the acrid scent in the air and he was seized by a sense of unease, wondering if he could undo the qualities in him that led her to use that word, qualities that had become fundamental to his being. The feeling of unease intensified, but he began clenching his right hand, wresting control of the feeling and burying it.

**

When he returned to the apartment, a tenuous internal balance had been restored. Lara appeared self-possessed, digging intently through a box and pulling out a CD. "What do you think?" she said, holding up her selection.

The plastic CD case was marked up and had no inner packaging. "What is it?"

"Some delta blues. Old recordings, the real deal."

He found enormous comfort that their tastes about so many things seemed similar. "God yeah. Food?"

"How about pad thai with chicken? Or a curry? Just down the street. They deliver and the portions are big. We can share."

"Of course," he said. "Of course, it sounds terrific. How about we go with the curry? You decide the rest." She went to the kitchen to order and he remained standing in the middle of the room. Whatever fears that lingered in him were cast aside. He thought this particular moment ridiculously easy, as if they had been a couple for years. "I think it's a date, girl," he called out after her.

She had ordered and was back in the living room in less than a minute. "So, let's eat, listen to some music. After we finish eating, let's watch a movie."

"What movie?" said Bobby.

"Something beautiful. You know, beautiful actors. Not a piece of crap. Maybe like *Notorious*."

"Is that the title?" She nodded. "Well, I like the title."

"Do you like Hitchcock?"

"I don't know much about Hitchcock."

"We should watch *Notorious*, then."

**

They ate off of white porcelain plates with an olive-colored trim, plates that were clearly decades old and secondhand, and they both drank Heineken from the can, the only two beers left in her apartment. After they finished eating, they resumed with the whiskey and turned on the movie. They were draped over one another, the black-and-white images alternating the room between darkness and light. Lara broke out a small tin of pot, which contained an already rolled joint, and they passed it between them.

Bobby whispered in her ear, indicating the joint. "Is this

the worst thing you do?"

"Yeah, pretty much." Lara glanced at him, then did a double take, a hint of intrigue in her voice. "Why? You got something else on you?"

"No," said Bobby, casually dismissive but concealing his disappointment, raising his arms slightly as if he were prepared to be frisked. In that moment, he thought it probably best that she confined herself to a softer drug. "You can search me, if you like."

"No," she said. "You're too clever for that, I think."

At first Bobby resisted the film, telling himself he did not particularly care for old movies, but as it continued, he found himself increasingly drawn in. Lara's head rested on his chest as he sprawled over the sofa, and he continued to drink, continued to find the world soft, intimate, and warm. At one point he coughed to cover up the fact that he'd choked back a sob. He thought to himself, *Could it be this simple? Just this simple?* He watched Ingrid Bergman and his lips moved wordlessly as he reached for the whiskey, Lara's weight a burden of kindness.

**

He opened his eyes and the room was dark save for the light from the street. He felt an odd radiating sensation in his chest, a disagreeable feeling he tried to suppress to no avail. He lifted his head from the pillow and saw that it was two forty-three in the morning. He placed his head back down and looked up at the ceiling, experiencing a sudden craving for a cigarette. Finally he resigned himself to being wide awake. He stole out to the bathroom and turned on the light, which cast a narrow beam over Lara's side of the bed, and he stood there and watched her. She breathed easily. Merely the sight of her created a storm of contradictory feelings, and he flicked off the light and made his way out of the living room in the dark, sat on the sofa, and smoked.

He burned his way through three cigarettes in silence. Somehow the placidity of night slowed his mind, and he simply stared at the window blinds and the black walls and noted the occasional sound—a car in the parking lot, a faraway siren. He stood up, crept back to her bedroom, and got dressed. He drew close to the bed and took her shoulder, shaking her gently.

"Lara," he said. "Lara, it's Bobby."

She opened her eyes, somewhat disoriented. "Bobby?"

"Yeah, hey." He paused, waiting for her to more fully awaken. "I can't sleep, sweetheart. I'm a night owl anyway and sometimes I can't sleep." She didn't nod or do anything to acknowledge what he said. "Anyway, I don't want to disturb you because I can't sleep. I'm going home to do a couple of things I need to do anyway. I'll be back tomorrow."

"You're leaving now?"

"Like I said, I don't want to keep you awake."

She checked her clock. "It's after three."

"Yeah, I know. Like I said, I'm a night owl."

She didn't seem suspicious, not exactly, but neither did she seem pleased by this development—perhaps not relishing the prospect of waking in the morning alone in a cold bed.

"Well, okay."

"Don't get up," he said. "I'll lock the door behind me." He bent over and kissed her. "I'll see you tomorrow."

He turned to leave the room, but at the threshold, he stole a furtive peek behind him. She had her head propped up on her hand and her eyes moved, watching him as he left the room.

**

The roads were largely empty and he made his way through downtown, black shadows alternating with pools of orange streetlight. Heading east, he turned up MLK, fighting a persistent question that refused to let him be: what the hell did he think he was doing? He tried to think through the multiple aspects of the question and suddenly pulled onto a residential side street, parked the car and got out. His footsteps crackled in the gravel. The only other sounds were the crickets and other nocturnal life eking out their perpetual nighttime melody. Bobby walked up the block until he was underneath the limbs of a tree over which shone a streetlight. He looked up. Individual shafts of orange light slid through the branches, and he blinked when he moved, and the light shone directly in his eyes.

**

He cleared his desktop save for a reading lamp, a pint bottle of Evan Williams, and several packets of cocaine from the closet. He cut lines with a bank card, sucking them up one by one with a short plastic straw. He had done a full gram and his mind was blank, his attention wholly absorbed by the aggressiveness of the drug. For a brief instant, he allowed himself to wonder what Lara might think if she walked in on this scene, but he drove further considerations of the matter from his thoughts. He lifted the pint and downed a swig, then did a couple more lines. He waited, the minutes passing. Finally, he reached into a desk drawer and pulled out the computer, plugged it in, and found a pornographic website. He got up and undressed. When he sat back down, he poured a gram, divided it into four large lines, and inhaled them all in less than thirty seconds. The drug acted quickly. He felt the oncoming rush and held the energy in his chest, navigating through videos under the rubric "two girl deep throat blowjobs." He created a series of them and poured another gram on the desktop.

When he realized his room was slowly filling up with morning light, he shifted the position of his desk chair away from the wall, away from the computer and whiskey and coke. It was not quite seven thirty and he hadn't slept. Out the window, dawn turned the sky into a cloudless overlay of baby blue and he blinked wordlessly at the heavens. Finally he stood and ferreted another pint from the closet.

Somehow the oncoming morning brought with it a small measure of peace. Bobby took a long breath after each sip and tried to forget the last several hours. He didn't attempt analysis. In fact, he didn't even search for words to describe what had just transpired, and further reflection was far beyond his capacity. Like a still image on a TV screen, he saw Lara's face; she seemed neither pleased nor displeased. She hovered on the edge of consciousness, then vanished. Bobby raised the window blinds. The morning sky seemed remote and mysterious and he took comfort in its vast emptiness.

**

Shortly after one thirty in the afternoon, his vibrating phone roused him from slumber. Bleary-eyed and disoriented, he answered.

"Hey, you," Lara said.

His head hurt remorselessly and he was very hungover. He tried to sound light and upbeat. "Hey to you, girl. You woke me up."

"Christ, Bobby, what time did you get back to bed?"

He tried to work through the ramifications of that question, but in his still semi-besotted state, his thinking was hardly state of the art. "Late," he muttered. "Or early. Depends how you look at it."

There was a moment's hesitation, as if Lara were weighing whether to ask him the question in the first place. "Did you get done what you needed to?"

"Oh, yeah. Yeah," said Bobby. "Like I said last night, it was just odds and ends, things around the house."

"Yeah?" said Lara, and there was another brief pause, as if she may have been evaluating whether to pose follow-up questions; but if she were troubled, she let the matter pass. "So, anyway, just by coincidence, a friend of mine texted me this morning. She wants to meet up for a drink or two. I texted her back and told her that I just started dating and, of course, she replied back that we should both bring our boyfriends along."

Bobby was hardly in the mood for a double date, but after the last several hours, he did not want to challenge her. He made himself sound agreeable. "Sounds like a hoot. When?"

"Tonight. Say about eight. Are you free?"

"Of course," he said.

"That blue shirt you wore the other night would be just about perfect."

He thought to himself that it was far too early into the relationship for recommendations about dress, but he said nothing. "How about we meet up about seven thirty? We can loosen up, have a cocktail before we meet them."

"Good idea," she said enthusiastically. "Let's do that. Pick me up about seven fifteen?"

Bobby calculated that he had at least five hours to pull himself together. "It's a date. See you then."

**

The restaurant Lara's friend, Vivian, selected was west of downtown, the sort of place where an appetizer cost at least $15, the drinks were in a similar price range, and the decor ran towards chrome and smoked glass. When Bobby ordered his usual cocktail, the uniformed waiter told him that the restaurant did not carry Evan Williams, hardly unusual for restaurants with far more humble aspirations than this one, but Bobby took it as a slight. Lara was dressed in khakis and a newly pressed black shirt, her black leather shoes a far cry from the sandals she had worn when she and Bobby met. Even her drink selection surprised Bobby, a pricey vodka martini. After a few minutes, a brown-haired woman led a man—a tanned, tall, athletic type—toward their table. Bobby had been told very little about the couple. He knew that Lara had met Vivian because they both did some design work for a local ad agency, but she'd said little about Vivian's date. It was unclear to Bobby if Lara knew anything about the man.

Lara and Bobby stood and there were handshakes and greetings all around. Bobby repressed a smirk when the man introduced himself as Ken.

"Ken or Kenny?" inquired Bobby.

"I go by Ken," said the man. His hair was sunburnt, a chestnut brown with lighter highlights. Bobby refrained from saying, *Ken as in the Barbie doll?* "Are you Bob or

Bobby?"

"Bobby." The two men stared at each other across the table. Ken wore a maroon polo shirt and brown shorts, his basic style of grooming seeming to derive from your average issue of *GQ*. There was something collegiate about Ken, a prep school air of entitlement that had persisted well into adulthood. It took Bobby only seconds to gather that he had little to say to this man, but he decided to play it by the book. "Let me get the first round," he announced. "Vivian, what are you drinking?"

"An appletini," said Vivian.

"A margarita," said Ken. "With Cointreau."

Bobby refrained from making a face at the drink selections. "You got it," he said, signaling the waiter.

Vivian wore acid-washed jeans and a black top with satin highlights, and it occurred to Bobby that her style seemed to draw more from North Dallas than the deliberately underdone sensibility of Austin. "Lara tells me you own a club on Sixth Street," she said.

"A bar," said Bobby. "On East Sixth. We're remodeling right now."

"Sounds expensive," said Vivian, her attention noncommittal. She had yet to make full eye contact with Bobby, and he thought there was something discursive about her style of speaking, a flippancy that bothered him. With no transition, Vivian pointed at Lara's wrist. "Where in the world did you get that, girlfriend?"

Lara wore a thick silver bracelet with Native American motifs that Bobby had never seen. "Taos," she said.

"You have to let me see it."

Lara handed it over. "I think this bracelet is the best thing that happened to me there."

"You've got to tell me about all that," said Vivian.

"Every yummy little detail."

"Yummy is not the word I would use," said Lara.

Ken wrested away Bobby's attention from the women. "So, a club, Bobby?" he said, an insistence in the way he leaned forward across the table. "How in the world did you raise the capital for that?"

Bobby wondered if Ken were trying to figure out how someone like Bobby, clearly not a newly minted MBA, might have come up with the cash for a downtown business. Bobby was only guessing, but he felt insulted nonetheless. He decided he needed to underplay himself, to not let on that he felt wholly alienated. "I know the owner," Bobby said, adopting a generic tone of voice. "It's a sweetheart deal."

"But I hear property in that part of town has gone through the roof."

"It's a small place. And I'm buying in."

"You must have a secret."

In multiple ways, that statement bothered Bobby. "I try to avoid having secrets."

The women were still talking but Bobby noticed his remark caught Lara's attention. She looked at him momentarily, although it was unclear what she was trying to convey. Finally, she mouthed at him, "Careful."

**

Ninety minutes later, Bobby was driving Lara back to her apartment. They were in the midst of a residential neighborhood and Bobby kept his eyes forward, watching the road. They had not spoken since they left the parking lot and Bobby thought the silence somewhat oppressive. At last, Lara cleared her throat. "They aren't all that bad," she said.

"Ken and Vivian?"

"I know, the names are . . ." Lara struggled for the right word before giving up in silence.

Bobby spoke up. "Well, you're right. They weren't all that bad."

She turned, her expression noncommittal. "But you had a bad time."

Bobby waited, feeling the silence escalate. Bobby's impression was that the dinner had continued on without any major developments, albeit awkwardly, and the couples were cordial as they parted for the night. He thought of any number of things to say before he settled on one, and as he spoke, he kept his eyes forward. "I guess I just didn't hit it off with them. I tried to put up a good front."

"Well, Vivian's actually quite talented. When I first met her, I was like you. She seemed like a sorority girl. But when I got to know her, she wasn't. And she's really a very talented designer."

Bobby waited a beat, letting the air clear. He glanced at her. "I didn't say they were bad people, Lara. Or that they were lowlifes, or talentless, or anything else. We just didn't hit it off."

"Oh, come on, Bobby. You were judging them."

"They were judging me."

"No, they weren't." Lara seemed to know he was refraining from argument. "What did you really think of Ken? In your own words?"

"Well, he's into money. Clearly."

"He's a corporate type."

"Is he?"

"I think he works for a bank." Once again, Bobby

desisted from further remarks. The silence ballooned. "And what about her?"

Bobby's patience was nearing an end but he decided to continue playing along. "She . . . Well, I'm sorry, but she seemed different than you."

Lara pounced on Bobby's observation. "Oh, so you know what I'm like. We've known each other less than a week and you know what I'm like." She waited a moment. "You haven't even seen my graphic novel."

Bobby waited, too. Finally, he picked his moment. "Do you want to fight?"

Lara took a deep breath. "It occurred to me earlier tonight that I feel all in with you and yet I haven't even seen where you live."

Bobby went silent once again. Finally, he looked at her directly, his demeanor frank. "Okay, let's fix that right now."

They continued onward through the dark streets, mainly in silence. They crossed I-35 and Bobby took Manor Road east, turning south on Airport Boulevard before taking a side street and heading east again. The neighborhood was old and trees grew in abundance. After several minutes, Bobby turned down his street. The houses seemed even more unkempt, more bohemian, than they appeared to him under normal circumstances.

He stopped in front of his house. "This is it," he said. "My castle."

"Two stories? A lot of space for one guy."

"I don't live alone."

"How come I didn't know that?"

"You never asked."

The band was away on a road trip and the house was dark. He opened the front door and turned on the lights to the living room. "Prepare yourself," he said. "It's a guy house."

"Well, you are a guy," she said.

There were shadows everywhere. The sofa appeared to lurk against the far wall, the chairs indiscriminately arranged in front of the television. Lara had taken only a few steps inside but she stopped, looking around her as if an owl might be hiding in the rafters. "Do you have only one roommate?"

"No, a handful. It kind of all depends, you see. It's a band. If one gets a new girlfriend, I might not see him for several months. Or I might see his girlfriend every day. Besides, they're out of town a lot."

"Are they any good?"

"You mean, are they good musicians?"

"Yes."

Bobby sniffed. "They're not terrible. Alt rock, they call it. They get songs played during the alternative segments on local radio, they have a bit of a following. I like some of their songs—a bit loud, but there's usually a reason for it. In the end, they manage to make a living."

"Not exactly an endorsement."

"They make things difficult by being drunk a lot."

Lara took a few more steps into the interior. "Where do you stay?"

Bobby felt a real misgiving. "Follow me," he said. "I'll show you."

Bobby turned on a desk lamp, which did not fully illuminate his room. There was the bed, the desk, the chair, the nightstand. Lara seemed to hesitate as she crossed the threshold.

"It's not much," said Bobby.

She stood, only her head moving as she appraised her

surroundings. "You're twenty-three. It shouldn't be much." She paused. "You're not into material things."

"No," said Bobby. "I guess not."

She paused again. "Neither am I, I guess."

Lara's eyes continued to dart around the room. To Bobby the silence seemed so acute that he imagined he could hear it. "I've forgotten my manners," he said, his voice far too strident in the quiet. "Can I make you a drink?"

Lara seemed to think about it. "Yes," she said. "That would be nice."

She sat on the sofa in the living room, Bobby in a chair, each cradling their respective drinks. The pluming darkness appeared to frustrate the thin light cast by the ceiling fixtures. She took a sip of her drink, seemingly as much out of obligation as a real desire for alcohol. She seemed distracted and neither one of them spoke. Bobby rattled the ice in his glass.

"I can add more ice if that's too strong," he said, indicating her drink. She did not reply immediately. Bobby's voice trailed away. "Sometimes I make them too strong."

"What's Cuero like?" she said.

Bobby looked at her. He straightened a bit in his chair. "Small."

"Small? Is that it?"

"Pretty much."

"Did you like living there?"

"Well, I didn't exactly live in town. I lived on a ranch. A small one."

"See, I didn't know that."

"Well, it was my grandfather's ranch. In large part, it wasn't even his cattle. He rented out the property to other ranchers. We were real country, if you get my meaning."

"I would have never guessed you came from a rural background."

"That's because I spent my formative years in Corpus. I never really stopped being a city boy."

"Why did you move to Cuero, then?"

Bobby paused. He saw no clever way of being evasive. Finally, he swallowed, clearing his throat. "It had to do with my mother." Lara continued to make eye contact and Bobby could tell she was going to wait him out. Bobby swallowed again. "I guess you could say my mother got sick, unable to take care of me. So I moved in with my aunt."

Lara asked the question as if she were being guided by a higher instinct. "Did your mother get better?"

"Not really."

"When did you leave Cuero?"

He paused. "Summer of 1998." Lara opened her mouth to say something. Bobby held up a hand. "Please don't ask."

"You have no idea what I'm about to say."

Bobby shook his head. "Just don't say anything. I've heard it all." She looked him over, large, uncertain eyes. Bobby struck an apologetic note. "Come on, let's get out of here, go back to your apartment. The energy in this place is bad right now."

Lara nodded. "You might have a point."

He approached her—whether for a quick kiss or a short hug, he was unsure—but her body language indicated she preferred to be left alone. This small rebuff caused his anger to flare, if only momentarily. Before he realized it, the words were issuing from his mouth. "I need to go back upstairs. Get a few things. An extra shirt, a toothbrush."

"Of course."

Bobby made a short hand gesture. "I do want to have the conversation. The life story conversation. Just not tonight."

Her statement was disarming in its concision. "I shouldn't push."

Bobby nodded, wondering if he should say something else. He smiled, then turned and ascended the stairs.

He grabbed his toothbrush from a cabinet, taking in his reflection. He almost immediately averted his gaze, but then he stopped himself. He straightened slightly, as if he were hardening himself. He then looked at himself again, even tilting his head as if that might change his perspective. He remained stock-still, his hands forming into fists. He cocked his right arm back as if he were going to smash the mirror, but after a time, his arm lowered and he left the bathroom hurriedly.

In his bedroom closet, he grabbed a shirt by the hanger and threw it on the bed, pausing to look down the hall as if confronting the barrel of a shotgun. The combination box was hidden under a blanket. He removed a gram packet, lunging for the nightstand to find a straw. In three large inhalations, he finished off the packet, debating whether to take another with him. The coke was strong and surged through him, and the thought crossed his mind to take five grams with him. He hit the flat of his palm with his fist, furious at himself for ever entertaining such a ridiculous thought, knowing he would be found out. He desperately wanted another bump, but summoned all his will and desisted. He put away the packets and the combination box, grabbed the toothbrush and shirt, and stomped his way down the hall, pausing at the head of the stairs to take a deep breath. After a couple of moments, he descended the stairs evenly.

She sat forlornly on the sofa while he grabbed a liter of Evan Williams from the kitchen.

"Come on," he said, not meaning to sound impatient.

He got into the driver's seat and nestled the whiskey between his legs.

"I'll take that," she said.

"I've got it," he said. "Don't worry, it's fine."

He raced up the street. When he reached the stop sign at the end of the block, he braked, then undid the cap to the whiskey and took a swig.

She didn't sound angry, but there was a persistence in her voice. "If you're going to do that, I'd prefer to drive."

"I'm just going to have a swig or two."

"I don't think I feel comfortable with this."

He downshifted and engaged the parking brake. "Fine then," he said. He sat immobile, embroiled in his own concerns. All at once, he made a face as if he smelled something rancid and opened his door. He stomped back and forth in front of the car, and Lara watched him through the windshield. He then marched to the sidewalk and sat down on the curb, his head in his hands.

She rolled down the window. "What the fuck is wrong with you?"

He gestured with his right hand. "You wanted to see my house. Now you've seen it."

She got out of the car. "If I thought it would do this to you, I would have stayed home."

Bobby spread his arms, his palms upwards. "Well, maybe we should have, but you sort of insisted."

She appeared at a loss. "What's your fucking deal?"

The tone of her voice galvanized something deep inside him. He stopped and hung his head. "Fuck," he muttered. He shook his head again, suddenly aware of the anger roiling through him that he'd been blind to only moments before.

She bent over him slightly, her anger mixed with an unwanted concern. She wished she were angrier with him. She asked herself how someone she considered so masculine could appear as vulnerable as a child. "Bobby?"

He looked down at the street. Lara bent over him but he did not look up. When he spoke, Lara flinched slightly, as if she were watching a wax figurine come magically to life. "Maybe I should go home," he said. "The last few days have been awfully intense. Maybe we need to take a step back. A day or two apart."

She looked back and forth up and down the street, apparently considering his suggestion. At last, she nodded, if ever so slightly. "Maybe you're right."

He felt a sharp craving for more coke. He stood up to begin walking home but it occurred to him through his impaired state that it might be considered a slap in the face. He fought against the craving, clenching his hands. "But let me drive you, at least."

Lara held her ground. Her voice was subdued, but direct. "Bobby," she said. He looked at her. "I don't mean to insult you, but I'd rather take a cab."

Bobby turned to look at his car, then turned back to face her. "Lara, I'm fine."

"Are you?"

Bobby did not move. His expression did not change but she could see his eyes cloud, a kind of darkness entering them. "Do you want to come wait at my place?" he said.

She already had her phone out. "What's your address?"

Lara allowed Bobby to drive them back to the house halfway up the block. They waited in the living room together, Lara on the sofa, Bobby in a chair. The only light came from a fixture in the small entryway, and it hardly penetrated the darkness. Bobby's face was an expressionless mask and he stared into the darkness.

"I'd like to pay for the cab," he said, his voice small. Lara didn't say anything.

Her phone rang and she stood up. "He's here," she said, not looking at Bobby. "The cab's here."

Bobby opened the front door and she didn't look back. He thought about calling after her, making some remark that was apologetic and connective, but he didn't. She got inside the cab without a backwards glance. Bobby raised his hand to wave, then felt foolish. The cab sped away and he was left in the dark, listening to the night sounds and looking at the canopy of the heavens. He was angry with her, but that emotion gained little traction as he considered binging on coke with abandon.

Back inside, he went through a gram in a couple of minutes. He stood in the bathroom with the faucet running and made lines on the counter. He left the bathroom, the faucet still running, and sat on the bed, his mind empty. The rushing, tremulous sensation of the drug took full effect. He made his way down to the kitchen and took a swig of Evan, the bottle making a familiar popping sound as it left his mouth. Somehow things were not to his liking. He retrieved four more packets of coke, grabbed his keys, and left the house.

He found his way to a neighborhood bar with cheap wood paneling covered with multiple beer gewgaws. It was not quite eleven. He ordered a house bourbon and a tequila shot and stared into the smoky mirror behind the bar. Without further ceremony, he downed both drinks and reordered. He stood up, his balance not yet affected. Inside a stall, he breathed in another gram and returned to the bar stool and polished off another bourbon, getting the bartender's attention and asking for a bourbon neat. He recalled thanking the man. After that, his recollection faded like a screen going blank.

Consciousness came back to him in fits and starts. He felt distinctly alone, even among other patrons two stools away. The bartender asked him questions periodically to test his sobriety but he answered them easily, even if he couldn't remember the questions thirty seconds later. He stepped out to a patio in the back, drink in hand, and smoked a cigarette, which brought him out of his stupor somewhat. But he finished his drink in a swallow and the stupor returned.

There was a woman's voice, subdued but immediate. He realized she was sitting next to him, addressing him. She said something about the Black Cat being her all-time favorite joint. He laughed, agreeing with her that the place was great, just great. He ordered another drink and tried to focus. He thought the woman pretty, large eyes and an indistinct blur of dark hair. She drew close and whispered, asking if he could help her out. As disoriented as he was, nobody had to tell him what that meant. The next thing he knew he was in the parking lot starting his car, the woman next to him.

As he drove, he pretended he was in a video game. He passed her his two remaining packets and she poured some on the back of her hand and inhaled. She waited in the car while he grabbed more drugs and whiskey from the house, then they were on the road again. She directed him under the freeway to a neighborhood just off Lamar. Her apartment complex was tiny, the parking lot dirt and gravel. He took a giant swig and he was aware of himself as he climbed some wooden stairs.

THE THIRD DOOR

They were doing lines and he was drinking. He couldn't remember her name and he tried to ask. He either could not get the sentence out or he could not remember what she said. He found her in the darkness and he held her close, humming a tune, the whiskey bottle in hand, his arms wrapped around her. She pushed him away, gently. He took another long, lingering swig and a void opened up, black and unrelenting, and he was consumed by it.

He awoke with a gulping breath, as if emerging from a deep body of water. The room was filled with the gray light of morning and he was sprawled on a sofa. His shirt and shoes were on the floor, but he was otherwise clothed. The pain in his head was almost unendurable. When he raised it, he was overcome with dizziness and nausea. He breathed steadily, attempting to form some semblance of inner balance. After several minutes, he stood.

She was on her bed, wearing pants resembling black fatigues and a black bra, her name still lost to him. She had dark hair and her pale skin was luminous in the subdued light. He studied her, but couldn't recall ever seeing her before. He touched her shoulder gently, hardly shaking her, and she moved but didn't wake. He gathered up his shoes and shirt and put them on, throwing one last backwards glance at her. She had not stirred. As he headed for the door, he saw her phone on a table and he picked it up and called his phone, which was next to hers. He immediately killed the ringer on his phone, looking to see if the noise had awakened her. It had not. He saw an electric bill on the table, a bill that had been pulled apart by someone tearing it in half. There was a single name on it, "Sylvie." He looked at the name, then looked at her. Finally, he crossed the room and opened her front door, locking it behind him with the knob lock, and then shut the door.

BOOK 3, CHAPTER 9
November, 2003

He shut Sylvie's apartment door behind him but stopped on the landing of the stairwell. He paused, his hand on the loose railing, and he attempted to assimilate the last several hours. He stood for several seconds, then he shook his head, denying a question he was never asked. He proceeded down the stairway but found his balance unsteady and he almost tripped. When he got to the bottom, he blinked. In front of him was a chain-link fence demarcating the gravel driveway, the bottom of the fence overgrown with grass and littered with gum wrappers and an empty pack of cigarettes. He looked back up the stairway to Sylvie's apartment, and for an instant, he imagined he could see her face. He reminded himself that however far he'd gone with her, they hadn't slept together. So forcefully did he internalize the thought, and so great was his relief that he had not cheated, that he almost said it out loud to himself: *I did not sleep with her.*

**

As soon as he got home, he sent Lara a text, a simple

question—*Can we talk?* He sat alone at his desk in his room, fragments of memory from the night before bursting across his field of vision like flash segments from a video. He was plagued by two moments in particular—Lara clambering into the cab without so much as a backwards glance, and his arms around Sylvie in a short-lived embrace, humming a scarcely recalled tune. Within moments, he grew angry and found himself tired of sifting through his past with a guilty bent, tired of picking around the detritus of his regrets and apologizing along the way. He pulled out his notebook and wrote.

What happened last night? What the hell happened? I guess it's really very simple—I lost it because I got high. (Or at least getting high greased the wheels—I think I could have controlled myself otherwise.) So, would behavior like that end if I simply stopped with the coke?

He stopped writing, evaluating the entry, then continued.

So, not getting high. How am I supposed to stop when I keep a couple hundred grams not five feet away from where I sleep? Is it realistic not to use with that sort of temptation so close? Probably not. So, I'd have to get rid of the stash, which presents its own problems. Throw the combination box away? (What if some youngster dumpster-diving finds it and cracks the box open? How would I feel about that?) Flush it? (Not so good for the fishes and our precious creeks and I'd be out a considerable sum.) Just hand it off to Jason? (Give 200 grams of coke with a street value of close to $8,000 to that prick? Are you kidding?) Sell it back to Ray? (Well, maybe.)

Once again, he stopped writing, concentrating.

So, I sell it to Ray. The streets being what they are, I would have to tell Tim. What would Tim think of that?

Would that be a basis for conflict in our business venture? So, that's an open question. But say I do all this. I stop using; I sell the stash to Ray; Tim blesses the deal, a one-time-only deal. Am I home free? If I do all that, will I change? Will I become the kind of guy that Lara—or a girl like Lara, just your average, ever so slightly fucked up, normal girl—expects?

The pen went still, and his eyes coasted across the surface of the paper. He reached for a whiskey but then stopped himself, swirling the brown liquid at the bottom of the glass. An old thought occurred to him, one he had played with before but had never taken seriously. A sentence formed in his mind and he balanced the considerations inherent in it. He picked up the pen again.

Today may not be a day for half measures, he wrote.

He puzzled through the sentence, then underlined it twice. He swirled the alcohol again, but then placed the glass back on the desk. He began a new entry.

The alcohol and the cocaine are fundamentally linked, but the alcohol is a more deeply ingrained habit. How long can I go without a drink? A day? A week? Longer? Let's find out. I'll aim for a week and see what happens. The next time I see Lara—assuming I do see her—I'll be drug and alcohol-free. I'll be sober, I'll be clean, I'll be directing myself toward a new life, a new me. Next time we meet, will she be able to deny that I am different?

He sat back in his chair, glancing over the entry, then once again confronted the glass of whiskey. He looked hard at the glass, as if he were about to negotiate with someone he did not like. Reaching down into a desk drawer, he pulled out a half-full liter bottle and uncapped it, carefully placing the side of the glass to the mouth of the bottle, pouring. The whiskey dribbled into the bottle and Bobby closed his eyes, barely tolerating the sound, in that moment the craving for the alcohol more pronounced than he imagined it would be.

**

Bobby pushed open the metal door to the El Dorado, the hinges squeaking. His eyes adjusted to the low light and he saw day-drinkers congregating at their tables as he traversed the main room, edging toward the bar. He detected the heavy odor of limes and simple syrup and he was seized by a decisive impulse to buy a drink. He stood still, managing the impulse. He moved to an adjacent room that housed a new lounge leading to an opened door, outside of which lay a freshly poured concrete patio. The lounge area was half lit, with a hectic gathering of wires dangling from a newly constructed section of ceiling. Bobby gazed at the exposed panels.

"The wires are for the light fixtures," Tim said. Bobby turned to find him at the lounge's doorway. "They also have something to do with the wireless connection. I'm not sure how that works since the modem is behind the bar." He advanced toward Bobby, wearing black khakis and a freshly laundered, long-sleeved gray shirt, his hand extended with assurance. Bobby noted the hand, the confidence behind it. The two men shook. Tim then swept the room with an outraised arm, obviously pleased with the sight. "I'm told the wires will be put away by the end of the day. As you can see, it's coming along."

"Looks like it," said Bobby. "We still on schedule?"

"Maybe a little ahead. Last they told me, completion in five weeks, maybe six."

It suddenly seemed very close to Bobby, his day-to-day

involvement with the business, and to his consternation, it felt like an enormous amount of responsibility and effort. "During the holiday season?"

"Well, the way I look at it, we can make New Year's a grand reopening. I'm seeing opening night with a good local band, maybe an ad or two in the *Chronicle*. What do you think?"

"I think it's great," said Bobby, hiding his ambivalence and nodding affirmatively, finding that he could not quite duplicate Tim's quiet exuberance. "Just great."

"Where are my manners?" exclaimed Tim. "What kind of bourbon do you want?"

Bobby stiffened, but after some uncertainty, he relaxed his shoulders. "I'm good right now, Tim. I'm fine."

Tim's eyes were purposefully blank but they moved over Bobby carefully. "You sure? Just a friendly drink?"

"I appreciate that, Tim, but not right now."

"All right," said Tim, clearly confused by Bobby's refusal of a drink. "You called me."

"You got a minute? In private?"

**

Tim's desk was piled high with Manila folders, invoices, a scattering of sticky notes and ballpoint pens. Both men sat down; Bobby immediately began fidgeting. Tim pulled a bottle of Maker's from a desk drawer. "You don't mind if I take a snort, do you?"

"Of course not," said Bobby. He snuck a glance at the bottle, at the alcohol splashing into the glass, then averted his gaze. "You picked up on it immediately. I knew you would."

"You mean, you turning down a drink?"

"Yeah, me turning down a drink."

"It's not that hard a thing to notice," said Tim. "It's kind of like the Mona Lisa without a smile."

"Well, I was just thinking that maybe it's time for a change."

"Is it?"

"Maybe."

Tim raised his glass, sipping, a neutrality to his aspect. "You said you wanted to talk about something."

"Context," said Bobby, instantly. "I think I want to talk about context."

"Context?" repeated Tim. He sat straighter in his chair. "You've got my attention."

"I had a fight last night, Tim. A fight with my new girlfriend."

Tim leaned forward. "Am I supposed to be surprised by that?"

Bobby reciprocated, leaning forward as well, extending a hand outward for emphasis.

"Well, now, listen. I don't do confessions but let me get this out. The fight was my deal, not hers. A bad moment, especially when combined with a little powder. She didn't even know about it and still doesn't, the powder. So anyway, I go into this dark place and the next thing I realize I'm yelling on the street and she winds up leaving in a cab. Hard to blame her. I'm left alone so I do more powder, get to drinking in a neighborhood bar, and I run into this girl that maybe I met once at a party. Nothing happened other than I slept on a couch in a strange girl's place, but the next thing I know I'm waking up, the girl's there, my head's a wreck. So I get up, get out of there, and then I get home. That's when I knew, I'm done with it."

Tim blinked. "Done with it?" he repeated.

"Yeah," insisted Bobby. "Done."

"Done with what?"

"Any of it, maybe all of it. As of right now, I'm on the wagon. With alcohol, I'm quitting for a while, trying it out. With the powder, I'm finished. Finished absolutely."

Tim didn't sound doubtful, merely curious. "You mean that?"

Bobby remained leaning forward, his pent-up feelings about the night before spilling out. "I'm trying to be straight, Tim. I've got a girlfriend now. All that time you knew me, a single guy, tomcatting and carousing, who gives a fuck, right? I sure didn't. I didn't care what I did. But now, I'm sick of it, Tim, and I don't want anything more to do with it. It took a night like last night, but yeah, Tim, I want to quit the life."

Tim crossed his legs, sitting back in the chair, regarding Bobby dispassionately but with concern. "Just going to walk away? Walk away like that? Not even a friendly portion of whiskey to help you out?"

"It's not an all at once thing, Tim. It's kind of been building these last several weeks. I've reached a tipping point, that's all."

Tim frowned, if only slightly, seeing an upside and a downside. If Bobby really were trying to quit, it might be the best thing for all involved, and god knows, he knew plenty of dry-drunk bar owners. On the other hand, he had been around enough to know that chaos might ensue when drunks engaged in nothing more than simple alcohol reduction. When giving up altogether, he had seen stronger men than Bobby fold like aluminum foil. "Bobby, I know you know this, I know you do. All this, all those cravings and feelings, they don't really stop. They don't stop until you quit breathing, whether that's tomorrow or fifty years from now. That's when they stop."

The two men stared at each other across the desk but it was Bobby who blinked first, looking away. Tim tried to resume eye contact but Bobby avoided looking at him directly. "Tim, listen to me. I came here for a reason, one single reason. I'm trying to lay off the alcohol, sure, but I'm quitting the blow, too. I'm quitting that shit and that's it. I would have never involved you in this decision, but I'm presented with one logistical problem. I have a personal stash, which was once a working stash. Not a crazy amount but real weight, or at least real weight in the eyes of the law. So, I'll probably be calling Ray, setting up a meet, and selling back. It's the safest way to dispose of it, and that's all I'm trying to do, dispose of it. Now, when I came to you I said no more deals, and yes, this is a deal, but it's a personal one, not a business one. I'm just making sure. There's not a problem, is there?"

Tim's elbows rested on the desk, his hands folded, and there was care in his gaze. "Bobby, I came into this partnership with my eyes wide open. Wide open. I never wanted to make it contingent on your personal habits, because as long as you're here when you're supposed to be, I really don't give a damn what you do. And listen, there are still nights when I unplug the bottle, let my hair down. Janine doesn't like it much but she kind of accepts that I'm blowing off steam. I don't know what she'll do when the kid's there. But anyway, I assumed coming into this that the feeling between us is mutual: business is business, personal is personal, and never the two will meet. So, this thing with Ray, I understand what you're telling me. And it makes sense, it does. So, I can't argue, and I wish you all the best."

Bobby opened his mouth, audibly exhaling. "That's

good to hear, Tim. It is."

The two men smiled a little, glad the talk was over.

Tim spoke, his voice confidential. "But just one more thing, Bobby. It's not actually the deal with Ray that concerns me. I know from long personal experience—it's a lot easier getting out than giving up, and the way you're talking about quitting, the overnight nature of it, I've heard famous last words like these before. Maybe not from you, but I've heard them."

Bobby's relief that their venture hadn't hit a snag elevated his mood and he spoke a touch glibly. "Tim, if you think you're preparing me for the worst, I know better than that."

"I'm not trying to argue, Bobby. But you see, you're my partner now. I don't want you to set yourself up for something you can't handle."

Tim's assessment created a momentary unease in Bobby, which he immediately fought off. "I'll handle myself, Tim, okay?" he said, a touch brusquely. "I'll handle myself just fine."

**

It was approaching ten p.m. and Bobby was alone on the sofa in the darkened living room, the TV tuned to a football game that he ignored, cradling his skull in his hands, trying to manage his craving for a drink. He felt adrift. His usual haunts, the bars, were off limits. He'd tried to take a nap, but inner tranquility, much less sleep, eluded him. The minutes crawled, and Bobby was fixated by a craving for alcohol so keen that his mouth watered. He rubbed his palms together, trying to maintain an inner equilibrium. But at last he went to the kitchen and opened a cabinet, taking a liter bottle by the neck and lowering it to the counter.

He considered taking a few drinks, physically feeling the soft inner glow they induced. He told himself there were plenty of times he managed to stop after only a few, but he also knew there were plenty more times he hadn't. His anger lit, like a fuse. "You don't own me," he heard himself say belligerently, presumably addressing the whiskey but speaking as if he were trying to engage something inchoate, the ether around him. "Did you hear me? I said, you don't own me."

He returned the bottle to the cabinet and paced the kitchen, then the living room. Lara had not answered his earlier text, so he texted again, not even taking a moment to evaluate his message before he sent it. *At least reply back,* he wrote. *If it's over it's over, but don't ignore me.*

He reread the message, finding it distasteful then made his way up the stairs to the musty quiet of his own room. He yanked open a desk drawer, the bottle of Xanax spinning to the front. He opened the bottle, trying to think through the implications if he took a single pill, but at last, he downed one, then another, and then another. He breathed out, a tremulous sound, and kept hold of the plastic bottle, returning to the sofa. He waited. Slowly, his agitation waned. When he felt a wave of tranquility, he swallowed another pill. His phone vibrated and he picked it up.

Let's talk, read the message. *Tomorrow afternoon, at my place.*

He reread the text several times, scrutinizing the placement of words, if anything might be discovered if carefully parsed. But the Xanax continued to work on him; his head bobbed, then nodded. He realized he was slipping under and he moved his thumbs eagerly over the display. If he awoke late in the early afternoon, he wanted to make sure he was not rushed.

I'll be there at three o'clock. Just text me back if another time better suits you.

In seconds, she replied. *Three o'clock works. See you then.*

He latched onto the last three words, seeing a kind of hope in them, and that murky sense of optimism melded with the Xanax. He began to nod involuntarily again, once, twice. His eyes closed, but he opened them with a start. "I know who I am," he said, haltingly. "I know who I am and I'm better than this."

**

Once again he strode down the shaded, mossy walkway, the heavy odor of dampness marking his passage. Bobby knocked on Lara's door. He heard a voice, what sounded like nonverbal assent, and he turned the knob and pushed the door open. In the half-light, motes of dust floated in the air and a single horizontal shaft of sunlight glowed on the tiled, dusty floor. Lara was still in her nightwear—a gray T-shirt and flannel pajama bottoms, her hair unkempt. He preferred her informal attire. She faced the door, her eyes dark, and he imagined that they were eyes that had resolutely pondered his behavior from two nights before. Whether this was true or not, he did not know, but merely the possibility of it moved him.

"Hey," he ventured, shutting the door and sitting down, facing her.

"Hey," she repeated.

A moment's hesitation and Bobby shrugged. "I don't

quite know where to begin."

"Neither do I," she replied.

"I guess I made something of a scene."

Lara nodded but showed no outward ill will. "A bit."

At last, he brought his palms together. "Well, let me just put this out there, okay? It was my fault and I readily acknowledge it. It was completely my fault."

She sat without expression, then she creased her brow. "Not entirely."

"No, I'm a big boy," he said. "I'm an adult and I acted like a child."

She appraised him with a steady, soft stare, her words quiet, somewhat detached. "I know I pressed, I see that now." She had something else she wanted to say and she stumbled in search of it. "I guess what I'm asking is, what happened? From your point of view?"

"What do you mean?"

"What do I mean?" She seemed surprised he would ask and turned her head from side to side, as if the room contained a small audience who would help her find the right words. "One minute we're at your house and you're making me a drink." She paused, clearly estimating the impact of her next statement. "The next minute you're foaming at the mouth out on the street."

Bobby winced, closing his eyes briefly. "I think I was embarrassed."

"Really?" she said, tilting her head. "What on earth about?"

"Come on, Lara, you know. At where I live."

She sat up in her chair, donning a half smile, as if she did not quite believe him. "Bobby, I've got to say, it was a pretty typical guy place."

"But you looked disappointed."

"Disappointed?" She contemplated the multiple aspects of the word. "No, not particularly. And even if I were disappointed, I don't see how it led where it did."

"Well, truth be told, the little date with Ken and Vivian didn't help—"

She cut him off. "Before you say anything further, Bobby, Vivian is a friend of mine."

Bobby answered immediately. "And she seems like a perfectly decent person." Lara absorbed his statement but he could tell this particular issue was far from being settled. "I think they simply took me by surprise—I was expecting something more along the lines of your Utah biker couple."

"Bobby, I don't know about you, but I have all kinds of friends."

"I do, too."

"Whatever Ken and Vivian's shortcomings, I still can't figure out why you lost it in the middle of a street."

Bobby thought she argued with the bent of an artist, someone not necessarily trying to prevail in the argument, but refusing to concede what she felt was the one insoluble truth—he had, in fact, lost it in the street, and she wanted some semblance of an explanation. He searched for a point of reference, a place to begin. Should he admit the drug use, following that confession with the optimistic projection that he was going to quit? Should he allude to his day-old pledge to stop drinking, a pledge he was far from sure he could fulfill? Should he attempt to explain that his awkwardness around Ken and Vivian stemmed from years of social dislocation, years in which he feared the little judgments of so-called normal people like them? His inconstant thoughts swirled about, not leading anywhere in particular, until suddenly he discovered a path.

His voice changed, becoming softer and more intimate,

and he asked, with a quiet insinuation, "What do *you* think happened?"

She picked up on the change of voice and appeared to follow the contours of the query, concentrating. "I don't know."

Despite her frustration with him, Bobby realized that categories of judgment were her last recourse. "But certainly, you've made guesses. If not about the night before last, then about me. About who I am."

Her dark hair ringed her face and the lids of her eyes sank, forming a hard tortoise shell. Her empathy competed with an impulse to argue the point. "It's like you're two different people; I see that. Two, three, four, I don't know." She reflected. "When it comes down to it, I like that about you. In fact, it's one major thing that we have in common, I think."

Bobby listened closely, feeling an inner chill. Now that he had teased the conversation to this point, now that the moment had arrived, he felt unsure, his throat tightening. "I don't usually talk about this shit with people," he said, the spoken words cramped and uneven. "You see, all this started a long time ago."

She waited, her expression shrewd and self-aware, but he didn't continue. She opened her mouth to speak, closed it, then opened it again. "I look at you, Bobby, and sometimes I feel safe," she said. "I'm almost embarrassed by it, I feel like such a girl, but you seem like someone who could face down anything." Her voice was low, as if she were talking to herself. "I think about that manager at the club. I get the feeling if you had been anyone else we would've been thrown out. But with you, the manager turns tail. Like he's scared. I've thought about that a lot, Bobby, both sides of that same coin, that maybe I feel safe because you—you yourself—are dangerous." She seemed to break out of her mini-trance and looked to him. He simply eyed her in return, and she looked down. "Then I look again, and I see this little boy, this scared little boy, without refuge other than evasion and a hair-trigger temper." She waited, her next statement a reluctant afterthought. "The worst part about it is that it's sort of fascinating."

Bobby sniffed, not quite defensively, but with dismissiveness. "I'm not a case study, Lara, and I have no interest in being one."

"And I have no interest in dating one." Lara gently bit her lip. "So, let's have it, Bobby. What happened? What happened long ago?"

He saw no clear way forward. He breathed in deep, then exhaled loudly. "It had to do with my mother," he managed. "Some shit having to do with her, and things got fucked up for a while. Then I went to live with my aunt and things got better."

Lara seemed to wait for more, then realized there wasn't any. "Okay, that's good," she said. Somehow she didn't make it sound patronizing. "It is, it's good. It's a start. But let's take it from the beginning. What happened to your mother?"

He felt a momentary panic and searched for words, dismissing them as fast as they occurred. At last, he shook his head in frustration. "God, Lara, fuck all if I know where to begin." He seemed to think, but the resulting statement was underwhelming. "She got sick."

"Cancer?"

He could see her trying to fill in the blanks. "No, no, not sick like that. In the head, something was wrong."

"Depression?"

"I'm not a doctor. It was hard to tell."

Lara waited, but her patience began to wane. "Come on, Bobby, I'm a big girl. If it's weird, I can take it. I've heard any number of fucked up things in my life. What happened?"

The words came in fits and starts. "God, you should have seen it with your own eyes, all fucked up." He paused, thinking this was not the right beginning and trying to formulate a new point of departure. He tried again. "It was like each new boyfriend, a bigger dickhead. Worse than the last." He paused, looking at her. He could tell by her noncommittal, stony expression that he wasn't being sufficiently revealing. He searched for something, an anecdote, when he thought of a story that he could stomach telling. He smiled, just a little. "One time," he began, a little slowly, "this one boyfriend, he took us to the Pecos River near Del Rio. This trip was supposed to save their relationship, and the boyfriend talked up the trip like it's a great big deal." He liked the beginning he had created. "And sure, we get there and there are huge limestone canyons, and we're walking on the canyon floor next to the river. Really quite beautiful. But of course, this boyfriend and Mom start at it, they couldn't not fight for more than ten minutes, and Mom gets so worked up that she trips over a rock and twists her ankle. Bad. Swollen like a softball, black and blue. She can't walk, at all. Well, the boyfriend, he's beside himself, because it's miles just to get back to the car, much less coming back with help. This guy is just walking in circles, angry as shit, and finally he says, 'This sums it all up, doesn't it, sums it all fucking up.' And he just starts walking away. Well, I couldn't believe it. Mom's cussing at him, and I call after him, yelling, 'You're just going to leave us here?' And he says, 'I'll send out a doctor, but she's your problem now, little man.'" Bobby chuckled, a bit regretful, but, with hindsight, seeing the fun in the situation. "The boyfriend returns with this park ranger in less than an hour. I was surprised to see him again, quite frankly. Anyway, the ranger knows first aid, braces her ankle, and we all walk out of there. Of course, Mom and the boyfriend reconcile after about five minutes, but the way I remember it, they broke up for good within a week."

Lara was smiling. Bobby could see she was glad he was revealing himself, but he could also tell she wasn't satisfied. "That is a little fucked up," she said. "Funny, too."

"Yeah, it is kind of funny, isn't it?"

"I mean, I'm glad I wasn't there, that's for sure."

"It was a pretty day, it was West Texas. It wasn't so bad."

"Is that what you wanted to tell me? Stories like that?"

Bobby was still caught up in the afterglow of the telling. "Well, yeah."

She turned her palm upward, her fingers curled, seemingly assessing her fingernails. "Bobby, I don't mean to be callous but I'm pretty sure I've heard worse."

His good-natured feeling disappeared. "What are you saying?"

She half shrugged, revealing a touch of resignation. "Well, I'm saying that I don't think you're telling me everything."

His thoughts rushed forward, his better angels advising him to be more forthcoming, but his lesser lights quiet, content with silence. His thoughts jumped to Larry—how his mother used him in trade as a drug mule to afford her ridiculously expensive habit. Is that what Lara wanted to hear? Should he begin with that? He thought about it but he knew there was no way he was going to tell her that story, at least not then and there. He felt a flash of anger but wrestled hold of the feeling, muffling it. The words came tumbling out. "You know, it's just a lot, Lara, a lot to talk about. And here it is, all of it—I'm not trying to be evasive, but I just want to move forward. The past has its place and you deserve to know everything, but some days I just want to leave it behind. I mean, there are things I want besides talking about this sort of thing. I want to get my bar off the ground, I want a decent life, I want to share it with someone. And what you need to know is that no matter how fucked up it may have been, whether it's ten years ago or two days ago, is that I'm trying to change. To take the past and look it in the eye, but then to finally put it away and leave it where it belongs, in the past."

Lara put a balled fist to her mouth, and at last, her frustration got the better of her.

"Christ, Bobby, what do you expect of me? Am I supposed to ignore that there's a part of your life you won't talk about?"

"I'll get there, Lara. Give me a little time."

Lara's face clouded. She seemed to regret her outburst. "Bobby, part of what you just said, the words were beautiful. They were, they were beautiful. And I get that you're trying to change. I can see that, I can."

"But . . ."

"Well, yes, *but*. What if I come to know it all, whatever it is, and then I can't handle it?"

"Then you walk away."

"Well, yes, I'll walk away. After what? After investing what? A couple of weeks? A month? Six months?"

"Six months seems a little extreme."

She repositioned herself at the edge of the chair, as if she were going to reach out and take his hand. "Don't you realize that I just left someone because I was waiting? I drove into the desert and searched my soul over some fucking guy who didn't have it in himself to change."

"You yourself said it, Lara; I'm trying to change. No, strike that, I am changing. I'm becoming someone new. I'm becoming myself."

Lara's voice turned sour. "Well, if becoming yourself leads to what happened the other night . . ."

Bobby's anger stirred in him again, but he buried it, attempting to sound light and dismissive. "A stumble. That's all."

Lara appeared more divided than ever. She sank to her knees beside his chair and took his hand. "What was your job again? Before this bar thing?"

He knew she could see through him and acid roiled in his stomach. He told himself that if he made a deal with Ray it was so he could walk away from the life, and that this final sale shouldn't count against him. He spoke in the past tense. "I was a salesman."

"A salesman? And tell me again, what did you sell?"

"Does it matter?"

A flash of impatience. She threw away his hand and stood up. "No, Bobby. Can't you at least answer that question? That one question?"

"What does it matter what I used to be?"

"Just tell me what you sold and I'll wait."

For a moment, he was overwhelmed—he heard nothing, thought nothing, aware only of a whiteout in his head. He almost left the apartment. Suddenly he hit upon something, a new direction that found form as he articulated it. "Okay, I'll make you a deal. On Saturday afternoon, we'll have a nice lunch, then we'll drive to Cuero. You can see my aunt, witness a better side of me." As he spoke, his thoughts turned to his mother, bedridden in his aunt's house. He reasoned that his mother's condition was so extreme that she would be entirely incapacitated and out of sight in her bedroom, and therefore, fairly easily ignored. But then, would Lara still want to see her? He thought his aunt might be better situated to help him think through that problem, so he continued on. "You can see where this all started with your own eyes. And then afterwards, after that, I'll tell you everything. And then I'll answer your question."

He knew this proposal was the sort of thing Lara would enjoy—a road trip, an unfamiliar part of the state, a chance to meet new people. "Okay," she said, after a moment's reflection. "You're on. I accept."

**

They made small talk for the next few minutes, hardly a resolution, but it was followed by a series of short hugs. Neither one was ready for an evening together and they seemed to communicate this without saying it. Although she did not intend it, Lara eyed Bobby carefully as he backed out of the apartment, and he took note of it.

As he drove, he paid little regard to his immediate surroundings—the college town, the capital city, with its pristine sky, its businesses, its residences, the Middle America ordinariness of it. He pointed his car north and began driving, considering the issues. What was he accomplishing by bringing Lara to Cuero? Would his aunt reflect well on him and give Lara the confidence to continue onward? Was that the problem he was solving? Or was he merely delaying the explanation she deserved? The more he pondered that last question, the more he mulled over strategies to deliver his life story to Lara by degrees.

He passed a dying shopping mall, the flagship stores long gone and the mall itself about three-quarters empty. Soon he found himself at the intersection of Airport and Guadalupe; he didn't question the wisdom of his unconscious, just maneuvered his car up Guadalupe until he came to the gravel drive and pulled into the tiny earthen parking lot. It was a warm November day and he killed the engine. Air conditioning units whirred, and large floor fans blew behind latched screen doors.

He found his phone and selected the number, waiting. She answered on the second ring.

"It's Bobby. The guy from the other night."

"You left without saying goodbye," Sylvie said.

He didn't hear animosity in this; she seemed hardly the type to be unduly bothered by a lapse in protocol. In fact, her voice sounded flat, almost entirely devoid of affect. "I tried to wake you," he said. "You were out cold. I'm in the parking lot downstairs."

Her face appeared in the window. "Well then, come on up."

He ascended the stairs, each footfall bringing him closer to a situation he was approaching without plan or agenda. Her front door was parted and he pushed it open. The blinds were raised and the room was awash in late-afternoon light. She sat on a bed, small but well-proportioned. She wore a black T-shirt and black shorts and was smoking.

"Am I interrupting?" he asked, shutting the door behind him.

Sylvie looked about the empty room, at the dust bunnies on the marked wooden floor. "Does it look like it?"

"Well, no."

"Then I guess you're not interrupting."

She ashed her cigarette into a black ashtray on the gray windowsill. He crossed the room, taking in the details, details that he'd been far from capable of discerning two nights before. The lack of furniture and the overall impression of emptiness suggested that she made little money, or that whatever money she did make went to her habit. At one point he thought she was parsing him with her eyes, and the next moment he thought she was not. He pulled a chair out from a card table and sat down, not wanting any overt gesture on his part to reveal his judgments. At last, he concluded that the apartment was in a state of transition—it was not yet a full-blown drug house, but with only a slight tipping of the scales, could easily reach that point.

She looked at him, her gaze simple and direct, her expression neutral to the point of indifference. She had elaborate tattoos on her forearms—a large-eyed owl on her right arm, a butterfly with a human skull atop a purple flower on her left, along with a scattering of multicolored stars around her shoulders and lower neck. Although he knew next to nothing about her, he felt as though he had known her, or others like her, for as long as he could remember.

"I got into a fight the other night," he said.

She seemed to take little heed of him, staring out the window down at the small courtyard. "You don't look the worse for wear."

"It was a fight with my girlfriend."

"I see." She took a drag on the cigarette and reflected, blowing out smoke. "And you drove across town to tell me?"

"Well, looks like it. In fact, I might have just done something really stupid trying to make up with her."

Her voice remained affectless—not bored or uninterested, simply devoid of feeling. "Sounds like you want to talk about it."

"I think I might."

"Did you bring any?"

There was no question about what "any" meant. "No, I didn't."

"Well, let's go get it. Then, we'll talk."

Bobby smiled sheepishly. "You got to know, Sylvie, I made a decision yesterday. I'm trying to lay off coke. I'm trying to quit."

If she was surprised by this change in habit, she didn't show it. Bobby regarded her empty expression and wondered what genuine surprise would look like if she expressed it. "Well, that's you," she said. "But as for me, do you mind? I'll keep it friendly, I'll keep it discreet."

He thought about it and told himself he could keep it together, even in the presence of the drug. He felt as though he really needed to talk to her. "No, I don't mind."

**

As they drove, tree-dappled sunlight shone through the windshield, the sky turning an even deeper blue as day gave way to evening. The East Side neighborhoods rolled past—all of them uniformly less prim, less well-kept than their West Side counterparts, an occasional unruly lawn, a house with peeling paint. Sylvie sat up straight in her seat, like a child peering over the lip of the dashboard. With her hands in her lap, she seemed composed, her presence without emotional adornment, as if there were nothing more to her than what was conveyed at any particular moment. Bobby found her a distinct type—the woman from nowhere, without immediate plans, moving headlong toward an unknown future. Bobby recognized in her a duality, how she could seem worldly and utterly adult one moment, and the next moment, a young girl, a waif.

They passed the bar where they met. "This bar is a long way from Guadalupe," Bobby remarked, not trying to lead in any particular direction.

She remained still, her head hardly moving as she spoke. "I had a friend who owed me a favor and he gave me a lift to the HEB. The bar was just around the corner."

Bobby smiled good-naturedly. "Getting groceries at the HEB after ten o'clock, on the far East Side?"

"Well, my friend and I waited but he never showed."

Bobby knew that the "he" in question was her dealer. "And you saw me? How did you know me?"

"You don't remember?" She shook a cigarette from a pack. "You mind if I smoke?" She lit up. "You were at one of Jason's parties, about a year ago."

"I suppose I was fucked up."

"I suppose you were," she affirmed. "You hooked up with Amber that night. Does that ring a bell?"

"Yeah, it does." Bobby watched the bar recede in his rearview mirror. "What happened to Amber? She seemed nice, but a bit lost. That was the last I saw of her."

"She kind of dropped off the radar for a while."

"That bad?"

With all the emotion she showed, Sylvie might have been commenting on the weather. "She's better now. She's in a detox. Court-ordered."

They approached Bobby's house, and the juxtaposition of Sylvie's last remark and the task at hand was not lost on him.

There was no question that the coke was free; Sylvie's time and company as he regaled her with anecdotes about his girlfriend was compensation enough. Back at Sylvie's apartment, they talked at a secondhand dining table with mismatched wooden chairs, and Sylvie did lines off the kitchen counter. Bobby blunted his craving for a hit by swallowing a Xanax. When Sylvie went to the counter for a second helping, Bobby took in the emptiness of the apartment. Although there was so little inside the main living area to delineate her, Bobby felt he was acquiring a better read on her. Most prominent, in his judgment, was absence—an absence of affect and an absence of association, as if the present moment unaltered by drugs were less immediate than a reality coincident with a high.

She powered through a gram and Bobby did his best to ignore her, standing up and peering out the window. He found Xanax a poor substitute for whiskey and coke, but he was determined to hold his present course. Only the faintest traces of daylight could be seen in the night sky and the courtyard was filling with fluorescent orange light.

"I'm going to Cuero with my girlfriend on Saturday," Bobby said, his skin turned an amber-tinged yellow from the light. "That was it, the stupid thing I proposed."

Sylvie was a shadow in the near darkness, and it seemed she hardly heard him, so inwardly-directed did she seem due to the coke. But she answered immediately. "Why are you going there?"

Bobby touched the window glass with his fingertips, thinking. "I'm from there. My aunt lives there. After our fight, my girlfriend wants to know more about me, but it's hard to tell her things because I only recently quit the life.

I want her to meet my aunt, I think, show her a better side of me."

"Didn't you tell me your mother lives there? In Cuero?"

Bobby felt as though he had been splashed with cold water. He took his hand off the window glass. "How do you know that?"

"You told me," said Sylvie. "You told me about your mother the other night."

He turned to Sylvie. "I did? What did I say?"

"Enough. Enough for me to get the picture. The crazy thing, right? Medicated to the max, half out of it when she's not sleeping, just a shadow of her former self."

Bobby was perplexed, at a loss. "But why would I tell you all that?"

"You seemed worried. You said you were afraid you were your mother's son."

Bobby blinked and turned to her, to the small black figure at the table, her head cocked like a sparrow. "I said that? I used those words?"

"I knew what you meant, Bobby. It's true of most of my friends, the crazy parent thing. I think you wanted to be with somebody who knew what that meant."

From so many women in his life he had withheld this critical information, but with Sylvie he'd opened up as if it were an everyday act. "How did you know what I meant?"

"Because I'm my father's daughter."

Sylvie's face was china-doll empty. He once again looked out the window and asked what he knew was an ill-considered question. "Is he okay?"

Sylvie shifted in her chair, peering resolutely at the wall on the other side of the room. "You mean my father?"

"Yes, your father."

"I don't want to talk about my father." She appeared

oddly immobilized. At last, she raised a cigarette to her lips and inhaled. "What do you think will happen there, in Cuero?"

"I think I want Lara to meet my aunt. Provide her some background." Bobby touched the glass again. "I know I hardly act the part at times, but I think all I want is a way out of this."

"This?"

"You know," said Bobby, gesturing around the room, noncommittal. "This. And my past, I guess."

"The third door."

"The what?"

"I said, you're trying to find the third door."

Bobby had no idea what this meant. "What's that?" he said. "What's the third door?"

Sylvie looked out over the courtyard again, her skin tinted orange, her hair a dark mop atop her birdlike head. She spoke declaratively, in a rhythmic cadence. "During my first rehab, I hooked up with a girl from Abilene. One day, we fled the center and we found ourselves downtown. She took me to the freight yards and we sneaked on a train. A cargo train. She said she knew how it all worked, the train's system of tracks. So we're sitting in an empty car and she pulls out some heroin she'd stashed and we shoot up, and remained high all the way into Abilene. I have a hard time remembering the particulars of that trip, but I still remember what she said." Sylvie took a drag of her cigarette and cast Bobby a weighted glance.

"She said addiction is a room with three doors," she said. "At first, the room's kind of cool, but then you soon understand that the room's empty and there are only three ways out. There's the first door, but it's a revolving door. You can leave through that door as often as you like, but you always end up back inside the room. There's a second door, but nobody wants to leave through that door because it leads to the void. The end. Which means there's only one more door. The third door."

"And what's that?"

She looked at him as if the answer were obvious. "Recovery," she said. "If you manage to leave through the third door, you've recovered."

Bobby thought about all of the usual things that separated him from most people, and he realized those barriers didn't exist with Sylvie—he would be unable to tell her anything about his past that she could not fit into some compartment of her own personal story. She sat there, loose-limbed, strangely desexualized, as if she had leapt clear of puberty and attained adulthood untouched by adolescent suppressions. Still, he couldn't deny that she was attractive, and her disembodied, starry gaze intrigued him more than ever.

"Listen to me," he announced. "Me and my girlfriend, we're going to Cuero. Maybe things will work out, maybe they won't. If they don't, I want to come back here."

"You can come back anytime, Bobby."

"Not like this. Not this way."

"What other way is there?"

"Sylvie, I'm not a john, and I'm not an easy access to supply." Sylvie cut away her gaze and resumed looking at the dark wall. "Come on, girl, you know what I'm asking here."

Every time Bobby thought she wasn't listening, that she was wholly engaged in her internal world, she answered immediately. "You're asking if I want someone."

"I'm asking if you want to try."

"Bobby, at this particular moment, you still have a

girlfriend. At this particular moment, your question is premature."

If she accepted his proposal, he knew the relationship would be a difficult one. Two years earlier, he had tried to make a go of it with a woman with one foot in the street, one foot out, and it had ended quickly. But it was appealing, not having to worry about sharing his life story with Sylvie. "I'm not trying to pressure you, girl."

"I think you should go to Cuero, see your mother. I think you should focus on that."

"But I'm not going to see my mother, I'm going to see my aunt. I'm taking my girlfriend to meet my aunt."

"Well, believe whatever suits you. But my advice is to watch your step when you're there."

**

That same night, Bobby wrote the following email:
Aunt Tilda,

I apologize for not calling more. "Self-involved," I think, is a term you've directed my way before, but still, you've always judged me with an enthusiasm for the better part of me (as if anyone else could know as well as you).

I'm in a state of transition right now, one I think you'll approve of. I'm trying to finally work my way through all that Corpus Christi nonsense. I'm starting a business, I'm dating a girl, I'm trying to do away with what hasn't ever really served me in the past. The other night, I fought with my girlfriend. I want to show her that that side of me is disappearing. I want to show her who I think I really am.

Would it be too much to drop by for the afternoon on Saturday? I know it's been five years since I've been back to Cuero but I'm trying to chart a new course for my life and I should come home more. I would like to bring the girlfriend. I think you would like her, I think she would like you. Just an afternoon, maybe some of those peanut butter cookies, some iced tea? I just want to show her how I was raised, even if the raising came a little late.

As far as all that history that predates my return to Cuero, I think it may be too early to share all that with Lara. I'd like to bring her along slowly. Is Mom still in the reconverted work room, or has she moved back into the house? As far as I'm concerned, they don't have to meet, and if she comes up in conversation, we can tell my girlfriend the truth—my mother is sick, confined to bed, generally not very lucid. If Lara insists on meeting her, I'll draw my cues from you, seeing that I haven't visited her since I left home.

Thanks for being good about that, thanks for understanding that I probably don't really hate her, but that for right now it's just next to impossible for me to be around her.

I want my girlfriend to see your influence, not hers. Would it be too much trouble?

All love,
Bobby

**

Saturday arrived and Bobby and Lara drove down 183, heading south. Within twenty minutes the scenery went from city to scrub and long yellow grass. It was a cool day and Bobby cracked the windows, the crisp air whistling into the car. He had remained true to his pledge not to drink, although he had taken a couple of Xanax that morning to blunt his anxiety. He watched Lara out of the corner of his eye. Her hair was darker than Sylvie's but her skin not quite as pale. He pushed Sylvie from his mind.

"Cuero's only ninety minutes by car," he said. "But it's a different world."

"That's what I hear," said Lara. "Germans, Czechs, and beer, right?"

"Part of it, definitely. My aunt could tell you more about that; she knows quite a lot about local history. In fact, when I was young, it was how she got me to quiet down at night, telling me stories about how the area was settled."

He wondered if he was hitting all the right conversational cues. He even tried to weigh the quality of his voice. He had planned this moment, picking out a subject he knew would interest her. "Speaking of which, my aunt has this book you might like. It's a collection of translated church records. You should see it—it's just copy-store printed with a plastic binding. In any event, the records start about mid-nineteenth century and continue into the 1980s. They're just minutes, but they go from being simple church records into forming a kind of history of the community. My aunt used to read from this book, trying to hook me into the town. A great idea, because I had lived in Corpus so many years, I didn't understand any of it, the area, the people. Nothing. My aunt was—" He corrected himself. "*Is* good like that."

"What's this book like?" said Lara, her interest seeming genuinely piqued. "What are the stories?"

"Droughts and floods, crop yields and church business, but also local politics. What it means to be German in a state where English is the official language. The older folk still speak a little German. My aunt may be among the last of them. My generation, the only thing German about us is our last names."

"I've heard stories about all this," said Lara. "You've got

to show me this book."

"Of course," he said, noting that the heaviness in the car had diminished. He couldn't repress a smile, and he faced the day with a guarded confidence. "We'll be there soon."

**

An hour later, he could see a flat shadow on the horizon. After a couple of minutes, it acquired substance and became a scattering of low-flung buildings. Soon they were driving by a mom-and-pop motel and a local hospital, gas stations and fast food places and diners, glass-fronted retail shops and unmarked, nondescript warehouses. Bobby felt a pall.

"This is it," he said, his voice low. "This is Cuero."

They stopped at a light. Lara looked at a crumbling Victorian mansion along the main thoroughfare, the fruit of cotton fortunes from another era. "Where are we stopping?"

"We're not. Not here," he said. "We're not going to Cuero proper. My aunt lives in a place about fifteen miles from here."

"It's not the same town?"

"Technically, no."

Ten minutes later, Bobby turned off 183 onto a two-lane road that wound through fields with bundled bales of hay and scattered with livestock and the occasional derelict oil pump. Bobby spotted an old farmhouse amid the live oaks, well-kept and rural-prosperous.

"We're here," he said, rounding a bend that opened out onto more fields, more cattle.

"We are?" said Lara. "I thought this was supposed to be

a town."

Bobby indicated a small cluster of one-story buildings and some playground equipment. "There's the school." They continued around a bend in the road, which revealed a church with a high steeple. "And there's the church. A little ways further, there's a general store, of sorts."

"Is that the church you were telling me about?"

"It is."

"We have to stop, then."

They pulled into a gravel lot, the tires crunching on the gravel. Bobby shut off the engine and became aware of the general quiet, the absence of traffic and commerce. Lara studied the church. It was not a small church by any means, its brick edifice substantial, its peaked roof reaching over fifty feet into the air. A groundskeeper tended some shrubs next to the parsonage.

The front door opened and two kids burst out, a boy and a girl, both younger than ten. They waved enthusiastically, and Lara raised a hand to wave back. Bobby walked around the church to a park area in the back, and Lara trailed after him. Sprinklers were engaged in their rhythmic revolutions. Behind the parsonage was an old, wooden building, next to which was an unfenced cemetery. Bobby stopped before a headstone.

Lara strolled up next to him as a live oak branch swayed in the wind. She looked at the name inscribed on the headstone: ELIAS KAUFMANN, 1930-1998. Bobby stared at the ground.

"Your grandfather, I take it," she said, putting a hand on his back.

Bobby found the pressure of her fingers light and curiously intimate. He nodded.

"How did he go?"

"Quickly. Heart failure, probably complicated by cirrhosis. He more or less dropped dead."

"I'm sorry."

"It was five years ago. Once he was gone, my mother moved back." Bobby could see Lara looking at him. He thought about what Sylvie had said to him, about the true nature of this trip. He changed the subject. "That was 1998, when I left home."

"Did you leave home because your mother returned?"

Bobby didn't answer right away, which made him experience a sudden empathy with Lara—it must be aggravating getting to know him. He shook his head. "Mom was really sick. I couldn't do anything for her. I was eighteen, I wasn't going to college. It was time." He waited a beat. "She's still there, at the house. I wanted you to know that. My aunt doesn't recommend that we try to see her. She's heavily medicated and just kind of out of it."

The breeze blew Lara's hair into her eyes. "You don't want to see her? Your mother?"

He waited. "I get really reactive around her, you know."

"Still, she's your mother."

"Well, be that as it may . . ." His voice trailed off. "Let's see what my aunt says." He sought a diversion, pointing at the church. "Do you want to go inside?"

"It's Saturday. I know a lot of churches used to have an open-door policy, but I thought that was a thing of the past."

"This is a different world, Lara. If it's daylight, the church is open."

They crested the concrete steps. The wooden doors were heavy, Bobby pulling hard on the metal handle. The interior of the church was dim, wooden pews proceeding to a white altar, stained-glass windows looking down over it all. Bobby noted the musty smell, the tranquility in the air. Bobby sat. Lara did a double take, then sat down beside him. He was hunched over ever so slightly, his eyes empty but directed at the altar in the front. Lara put her hand on his forearm.

"I'm fine," he said, rather insistent. "Really, I'm fine," he repeated, realizing that he was never asked the question. "You're going to like my aunt."

"I never doubted it, Bobby."

Bobby stood abruptly, not understanding why. "Anyway, this is the church." He tried to retrieve the thread of the conversation. "It's been here, on this site, for over a hundred years."

**

As he came to the little lane leading to the long driveway up to his aunt's house, he felt as though he was disembodied, with the strange sense that he could see himself, even though he couldn't. He turned up the driveway, the grass high all around, and he reminded himself to relax, knowing implicitly that his aunt would help see him through the afternoon. He rounded a bend and the house came into view, seeming smaller and more worn than he remembered, the white paint coming off in large, cracked pieces on the sideboards. He stopped the car, driveway dust floating all around, kicked up by the tires. His aunt appeared at the screen door. He hadn't seen her since she'd visited him on Christmas Eve. She wore khakis and a wine-red shirt, her hair salt and pepper on top, but now fully gray at the sides. Bobby was the first out of the car, and as his aunt approached him, whatever anxiety he felt about the trip disappeared, if only for a moment.

"My young man," she cried out warmly, her arms extended.

From the corner of his eye, Bobby could see Lara taking in the scene. "It's good to see you, Aunt Tilda," he said, his voice muffled in Tilda's embrace.

"Thank you so much for coming," exclaimed Tilda, letting go of Bobby and turning to Lara. "Tilda Kaufmann," she said, beaming, taking hold of Lara's hand. "I'm Bobby's aunt."

Lara seemed disarmed. "Bobby's told me a lot about you."

"Please," said Tilda, gesturing toward the house. "It's not much, but it's comfortable. Please come in."

Tilda held open the screen door for Lara, Bobby following. Tilda put her hand on Bobby's shoulder, stopping him. "She's in her room. She won't bother us, I gave her her pills with lunch like I do every day and she's pretty much out cold. Even if we woke her up, she wouldn't be very lucid."

"Lara might want to see her, at the very least. Is that possible?"

Tilda nodded. "If we stay quiet."

"Okay then," said Bobby. "Let's just see where this leads."

When he entered the living room, he experienced minor disorientation. While he recognized that the room was almost exactly as he'd left it five years earlier, the furnishings seemed far older and distinctly rural—the blue upholstered sofa, the armrests frayed and worn and covered with an oily deposit from decades of use; the satellite TV with a fine dust on the screen; the wooden dining table, polished to such a degree he saw his blurred reflection in the grain. He detected a lemony scent in the air and realized Tilda had spent some time cleaning the house, an activity she was rarely inclined to perform, much preferring a good book and a cup of tea while sitting on the wooden rocking chair in the corner.

Tilda indicated the dining table and Bobby and Lara sat down. "Lara, would you like tea?" inquired Tilda.

"Please," said Lara.

They could hear Tilda as she rummaged through the kitchen. "I have cookies, too, if you would like. Peanut butter, Bobby's favorite, and chocolate chip." Tilda returned bearing aloft a tray on which rested a plate of cookies and a pitcher of tea, along with glasses, ice, sweeteners, and lemon slices.

"Oh, this is so lovely of you," said Lara.

As Bobby gradually regained his bearings after the initial disorientation of returning home, he looked at the two women and noted a resemblance he'd never discerned before, not so much a physical resemblance but one of personal style and temperament. He thought to himself that Lara could easily be one of Tilda's teacher friends from the high school.

Lara took a chocolate chip cookie from the plate. "On our way here," Lara said, "Bobby was telling me the most interesting story—that you have a book of church records, from the church we stopped at driving in."

"Oh, did you go inside?"

"I insisted," said Lara. "After what he told me about the book."

"Oh my goodness, yes," said Tilda. "The volume of records. Actually, translated records, at least the first seventy years or so. Until World War One, all the minutes were in German, and until then, even the Sunday early services were in German. The war ended that for good, although I think I learned enough in Sunday school—there was this schoolmarm who insisted we study some basic German after Sunday school classes—that I could probably get by well enough if I were plopped down in Berlin. Bobby never learned a word of German but I thought that was probably just as well."

"I would love to see this book," said Lara.

Tilda pointed at a weathered chest of drawers in the living room. "Bobby, it's in the middle drawer over there. Would you mind getting it for us? I've got to find my glasses."

Bobby stood up and went to the chest of drawers, feeling a moment of buoyancy. The two women were getting along famously, and the homey trappings—the tea, the cookies, the overall domestic air of the scene—he thought it all reflected well on him. He had established his street credibility to Lara, now he wanted to demonstrate his capacity for domesticity. He pulled the middle drawer, which made an abrasive sound. The volume of records sat amidst a mosaic of notebooks and papers—Bobby immediately recognized the Manila cover with a photocopied etching of the church emblazoned on the front, the black plastic spine which held it all together. He picked up the volume and was turning toward the table when his eye was caught by a spiral notebook, the kind an elementary school student might use, its yellow cover faded with age. The name on the front was printed in block letters: REGINA K. MAY, 1986. He managed to pull himself away, but he left the drawer open.

He stood between the two women, who had pulled their chairs together, Tilda with her reading glasses dangling around her neck on a chain, Lara holding a black magnifier that Tilda had provided her. "Bobby said parts were historical," said Lara. "Like how?"

Tilda cracked the volume, the plastic spine creaking. "Well, it's interesting you bring it up," said Tilda, speaking as if she were going to direct a class. "For example, during the First World War, whoever kept the minutes made several references to the war, especially as it pertained to German-Americans. Warnings, basically, not to say or do anything that might be construed as disloyal. It was just short of an entreaty to deny their heritage." Tilda pointed to a shelf in the living room on which rested two ornate beer steins. "Apparently Bobby's great-great-grandfather nearly threw those away in 1915, but my great-grandmother, who had an English heritage, talked him out of it. But anyway, there's no mention of the Second World War in the records. Only the minutia of church business. I've always wondered about that, about the record-keeper's state of mind. Was it the same record-keeper? If so, why talk about one war but not the other, especially when they're both perceived to be German wars?"

Bobby sat at the end of the rectangular dining table while the women took up one side of the middle. He found it difficult to concentrate on Tilda's disquisition. However faded the memory was, he recalled May of 1986, the month his mother had taken him and left Cuero. He wanted to know what was in the notebook—his mother's take on the early days in Corpus Christi—but he didn't want to seem rude by ignoring his aunt. He paid half-hearted attention, but his mind was turning rapidly, and he was suddenly possessed by an intense craving for alcohol. His mind swirled, and before he realized it fully, he got up and grabbed the yellow spiral notebook and returned to the table.

Tilda was telling Lara about a passage in the church

book concerning a flood along a creek when she saw what Bobby had retrieved from the drawer. "One of your mother's old notebooks," said Tilda, momentarily diverted.

"It was underneath the book of records."

Bobby saw Tilda glance at Lara from the corner of her eye. "Oh yes, Bobby, you know your mother. She was always one for a journal entry, or a story or two."

Lara picked up on Tilda's remark. "Your mother kept a journal?"

"Don't you remember?" Bobby replied, slightly annoyed. "I told you she tried her hand at writing." The attentions of both women were trained on Bobby and he soon felt distinctly uncomfortable. "I'll put this away in a second," he said. "You two go on about the church."

Tilda and Lara traded a glance, one Bobby tried to ignore. Tilda picked up where she'd left off, and Bobby relocated to the sofa, the notebook nestled in his lap. He opened it to the first page. At the very top were two or three doodles, one of which was a fairly rendered Mickey Mouse. Underneath the doodles was some spidery handwriting.

June 1, 1986:

Took to drinking last night here at home, started with beer but that seemed tame so moved to Evan Williams. In my genes, I suppose. I just had a few but Kurt kept telling me to take it easy, which got annoying fast, and Bobby was still awake, so we stayed away from the herb, but I couldn't wait to bundle him off to bed and turn on some music, get the party started.

I've been trying to write, bought this notebook to help organize it all since I'll write on bits of paper but then lose them and nothing gets any traction. I've got a story in me, I know I do. He thinks I can't do it, the old bastard, one of the last things he said to me before I left. Called me a fool, but he was drunk as he always is, and Tilda was in her room writing some goddamn piece of shit—what's she call it, her "thesis"—but it's all just college bullshit. Something about Thoreau. I can't believe Tilda's writing about him, since she rejects personal freedom at every turn, taking orders from that bastard. She doesn't understand real life, when you've got your snoot down in the mud, when you're caught up with it all with some guy, trying to work it out, trying to find that balance. Kurt, he's a good man, a decent man. Is he what I've been looking for in the first place? Not like that fucker at home—fuck all with his cows and his booze and red, red face like a piece of raw meat. Fuck him, his world about just this big, the size of a dot on this paper. And then there's Tilda, miss perfect. I don't think I could stand her if she weren't so good to me, listening when he gets me down, talking through it all—but she never says shit to him even though I know she sees it, too. Sometimes I just want to scream at her as well. He'll drag her down, too, I just know it, if she can't find her way.

I want to write about being pregnant, and alone, and the whole world judging you. That reproach of strangers who barely know you. The day after I told him I was pregnant with Bobby, Kyle said he wanted to marry me, then the next thing I knew he couldn't stand the sight of me. It seemed like we were at each other's throats in less than a week. For the first couple of days, he's fine, then he's wondering out loud if the baby was really his, saying that I lied to him about the birth control. I never lied, not about that. Will it be the same with Kurt? Sometimes I think so, sometimes I feel like I can see these things coming at me. The headaches are getting worse, if that's what they are. I told Dr. Schwartz about waking up and being unable to fall back asleep, like I'm being pursued, hunted even, this formless thing which is as real to me as the nose on my face. It feels like it's been there just as long. Sometimes it gets so loud in my head that this is my only release, this notebook, these bits of paper, the only way I can talk about it, but the next day I'll wake up and the sun's bright and the sky so blue I feel my heart breaking, and I get carried away with enthusiasm, and this stupid scribbling so sad, the refuge of lonely girls who can't find a man to love them.

Kurt will be awake soon, I should clean up. Maybe I should cook something. He seems like the type who would appreciate a plate of eggs and sausage. How long have I known him, less than two months? Are men that simple? I don't know. I don't know anything. Bobby just woke up, he just came from his room and he's standing right beside me. Would Bobby appreciate eggs and sausage, or would he like something else?

R

**

Tilda did a double take when she realized that Bobby was at her shoulder, then she saw that he had folded the notebook into a tube, his knuckles white from the exertion. "Bobby, you startled me," said Tilda.

"Which room is she in?"

"Who? You mean Regina?"

"My mother. Down the hall? Outside? Where do you keep her?"

"She stays in her old room, Bobby," said Tilda. "And I don't keep her anywhere. She can go where she pleases."

Bobby saw that Lara was looking between them, trying to determine why Bobby was being abrasive. Bobby felt a moment of frustration, of second-guessing. "I apologize. I don't mean to be abrupt."

"You seem keyed up," said Tilda. "Why don't you sit down? Have some tea."

"Some tea," said Bobby, nodding. "Do you think I need some tea?"

"Maybe just half a glass," said Tilda.

"I'll have some tea," said Bobby, pulling out a chair from the table. As soon as he sat, he began fidgeting. "I've interrupted."

"Did you read part of the notebook?" asked Tilda.

"I did."

"I don't know if she wrote it with you in mind, Bobby. Certainly not you as an adult, I'll wager."

"Have you read it?" he asked.

"I've glanced at some entries here and there."

"What did the notebook say, Bobby?" inquired Lara.

Bobby shot a glance at Lara but then looked away, unsure how to respond. The women continued to watch him, which induced more fidgeting, a light shaking of the right leg. "Do you remember a Kyle? One of Mom's boyfriends?"

"Kyle?" said Tilda, concentrating.

"Yes, she wrote about a Kyle. Maybe someone special? Someone she brought home?"

"She didn't bring home many boyfriends, Bobby."

"But do you remember the name? Remember her talking about him?"

Tilda took note of the rapidity of the questions and she turned to Lara as if she expected assistance. "Has he talked about Kyle with you?" she asked.

Lara's mouth was half open in surprise. "No," she said.

"She knows nothing about this," interjected Bobby. "Do you remember a passing reference? Anything?"

"Bobby," exclaimed Lara. "Slowly, now."

"I don't, Bobby," said Tilda.

Without a moment's hesitation, Bobby stood up and began taking small, rapid steps to the hallway leading to the bedrooms at the back of the house. At that instant, he wondered if he was destroying what he thought he was trying to build. "You said she was back here, right?"

"Well, yes, Bobby, but she's probably asleep. She had her pills at lunch." Tilda stood, crying out after him. "She's not going to be able to say much."

"I think that might be preferable," Bobby muttered.

He stopped at a closed door and looked back down the hallway. By this point, Lara was standing as if she were ready to make her way down the hallway, but Tilda had put her hand over Lara's, indicating it was best to leave him alone. Bobby knocked on the door and turned the knob. A heavy odor billowed out into the hallway, a dank urine-tinged reek that left Bobby momentarily gagging, trying to expel the offense out of his mouth. The room had two windows but both were shuttered by plastic blinds that left the room in a gray pall. In the center of the room, a king-sized bed faced a TV, the screen animated but the volume off. Bobby absorbed these details one by one and blinked as he peered at the bed, as if he had to manage the intake of the scene by degrees. Regina's thin form rested lightly on a number of gray pillows propped up by the headboard, and she stared blankly at the TV. Bobby walked to the foot of the bed, clasping his hands in front of him.

"Hello, Mom," he said, the sound of his voice subdued.

Regina's eyes widened when she heard the unfamiliar voice, and she concentrated, which looked as though it caused her pain. Her arms were spindly and long atop a heavy blue blanket, her face pinched, her hair gray and stringy. She looked elderly. Bobby unclasped his hands and placed the fingers of his right hand to his chin, as if this were a museum diorama depicting a ruinous scene of state-enhanced home care for the infirm. It was unclear to Bobby if Regina had recognized him yet, then the appearance of concentration waned and she turned to the TV, staring remotely at the moving screen.

"Do you hear me, Mom?"

"I hear you," announced Regina to the room, her attention still diffuse.

Bobby began by following the general rules of decorum. "How are you? Do you feel any better?"

"I feel fine," she stammered.

It was unclear to Bobby if she fully understood what was happening, but he could wait no longer. "Who's Kyle?" said Bobby, softly. "Is Kyle my father?"

Regina's eyes widened again as she tried to focus on Bobby's voice. When she spoke, her eyes passed over nothing, as if she were addressing a disembodied spirit, a restless one that caused her unease. "Who are you?" she managed.

Bobby closed his eyes briefly. "You don't know me?"

"No, I don't," said Regina.

Bulbous blue veins snaked through her forearms and there was scarring in the nook of her right arm, the track marks from long ago healing into a thin uplift of skin splayed vertically. Her lips trembled as her eyes lingered over him. "It's me, Mom. Bobby. I've come home."

Regina's head sank back into the pillow and she stared upwards at the ceiling. "I have a son named Bobby," she said. "He lives in Austin."

Once again, Bobby closed his eyes, but he took another step toward the bed. "That's right, Mom, I do live in Austin.

I'm opening a bar and I'll be the owner." Regina did not seem to hear him. Bobby threw back his shoulders and straightened to his full height, adjusting his short-sleeved golf shirt as if it were an overcoat. "I just realized, Mom, that I've brought someone to meet you. I've brought a girlfriend."

Bobby backed out to the hallway, his eyes never leaving the bed until he made eye contact with the two women, both of whom were now standing. He waved Lara toward him, and Tilda followed. The three of them congregated before the open bedroom door, and then Bobby stepped inside. "Lara," said Bobby, "this is my mother."

Lara beheld the woman resting on the bed, the shriveled arms, the eyes open wide but devoid of animation. Lara looked like a dispassionate inspector assessing a car wreck. She took a couple of steps toward the bed, her hand extended. "I'm Lara," she managed.

Regina made no attempt to take the proffered hand and coughed. "Who?"

"Lara," she repeated, continuing to hold the hand out. After several seconds, she shot a backwards glance, not at Bobby but at Tilda, as if asking about proper protocol. Tilda's eyes were awash with sympathy, but she offered nothing, and touched her nephew on the shoulder.

"Bobby," said Tilda, "are you sure this is the right time for this?"

"She needs to know," said Bobby, staring at his mother. "If this is going to move further, she needs to know."

Lara looked between Tilda and Bobby, seeming a bit unnerved that they talked about her as if she weren't there.

Tilda picked up on Lara's disquiet. "I don't think this is fair to Lara, Bobby, and there are probably better ways of handling this."

Bobby breathed through his nose and furrowed his brow, and a long moment passed in which he did not respond. He then stepped toward the bed and stood directly beside Regina. "Mom, can you hear me? Can you?" Bobby waited. "Who's Kyle? Who is he?"

The two women looked between Bobby and his mother, at the preternatural intensity of Bobby's posture and the woman who lay prone and absolutely still beside him. Bobby cast a sidelong glance at the women, indicating self-doubt, but he once again turned to his mother. "Kyle, Mom. Do you remember a Kyle? His last name? Where he's from? Anything?"

Regina's eyes were blank and she turned her head away from the persistent voice.

"Bobby," said Tilda, quietly.

"Is Kyle my father?" demanded Bobby, his face growing red. "Goddamn it, this is so like you, Mom. I know you can hear me in there, I know you can hear me. Is Kyle my father?"

Tilda moved beside Bobby and took his arm. "Come on, Bobby, you need to leave her."

"She'll answer me, goddamn it."

"Bobby, you need to leave her now. You're upsetting our guest."

Tilda led Bobby out of the room. "I'm coming back, Mom," he said. "I'll keep coming back until I get an answer."

**

Moments later, Bobby sat in a chair at the dining table and stared down at his reflection in the wood grain. Tilda had taken possession of the yellow notebook and returned it to the chest of drawers, out of sight. Bobby remained silent, his hands fidgeting.

"Can I get you anything, Lara?" said Tilda, at last, her voice exuding an artificial decorum. "Some more tea perhaps?"

"Some iced tea would be very nice," Lara said, appearing grateful that Tilda was trying to restore a basic sense of social normalcy.

"Bobby," said Tilda, "do you want some tea?"

Bobby continued to ponder his reflection, but finally, he nodded.

Tilda fussed around in the kitchen. She came back with two glasses and handed them to her guests. "Aren't you going to join us?" said Lara.

"In a while," Tilda said. She looked at Bobby, then placed a hand on his forearm. "Bobby, you don't want to be rude."

"I'd like to take that notebook with me," he said, his fingers interlaced.

"I don't think that's a good idea, Bobby," replied Tilda. "I'll read it tonight to see if I can't find out more about this Kyle fellow. And when she's lucid, I'll see what I can learn from her."

Bobby closed and rubbed his eyes, trying to process the day's events. He turned to Lara, the question arriving in a bundle of words. "Do you think we should start heading back?" Lara looked surprised she'd been spoken to. "It'll be getting dark early."

"It's not even three o'clock, Bobby," said Tilda.

"It'll be close to five before we get home."

The two women eyed the space between them. Tilda tilted her head, her half smile sympathetic, and Lara nodded, as if she could hear Tilda's voice in her head. Their eyes lingered over one another, as if sending messages. "Bobby might have a point," said Lara, at last. "Driving in daylight is safer."

Bobby could see the women communicating with their eyes; he picked up only a slight exaggeration of voice when Tilda said, "I was having such a lovely time getting to know you, Lara."

"Well, the way I look at it," said Lara, "a lot has been cleared up for me today. If not the details, then the big picture."

Bobby turned to Lara, a bit aggressively. "And how's that?"

Lara looked between Bobby and his aunt. "We'll talk about it in the car, Bobby, if you don't mind."

Tilda looked her nephew full in the eye. "Bobby, you need to take care of Lara now."

Bobby dropped his head, as if Tilda had admonished him, but then he stood, his posture once again defiant. Before leaving, he took a long look back down the hallway to his mother's room.

**

The afternoon sunlight had warmed the car's interior. Tilda stood in the front yard and waved at the couple as they backed out, but then they turned a bend in the driveway and Tilda and the house were both lost to view.

"Mom's notebook," said Bobby, seeking to reign in his disordered feelings. "I didn't expect that. Sorry. I was taken by surprise."

"What's wrong with her, exactly? What's wrong with your mother?" said Lara.

Lara seemed genuinely empathetic to his mother's

plight, and by extension, to his. He maneuvered the car onto the county road from the dirt driveway, his expression noncommittal. "The doctors, the shrinks, they don't agree. Last Aunt Tilda told me, they're treating it like a major case of manic depression. I'm not sure what that means exactly. I wonder if more could be done for her with private care but my aunt can't afford it and neither can I, so she's receiving state care."

"Are they helping her?"

Bobby blinked hard. "Judge for yourself."

"I didn't realize, Bobby," said Lara, "that your mother was so sick. It explains so much."

Bobby nodded as if Lara's last statement was to be expected, then he slowed the car somewhat. "Explain? How do you mean, explain?"

Lara turned her head, seeming to wonder if she'd detected a hint of provocation. "Oh, come on, Bobby. Why are we down here in the first place?"

They were still on the county road, fields with autumnal yellow grass rolling past. In the distance, Bobby could see the line of trees he remembered from his teenage years. "Okay, point taken, but I've already said, don't think I'm a case study either, Lara."

Lara turned back to the windshield, back to the dusty road. "I never said you were."

Bobby told himself to let this matter go, and for a minute or two, they drove in silence. Bobby was embroiled in deep reflection, but then his eyes narrowed and he spoke as if they had never stopped speaking in the first place. "No, actually, I don't think I get it. What does my mother being sick explain exactly?"

Lara looked to the driver's side of the car, her lips parted, a quiet concern to her expression. "Well, maybe it explains moments like this. You're making something out of nothing, Bobby."

"Am I?"

"Yes, I think you are."

Bobby turned in his seat as much as the seatbelt would allow. He was suddenly angry. "And now that you know a little about my mother, is this subtle condescension going to continue? Like every time I get mad about something, it's just Bobby being Bobby? It's okay that he's throwing a tantrum because he's not really angry at anything specific, it's because his mother's fucked up?"

Lara leaned forward, as if she wanted to confront him head-on. "Bobby, you're getting ahead of yourself and you're starting to piss me off."

"Oh, so now you're pissed off?" he said mockingly. "Is it because you're still angry about the boyfriend in Taos? Or maybe because your father got sick and the family got poor?"

Lara balled up a fist and made a short punching motion. "You of all people have no business attributing motives to me based on anything having to do with my father."

Bobby was equally angry and he had stopped looking at the road. They stared at each other across the short distance between them. "Does all this explain why I sold cocaine?"

Lara barely reacted, a stunned blankness in her eyes. She pulled her arms into her chest, her head not moving.

Bobby turned back to the road. "You said you wanted to know what I sold. Before the bar." In that instant, he realized this moment could never be taken back. His anger transformed to defiance but carried with it a suggestion of fear and dismay, scarcely believing the baldness of his words. "I sold cocaine. For about five years." His deflated anger blunted his speech, which had become detached. "I worked for a supplier in town who provided it to me wholesale and I sold it. Grams at a time." He paused again; he seemed disgusted. "And I guess now, by your own admission, you don't have to ask why."

Lara's eyes glazed over. "I thought your aunt was very nice, Bobby."

"I'm not talking about my aunt."

"I know what you're talking about, Bobby."

He faced the road, his hands gripping the wheel. Then he shook his head, as if he were expelling his negative body language, his abrasive tone. "Goddamn it, Lara," he said. "Look, I just need you to know. I'm through with it. The coke, the dealing. All of that's behind me. I'm putting my punk-ass past behind me and all I want to do is look to the future, keep my eyes on the prize." He looked at her. "You do believe me, right?"

Lara's lips were again parted, her eyes trained on Bobby. She nodded faintly. "Of course I believe you." The moments passed. Lara turned away, but after several seconds, sneaked a sidelong glance at him, only to discover that he had been observing her the whole time. Her head swiveled rapidly and she put a hand to the cleft of her chin and conspicuously looked out the window. Bobby felt his stomach knot and he turned back to the road. He suddenly felt an overwhelming craving for alcohol, one so intense that it resulted in nausea.

**

They passed the next fifteen minutes in a largely uncomfortable silence. As they neared Cuero, Bobby slowed down. When he spoke again, it was as if he were continuing on with a conversation that had never stopped. "I stopped selling before I posted my dating profile on the site. I didn't want to lie to anyone. And I haven't, really. And that's a good thing, because I'm tired of it. Progress, you see. But I guess when I pull back entirely, I know there's the third door out there somewhere and I'm not through it. Not through it, maybe nowhere near it."

Lara seemed puzzled. "What's the third door?"

Bobby wondered if he should explain it to her, if it would bring further clarity. He realized it probably wouldn't. "It's nothing, a story that someone told me."

They had pulled into town and were heading along the main highway. Bobby looked at Lara again, and again she cut her eyes away from his. Bobby could see that she was using a great deal of energy to control her expression, and he guessed at what underlay that attempt at control. He swerved suddenly, nearly colliding with an oncoming car, and screeched to a halt in front of a strip mall liquor store.

"Jesus, Bobby, what the hell?"

"I'm admitting defeat."

"What?"

"I'm getting a liter."

"Christ, Bobby, can't it wait until we're home?"

"Where you're going to end this?" Lara started to speak but Bobby cut her off. "Don't shine me on, Lara, it's all over your face." He cut her off again. "You want me to sit here quietly for the next ninety minutes knowing you're going to end this? Well, it's not going to happen."

"And where will you be?"

"I won't be in the car with you."

Lara couldn't disguise her incredulity. "What are you saying?"

Bobby eyes were trained on the strip mall. He spoke

with resignation. "I'd call a cab but I doubt there's one that would take you to Austin." He took the keys from the ignition, jangling them. "Take the car. Drive yourself home."

"What are you saying?"

He passed the keys to her. "Take the car to your apartment, leave the driver's side door unlocked and the keys in the glove compartment. I'll pick it up later."

"And how are you getting home?"

"I'll find a way."

"That's ludicrous."

Bobby cut his hand through the air, a sharp gesture. "I can't be sitting next to you, waiting for the knife. I really like you, but we both know it's over. Right? It's over?"

Lara shook her head, hardly disagreeing but confounded nonetheless. "For god's sake, Bobby, quit your showboating."

"I'm not showboating." He raised his chin, appraising her carefully. "It's too much, isn't it—me? Too many questions, too many moving parts, everything so raw."

Lara narrowed her eyes, manifesting a real aversion. "How dare you put me through this, break up with me and then make this sort of scene because you can't handle a little discomfort?"

"I'm breaking up with you? That's a joke. Besides, haven't you figured it out yet?" He pointed a finger, underscoring each word. "I . . . can't . . . take . . . discomfort. I've hidden from discomfort since I was twelve." He dropped the keys in her lap and she looked at them as if they were an alien technology. "Now if you'll excuse me, I've got some drinking to do."

He got out of the car and without so much as a backwards glance strode to the liquor store, half aware of strands of wires with multicolored plastic flags fluttering in the breeze just above his head. After the turmoil of the last half hour, he felt utterly detached, entirely devoid of sensation. He climbed the wooden steps to the liquor store's entrance. He heard Lara slam the passenger door, her angry footfalls on the pavement. He kept his head level, his gaze forward. He heard the engine rev and the screeching of tires on the pavement. The car raced away.

His head remained steady as he walked inside and up an aisle, selecting a liter bottle of Evan Williams with a misplaced care. He walked a straight line toward the clerk.

Bobby reached for his back pocket and removed his wallet, only to realize his hands had lost their usual dexterity. He grasped the wallet in his left hand and beheld his right. It shook violently. Bobby was aware that the clerk could plainly see this and he experienced a wave of embarrassment. The embarrassment quickly gave way to a surge of rage that started in his chest and flowed outward. He cleared his throat, once, twice, three times, handing the clerk a twenty. "That motel, around the corner," he managed to say. "Is it still operating?"

BOOK 3, CHAPTER 10
November, 2003

A square of sunlight against the fabric window blind, the whirring of a window unit. The absence of artificial light turned the motel room gray and Bobby sat on a queen-sized bed, ashing his cigarette into a black, plastic ashtray. He had checked into the motel, intending to stay the night and then take a bus into Austin the following morning, but after only two hours in the room, the space felt constrictive, the whirring of the air conditioner high-pitched and offensive. He took a swig from the liter bottle and crossed the room to the window, peeling back the edge of the fabric blind. His room faced the parking lot, sunlight glancing off of a garbage bin. He considered the parking lot, the expanse of concrete leading to the ceaseless ribbon of the highway, and he returned to the bed, sitting hunched over, his shoulders bunched up and narrow.

As he sat, his thoughts retreated back to the guarded optimism of the morning, the fact that somewhere deep down he believed this day might prove to be a turning point, that the worst might be behind him and the future was beckoning with new possibilities, an expanding horizon. His thoughts slowed, a jumbled collage of memories and impressions. On the plus side, he remembered how he felt listening to Tilda and Lara talking contentedly over the book of church records, revealing to himself that he was capable of fashioning a low-key domestic scene, a quiet familial chat. To him this suggested that there would come a day when he might return from his ordinary job in the midst of his ordinary life, greet his wife, have dinner, watch TV and be early to bed, and repeat that same satisfying sequence day after day. Then, like a counter-melody, he saw the yellow notebook in the chest of drawers, the breakup, but most of all, his mother stretched out in the sour reek of her bedroom. He felt once more his impotent anger as he confronted the notion that his mother would fail him again—she could not provide even a modicum of information about the father he knew nothing about.

At that point, considering his father, his thoughts stopped. Of course, intellectually he knew he had a father, that he was not brought to his mother's doorstep by a stork. But while he knew that ghostly figure existed (or at least, had existed), he had remained for Bobby just that, a ghost— a figure ill-defined and spectral, vaguely haunting, something that had troubled his dreams as a child but that he grew to ignore as an adult. He blocked it from his conscious thoughts so completely that it might as well be that he had no father at all. But now, Bobby knew the man's name. Rather than producing a milky, normative hope of meeting this man, it produced a burning in his stomach, an acute sense of disorientation. The possibility that he might actually meet the parent he never knew filled him with a storm of contradictory feelings and he imagined that the actual meeting could be awkward and rather horrible, each man at a loss about how to feel, what to say. He grabbed the liquor bottle and shotgunned it back.

"I've got a father," he muttered, unplugging the bottle from his mouth, his breath shallow. "A fucking father."

He tried to back away emotionally, to assert that the breakup was only a minor setback—he could go on from here, he would get back on the dating site, find a new girl; he would be starting a new vocation before Christmas; he was more than capable, like Tim, to leave his personal shit behind him, to become a confident man with a firm, genial handshake. He reached for the liter bottle and upended it again.

Then, finally, the direction of his soul-searching changed, spurred on by the terminally negative perspective he'd acquired as a child and had been unable to let go as an adult. He sat for a long moment as the thought acquired definition and substance—a simple idea, with simple words. *There will always be something*, he said to himself. As the thought rattled in his head, he nodded. There will always be memories tinged with regret, a yellow notebook to discover, a new reason to binge. And it will go on like that, he thought to himself, day after day, year after year. So why give a fuck? His eyes emptied out and he nodded again, reaching for the bottle and taking a swig—one, two, three, four. Then he was aware of the inessential room, the bright fabric blinds and the whirring of the air conditioner, and suddenly he could not stand being there.

**

He checked out of the motel and paid a second visit to the liquor store. It wasn't quite five. He walked beside the highway, his thumb out, with a brown paper sack containing two liter bottles of Evan Williams. There was no walkway and he passed fast food drive-throughs and parking lots scattered with bits of gravel and long-forgotten pieces of broken glass. The draft the passing cars produced felt oddly pleasant, blunting the smell of tar and exhaust. A gray Mustang stopped fifty feet ahead of him and Bobby trotted to the passenger window. There was a boy in the driver's seat and a girl riding shotgun. They were both very young, barely drinking age, he guessed. Even a couple of feet from the car, Bobby detected the faint scent of marijuana.

"You look like a fellow traveler," said the boy. He had light-brown hair and his top lip curled upward, revealing his front teeth. He wore a light-blue button-down shirt with the top three buttons open, revealing a hairless chest—not quite a punk, but no Boy Scout either.

"How far up 183 are you going?" said Bobby.

"We're going to Austin," said the girl. She was dressed all in goth black, a couple of black teardrop tattoos descending the length of her cheek down from her right eye. In high school, Bobby remembered, he had been equally attracted to and repelled by such girls.

"Well," said Bobby, "it just so happens I'm going to Austin, too."

"Where else would you be going on this road?" said the girl.

"I feel that," he replied. "I'm Bobby."

"Nick and Rebecca," said the boy, who leaned toward him. "What do you say—maybe we can help each other out? As it turns out, we're a little short here."

A simple bartering situation. Bobby decided to seal the deal and get off the road by throwing extra honey into the pot. "I've got fifty bucks in my pocket," he said. "And if you take me to the place I say once we're in town . . ." Bobby reached into the sack and pulled out the bottle of whiskey, revealing only its neck. "I'll throw this in for good measure."

**

The couple listened to a Grateful Dead cassette tape. Once they were well clear of town, they relit their half-smoked joint and passed it back and forth, Rebecca offering Bobby a toke. Bobby declined. Instead, he uncapped a liter and took a swig, watching the familiar terrain advance before him. After a while, the couple took little heed of their travelling partner and started talking between themselves, strategizing what they would do once they were in town—the friends they would see, the clubs they would frequent. Bobby listened to them converse. It turned out they were from Goliad, the site of a decisive juncture in Texas history, but to Bobby's thinking, little else. Bobby was once again reminded that for much of the state, Austin was a destination location, a place where one could shed the confining remnants of a small town and become, even if only for a night, someone new.

In the midst of all the turmoil he was feeling, the pain and emptiness he could not shake, not even in motion, the singular idea of losing oneself in Austin, if only for a night, cut through the dissonance in his head. He told himself he could deal with the claustrophobia of loss. He would descend headlong on the city and not care what tomorrow might bring.

**

They pulled into Austin and the couple deposited Bobby

in Lara's parking lot. There was a slight chill to the air, the permanent rushing sound of a city at mid-evening. Once Bobby handed over the money and the bottle, Nick sped away. He found his car with the door unlocked and the keys in the glove box, just as he instructed. He stopped, looking at the mouth of the passageway to Lara's door, imagining the number of the times she would tell the story of their breakup, how the incident in Taos was tame in comparison to the fiasco in Cuero with the alcoholic cocaine dealer. Placed in that context, Bobby felt overawed by feelings of regret that the alcohol had dulled during the car ride into town. He began walking down the damp passage, and for several seconds, he stood before her door, his hand raised to knock. He stood there, trying to determine what he would say if he did knock, wavering, almost visibly bending one way and then another. He lowered his hand, only to raise it again, but then the next thing he knew he was walking back up the passage to his car, not once looking back.

**

He weaved in and out of lanes, both hands on the steering wheel, leaning forward. He found a place to park on Ninth and San Jacinto and he whirled into the space with a single turn of the wheel. He began walking south, his footsteps short but rapid. As he walked down a hill, he could hear Sixth Street, the music and the low-level din of thousands of people, the sonic accumulation of their voices and footfalls, the clink of glasses and raucous laughter and the myriad other sounds of bars and clubs. There was an energy in the air, a barely restrained exuberance. Bobby kept walking and breathed deep, taking it all in, and as he walked, he felt an acute craving for cocaine, which he had not used in almost a week. Merely a few days earlier he was sure he had given up the drug but now, he told himself, he just didn't give a fuck.

He walked along, trying to devise a strategy for the night. He searched his pockets to determine if he had any misplaced or overlooked packets but found nothing. The craving became so intense that he stopped at an ATM and withdrew $400. He had held on to a stash of $20,000 when making his offer to Tim, a rainy-day fund. He ducked into a typical college bar with limestone walls and a raised wooden stage where a young cover band played obvious '90s fare: Nirvana, Guns N' Roses, Soundgarden. As much as Bobby hated such a scene—the homogenized college kids and the young adults, most of them white and hailing from insulated city suburbs—he knew this crowd to be more generally affluent, and consequently, the type of place where Jason would set up a distributor.

He stalked the dance floor, scanning the crowd, looking for a face he recognized. It did not take long before he saw one. Their eyes met, both heading out to the smoking area in the back. Bobby thought the dealer a bit too conspicuous, the smug mouth and the punk demeanor, black T-shirt with a Jack Daniel's logo untucked over long red shorts, in contrast to a good portion of the clientele who wore jeans and some brand of designer shirt. He glanced once behind him to ensure the rep was not being watched, but Bobby saw nothing out of the ordinary. He bought two eight balls under the pink light of a beer gewgaw, nodding at the dealer wordlessly. In a bathroom stall, he flushed, then stuck a small drink straw into a packet and inhaled.

The coke redirected his thoughts; he began telling himself that this was not a night he wished to spend alone.

He left the college hangout and walked up the street, coming across a bar adorned with Mexican motifs, snakes and lizards and strange winged birds, the kind of place where the drinks were $2 more than the norm and the patrons were largely young professionals, not vacuous college types nor hard-bitten loners—a bar, he thought to himself, where Lara would feel right at home. Merely the mental reference to Lara caused him a sharp jab of pain but he ducked inside the bar regardless.

The interior was dimly lit, the ceiling the color of adobe with Mayan ruins painted on the wall furthest from the entrance. Bobby bellied up to the bar, and in keeping with the room, ordered a shot of house tequila. There were several couples seated at tables, groups of men and women in wooden booths. He downed the tequila and surveyed the room, seeking out any likely prospects. He saw three attractive women who appeared to be in their late twenties seated at a table and he slammed another tequila, then proceeded to the table with an even step.

He sought a jaunty, devil-may-care air as he closed in. "The worst thing a guy can do in a place like this," he began, "is approach a table full of ladies without being invited."

The women stopped talking, turning to appraise him. Two of the women traded a glance, the third woman appeared amused—she was a brunette with large eyes in a narrow face—and she suppressed a smile, a playful air to her demeanor. "Surely that's not the worst thing a guy could do."

"I think it's right up there," said Bobby. "Right up there with spitting on the floor or cussing out the bartender." A moment's hesitation, an attempt to determine if he saw any signs of welcome. Bobby pressed on. "I'd be happy to buy a round or two if you guys want to hang out."

"What's your name?" inquired the brunette.

"Bobby. Yours?"

"Deborah. And these are my friends—"

One of the other women cut in, looking at Bobby suspiciously. "We're having a girl's night out, and though Deborah here seems optimistic, I don't think we're looking for company."

While it was hardly a feeble rebuff, he had certainly been subject to far rougher treatment, which was why when he heard the bitter, jarring retort, it took him a moment before he realized it was he who had made it: "It's just a goddamned round of drinks, not a fucking lifelong commitment."

All the women drew back, even the brunette, startled. Bobby stared at them blankly as he tried futilely to minimize his anger. He mouthed the word "sorry" but no sound came out and he turned from the table, beating a hasty retreat to the exit. Out on the street, he far outpaced his fellow pedestrians, almost trotting, coming to an alley and ducking into it, striking a brick wall with the heel of his palm. He stood there in the unlit alleyway, placing his forehead on the wall and remaining like that for almost a full minute.

He came out from the alley filled with a new resolve, thinking that he needed to press his advantage, find the right kind of woman, and close fast. He began to barhop, doing a shot of bourbon on the barstool and a hit in the bathroom. The night was accelerating, becoming less linear, unfolding like Polaroid pictures, acquiring focus but then blurring at the last instant. He found a two-story club with a wooden balcony, high ceilings, and limestone walls. The bottom floor was fairly well-lit but the second floor was mostly dark. The patrons were a diverse lot, college kids and professional types, but also biker sorts with bandanas and black leather. There was no dance floor and little decor, and Bobby wondered what accounted for the crowd. Ordering at the bar, he discovered the club's secret—cheap drinks, and they did not skimp on the alcohol. He downed two bourbons at the bar, then turned on the bar stool, scanning the club.

He saw her—a girl with a chipmunk face, short brown hair, and a small bump of a nose. Bobby imagined he could see it in her posture, in the slump of her shoulders: a college-aged looseness and wildness, a girl who would be open to the possibility of a risky trip, an indiscretion she might regret but too tantalizing to turn down. She sat at a table with a young man who likely went to the university, a suburban type with short, feathered hair and a maroon Izod shirt, jeans, and tennis shoes. They were seated with each other but physically separated and seemed a bit self-conscious. Bobby concluded that they were hardly together; a first date maybe. He waited, watching them. When the guy got up to go to the bar, Bobby hopped off the stool. He crossed the room, a feline quality to his step. He came up behind her, gathering up a chair and sitting next to her. When she realized he had pulled so close, she turned, a kind of alarm in her eyes, but Bobby leaned into her, quiet and conspiratorial.

"I come in peace," he whispered, his mouth just inches from her right ear. He gestured with his head toward the guy at the bar. "Who's the stiff?"

She looked at him, saw the cavalier half smile, the aggressive vibe. Bobby perceived uncertainty but he could also see the alarm give way to a glimmer of intrigue. "You mean, my date?"

Bobby leaned even closer. "Oh, come on, you seem

bored. Let's you and I have some fun. Look." Bobby half opened his hand, revealing a packet of cocaine. Her eyes widened. Bobby guessed this was the first time she'd ever been offered. She suddenly seemed very young, usually a real turn-off for him, but he was in full predator mode and her youth, her inexperience, brought out a deep-seated taste for the jugular. He thought quickly, reasoning that he needed to moderate the risk. "We'll club-hop along this street only, always in public, I promise."

He could sense her coming around. Her shoulders lowered further, youthful and vulnerable. "I don't even know your name."

"Do you really want to know? Or would this be more interesting if you don't?" Her hesitation showed equal parts doubt and arousal, and he concluded he was giving her too much time to think. He stood up, extending his hand. "Come on, he'll be back from the bar in just a second. We need to leave." She hesitated once more, but then she stood up and took his hand. "Let's go across the street. I know a place. I'll buy the drinks."

They headed to the door hand in hand, both glancing toward the bar—her date was paying the bartender and didn't see them leave. Outside was chaos, pedestrians of all kinds swarming the sidewalks, cops on horses, the street barricaded at the freeway and sealed off from car traffic. Bobby moved through the crowd with the young woman in tow. They came to a bar with wood plank floors, the bar and a mirror running the full length of the room. Bobby still had the woman's hand. "Let's go to the bathroom first, powder your nose," he said.

The woman seemed doubtful but somewhat mesmerized, her startled curiosity apparently erasing the need to speak. Bobby ushered her into the men's room;

none of the men appeared concerned in the least that a woman had been brought into the lavatory. Bobby pulled her into a stall and shut the door behind them. They stood face-to-face. Bobby reached into a front pocket and produced the coke and a straw. "Okay, quiet. We don't want to attract further attention. It's like this." He put the straw into the packet, inhaling lightly and taking a good-sized hit. He handed her the packet and straw. "Now your turn."

She took the packet warily, yet wearing the slightest of smiles. She inhaled tentatively.

"No," said Bobby quietly. "You're a little nervous, I understand. But just rear back and inhale."

She hesitated but did as instructed, then shook her head, rocked slightly by the drug and the strength of her inhalation. She started rubbing her nose. "It burns a little," she said.

Bobby concluded that his initial estimation of her was correct. She had never tried coke. "The first snort is always a bit harsh," said Bobby. "Give it a minute." He watched her expression give way to a sense of alarmed wonder as she felt the rush come on. "Again?"

His inquiry and the oncoming high fully reawakened her doubt, he could tell. Was the drug safe? Was this strange man safe? Where will this end? But those questions, however pressing, were altogether muted as the drug made further inroads and she felt the high beginning to take real effect. She took the packet from him, inhaling with gusto, once, then once more. She swallowed, continuing to rub her nose. Bobby leaned into her slowly, putting his face inches from hers. He then kissed her, gently. Initially she didn't return the kiss, but soon he felt her lips begin to move over his. Bobby opened his mouth wider and he felt her tongue, and finally, she kissed him hard, pushing him backward until he was pressed against the metal wall of the stall.

Bobby produced another packet and they both took some more, the bar's ambient music muted in the bathroom. He took her by the hand and led her to the bar, ordering two bourbons and two shots of tequila. They sat side-by-side in a black booth next to the window, pedestrian traffic a constant out on the sidewalk. She leaned forward and kissed him again.

"When are we going back to the bathroom?" she whispered.

"Easy, girl," he said. He brushed the side of her cheek gently with his knuckles. "This is not popcorn; you can't gorge on it."

"A bit more? Soon?"

"Have a drink first. Relax a bit."

The girl downed her tequila shot. "Come on, you started this," she said, her eyes intent on his. "What do I have to do to get more?"

Bobby realized that she had turned completely, an enthusiastic initiate into the world of white, and that the manner in which she entreated him indicated she was probably up for just about anything for a further taste of the drug. There had been times in the past when he would cut off anyone exhibiting such unabashed enthusiasm, concerned not only for the user, but also thinking of his own soul; he was not in the business to place people in harm's way. But on this night, his rules of etiquette were out the door, and her desirousness only increased her vulnerability, further intriguing and sexually exciting him. He got the attention of a waitress. "I left something in my car," he said to the waitress. "We'll be back in about five minutes. Save our table, all right?"

He handed the waitress a $10 bill. "I'll look after your drinks," she said.

"Thanks, darling," said Bobby, who turned to the girl. "Well, come on," he said, fully aroused. "Come on if you're coming."

They left the bar through the back, coming out into an alley. They were about a quarter way down the block. Bobby and the girl were hidden in the shadows from the solid mass of pedestrians that passed along the sidewalk at the end of the block. Bobby looked once about him, seeing nobody else in the alley. He backed up against a brick wall and pulled out a packet and the straw, handing her both. "Now, look here, there's more," he began. "But I want one thing."

He leaned over and whispered in her ear, and she smiled deviously, seeming aroused by the brazen request. She devoured the contents of the packet in less than thirty seconds, rubbing her nose. Bobby gave her a few seconds to recover, then leaned into her and she pushed back into him, kissing him hard, her tongue exploring his mouth. She then drew back and fell to her knees, undoing his belt and his trousers. Bobby felt her mouth on him and made a plaintive sound, and he arched his back, his neck and shoulder against the bricks. She continued on, Bobby's pleasure increasing, when suddenly he felt a rapidly escalating sense of something different. At first he was unsure what it was, but then he realized that it was an overwhelming sense of pure self-revulsion. Images from the afternoon crashed through his mind—the breakup, his mother, the discovery of the yellow notebook—and he found himself zeroing in on a most unpleasant thought, that he was merrily taking this girl down the passageway toward drug enslavement for a momentary gratification.

Then the agitated turning of his mind stopped, and he realized he was pushing the girl away, telling her to stop, his erection disappearing. She looked up at him, baffled. He then reached into his pocket and threw a single packet on the ground.

"Come down with this, if you can," he said, meaning the lone packet, buttoning his pants, securing his belt. The girl was beginning to stand up. "Use it slowly, measure it, at home preferably, and take your time. Drink beer, it helps. I'm really very sorry," he said.

She was stunned, her mouth pained and open and her eyes awash in naked disbelief.

Bobby imagined her dalliance with the dark side would end right then and there, at least for this night. He couldn't stand to look at her. He shook his head, then turned down the alley.

**

He hurried north back to his car, his arms swinging, his mind blank. He felt around in his pockets and found a couple more grams. Back in his car, he stared straight ahead up to the Capitol building. His hands remained where he first planted them, his gaze fixed but his eyes dull. During the last few hours, he had pushed out conscious thought with constant motion, but now that he was still, all the events of the day crowded in and he could not keep them out. He shook his head, incredulous on several levels about his own conduct. His anger mixed with self-disgust and he pressed the horn repeatedly, the blaring noise echoing out over the street but scarcely reducing the burning inside him. He began to cry and the pain accelerated with the tears.

He sought refuge, a safe harbor, not wanting to be alone if he could help it. He reached for his phone. His first impulse was to call Sylvie, but once he had the phone in hand, he changed his mind. He keyed in a number and put the phone to his ear.

"Ellen, it's Bobby. Hey, look, girl, if it's not too much trouble, I was wondering if you might have some time for me tonight."

**

He pulled up in front of a modest but homey one-story house just west of Mopac on a quiet, leafy street. A lamp had been turned on behind a curtained living room window and the porch light was on. Bobby sat in the car, teasing out his thoughts. He had assumed that in calling Ellen he'd been seeking simple companionship and counsel, the advice of an old friend. But as he drove, he began questioning his motives. He knew nothing of how Ellen's dalliance with Hannah had progressed, and he wondered if he had chosen Ellen because he thought she would have yet another lovelorn tale to tell and vindicate his waste of a day. If she did, what did he think would happen next? Did he expect merely to commiserate with her, or did he think perhaps they would party a little bit and fuck in their mutual grief? He held on to that final thought before discarding it.

He traversed the lawn, his steps ponderous. At the front door he knocked twice and entered, crossing a tiled entry hall that opened out into a carpeted room. Ellen was sitting on an upholstered sofa in a spare but elegantly furnished living room. She stood up, her expression cordial, but she could not quite conceal a lingering trace of guardedness.

Bobby tried to assess her eyes and imagined he could read her thinking. Was he drunk, high, or both? Were his motives for being there going to lead to an awkward situation? But Bobby was so accustomed to emotional fragmentation and self-abuse that at first glance he did not seem much the worse for wear and he could see Ellen's shoulders relax, if only slightly. "I guess I shouldn't be surprised when you call after ten out of the blue," she said, hugging him.

"Hey, girl," he muttered, lingering over the warmth of her embrace.

"Can I get you anything?" she said, parting with him cheerfully but decisively. "A drink maybe?"

Bobby noted her wardrobe—a long and loose-fitting T-shirt depicting Tweety Bird, flannel pajama bottoms, fluffy black house shoes. If she was trying to send him a message with nightwear that de-emphasized any hint of sexuality, she was sending the right signals, but perversely, it wasn't working—he could still make out the outlines of her beguiling figure, and he felt more than a remnant of libido. He again became angry with himself, thinking about the girl in the alley, confused about what led him here in the first place.

"I guess I wouldn't mind a little bourbon if you got it," he said.

"I know you all too well," she said, pointing to a small, round table between two chairs. On the table rested a coaster and a sweating glass of bourbon on ice.

Bobby smiled wanly, taking a seat and lifting the glass, swallowing a quarter of the alcohol in a single pass, hoping that a basic sense of social decorum might bring some order to his riotous feelings. He sank deeper into the upholstered chair, taking in the details of his surroundings.

The living room was immaculate, which Bobby had anticipated—despite all of the past relational chaos in Ellen's life, she was particular about the tidiness of her home. He led with the question foremost on his mind. "I suppose you're still with Hannah?"

"Yeah," said Ellen, her voice deliberately understated, though she seemed delighted by her answer. "She's out right now. Studying. She stays late at the library."

Bobby felt a gaseous churning in his stomach, which he tried to cover up by sounding light and glib. "On a Saturday night? You really believe that?"

"She's not nineteen, Bobby."

"I know," he said, immediately regretting the offhand teasing, not wanting to sound as if he were scratching in the dust for faults in their relationship. "I'm just playing with you, girl."

"Another year and then she's done, you know. She'll be a Ph.D."

Bobby saw that the visible frustration that clung to her only weeks ago had given way to something new, a fresh lease on things. "Then what happens?"

"We've decided to stay here. Hannah will teach somewhere, anywhere, and I'll keep my sales job."

"Well, that's great," said Bobby, his words trailing off—Ellen, the perennial loser at love, and now she sounded happy. He looked at her sidelong, then mustered himself, nodding. "It is, sweetheart, it's just great, great to see you like this." He managed a smile. It lingered, then faded. He noticed Ellen eyeballing him and he shrugged, self-conscious, attempting another smile but it seemed misplaced. He shook his head. "I was simply thinking just a while ago, thinking that you're about my oldest friend here in town. Well, the oldest friend without a rap sheet, maybe."

Ellen nodded evenly, but she was clearly trying to determine the meaning behind his words and the fuller context, the reason behind his sudden visit. "Am I?"

"Well, the others—lots have pretty much moved on. Some are in jail, or dead. The rest are still being punks." He considered his own observations. "I'm so tired of punks, Ellen. I've had a lifetime of them. You just don't know."

Ellen nodded again. "Understandable."

The words were out quickly, before he realized what he was saying. "Do you think I was a punk?" he said, under his breath. He hesitated. "Do you think I am?"

Ellen furrowed her brow, clearly concerned by the line of questioning. "I never thought you were a punk, Bobby."

He pounced on her comment. "You didn't? You're sure? Not even at first?"

"Christ, no. I wouldn't have slept with you."

He pressed his lips together, a discerning undercurrent to his gaze. "That wasn't part of the attraction? Slumming it a bit?"

"Oh, for god's sake, Bobby."

"Is that a no?"

"Okay, what has gotten into you tonight? Why are you here?"

He took a long moment, then he looked at her. "The reason I'm here, I guess, is because I've known you through more than one breakup."

Ellen half smiled, a little embarrassed but good-natured about it. "Well, that's an understatement."

Bobby chuckled mirthlessly. "Yeah, I guess it is. I guess there was more than one, wasn't there?"

Ellen didn't seem pained in the least. "I think it was about a dozen over three years."

Bobby recognized that the hard-bitten air that had twisted her face into a mask of regret only weeks before had dissolved entirely. "Sounds about right."

"Spilt milk under the bridge, as they say," said Ellen, rather cheerfully.

"Good attitude," said Bobby, chuckling again. Her equanimity caused his anger to flash involuntarily, but he hid it completely. "What I don't understand is . . ." He waited. "What I never understood is . . . how did you keep from becoming overwhelmed?"

Ellen, perhaps thinking that he was putting her on, appeared to wait for some sort of punch line. It never arrived. "Tell me, Bobby, what's going on right now?"

He paused, glowering. He started shaking his head, his hand forming a fist. "Girl, I've had a mind-fuck of a day."

"Did you just break up with someone?"

"Brilliant deduction," he said, with a bitterness that disappointed him.

"Well, Jesus, Bobby, I'm sorry. I really am. Do you want to talk about it?"

"You know, Ellen, I've made some big changes since we last saw each other. Looks like you have, too, if I'm guessing right. In any case, the big news is, I don't sell anymore." He looked to see if she would say anything. She waited patiently. Bobby continued. "Bought into a bar with an old friend. And I started dating, the real deal—not hookups over an eight ball and a bottle of bourbon. So, I make these changes and I feel pretty good about it, like I was leaving the worst of my past behind. But then days like today, I find out it's just a trick, a hall of mirrors."

He spoke calmly, but the words touched something deep inside him, and he bent over and put his head between his knees, grasping the back of his skull with both hands.

Ellen watched, almost standing to comfort him. Finally, she spoke. "We can take this slow, Bobby. We can take this step-by-step."

He remained bent over, shaking his head. "I don't know, Ellen. I don't know if there's any use talking about it."

"Of course there is. Don't be daft."

"It'll just come at me from another direction. A direction I don't expect." He hesitated, then sat up once more. He shifted in the chair, scrutinizing her. "You see, just weeks ago, you seemed to be in so much pain. And now look at you."

She sensed an opening. "Well, Christ, Bobby, that's fundamental. You gotta move on."

"Move on?"

"Yeah. Move on, put it behind you."

Her observation was simplistic and trite, but at the same time, he knew she was essentially right. He began slowly, but as he spoke, the words increased in tempo. "I get that, I do. I get it. But which 'you' do you put it behind? The one who gave up coke but was sucking it down in a club bathroom just an hour ago? The one who made such a fucking juvenile scene during the breakup that it will probably become the stuff of urban legend? Or maybe the guy who turned a college girl into his own personal coke whore? Or maybe, just maybe, it's the fucked-up little kid, fatherless, with a mother so crazy she's bedridden?"

Ellen got up and knelt next to him, putting her hand on his back. "Bobby, you're in a dark place. And I've been there, you know that."

He felt her hand and was seized by an intensely sexualized feeling, longing for her to touch him elsewhere, to touch him all over, but he buried the feeling and turned to her, addressing her frankly. "I mean no offense when I say this. As crazy as you are, you don't know the kind of crazy I'm dealing with."

Ellen left her hand on his back, patting him twice. "Let's get you settled down tonight. You're welcome to stay here, if you like."

Bobby thought she was moving ever deeper into a sisterly mode, which he immediately found repulsive, and the churning in his stomach began anew. "I appreciate that, Ellen, I really do." He couldn't stand to be a desexualized object in her midst. "I should go."

"Didn't you just hear me?" said Ellen, putting a hand on his shoulder, as if she were a cop seeking to detain him. "You're welcome to stay."

He moved his shoulder out from under her hand with a violence that startled them both. She looked hard at him but he raised a palm in reconciliation. "I appreciate that, I do. But I can't."

"I want you to stay, Bobby."

"You have Hannah to think about. I don't want to screw things up."

"You're not screwing up anything, you asshole. And Hannah would feel the same way."

"Ellen, believe me when I say this—I gotta get out of here."

"I really don't think you should be alone right now."

The words came out with a high-pitched edge to them, a barely contained hysteria. "Listen to me talk, girl, because this is all crazy-making. Right now, I'm doing everything I can just to keep my self-control around you."

She had never seen him quite like this, teetering on an emotional precipice. She drew back. She had always recognized his underlying street toughness but she had always believed he was fundamentally decent and not terribly threatening. Now, she was unsure. Still, at the most basic level, she trusted him, and whatever threat he posed was subsumed by her concern for him. "Bobby, I would never forgive myself if something happened to you tonight."

He got eyeball to eyeball with her, disgusted that he'd allowed his vulnerability to show so readily. "What I do tonight, it's not really your decision to make, Ellen, now is it?"

For an instant, she was scared of him, and even though he had sought her out, she wondered if she were only making matters worse. This notion cut through her confused impressions and she went with it. "Okay, you can go. You can fucking go. But you're going to call me, if you need to." Bobby seemed to mull that statement, but stood up, nodding his head. It was unclear to Ellen if he even heard what she said. She hesitated, stopping him once more. "I'm serious, Bobby. We have an extra bedroom, with a sleeper. Hannah will be here any minute. It's Saturday night. It'll be safe here. We can get a little drunk and watch a movie."

Bobby took Ellen in his arms, shaking his head, whispering in her ear. He had turned once more—the anger gone, the compassion real. "I won't forget this. You've always been good to me, girl."

He strode out the door with Ellen trailing him, then crossed the lawn to his car, not once looking back.

**

His eyes adjusted to the dim of his house's entry hall. He could make out the ghostly outlines of living room furnishings, the stairs at the end of the room, the sliding glass door out into the backyard. As it always did, the oppressively unkempt quality to the downstairs, which he thought indicative of a bunch of unruly young men, darkened his mood further. Bobby took several tentative steps through the living room, as if he were afraid he would trip on unseen debris. He picked his way to the stairs, then took them purposefully, two at a time. The upstairs hallway was almost pitch-black, but Bobby felt his way past the first three bedrooms and the bathroom until he arrived at his room at the end of the hall.

He could see the faded shadow of his bed, almost consuming the entire room. He walked over to it, flopped down and hunched over at the waist, taking his head in his hands, remaining like that for several seconds. Then he opened the bottom desk drawer and heard the familiar rattling sound of the plastic bottle of Xanax. He guessed that it still held about forty pills. He sat back on the bed with the pill bottle in hand, holding onto that number, thinking it through. Surely forty pills, he thought, combined with a liter of alcohol, surely that would be sufficient.

He stood up and went to the closet, finding a liter lodged in a folded blanket, and returned to the bed. In the past there had been fleeting moments when he considered ending it all but they were just that—fleeting and vaporous, a momentary dalliance with the idea. This particular line of inquiry went deeper, settling in his mind to such an extent that he could feel the psychic contours of the issue. A series of questions occurred to him. How long would he lie in this room before he was discovered, hours or days? Which unlucky member of the band would find him? Would that person ever forgive him? And not least of all, how would it feel? How would it feel approaching permanent darkness, a darkness more complete than any he had ever known?

He sat with these questions and others. Then he typed a text message into his phone: *Sylvie, may I come over? Right now, you're my last stop on earth.* He looked at it for a minute, then sent it. Then he simply sat, the bottle of pills in one hand, the bottle of alcohol lying on its side by the bed. He did not know what he would do if she didn't text back. He waited, the moments crawling forward. Finally his phone vibrated.

What do you mean, last stop on earth? Sylvie replied.

He took a long breath through his nose, hardly inclined to explain himself. He wrote a message, minimizing the situation, and sent it. *Nothing special, just alone and fresh out of places to be. I just feel like it would be nice to see you.*

He thought she might ask about Lara, insist on further context, but the text returned in a flash. *You're welcome to come over, but please bring a good bit with you. That would be most welcome.*

**

The trees along Guadalupe seemed to him crowded and close in a way he had never experienced, the shadows of the leaves under the streetlights passing across the windshield. He had brought with him the combination box, which he placed in the trunk, and a fresh liter of Evan Williams and the bottle of Xanax, which sat next to him on the passenger seat. He drove, his face grave, his right hand gripping the steering wheel, his knuckles white. He was very much aware that he approached what could prove to be a fluid situation without planning and agenda, and he barely slowed as he came to the driveway of Sylvie's tiny complex, the left wheel bumping the curb, the gravel grinding beneath his tires. He braked hard.

He scrambled out of the car, popped the trunk, and opened the combination box, snapping up packets two at a time. He removed just short of ten packets to supplement the two in his pocket—he had decided he would join her in any reckless binge—and then he collected the whiskey and Xanax. He scurried up the stairs and knocked.

She stood there, slender and dark-haired, her expression nondescript but her eyebrows raised, poised like an impending question. Once again, he was struck by her delicate facial features and small breasts, by the energy of her form. She stepped back from the doorway without a word, and he hurried inside. The room was mostly dark. On a card table he poured two grams of coke, cut it into six lines, and inhaled three. Sylvie opened another packet and took three lines in succession.

As the rush commenced, he slowed somewhat, his agitation temporarily mollified, the action of the drug blunting his thoughts. Sylvie sat down at the table, her large, dark, inscrutable eyes dominating her heart-shaped face. She wore only black shorts and a gray T-shirt. For a moment, her eyes darted about without purpose, but then they fixed on him. He shook off a spooked feeling, guessing that she'd simply been impatient for the drugs, but now that she'd had a little and access to more, she had calmed down. She poured out another packet, formed one enormous line, and hit it, rubbing her nose, snuffling.

"You're not with your girlfriend tonight," she said, looking down at the table, her observation noncommittal.

"No," said Bobby, eyeing her. "I'm not."

Bobby made no attempt to amplify or to contextualize, wanting the present situation to unfold gradually. He hit the three remaining lines, inhaling them through a $20 bill. He remarked to himself—two grams apiece, gone in under a couple of minutes. He uncapped the whiskey and downed two large swigs straight from the bottle. He extended it to Sylvie, who declined.

She pointed to the bottle of pills. "Are those Valium, Xanax?"

"Xanax."

"Do you mind?"

"It's why I brought them."

He shook out a couple of pills and passed them to her. She took one, swallowing it. Then she opened another packet, this time forming only one line, a modest one. Still, she hit it without hesitation.

Bobby watched her sit back in her chair, her chin raised, a curiously genteel mannerism, as if they were at a tea party. He remarked again at her odd engagement with the moment—how she could seem absent, but in the next instant he would come to understand she had been entirely present all along.

He considered his statement before he said it. "It didn't work out with my girlfriend in Cuero," he said, controlling his voice so it wouldn't crack. He half shrugged. "It just didn't."

"I'm sorry," she said, as if it were an afterthought. "You seemed to like her."

"I did." The moments passed in silence. As he sat, the rush magnified, and he reached for the whiskey and took another enormous swig, then wiped his mouth with the back of his hand. The whiskey countered the coke, but then he knew the coke was really starting to take effect because his libido magnified in an instant, and he found his eyes moving over her. She watched him, carefully, hitting another line, sitting back in the chair. His sixth sense told him that a pass would not be welcome, at least just yet; he knew he had a point to make and he stumbled in search of it. He sought a moderate tone. "When I started doing this, this dating thing, I told myself I wanted a normal girl. You know, Saturday night dates—restaurants and music and downtown. Cut back the drugs, cut back the drinking. I don't know. That was the general idea. But maybe I was wrong."

She emptied more from her packet, her third, forming a line but hesitating. Her hollow eyes turned reflective. "How were you wrong?"

Bobby regarded the slender, angular face, parsing his words so that they would not be overtly sexual. "Because maybe what I was looking for in the first place is this."

She looked away from him but her voice changed, became stronger, as if she were making a point. "This speculative relationship, would this be the basis? Gram after gram?"

"With a bottle of whiskey thrown in." He smiled sheepishly. "No, it wouldn't be. I was just playing."

"Then what would be?"

Bobby sat back in his chair, looking at her. "We're alike."

She seemed almost amused. "We are?"

"Yes."

"And how's that? How are we alike?"

"It's obvious—a child could see it."

She paused, as if she were postulating. "You mean, like, we're both damaged?"

Bobby flinched slightly, her words biting into him, but he deftly brushed aside the question. He looked around the dark room, encapsulating his answer by calling attention to the emptiness of the place. "No, we're both alone." She, too, flinched. "Come on, Sylvie." He wanted to reach across the table, take her hand, but he kept to himself. "I think we're alike, that's all. Enough alike. Common experience, common vocabulary."

She closed her eyes again, momentarily hanging her head. "I don't think you know what you're saying." Her brow furrowed, signifying a faint projection of disquiet. She took the second Xanax, swallowing, again averting her eyes.

Bobby felt a sudden need to burrow further, to defend himself. "You were talking about your father the other day." Bobby waited, allowing her time to speak, but she didn't, and he continued on. "Or rather, you didn't talk about him. I notice things like that."

"Good for you."

"So what happened with your father? Did he do something to you?"

She winced and Bobby felt embarrassed that he had asked such a direct and impolitic question. Sylvie folded her hands on the table. "No, he didn't. He was a very decent man."

"Then, what happened?"

Her voice again changed in volume, a force underpinning her words. "I don't talk about my father, Bobby."

He felt rebuffed, but his anger didn't flair, the curious intimacy of the scene creating an abiding calm. He waited. "Funny," he began. "That's funny, because before today, I didn't talk about my father either." His voice lowered involuntarily. "I think I know . . ." He reached over and took the whiskey, taking one great swallow. He breathed out. "The thing is, I think I found out the name of my father today. Kyle. I'm pretty sure his name is Kyle."

Silence pervaded the room, and then Sylvie sought eye contact. "How did you find out?"

"Mom kept a journal. For a while, at least. I ran across it."

"You didn't know his name until today?"

"No, I knew nothing." He thought, then shook his head. "I suppose, with my aunt's help, I'll find out his full name."

Sylvie was as still as a cat, her face revealing nothing. "And assuming you find out, what are you going to do?"

"I don't know," said Bobby. In a moment, like Sylvie, the affect had left his voice. "Maybe nothing."

She countered, more engaged with him than ever. "Funny, that doesn't sound like you."

His shoulders tightened, bunching up together. "Well, what would be the point?" he said. He turned to the bank of windows and stood, the lights of East Austin blinking against the backdrop of the dark horizon. He put his fingers to the glass. "You see, Sylvie, I'm tired of days like today." He took an awkward step backwards, almost as if the urgency of his emotions affected his balance. He was unsteady, and returned to his chair. Sylvie was motionless. He considered the situation, then opened a packet, cut two lines, and hit them both. He leaned back in his chair, trying to reorient his feelings. He looked at her, at her fragile, perilous beauty. The coke took immediate effect; he knew he wanted her. But he also knew that he wasn't reaching her, that they were somehow separated. He thought quickly, then he told himself that unlike most other women, his past would not divide them, but join them, and he formed a plan in a moment. The words began slowly. "She said she'd take me to the beach," he began. "No, not the beach. To the ocean, I think she said. Funny, I still remember that, in Cuero, a long time ago." He drank from the bottle, swallowing once, twice. "I was six years old. That was the beginning."

He looked down at the tabletop and saw a sticker depicting a little red demon woman with a pointed tail and small horns. The demon woman smiled coyly, as if letting him in on a joke. He re-evaluated, then continued. "There was a boyfriend. He wasn't so bad, the first one. I'd forgotten his name until today. Kurt. Saw it in Mom's journal. It didn't take long before he saw the handwriting on the wall, so he left. She was rarely ever single more than a month. So, there was another boyfriend. Then another. They began to run together.

"The boyfriends I could deal with. But it was her, you see. Her. I was so young, but I could see it. Like when someone goes blind, their other senses heighten. A different awareness. And she was losing her grip, a tiny bit every day. So slowly, it was hard to see. But I saw it, I watched it. I laid awake at night. I wanted her to get help, but then sometimes, I just wanted her to go away."

He stopped. In the thin pool of lamplight, Sylvie held the straw over a line but her eyes were trained on him. With her gray shirt and moon-white face, she looked vaguely spectral, and Bobby could not tell if she was connecting to his story. His voice lowered, as if he were starting a new thread of exposition. "I thought about that often, over several years. How old I was when I first thought it, I don't know. How badly I wanted to get away from Corpus. Never seeing her again." He paused. "Hating her."

Sylvie sat up straight, easing her shoulders back, her lips parted. She was listening, he could tell, and this emboldened him.

"There was one time, before the hard drugs started. We still had a relatively decent apartment, the boyfriend wasn't that bad; he had a real day job. I think I was almost twelve. I woke up one night needing to piss and walked out my door and she was in the living room. This was like three o'clock in the morning. She was on the sofa, the TV wasn't on, and she was smoking. Chain-smoking, the ashtray was filled to overflowing. She was staring straight ahead. I must have made a noise, something, because she was suddenly aware of me. Her face was drawn, white, her eyes just sort of dead. She said to me, 'I seem to be having trouble sleeping.' Then she turned back to the wall. That was it. Just that.

"Things got worse. Fast. It was almost bewildering. At first, she was always drunk. Hardcore. She stank of alcohol all the time. She couldn't hold a job for more than a few days, the boyfriends dried up. We lived off peanut butter, white bread, oranges. But then something changed. Not with her so much, but the money returned, just a little bit. She was now gone most nights, all night long, and if she came back, it was always with a guy who was gone in the morning. I didn't care because we could afford luxuries like canned ravioli and basic cable.

"Life got all out of whack. I started staying up late watching TV, I stopped going to school. She didn't care, so I didn't care. We got calls. Someone from the school, I think, I don't know. Not a cop exactly. For a couple of days, someone would knock on the door mid-morning. I didn't answer and she was out like a light. There was a call, this time from the police. Then we moved into a hotel room, then we moved again, this time into another apartment. She was still gone nights. She barely said a word to me. The calls stopped.

"Then one time she was gone for two nights straight. After the second night, I got up and she wasn't there and there was a stash of whiskey. I started drinking, watching TV, and got plenty drunk, fast. Sometime in the afternoon, I could hear laughter outside, loud and ear-piercing, like a bird shrieking. The lock turned and it was her. She could barely stand up straight and she staggered and she was with this little white guy not much taller than me. As soon as I laid eyes on him, I didn't like him. Her face was thin and her eyes were clouded but she laughed, and she said, 'Bobby, I want you to meet Vyasa.' And I said, 'What the hell?' and she repeated herself, 'I want you to meet Vyasa.' And I said, 'Is that a name?' and this time the little guy answered, his chest puffed up, and he said, 'Yes, it is. A holy name in India.'

"The next thing I remember, we were living with him. It happened so fast. He wanted me to do these little 'errands,' he called them, just taking these packages to this woman's apartment. The woman had a son my age, and she would take the package and call to her son and ask me to stay and watch TV for a while. After about thirty minutes, the woman would say, 'Okay, you can leave now.' It took a week for it to sink in that I was a mule.

"Meanwhile, my mother, she . . . she . . . she was staggering about, speechless. She was now neck-deep in the hard stuff and it immediately took a toll. At first, I was afraid—for me, for her. Then I got angry. But I just buried it, deeper, the anger, and then I put two and two together. She didn't work anymore, and even if she did, there was no way she could support that kind of habit, and it became clear to me I was the trade-off."

He wondered at the sound of his voice, if he was so caught up in the telling that he would fail to moderate himself, as if his hatred might spill over and infect the entire room. Sylvie had returned her gaze to a blank wall, her expression empty and unknowable. Bobby was sure she was listening, and he continued. "I had friends who told me Austin was the only place within 500 miles of Corpus that was cool. I began to think of Austin. Dream of it. So I made contacts in the neighborhood, asked around, made a plan. I had a notion to stay at it as a mule once I got here. It was the only job I'd done. I'd gotten about halfway here when I crossed the wrong guy; I was being a little punk, just young and stupid, thinking the guy was too spaced out to count the number of rocks I had smoked. He didn't take kindly to it. The police found me, all beat up. Funny enough, this was just outside of Cuero, so I told them to call my aunt.

"I was halfway an addict, probably would have been a full-on crackhead but I had no money. My aunt took me in, warts and all. She got me back in school, began to turn me around. Ever since then, I've been at least two different people, and I never know which one is going to show up—the boy raised by my mother, or the boy raised by my aunt. I thought I was close today, walking through that third door you talked about, walking through it and not looking back. But I'm thinking it will never end, there will always be something to stare down, some fuckup to amend, so why keep trying."

Bobby stopped and the apartment went silent. He could see Sylvie in the half-light, and once again, he noted her lightly muscled limbs, her slender torso. In an instant, he stood, not worrying about the consequences of an approach. He rounded the table and dropped to his knees, cupping Sylvie's chin in his fingers, then placing his head in her lap. He looked up at her and she returned his gaze. She spoke first.

"Why did you come here tonight?"

Bobby noted where he knelt, almost supplicated before her. "Come on, girl, you know why I'm here."

Bobby thought her poise indicated a sophistication of perception that rivaled, perhaps exceeded, Lara's. She shook her head, almost imperceptibly. "Do you really think we're alike? Really alike?"

"Yes, I do."

"I wonder." She waited. "Have you ever hurt anyone? Really hurt them?"

"You mean, like girlfriends, breakups?"

"No, that's not what I mean."

For as long as he had known her, Sylvie had been resistant to talking, but now he could see she had something to tell him. She began, speaking quietly, almost in a monotone.

**

"My father died when I was fourteen. I didn't handle it well. This was in San Antonio. I was in eighth grade with kids I'd known for years, but suddenly, it was like there was this barrier between me and them. A glass barrier; you could see through it, but you couldn't touch. I stopped hanging with my friends. There was this guy; he was a bit older. Nineteen, or that's what he told me. We started up a thing but I had to keep it quiet for obvious reasons, keep it secret. Mom wasn't doing too well, either, sort of vacant. So, this guy and I have this thing—I'd go to his house and we messed around, listen to albums. He was into the Sex Pistols, so then, so was I. Blondie. The guy said he was post-punk, had these black leather pants, shirts with the sleeves ripped out, a poster of Sid Vicious.

"He showed me speed, coke. I guess it was fun, but I came home one night and I was still creeching and Mother saw. She didn't get angry, she got scared. For me. She was already fucked up enough about Dad, and I couldn't look at her, couldn't be in the same room with her, not with her like she was. The dishes piled high in the sink, the roaches everywhere. She had always been a housewife, the whole place nice and neat, sack lunches, now there were times she wore the same shirt for days. There was a visit by a woman from the state. This woman took me in a room, asked me the last time I wore clean clothes, stuff like that. I didn't like how this was going, so I got together with a friend and she knew a friend of her own here in town, and her friend had a friend, said she had a room for me in Austin. Said she could get me an ID. I made the decision to move, broke up with my boyfriend. I was fifteen.

"I left Mom a note but didn't tell her where I was going, told her I was old enough to take care of myself. I remember the ride here like it was yesterday. The hills off to the left, distant, sometimes close. When you come at Austin from the south, sometimes it feels like you're going downhill, like you're descending on the city. It was different here, had a different feel. I got the ID, got a job washing dishes in a club, the after-hours parties with employees, musicians, a little bit of coke now and then. People didn't treat me like a kid, I think, because I didn't act like one. There was this guy, Stan; he was in his thirties. It wasn't like that—he had a wife, Margaret. They were completely cool; they were trying to help. They asked me why I wasn't in school, and I said because I didn't want to go. They had an extra room. Stan was a musician, his wife was a painter. She began to show me these art books—Rembrandt, Vermeer, Van Gogh, those are the ones I remember best. I would look at the Van Goghs in the book, the swirling colors, and she set up a canvas for me in an empty room. Said I should try to paint whatever it was I was feeling. The paintings never really came out right.

"I was working at Lucy in Disguise, a costume shop. It was a part-time day job. There were these kids working along with me. They were a couple of years older, although I didn't let on that I was younger. But they seemed older. Three of them, two boys and a girl. They could get alcohol, they could anything, it seemed, and that's when they showed me heroin. I was still living with Stan, washing dishes on the weekend, working at the costume shop during the week. The first time I tried heroin, I passed out in just a few minutes. The girl said I did good because I didn't throw up. The second time, there was some coke there, and I knew. I knew this was it, what I was looking for in the first place. I remember what it let out—all that with my father, it was forgotten, in the moment at least. The night just before me, like it was something wild and unknowable. Then things progressed, just shards of memories, then I came to. It was three days later, I was in a room in a house I didn't know.

"I returned to Stan's place and they listened to me, they were respectful, but they told me what had happened was dangerous. I couldn't disagree, so I went back to work. Stan and Margaret made me promise I would leave Lucy in Disguise, and I did. I washed dishes, and by then, I had gotten to know restaurant work, so I started waiting tables. Don't get me wrong, I still used. I still did coke and pot and drank any chance I got. If someone had speed, all the better. I was young. I could go all night and go to work the next day, no problem. As for Stan and Margaret, I kept my habit secret from them. So, I had a place to sleep, I ate at the restaurant, I had some friends, kind of. I mean, they were a lot like you. We had certain things in common. Things were all right but I knew I couldn't keep away. I got hold of one of the boys from the costume shop, we agreed to meet, and all three came. We divided up a couple of balloons; I made sure there was plenty of coke. After the third day, we had run out of money, and I turned my first trick, a middle-aged guy off South Lamar. I just hung out on the sidewalk as cars went by. It's like magic; guys know somehow. Maybe it's in the walk. So, I turned a couple more, and I kept going.

"When I came back to Stan and Margaret, she was in tears—she had never been there, but she knew people who had. They called a city-funded rehab center, tried to get me in, but by that point, I had gathered my clothes, left them a note, and climbed out of a bedroom window. I never saw them again. I met another street girl. She was a couple of years older, she had a room. Bianca. I stayed there. I got a new ID that said I was eighteen, so I got work at a strip club, turned tricks on the street if I needed extra money. By this point, I was sixteen, and knew any number of people in town. At the club, I made good money, so I could work one night, and go all day and night the next day, then come back to the club. I shot up in between my toes so my arms weren't bruised. But then one day, I started going, got hold of some really good coke, and it was a whole other level, and then I woke up the following week.

"I was in Midland, five hours away. In the desert. I had only a vague recollection about how I got there. I was pretty fucked up. There was this couple. They said we could score big for cheap, they said they knew people out there. Hours in a pickup truck, the dead of night. A faint sunrise as we approached the town. Their connection was a waste—

terrible, shitty coke and no heroin. Shitty like everything else in that godforsaken town. I hitched back, returned to the club, put an ad in *The Austin Chronicle*. You know, *escorting*, the polite term for a trick. At first, most days I found a balance. If I got off, I could always return to the club. And so it went. A couple of years go by. I kept in contact with Bianca. I had access to money. That's when I met Will.

"For a trick, he was younger than usual, in his early thirties, I think. Attractive, polite. He had his own place, a dog and a cat, but one look at him, you knew there was something wrong. He seemed to enjoy paying for sex, but at the same time, I could somehow sense he hated what he was doing, like he was acting against his will. Still, he was very sweet. He had all these books, history books, books about the world wars, Hitler, Stalin, books a thousand pages long. I saw him a handful of times as an escort, then one time, he asked me what else I did. I asked him what he meant. He said he could tell, could see it on my face—the coke, the heroin. He said he was curious, would pay me extra if I cut him in when we saw each other. I had been having ups and downs at the one club, so I moved on to another club, but then I had the same problems. I had lost weight, managers looking at me funny, like my drug use was taking too obvious a physical toll. But I needed the extra money. So I agreed to cut Will in a little, with the coke only, not with the heroin. Something about him told me he couldn't handle smack.

"Days were starting to blur together. I would nod off in the afternoon and wake up the next day. It was Austin, so it was safer than a lot of places. I was never robbed, beat up, whatever. I passed by a window down on South Lamar and saw my reflection. That's what the managers saw, too, how much weight I'd lost. I took cabs all over town; cabbies were cool. I did more coke than heroin and had one source for the brown stuff. He was crazy unreliable. He was an addict, so I did less of it; I wasn't hooked, not quite. I always managed to have money, I managed to keep it together, and if I got out of whack, it wasn't that bad. There was even a month or two, a lull, I just kind of got tired of using. I put weight back on, even did these kickboxing classes, had extra money to eat out. It got so far I thought that maybe I was going to kick. I guess that was probably far-fetched but I thought it at the time.

"Will called and I thought it would be cool seeing him, that I could make a little money with someone nice, do some coke, chill. He was watching *Titanic*. He was a real movie buff, too, and so we fool around, do a little powder, and I have some brown with me, so I go to the bathroom. I'm not going to do it with him. I have a spoon, all the works, and I use a candle for the cook. It's no big deal, I've shot up in a client's bathroom lots of times, so I do it. It must have been strong. I was so far out of it I didn't hide the candle, clean up after myself. I come out of the bathroom and we do some more coke. I did more, so did he, but then I'm nodding off. I wake up in the dead of night and turn on a light. Will was in bed, his head slumped in a pillow, his face turned. That's when I see it. The bloat, the purple face, the white shit in his mouth. He was stiff already. The dog on the floor whimpering, the cat pacing around the bed. I must have left some heroin and he did it, just like he'd always wanted. I'm not sure what to do. But then, I get scared, I get my shit, I got out of there. I called 911 from a payphone at a gas station. This was two years ago.

"I tried to forget about Will. There are days, maybe only

hours, when he is out of mind. I told myself I didn't cook the dope, didn't put the needle in, didn't even offer it to him. That's what I tell myself. Sometimes I can see his face there at the end, so clearly I can see it—his eyes open, sightless, as if at the end he was fighting the inevitable, trying but failing to find it in himself not to die. There are days when I begin to have little regard for myself. There was one month, about a year ago, that I just went and went. I ended up in a motel room in El Paso; a pimp tried to lure me to Juarez. I told myself that I had to put this behind me, that it would be the end of me. I try hard and find I can lay off, at least for a while. But then things build and build and I see Will again, see his face, and maybe I can handle it and maybe I can't. Maybe I go off. I was in a lull when I first saw you at the bar, but I can feel it now. Things are building."

**

As her story ended, Bobby returned to his chair at the other end of the table. Neither one of them did any coke. Bobby opened the bottle of Xanax, took two, and drank whiskey straight from the bottle. He passed the bottle of Xanax to Sylvie, and she popped one pill, then another seconds later, then one more. She refused the whiskey. Out the window, the East Side lights flickered like fireflies.

"I know there are just a handful of people who can hear that," she said. "Can hear that story and know there's not a lot for me to do."

Bobby immediately understood she was talking about herself, about her addiction. "But there are doctors," said Bobby. "There are facilities. You can get help."

"I would do it if I thought it would work, but I don't think it will."

"You don't know that."

Sylvie talked to a wall, facing away from Bobby, but her tone was curiously intimate. "Don't tell me there haven't been times when you've thought the same thing. Maybe, in fact, you were thinking that way even tonight."

Bobby looked out at the expanse of glowing lights. "If I were, it doesn't mean I was right about it."

The intimacy to her voice remained, but she also sounded removed, investigating something deeply interior. "You don't feel resigned? Trapped?"

"At times I do. But I guess it passes, eventually."

Her eyes were wide, absorbed. "And you come to your better senses, right?"

"Something like that."

"I don't think I do," said Sylvie. "Come back to my better senses."

"The doctors could maybe work with you on that."

Her mouth moving dismissively, as if she were expelling Bobby's idea. "Perhaps, but I'm not sure I want their help in the first place."

Bobby tried to stand up, alarmed, but his head began spinning and he sat back down. "You're not going to hurt yourself, are you, Sylvie?"

She waited a moment, considering the question. "I think the question is, are *you* going to hurt *your*self?"

He thought about it, then answered guardedly. "I was going to, maybe. I was thinking about it. But now, no, I'm not going to hurt myself. Not tonight." He waited for her to say something. "And you?"

"I would never hurt myself. Not directly." She paused. "But indirectly, that's another story."

"You should get help. You should try."

Sylvie stood and extended her hand in his direction.

This time he found a modicum of equilibrium, standing and taking her hand and trailing her as they made their way to the bed, sitting side-by-side. Bobby took off his shoes but nothing else, not feeling even a remnant of sexual longing. Sylvie wrapped an arm around his shoulders and gently pulled him until they were both lying down, face-to-face. Her expression was blank but her voice was soft.

"Sometimes I feel like I see things," she began. "Things that haven't happened yet. I feel like I see you, see you five years from now. You won't be the same person. It won't go by the book. It'll be hard, but I think I see you finding your way. Ups and downs, but finally you're going to come to a place, and you'll stay there. It'll be good, this place. A good place. The third door, you'll find it. I think I see that, Bobby."

Bobby reached out and took her hand, squeezed it. She squeezed back, the briefest of smiles. Between the whiskey and pills, Bobby was entering a phase of real disorientation. "What about you? What do you see for you?"

She cut her eyes away from him. "About what you were saying earlier, I think you're wrong. I don't think we're alike, Bobby, and I think if you're honest with yourself you'll agree. You see, I don't feel divided. I feel overwhelmed. And I don't see anything. That used to terrify me but now I find it rather comforting. One day there will simply be nothing, and that will be that. If anything, I won't think about my father, see Will's face any longer. There's peace in emptiness, in a void. I find that comforting, too."

Bobby reached over, moving a strand of hair off her cheek. He thought to himself that she was lovely. "Please, Sylvie, you just said you wouldn't hurt yourself."

"And I won't. Not directly." She smiled shyly and rubbed his cheek with her fingertips.

He shook his head, but the light-headedness accelerated, and his eyes closed. He opened his mouth to say something but his eyes closed involuntarily. "Tonight, Bobby, I am here with you. But don't look for me tomorrow. By the morning I'll be gone."

**

He awoke suddenly, shaking off a dream he could not recollect. He lay there, the vestiges of the dream dissolving, and he breathed. At last, he sat up. It was a bright morning and the room was filled with a grainy light. He turned to where Sylvie had slept but there was nothing there save for a balled-up blanket, and he looked about, seeing if she might be somewhere else in the apartment. His eyes darted into every corner, but the room was empty, the bathroom door open and that room dark. He stood, still fully clothed except for his shoes, and went to the table and checked his phone, which contained no voicemail or texts. It was eleven o'clock. He composed a quick text and sent it to Sylvie: *Where'd you go? Will you call me later?*

He remained standing, unsure what to do next. He continued rummaging through the table and discovered no note. He realized he was very thirsty, so he made for a kitchen cabinet and found a plastic cup, filling it with water and drinking greedily. He refilled the cup, drank half of it, then placed it on a cabinet, the sound of the plastic hitting wood strangely loud in the silent apartment. Suddenly, his phone vibrated—a text from Sylvie: *What would we talk about? I think we've said all we have to say to each other.*

He cocked his head, his hands moving over the display. He considered engaging her remark, wanting to argue that perhaps they did have something more to say, but he could not think what that might be.

I wish you had said goodbye.

It took only a moment for the phone to vibrate.

I'm not good at goodbyes, Bobby, and I thought it might be awkward in the morning light.

He was about to reply, sure that he had more to say to her, but he drew a complete blank. The phone vibrated again.

The bottom line, Bobby, is that you need to let go of me. We're different, you see, because I'm not tired of this shit. Not tired at all. Because I want it to go on. On and on. So we have no future. We won't meet again.

After a couple more seconds, the phone vibrated a final time.

I think you're closer than you realize.

He looked up from his phone. Was she right? He was unsure. The doubt it engendered created a momentary paralysis and he stood frozen by the table when, all at once, he felt as though she were right, that they *were* different—for all the past and present chaos in his life, her story was more fragmented, harsher, darker. Her next-to-last text had summed it up best—he wanted to quit the life, she did not. The realization left him strangely conflicted, since he generally felt far more connected to fringe elements like Sylvie than to ordinary folk. It twisted his bearings, produced a moment of minor disorientation. He shook his head, trying to dispel the confusion, and looked around the gray shell of a room—the table, the bed, the dresser, the emptiness and finality of the space. Gathering his things quickly, he headed for the door, locking it as he closed it and descending the stairs.

When he came to his car, he opened the trunk and made sure the combination box was still there. It was. He looked up to her window. Though he and Sylvie had hardly been together (Bobby would be hard put to say whether they could even be called friends), he felt as though their short-lived connection was intricate and unique, and he felt a pang of misgiving and loss. He opened the car door and got inside, adjusting the angle of his rearview mirror to look one last time at her window. He started the car, idling, still gazing into the mirror, then he backed up and turned the wheel, Sylvie's window disappearing from view.

**

An hour later, he was sitting alone on the sofa in the living room of his house, still dressed in his clothes from the day before. He stared at the TV, which was off, pondering his own reflection in the gray-black screen. At his feet rested a highball glass filled with ice and whiskey, but in his hands he held his phone, looking again and again at Sylvie's last texted remarks to him: . . . *you're closer than you realize.* He puzzled over the words. Contemplating the overall gist of the statement, Bobby was pretty sure she meant he was nearer to full recovery than he cared to admit, but the details of the phrase nagged at him. The word "closer," in particular, bothered him. How close was he? Actually close, or closer than he thought, which could still be light-years away?

Then, apart from whatever Sylvie said or meant, there was the larger matter. If he were really approaching full recovery, how did he explain the previous twenty-four hours? Surely, he thought, those were not the acts of a man on the brink of disavowing drink and drugs, perhaps on the verge of self-discovery. Sheer logic suggested that he was as mired in the swamp of his past as ever, and this mulling over things led to nothing.

His line of thinking continued uninterrupted—so he was trapped, as always. It was a familiar feeling, a familiar mode of thought. He embraced the feeling; the commonplace nature of it was almost comforting. For a long while, his aspect was impassive, impossible to read, but then he scowled. Is that really where he would leave matters? That things had always been this way, that he had once fucked up and so he will fuck up again, and why try to fight it? This led to a slow-building conclusion: *this sounded like something his mother would think*. His thoughts jumped about and he considered his mother, seeing her not as she was the previous day, but when she was young, how she could summon up vibrance at will, and he asked himself, where was *his* youth, *his* vibrance? Had his mother sucked it from him long ago? With that, he grew furious, his face turning crimson and his hands forming fists. With a sudden movement, he reached down to the floor for his whiskey and he brought it to his lips, but then he pulled the glass back, keeping himself from drinking at the last instant.

He lowered the glass to his lap, simply sitting there, his face impassive once again.

Finally, he stood, making for the stairway, the ice cubes rattling. He came to his room and immediately sat down at his desk, going for the bottom drawer and gathering up his black spiral binder. He opened the binder and a blank page confronted him and he took up a pen, sitting very still and placing the tip of the pen directly over the paper. He concentrated, and finally wrote:

Am I really just going to lay down and die? Give up without a fight? That seems pretty fucking weak.

He stopped writing and thought about his words. Then

he resumed.

But if I try, am I biting off more than I can chew? I mean, can I do it? Stop it with the drugs, the drinking? Do I even want to do it?

Another pause, more reflection. Once again, the pen engaged the paper.

Gramps used to say that it's always darkest before the dawn and I used to think that was really fucking dumb. In my experience, bad things lead to more bad things. But I don't know, maybe he knew more than I ever gave him credit for. In the final analysis, can you really tell if you've come to the end of something? If so, how do you know?

He stopped writing, looking at the questions, then he looked at the highball glass. It glistened, the bottom half of it beaded with condensation. He wrote:

The answer is, you don't know.

The pen dropped from his hand and he reflected on the notebook entry. Several variations of the same thought occurred to him. Yes, he probably should give it another go at abstaining from drugs and alcohol, but the catch was simple—for how long? A day or two? A week? Maybe abstinence days? Monday, Wednesday, and Thursday, leaving the weekend open? Maybe go long, go big, perhaps until the end of the year? As his consideration of the time frame increased, his thoughts slowed, arriving at a thrilling but nauseating prospect. For good. Forever. Never another line or drink again. Was it possible? Did he really and truly have it in him to finally quit? He pondered that question, cupping his chin in his hand, staring remotely at the white wall directly before him. He certainly could not quit for good with so much alcohol in the house. He looked again at the sweating glass on his desk, his eyes trained on it.

With little fanfare, he grabbed the glass and trotted it

to the bathroom. He beheld his reflection in the mirror—his hair in disarray, his clothes a mess from sleeping in them. Then he looked beyond the superficialities, into his eyes, and he saw doubt. So much doubt, in fact, that it scared him. He sat with his anxiety, then mustered new resolve. He poured the whiskey and ice into the sink and listened to it gurgle down into the drain.

He blinked, unsure how he was feeling. The doubt ebbed and then returned with unsettling speed, and his breathing increased. His mind zeroed in on the alcohol. To his way of thinking, this was his most fundamental problem. Through all this, he told himself he should give it a shot, not drinking, and he should learn to live with the uncertainty. But the alcohol had to go. He said it out loud: "It simply has to go." He returned to his room, an intensity to his motions. He reached up to the top shelf of the closet, pulled out a musty blanket, and unfolded it, and a glass pint fell to the carpet. Bobby picked up the pint and tossed it on the bed. He continued to rifle through the closet and took out a heavy winter coat, reaching into the inside pocket and taking out another pint. This, too, he threw on the bed. Down on his knees, he scoured the floor of the closet. A pair of boots, years old but still appearing rather new because he never wore them after the move to Austin, caught his eye. He pulled out one of the boots and this time found a fifth crammed inside.

He moved from the closet and began going through his desk drawers. A half pint was stored with the pencils, a pint was stashed inside a three-ring binder he never used, a liter turned on its side at the back of the bottom drawer. He dashed down the stairs and opened up a kitchen cabinet. He always kept a liter on the bottom shelf of the pantry but nothing more, afraid his housemates would pilfer the supply if the house went dry. At last, satisfied he had found them all, he took them to the bathroom and emptied them into the sink one by one, the tap going the whole time. He emptied each bottle and monitored his breathing, resisting the urge to take a swig as he did so, the craving for alcohol so acute his shoulders drew together and his neck lurched forward. He came to the final bottle, a liter. He reached for the cap but froze, shaking the bottle once, listening to the alcohol slosh around. He moved to the cap again but stopped once more, holding the bottle out at arm's length. This went on for a short while, but finally, he slid to the floor, cradling the bottle in his arms and choking back a sob. At last, he stood and poured, the liter emptying out, and he lowered the empty bottle to the basin with a loud thwack. His breathing was elevated, his heart racing. Stumbling to his room with the empty bottle in hand, he flopped on the bed, exhausted by the rigors of the last twenty-four hours. He dropped the bottle to the carpet, and within minutes, he was asleep.

**

He awoke just after six in the evening, the room enveloped in darkness. Although he had not partaken in drink all afternoon, the alcohol, the coke, and the pills from the night before all lingered in his system, and he was still hungover. He sat on the edge of his bed, his first thoughts turning to drink when he remembered what he had done earlier in the day. His next thought arrived unbidden but it was undeniable, a thought with which he knew he had to live—that alcohol could be easily purchased. He berated himself—he had come this far, at least he could give it a week. Evaluate how he felt at the end of the week and he could go on from there.

He washed in the bathroom, changed clothes, went downstairs, and turned on a football game. He ignored the game, unsure what to do with himself with no drink in hand. For years, the goal of each day had been to blot out the night, to achieve unconsciousness before falling asleep, certainly upon lying down. Now there was no goal, and he felt adrift, like a cork bobbing in the tide, meandering in whatever direction the current took him.

He reconsidered the situation, reminding himself of his other major problem and that he still had the combination box, and while the contents of the box did not lead to unconsciousness, they did alter consciousness, and maybe that was all he needed on this particular night. He held that thought, those feelings, simply letting them linger while he examined them, but he held resolute. Still, the craving persisted, the obsession of the mind refusing to diminish when a separate thought occurred to him—just give it away. Give it to Jason and be done with it. It would save having to go through the logistics of selling back to Ray, even if he would take a $2,000 to $3,000 loss. Just hours before, he would not have entertained the notion out of overweening pride, but he thought the immediate solution so simple, the answer so obvious, he would not allow ego to stand in its path. He considered the plan another second or two but saw no drawbacks. It was simple and direct. Standing and grabbing his keys off the kitchen pass-through, he went out to the car, made sure the box was in the trunk, then headed further east.

As always, the street was lined by a handful of pickup trucks, a stray car or two. Jason's mammoth black truck dominated the driveway. Bobby got out of the car, went to the trunk and pulled out the box, strode across the street and around the truck, and deposited the box at Jason's door. He returned to his car, picked up his phone and tapped out a text message:

Okay, now look, old friend. We've had our differences, and I accept my role in causing them. I don't want to get negative now that I'm trying to create my positive world. As a token, open your front door. You'll find a steel box, the combination is 36-24-5. You'll appreciate the contents, not really enough to sell in any major way, but plenty to use. Accept it as a kind of apology. We were friends once and things went south and I had plenty to do with it. I won't drive away until I see your dumb ass open the door, so do it now, do it quick. I don't want to have to be here all night.

Within thirty seconds, the door opened and it was Jason, who stepped over the combination box and trotted out into the front yard and began looking up and down the street. Bobby turned on the ignition and the headlights, pulling out from behind a truck, stopping the car directly before where Jason stood.

Jason peered into Bobby's car. "Bobby, what the hell is all this about?"

Bobby felt smug satisfaction despite angling for better angels. "Use it in good health," he cried out, before tapping the accelerator and disappearing up the street.

**

He arrived back at the house with a six-pack of Coca-Cola and some corn chips, placing the chips in the pantry and the Coke in the refrigerator, and sitting back down to the football game. For a few minutes, he negotiated triumphalist feelings, as if he were a Roman general who had succeeded in a major victory, but as the game progressed and the feelings diminished, doubt set in once again. Feeling plucky, he told himself he was more than ready for doubt as a constant companion.

His phone began to vibrate and he picked up. A familiar voice awaited him. "Bobby," said Tilda, "I'm glad you answered."

"Aunt Tilda," said Bobby, and he smiled involuntarily. Nobody would be more thrilled by the latest developments in his life, no matter how short-lived. "I've got news."

"I've got news, too, Bobby," said Tilda, talking over him, which was unusual for her. "I've got something to tell you that you need to know. Your mother wants to see you, Bobby. She told me herself."

Bobby was momentarily derailed. "What?"

"She has news about your father and she wants to tell you herself. In person."

Bobby paused, perturbed. "In person? Why in person?"

"Now, Bobby, don't take this the wrong way. I told her about your visit and she took an interest. I think she wants to begin trying to make amends."

"She wants to make amends?" said Bobby, repeating the phrase. "In person? I mean, can she? Can she even speak for herself?"

Bobby heard the agitation in his words, the excitability. Tilda's voice deepened as she sought to keep the conversation from escalating. "She won't take her medication when she sees you and she does have lucid moments when she's unmedicated. I've learned, in fact, that there is this different generation of meds. They'll treat her symptoms with less of the awful side effects and she'll be on those within a month. But the issue here, Bobby, is that she has news about your father."

Bobby heard the urgency in his aunt's voice and he

reminded himself that she hated confrontation. Yet in the moment, he was overawed by his feelings. "Really, she has news? Now? Today? Today of all days?"

"She knows his name. She's pretty sure where he lives. We checked."

In spite of his respect for his aunt, the aggressive line of Bobby's questioning continued. "So then, you know my father's name, where he lives? You know and you're not telling me right now?"

"Bobby, did you hear me? *She* wants to tell you."

He interrupted. "You call me to tell me that for all these years *she* has had some idea where my father might be and she never said jack about it—and today, today is the day I make a real attempt at giving up drinking? That's just special, Aunt Tilda. That is my mother in a nutshell, because the timing is just perfect."

"You're trying to quit, Bobby?" interjected Tilda.

"Yeah, everything. I'm trying to quit everything, but it turns out now, today might not be the day."

Tilda tried to redirect the conversation, her voice remaining low and in control. "Bobby, you're hearing this the wrong way. It might be a new start. It could change a lot of things. Maybe your father would be delighted to hear from you, maybe he's a great guy. We don't know that, but it's possible."

Bobby retorted in dismay, almost like a child making an emotional and fatuous observation. "I asked her a long time ago who he was and she wouldn't say anything."

"Maybe she didn't think you were ready."

"Well, you know, at the time her judgment was seldom questionable."

"Bobby, I swear, you're not hearing me. She wants to say she's sorry. She wants to tell you these things face-to-face."

His rage had built to a point where he had lost the capacity for self-censorship. "And you know what? I don't want to hear it," he said. "It's about the last thing I want to hear from her. I don't want her goddamned apology, Aunt Tilda. I just don't."

Tilda raised her voice, his anger infecting her. "Bobby, not everything is about you."

He knew at some level he would be ashamed of this exchange for years to come, but the day had been so fraught, his emotions so high, there was no containing him. "This conversation's over. I love you, Aunt Tilda, but this is over."

Bobby cut off the call, entirely caught up in his own outrage. He stalked the length of the living room, then stopped, looking at the phone. He began trying to unravel his feelings by confronting the idea of his mother showing remorse, imagining a scene of semi-coherent apology in the miasma of her bedroom while his aunt looked on earnestly. He did his best to visualize the moment, and as he did so, questions piled up in his mind like debris on a riverbank during a flood. What would be the words his mother would use? He literally could not imagine what she would say. What would he be doing? Standing? Sitting? Fidgeting uncontrollably? Pacing the room? What would he feel? Empathy? Sadness? For both himself and for her? A feeling of reconciliation? A feeling of desolate emptiness? Or would it simply be long-pent-up and unbridled anger and a dizzying sense of nearing the absolute limits of his self-control?

He could not be sure, and as the questions amassed, he set them aside to suppress the tornadic churning in his stomach, and in that instant, he wanted a drink. He *needed* a drink. His anger doubled him over and he wheezed, heading for the sofa and sitting down, trying to pull back to regain his bearings. He considered heading out to downtown, having a drink or two at a club or a bar, simply letting all the negativity drain from his body. A simple drink or two, no more, no less. He let the line of inquiry proceed. By itself it was such a harmless thing—a single drink. For millions the world over it was the fitting end to a hard day at work, a nightcap, a rather innocent way of lessening tensions and anxieties, a brief moment of respite and minor pleasure. This avenue of self-examination put a drink in an innocent context, a minor violation of personal code but ultimately harmless. But as he sat there, the context shifted and he knew, he knew this mode of thought for what it was. For him a single drink was the first step down a pitiless slope, one so steep that footing was instantly lost, the ground rushing up hard to meet him and the landing always painful, the only distinctions being gradients of severity.

The churning in his stomach ceased and he tried to recontextualize his situation. His mother was going to be an issue for him his whole life. He knew that with an intense conviction. If it led to this every time he was bothered by anger directed at his mother—if it led to him doubled over, craving drink—what chance did he really have? He held that question, affirming the answer again and again. No chance, no chance at all. He grabbed the phone off the coffee table and dialed Tilda's number.

"Aunt Tilda," he said.

"Bobby—"

It was his turn to jump right in and cut her off. "I'm very sorry, Aunt Tilda. I should never ever talk to you like that, but this goes so deep and I get angry when I should listen." He stopped, unsure what else to say. "I am sorry."

Tilda spoke evenly. "I know it goes deep, Bobby. You don't have to apologize."

"Yes, I do. I have to apologize."

Once again, she spoke with a measured cadence. "Well, there's no need, Bobby, not on my account. I know you're not angry with me."

Bobby thought his aunt was exhibiting her rational side, the place she went when escaping high emotions. Bobby's mind was reeling. He knew he had a reason for calling her besides simple apology, but the idea was elusive, the formulation receding like smoke. "Look, I need to do something," he said. "I've known this in one way or another for years, but this might be the time."

He stopped, silent. Tilda waited. "What is it, Bobby?" she said "What are you saying?"

He cut right to the chase. "I'll be there tomorrow."

"You're not saying that out of some misplaced guilt, are you, Bobby?"

"No, I am not. I need to spend a couple of days out there, maybe longer. I mean, it's so simple it's ridiculous. Drinking is a byproduct. A result. The first thing I need to do, the very first thing, is to get into a better place about her."

Tilda was quiet and Bobby could almost sense her parsing his words, looking at the situation from various angles. "It's not going to be easy, Bobby. Not easy at all. Certainly you can come down and I will try to make it as comfortable for all of us as possible, but if you're sincere about this, I would think hard about starting counseling. Ongoing counseling with a very good therapist. It's probably going to take months, Bobby. Years, maybe."

He was fully plucky again, his emotions volatile and his

self-confidence renewed. Amid his careening feeling, his mood had completely turned, now artificially high. "Be that as it may, it all begins tomorrow."

The line went silent. Finally, Tilda spoke hesitantly, with delicacy. "You know, Bobby, she might say some things you don't like tomorrow. If not tomorrow, then the day after, or next week, or next year. The two of you see this from very different perspectives."

Bobby once again began to pace the room, caught up in forming a plan for the next couple of days. "I'll be on my best manners. I'll be a big boy," he said. "A grownup."

"That's not what I'm concerned about." The cadence of Tilda's sentences slowed once more. "She describes years of pain, Bobby. A lifetime of it, really. And I'm not talking about her run-ins with Daddy. This thing that was always there, the shadow, the visitor—as a girl, I think I knew it, the illness in her mind. The illness is why I could never truly be mad at her." She paused, hesitating, but pressed on. "I sometimes wonder if you have some form of it, a less virulent form. At least it occurs to me to wonder." She paused again, then spoke as if she were intimating something sensitive and private. "She does feel terrible about you when she can focus her attention on it. But she's got real limitations, Bobby. So real that I can't say for sure if she'll ever be able to say what you want to hear."

Bobby took the phone from his ear, looking at it. He had never considered whether he might have a mental illness and it left him feeling empty, curiously hollow. He returned to what he considered to be the matter at hand. "Aunt Tilda, if I can't handle a little static from her? If I can't deal with that? Shame on me. Shame on me."

More hesitation on Tilda's part. "Well, maybe you're right." She paused but it was clear she had more to say.

"But come down. Yes, come down. The more I think about it, the more I like the idea. I think you should maybe stay in Cuero, in a hotel. I don't mean not to welcome you but you're going to need breaks from her, from this place. Maybe you should even stay in Victoria, drive here in the mornings. There are more restaurants, stores, other means of diversion, and I can imagine that if you're not drinking you're going to have to fill that time some way. I'll come with you in the evening, if you like, but I need to get back to her before too late. How does that sound?"

Tilda's gentle words brought a lump to his throat. "It sounds to me like you're the only real parent I ever had," he said.

When his aunt spoke again, she sounded disengaged. Bobby knew this meant she, too, was probably dealing with high emotions. "I tried to be, Bobby. I wanted to be. But I'm not, I'm just not."

Bobby realized that the moment had become too overwrought and left him with no outlet for his feelings. He spoke rapidly. "I'll call before I leave tomorrow. Thank you, Aunt Tilda."

He could barely hear Tilda as he pulled the phone away from his face and cut the call. "Good night, B—"

**

The sight of a packed suitcase standing upright next to the bed struck him as incongruous, the lone domesticated item in an otherwise unruly house. After the rigors of the evening, he felt strangely light-hearted, seeing the following day as perhaps the true beginning of something new, the first steps. He went back downstairs and found a football game on TV, which pleased him to no end.

Somehow the familiar sound of sports—the crowd, the whistles, the announcers further hyping the spectacle—it was all of a piece, a part of his past he did not care to discard. He went to the refrigerator, grabbed a soda, and poured himself a Coca-Cola from a can—the first of many, he thought—and started watching the game.

After a while, he felt hungry. In the pantry, he rifled through corn chips and crackers. When he moved aside a carton of wheat crisps, he found a pint of Evan Williams squatting on the shelf, its contents amber, the bottle resolute. He didn't remember this bottle but he knew it had to be his—despite his housemates being penniless, not one of them would condescend to drink a discount brand of bourbon unless there was no alternative. He looked at the bottle closely, tilting his head, then he raised it to eye level, almost as if he were Hamlet and this were the skull of Yorick. His eyes bored into the whiskey and he did not lower the bottle. It was a long moment before he realized he could not find it in himself to put it down.

THE END

ABOUT ATMOSPHERE PRESS

Atmosphere Press is an independent, full-service publisher for books in genres ranging from nonfiction to fiction to poetry, with a special emphasis on being an author-friendly approach to the challenges of getting a book into the world. Learn more about what we do at atmospherepress.com.

We encourage you to check out some of Atmosphere's latest releases, which are available at Amazon.com and via order from your local bookstore:

Mandated Happiness, a novel by Clayton Tucker
The Yoga of Strength, a novel by Andrew Marc Rowe
They are Almost Invisible, poetry by Elizabeth Carmer
Let the Little Birds Sing, a novel by Sandra Fox Murphy
Spots Before Stripes, a novel by Jonathan Kumar
Auroras over Acadia, poetry by Paul Liebow
Channel: How to be a Clear Channel for Inspiration by Listening, Enjoying, and Trusting Your Intuition, nonfiction by Jessica Ang
Gone Fishing: A Girls Can Do Anything Book, children's fiction by Carmen Petro
Owlfred the Owl, a picture book by Caleb Foster

Love Your Vibe: Using the Power of Sound to Take Command of Your Life, nonfiction by Matt Omo
Transcendence, poetry and images by Vincent Bahar Towliat
Leaving the Ladder: An Ex-Corporate Girl's Guide from the Rat Race to Fulfilment, nonfiction by Lynda Bayada
Adrift, poems by Kristy Peloquin
Letting Nicki Go: A Mother's Journey through Her Daughter's Cancer, nonfiction by Bunny Leach
Time Do Not Stop, poems by William Guest
Dear Old Dogs, a novella by Gwen Head
Bello the Cello, a picture book by Dennis Mathew
How Not to Sell: A Sales Survival Guide, nonfiction by Rashad Daoudi
Ghost Sentence, poems by Mary Flanagan
That Scarlett Bacon, a picture book by Mark Johnson
Such a Nice Girl, a novel by Carol St. John
Makani and the Tiki Mikis, a picture book by Kosta Gregory
What Outlives Us, poems by Larry Levy
Winter Park, a novel by Graham Guest
That Beautiful Season, a novel by Sandra Fox Murphy
What I Cannot Abandon, poems by William Guest
All the Dead Are Holy, poems by Larry Levy
Rescripting the Workplace: Producing Miracles with Bosses, Coworkers, and Bad Days, nonfiction by Pam Boyd
Surviving Mother, a novella by Gwen Head
Who Are We: Man and Cosmology, poetry by William Guest

ABOUT JIM WILLIAMS

Born and raised in Houston, Jim Williams received a BA in political science from the University of Houston, followed by an MA in political philosophy from the University of Chicago. In his mid-twenties he moved to Austin, where he grew interested in creative writing. Soon he became fascinated with—and resolved to portray in fiction—the endless diversity of the people he encountered in the Austin nightlife, a vibrant but shadowy subculture suffused with drugs and replete with all manner of talented but damaged people. These experiences resulted in this novel, *The Third Door*, a story he had to live before he could write about it authentically.

Williams is a sixth-generation Texan who has lived in Austin for more than twenty-five years. He is currently hard at work on his second novel.

CPSIA information can be obtained
at www.ICGtesting.com
Printed in the USA
BVHW071242311022
650744BV00002B/173